Praise

Ryan Steck is the real deal! *Gone Dark* powers forward, with each scene slamming into the next like colliding freight cars. Matthew Redd is my new favorite thriller hero.

ROBERT CRAIS, #1 *New York Times* bestselling author of *The Big Empty*

Things have *Gone Dark* up in Montana, but Mathew Redd has his hand on the switch and is about to shed some light on the subject. . . .The fourth in Ryan Steck's pulse-pounding novels, *Gone Dark* fans the flames of a wildfire of a series!

CRAIG JOHNSON, *New York Times* bestselling author of the Walt Longmire series

Gone Dark is wildly entertaining—Steck keeps raising the stakes, putting his characters into increasingly impossible situations, but Matthew Redd is a hero equal to every challenge. Vivid imagery, pulse-pounding suspense, and an all-time great dog—everything we read thrillers for.

JOSEPH FINDER, *New York Times* bestselling author of *The Oligarch's Daughter*

Set in Montana's breathtaking Big Sky Country and packed with intense, hard-hitting action, *Out for Blood* reaffirms Ryan Steck's prowess in the thriller genre, demonstrating once again why his character, former Marine Raider Matthew Redd, is a force to be reckoned with. If you're looking for action, this one's coming in hot!

JACK CARR, former Navy SEAL sniper and #1 *New York Times* bestselling author of the James Reece Terminal List series

Matthew Redd, introduced in Ryan Steck's debut novel *Fields of Fire*, is back and ready for trouble. Redd, a former Marine Raider turned Montana rancher, takes on a gang of outlaw bikers where the buffalo roam. The Wild West has never been wilder. Intense, brutal, and faster on the draw than a gunslinger; *Lethal Range* delivers a fresh take on your grandpa's Western.

NELSON DEMILLE, #1 *New York Times* bestselling author of *The Maze*

Intense, riveting, and ultimately wild escapist fun, *Lethal Range* is a powerful modern Western. It's *Sons of Anarchy* crashing into *Yellowstone*. Steck is a talented cinematic writer and has created a character in Matthew Redd that is both larger than life and remarkably relatable. Buy this book!

DON WINSLOW, #1 bestselling author of *The Force* and *The Border*

A white-knuckle ride from start to finish, *Lethal Range* takes off with one of the most intense scenes I've ever read, then builds to a thunderous crescendo. It's one of this summer's hottest thrillers. Like the best kind of roller coaster, the tension rises to an incredible climax.

T. J. NEWMAN, two-time *New York Times* bestselling author of *Falling* and *Drowning: The Rescue of Flight 1421*

Ryan Steck's latest *Lethal Range* is a high-stakes thriller that starts at a run and races faster with every flip of the page. The mix of spy tradecraft, gutsy action, and nonstop mayhem is what I love in a book. Pair that up with the return of Matthew Redd, a hero as ballsy as Jack Ryan and as street-smart as Jack Reacher, what's not to love? I can't wait to see what trouble Redd must tackle next!

JAMES ROLLINS, #1 *New York Times* bestselling author of *Kingdom of Bones*

Matthew Redd is a hero many readers will find comfortingly familiar while refreshingly different, and Steck wields him with precision in *Lethal Range*— a spectacular follow-up to his stellar debut. If you're a skeptic who thinks Ryan Steck can only write *about* thrillers, you're missing out on one of the hottest new authors in the genre. You'll be far from disappointed in this installment and eager for more.

JACK STEWART, author of *Unknown Rider*

[*Lethal Range*] contains all the danger, treachery, and intrigue that a thriller reader could hope for. It's a gritty tale, with tangled threads, full of action and drama. More than enough angst and adventure to keep you reading long into the night.

STEVE BERRY, *New York Times* bestselling author of *The Last Kingdom*

Steck and Redd are back! Crisply written and beautifully researched, *Lethal Range* rips the reader from Majorca to Big Sky Country. Packed with twists and cliff-hangers, this classic thriller from world-class thriller expert The Real Book Spy roars like a beast.

GREGG HURWITZ, *New York Times* bestselling author of *The Last Orphan*

Full of fists and fury, Ryan Steck's *Lethal Range* is a masterfully plotted battle of good versus evil. With unforgettable characters, lightning pace, and a story frighteningly similar to today's headlines, this book entertains and educates. If you like C. J. Box or Vince Flynn, you will *love* this book!

LARRY LOFTIS, *New York Times* bestselling author of *The Watchmaker's Daughter*

RYAN STECK

GONE DARK

A **MATTHEW REDD** THRILLER

Tyndale House Publishers
Carol Stream, Illinois

Visit Tyndale online at tyndale.com.

Visit Ryan Steck online at therealbookspy.com.

Tyndale and Tyndale's quill logo are registered trademarks of Tyndale House Ministries.

Gone Dark

Cover designed by Dean H. Renninger

Edited by Sarah Mason Rische

Published in association with The John Talbot Agency, Inc., a member of The Talbot Fortune Agency, LLC, 180 E. Prospect Ave. #188, Mamaroneck, NY 10543.

For information about special discounts for bulk purchases, please contact Tyndale House Publishers at csresponse@tyndale.com, or call 1-855-277-9400.

Library of Congress Cataloging-in-Publication Data

A catalog record for this book is available from the Library of Congress.

ISBN 978-1-4964-8602-8 (HC)
ISBN 978-1-4964-8603-5 (SC)

Printed in the United States of America

31	30	29	28	27	26	25
7	6	5	4	3	2	1

For Brynn Steck

Daughter. Sister. And one of the most loving, most caring, and funniest people I've ever known. I love you endlessly, and being your dad has been one of the greatest honors of my life.

Their crosses are quiet and a long way off, and from this remove their influence is quiet and seemingly distant. But quietly they are present on every fire-line, even though those whose lives they are helping to protect know only the order and not the fatality it represents. For those who crave immortality by name, clearly this is not enough, but for many of us it would mean a great deal to know that, by our dying, we were often present in times of catastrophe helping to save the living from our deaths.

NORMAN MACLEAN, *Young Men and Fire*

Some say the world will end in fire.

ROBERT FROST, *Fire and Ice*

Prologue

Montana was on fire.

The Big Sky was full of smoke, and the country beneath it was full of flames.

And that, thought Trace Hazlett as he shuffled across the flight line in his high-collared Kevlar jumpsuit, lugging more than half his body weight in gear, was not such a bad thing.

For Trace, fire meant work. Work meant money, and money meant freedom. Freedom from the grinding poverty of the reservation. Freedom to live as he pleased.

No fires, no freedom.

Oh, to be sure, fire was an enemy—*the* enemy that he and his team would fight to the literal death, just as his Blackfeet ancestors had fought against Shoshone and Kootenai, and later against white settlers trying to take their territory. Warriors needed enemies. Without an enemy, how could a warrior demonstrate courage and win glory?

Freedom and glory. That was what fire meant to Trace Hazlett. It was why he had left the rez at eighteen, worked his way onto a hotshot crew, and then, four years later, attended smoke jumper school at Missoula Base. It was why he was humping eighty-five pounds of gear—heavy-duty jump jacket and pants, a helmet with a steel face cage, main and reserve parachutes, and a personal gear bag containing, among other things, about a gallon of water and an emergency fire shelter—up the boarding steps of an idling Forest Service De Havilland DHC-6 Twin Otter, for yet another one-way flight.

Once inside, he collapsed onto the jump seat and slid over until he was pressed up tight against the jumper who had boarded just ahead of him. A moment later, the last jumper in the "stick"—the technical term for the number of parachutists who would be going out the door on an overflight—squeezed in next to him, completing the human sandwich.

The cabin of the Twin Otter was cramped to begin with, and with all the gear they wore, jumpers quickly got used to the idea of being packed in like sardines on takeoff. The jumpsuit, which was essentially body armor to protect the jumper upon landing, was like a personal sauna under the best of conditions, and the close quarters didn't help. But these were minor inconveniences, quickly forgotten when the command came to line up, clip in, and exit the plane.

As the plane lurched and began moving, Trace glanced over, curious to see who he would be snuggling with for the duration of the short flight.

At the beginning of the season, things had been very precise and disciplined, the team assignments carved in stone. But as things ramped up and the calls started coming in fast and furious, operations became a lot more fluid, such that he didn't know who he would be jumping with until the roster was called.

On his right was Terry Collins, a fellow "Ned"—newcomer—whom Trace had gone through initial training with. Although they both had about a dozen actual fire jumps under their belts, they wouldn't shed the loathed nickname until the start of their second season.

When he looked to his left, he did a double take.

Who's this guy?

There were about eighty jumpers at Missoula Base, and while Trace didn't know all their names, he did know their faces. This guy definitely wasn't one of them. His most distinctive feature was his blond hair, shaved on the sides but long on top and pulled back in a ponytail. That and a wispy, slightly reddish beard made him look like a Viking.

Trace stared at the unfamiliar face in profile for a moment until the man, sensing his scrutiny, turned to face him. Smiling, he gave Trace a nod and awkwardly reached across with his left hand.

"Hey," he said, almost shouting to be heard over the roar of the plane's engines. "Name's Josh. Josh Harris. I'm over from McCall."

McCall was the name of a smoke jumper base in central Idaho. As fire season got into full swing and resources were needed in different places, it wasn't at all unusual for teams to get moved around from base to base, and Trace supposed that, once in a while, that applied to individual jumpers as well. But that didn't account for why this guy hadn't been formally introduced to the team upon arrival. And although Trace had only been listening for his own name when the roster was announced, he was pretty sure he hadn't heard the name Harris.

"I just got in like half an hour ago," Harris went on. "I guess one of your guys got pulled out of the lineup at the last minute. I think his wife went into labor or something."

The man shrugged then grinned again. "Nothing like being thrown into the deep end and told to start swimming. But that's the job, am I right?"

Trace, feeling oddly relieved by this explanation, nodded back and accepted the handclasp. "Welcome aboard."

✳   ✳   ✳

Once they were aloft, Trace couldn't resist the urge to look out at the vast landscape below. He was no longer awed by the thought of moving through the sky, nor even very anxious about what would come next. Once you realized that anything, literally *anything* could happen on a jump, you either found a way to deal with it or you went back to fighting fires on the ground.

No, what Trace was looking for was the smoke.

Typically, smoke jumpers were called out to stop new fires from turning into big fires. From the air, it was easy to spot those fires—usually the byproduct of a lightning strike—because of the long plume of whitish smoke rising out of the forest. This was, in fact, why smoke jumpers had been created in the first place. Teams of two or four could drop in on a fire that was miles away from the nearest road and use traditional firefighting methods to contain that fire before it got out of control. Those callouts typically didn't last more than a day or two, with most of that time spent hiking out to different fire zones.

Sometimes, however, when an established fire threatened to move in a different direction beyond the reach of ground teams, a larger element of smoke jumpers was sent in to carve out a firebreak in the path of the conflagration and establish a landing zone so that additional manpower could be brought in by helicopter. Those jobs could stretch out for days—days of hard, hot, dangerous work.

Judging by the massive column of smoke dominating half the southern horizon, this callout was of the second variety.

The Twin Otter stayed to the right of the smoke, banking around it to approach the designated drop zone from the south. As the plane made an initial pass and the spotter threw out long bright-orange streamers to mark the DZ, Trace donned his helmet, took a deep breath, and said a short prayer. Then, at a signal from the jumpmaster, he and the others rose and began moving toward the open hatch.

When his turn came, Trace clipped his static line—a long yellow cord attached to his parachute—into a hard point inside the aircraft and sat down in the hatchway. His gloved hands gripped the doorframe. His lower legs, dangling out into space, were buffeted by the rush of air.

This was the part that never got old. The part that still took his breath away.

When he felt a tap on his shoulder, the jumpmaster telling him it was time to go, he leaned forward and gave himself to the sky.

He fell away from the aircraft, feeling the wind swirl around inside his face cage, and then felt a slight tug as the static line went taut and ripped open the deployment bag, releasing a small drogue chute. Trace felt his body being pulled into an upright position just as the trailing drogue pulled his main chute from the pack on his back.

This was the first moment when, if something was going to go wrong, it usually did. If the lines got fouled or, for whatever reason, the square DC-7 ram-air chute did not properly inflate, Trace would have to quickly cut away the main chute and deploy the reserve strapped to his chest.

Not today, though. The big orange-and-white canopy blossomed and inflated and, with a body-wrenching but oddly reassuring yank, arrested his free fall.

He quickly found the control toggles and began steering toward the line of square chutes descending ahead of him, turning like corkscrews as they drifted down to the drop zone. From the door of the Twin Otter to the ground was a journey of about ninety seconds. It was when he neared the ground that he realized just how close they would be to the burn.

Touchdown was the second chance for things to go wrong, though usually not disastrously so. Ideally, the spotter tried to situate the drop zone in a clearing, but sometimes nature didn't cooperate and the jumpers had to come down in the woods. That was when the Kevlar jumpsuit and the wire face cage on the helmet justified their existence, deflecting tree branches that might otherwise pierce the body or gouge out an eye.

If the chute got snared by a tree, leaving the jumper hanging, a self-rescue would be required. That involved using the safety rope tucked in one of his leg pockets and, if necessary, a small folding saw to cut away the branches in order to recover the chute. At more than a thousand dollars apiece, smoke jumpers observed a strict *no chute left behind* policy. Rips could be mended and broken lines replaced, at least until the master rigger decided the chute had to be retired.

Of course, there were other hazards upon landing. Sprains and fractures were the most common. Or a gust of wind could catch the chute and drag you across the landscape like cheese across a grater. Usually these outcomes, while painful, were survivable.

Usually.

Today, the fates were kind. Trace flared his chute, getting that last little bit of uplift just as his boots made contact with the ground. Without the additional gear, his landing would probably have been featherlight. With it? Well, it was a little like jumping off the roof of a one-story building. A jolt to the system—especially the knees, ankles, and spine—but manageable. A quick glance around showed that the rest of the eight-man crew had all made it down safely, landing within a hundred-yard radius.

Trace gathered in his chute, hugging the now-shapeless mass to his chest and squeezing the air out of the cells. He then shrugged out of his harness and began the necessary process of shedding his jump gear, all of which went into a stuff sack along with the chute to be stashed for later retrieval after the fire was contained. From the moment his feet hit the ground, he ceased to be a smoke jumper and became just another firefighter.

Wildland firefighting, at least for the ground crews, wasn't like battling a structure fire. The goal wasn't to put the fire out by smothering it with water, but rather to clear an area in front of the fire, removing all vegetation it might use as fuel, thereby eliminating one side of the fire triangle. It was a laborious process of cutting down trees, clearing brush, and basically scraping the ground down until it was nothing but dirt. Trace had once heard a veteran smoke jumper accurately describe the job as "extreme landscaping." The only difference was that while they were cutting and digging, an inferno raged a stone's throw away.

The plane made another low pass, dropping out several cardboard boxes attached to small parachutes. These contained firefighting tools—chain saws, shovels, and Pulaskis—along with enough food and water to sustain the crew for a couple days. The equipment drop was less precise than the smoke jumper insertion, so the first task after landing was to go out and collect all the boxes.

Once the equipment and supplies were gathered in the drop zone and the tools distributed, the supervisor for the drop—Jason Steen—began directing the crew to head out in teams of two and start establishing the break that would, hopefully, stop the fire in the event that the winds changed and began blowing it northeast toward Helena.

It was only as he was directing his crew to their designated work assignments that Steen realized a substitution had been made. Normally confident, the supervisor stared speechless at Harris for a moment before finally asking, "Who the hell are you? Where's Denny?"

"Josh Harris, boss. I'm over from McCall. I guess Denny had to drop out last minute, so they sent me to sub in."

"I'll work with him," Trace said, filling the awkward silence. Sometimes being the first to volunteer paid off later on.

Steen continued to stare at Harris, his face twisted into a look that said *this is definitely not okay,* but then he shook it off. Whatever irregularities had occurred back at Missoula Base, it didn't change the fact that there was work to be done. "Yeah, okay. Harris, you're with Ned. Go up about two hundred yards and start working back this way."

"Got it," said Trace, cocking his Pulaski onto one shoulder.

A hybrid of lumberman's axe and stonecutter's adze, the Pulaski was the quintessential tool of wildland firefighting. Named for its inventor, assistant forest ranger Ed Pulaski, who was credited with saving forty-five members of a firefighting crew during the disastrous 1910 fire season, the Pulaski could be used to chop down trees and break up hard soil—the two most basic tasks of the firefighter. If they had to, any one of the smoke jumpers could do his job effectively with just a Pulaski, and quite often, that was exactly what they did.

Trace immediately started off in the direction Steen had indicated, moving at a jog. Although he still carried his personal gear bag, which weighed in at about twenty-five pounds, and a STIHL chain saw that added another fifteen pounds, without the jump equipment he felt like he was floating across the forest floor. The illusion faded as he neared the edge of the fire.

It was a thing more felt and heard than actually seen. Overhead, smoke partially blotted out the sun, plunging the woods into deep darkness, and even though the fire itself was probably still a quarter of a mile away, he could hear its freight-train roar and feel its heat on his face. Thankfully, a light wind was blowing from the north, slowing the fire's advance and carrying away the smoke that would have otherwise turned the air into a choking miasma.

When he had counted off a hundred and twenty steps—roughly two hundred yards—Trace took his Pulaski from his shoulder and brought the adze end down, hoeing it into the dry soil as if marking a spot on a map.

"This is as good a place to start as any," he said, turning to Harris.

The blond man, who barely seemed winded after jogging through the forest, grinned. "You know, that's exactly what I was thinking."

Trace found the smile unsettling, but it wasn't until he saw Harris raise his Pulaski in preparation for a swing that it occurred to him something was very wrong about the situation.

But it was too late.

For the briefest of moments, Trace wondered what had actually happened to Denny.

A second later, his world faded to black.

ONE

The smoky haze, which did not quite erase but definitely obscured the mountains in every direction, gave the sky a yellow cast and transformed the late-morning sun into a red orb that could be looked upon with the naked eye without ill effect. In its light, the world looked like a vision of the apocalypse.

There were, at that very moment, twelve separate wildfires burning in the area designated by the Forest Service as Region 1—an area comprising all of Idaho, Montana, and the Dakotas. Five of the fires were in western Montana, and one of these, the Trask River Fire, which took its name from the site where it had first been reported, near the Trask River Trailhead in the Elkhorn Mountains, was of greatest concern because of its proximity to inhabited areas. If the wind blew north-northeast, it would push the fire toward the state capital, Helena. If it blew south-southeast, as it seemed to be doing, it would threaten Wellington, the county seat of Stillwater County, and the rural properties surrounding it.

There were no reports of lightning strikes—the second leading cause of wildfires—which meant the fire had probably been the result of the number one cause. Human activity, either through carelessness or deliberate acts of arson, was responsible for nearly eighty percent of wildfires.

Determining the exact cause would be a job for fire investigators in days to come. The immediate priority of the Forest Service and cooperating state and county agencies was to bring the fire, which had been burning for three days and had already consumed over three thousand acres of forest, under control before it posed a threat to nearby homes and communities. Presently, the leading edge of the fire was about twenty miles north-northwest of Wellington and about eight miles from a property listed on the county registry as Thompson Ranch.

Matthew Redd just called it *home*.

That had not always been the case for Redd. He'd come to the ranch at the age of eleven after the overdose death of his mother—the only parent he knew. He met his biological father, a man named Gavin Kline, for the first time right before Gavin arranged for his young son to be adopted by an old Marine Corps buddy—a Montana rancher named Jim Bob Thompson—and so for the next eight years, the ranch became the only home that mattered.

Once he turned eighteen, however, Redd had followed in his father's footsteps—actually, both his fathers', though it would be some time before he would think of Kline that way—by enlisting in the Marines. From that moment forward, the Corps had been both home and family until, in short order, his military career had come to an unexpected end and Jim Bob had been murdered, leaving Redd the sole inheritor of Thompson Ranch and a mountain of debt.

It was a homecoming he could not have imagined in his wildest dreams.

And yet, little more than two years later, he felt like the luckiest man in the world. He'd reconnected with his childhood sweetheart, Emily, the love of his life, and together they were building a family. Their son, Matthew Jr., would soon have a sister—name yet to be determined. And they had moved into their new house, built to replace the old ranch house that had burned down—not the result of a wildfire but of a vicious act of terrorism.

Redd had known plenty of loss in his life and knew better than to get too attached to material things, but losing the house where he'd banked so many memories with his adoptive dad had hit hard. The idea of losing a second home to fire in less than a year's time was almost too much to handle, so when he heard about the Trask River Fire and the possibility that they might have to evacuate, Redd had set to work with chain saw and tractor to create a thirty-yard-wide firebreak around the new house and the barn. Then he had called his friend and nominal employer, Sheriff Stuart Blackwood, and asked what he could do to help.

"Right now," the sheriff had told him, "the best thing you can do is see to your ranch. Leave wildfire fighting to the trained professionals."

While Redd appreciated the sentiment, he did not at all like the idea of sitting around and waiting for someone else to save the day.

Then Emily had reminded him that this wasn't a situation Matthew Redd could control through grim determination and sheer muleheaded stubbornness. One more body on the front lines wouldn't matter at all if the wind shifted the wrong way and sent the fire toward his ranch. Better to stand by with a hose and shovel and defend his home if it came to it.

Emily was right, of course. She usually was.

But then the sheriff called back. "Still interested in helping out?"

TWO

Within an hour of the sheriff's call, Redd was behind the wheel of his 2020 agate-black F-150 4x4 Ford Raptor, roaring north on the main highway, rocketing toward the heart of the fire like a heat-seeking missile.

It had turned out Blackwood wasn't looking for another firefighter. "Just got a call from the Forest Service," he'd said. "Seems they've lost contact with a group of smoke jumpers. Whole team's gone dark after being dropped south of the Trask River Fire and they want to know if we can deploy our SAR team to go look for them."

This was almost a laughable request because Stillwater County's search and rescue team was very much a work in progress and presently was able to field only one qualified rescue technician: Matthew Redd.

In Montana, as in most states with wilderness recreation areas, search and rescue was primarily the responsibility of county sheriffs, with the actual work of searching and rescuing performed by trained volunteers. The more populous counties like Yellowstone, Gallatin, and Missoula had an easier time coordinating and fielding volunteers, while rural counties like Stillwater, with a total population just north of a thousand souls, usually had to outsource SAR callouts. Sheriff Blackwood, however, wanted to change that and take advantage of some federal grant money that would become available once the county established its own SAR team.

In addition to teaching him dozens of ways to kill an enemy, Redd's training in the Marine Raiders had equipped him with the skills to save lives, not to mention a high degree of physical fitness. It was a relatively easy thing for him to take a few online classes and get certified as a technical rescue specialist so that Blackwood could officially hire him as the county's search and rescue coordinator.

It was a part-time gig with a very flexible schedule, and it paid well, which was not an inconsequential thing. Not with another baby on the way.

Besides, he enjoyed the work, which was kind of like leading a Boy Scout troop for grown-ups.

A dozen locals had attended his first volunteer meeting at the public library. Eight of those had shown up for his "selection" test, which consisted of a four-mile hike up the mountain road behind Redd's still-under-construction home, and five had decided to stick with the training program—a one-weekend-a-month commitment that involved long hikes into the wilderness, learning knots and wilderness first aid, climbing up sheer rock faces, and rappelling out of helicopters. Barring any unforeseen challenges, in another year or so, Stillwater County would have a fully fieldable technical rescue team.

Which was about twelve months too late to be of any use to the missing smoke jumpers.

Redd could have punted and told Blackwood to pass the request to the SAR teams in Bozeman or Helena, but fobbing off a call to action on someone else wasn't his style.

The turnoff to the staging area for the firefighting effort was only a few miles up the highway and another mile or two up an unpaved fire road. The camp resembled nothing less than a military outpost, similar to the sort of ad hoc constructs he'd occupied during overseas deployments in his early days in the Corps. The only difference was that instead of jarheads in cammies carrying M16s, the men ducking into GP medium tents or using the Port-A-Johns wore yellow shirts over brown trousers with full-brim hard hats and carried chain saws and strange tools that looked like a cross between an axe and a hoe. It occurred to Redd that, in his Wranglers, buffalo plaid flannel, and New Era Detroit Lions hat—a callback to his home state—he wasn't exactly dressed for the occasion. In his haste, he hadn't thought to change into the "official" uniform of the Wellington County

SAR team: brown Carhartts and a long-sleeved orange cotton shirt emblazoned with the word *RESCUE* and a blue asterisk—the Star of Life symbol indicating that the wearer was certified as an EMT.

"At least I didn't forget my gloves," he muttered, grabbing them off the passenger seat.

The camp was a few miles south of the fire, close enough that he could occasionally see what looked like red and yellow worms crawling in the midst of the massive smoke column rising from the forest but distant enough that the flames did not pose an immediate danger. Still, it wasn't a stretch for Redd to believe that he could feel its heat on his face. He cast a glance back at the Raptor and felt a twinge of apprehension about leaving it behind.

I should have driven the old dually, he thought miserably, wondering how much heat it would take to blister the immaculate matte-black paint job.

The truck, which he had bought outright not long before leaving the Corps, had been his most prized possession as a childless bachelor. Unfortunately, it had spent the better part of the last two years under a tarp out behind his father-in-law's auto body shop, totaled after a nasty rollover—an incident, not an accident. Since then, he'd been driving the old workhorse that he'd inherited from J. B. Thompson. The slightly rusted F-250 dually certainly didn't earn him any style points, but it was good enough for ranch work.

It had been his plan to restore the wrecked Raptor to its earlier glory, but a lack of both time and money had kept that project in perpetual limbo. Or so he had believed. Unbeknownst to Redd, his best friend, Mikey Derhammer, who managed the auto body shop, had secretly completed the restoration project, handing Redd the keys on his last birthday, less than two months ago. For someone who hadn't even thought about celebrating his birthday in years, it was the best present ever.

Redd considered moving the Raptor back to a safer distance but ultimately decided that, should the fire travel this far, he'd have bigger problems than cosmetic damage to his truck.

He trekked across the open field to the tent displaying a crude sign—written in Sharpie on what looked like a discarded pizza box—that read *ICP*. Incident command post.

After ducking through the tent flap, he took a moment to let his eyes adjust to the lower interior light level. As they did, he realized that he had become the focus of attention for nearly everyone inside the tent. At six feet three inches and two hundred sixty-five pounds of pure muscle, Redd did not merely occupy space, he dominated it. Flashing his best self-deprecating grin, he began scanning the faces, wondering who was in charge.

The enclosure was a maze of foldable tables upon which rested an assortment of computers, radios, maps, and binders. Another enormous map showing the entirety of the Elkhorn Mountains Recreation Area adorned one wall. Little flame-shaped decals showed what Redd presumed to be the current state of the fire, but his eye was drawn to the lower right corner of the map, to an area outside the public land boundaries. That was where Thompson Ranch was located.

"You the SAR guy?"

Redd turned to find a stressed-out-looking middle-aged man of average height and build with lank hair just starting to thin on top and a couple days' worth of stubble on his cheeks.

"That's me," said Redd, extending a hand. "Matt Redd."

"Frank Thornhill. I'm the IC." Thornhill accepted the handclasp. "I'm glad you guys were able to help out. As usual, we're spread pretty thin. I can't afford to pull any of my guys off the line for search and rescue."

"Happy to help," Redd replied, deciding not to point out that he was alone. "Just tell me where to start looking."

The incident commander ran a hand through his hair and then gestured to the wall map. "Easier to show you," he said, tapping a spot near the line of flame decals. "This morning, we dropped an eight-man team here to establish a break, just in case the wind shifts this afternoon and starts pushing the fire southeast toward Wellington."

Despite being aware of the threat, hearing it from the man in charge of the firefighting effort triggered a fresh wave of apprehension.

"How likely is that?"

Thornhill gave a helpless shrug. "That's the thing about a big fire like this one. It creates its own weather conditions, so you never can tell. Our main effort has been concentrated on the northeast flank of the fire and protecting Helena, and that's still our area of greatest concern, but make no mistake: we're going to stop this fire before it reaches populated areas."

Redd nodded. "Okay, tell me about your smoke jumpers."

"The team supervisor radioed in at about ten hundred hours to say that they were on the ground, no injuries or equipment lost, and moving into position." He shrugged again. "After that? Nothing. Zero contact. One of the Bambi Bucket birds . . . Sorry, those are the helicopters we use to drop water onto the fire . . . One of them did a flyover of the drop zone but reported no sign of anyone."

Redd checked his black G-Shock. It was almost one o'clock—thirteen hundred hours—which meant the smoke jumpers had been out of contact for three hours.

"Could the fire have . . ." He hesitated, unsure how to ask the question. Getting caught in a burnover and devoured by flames or left suffocating from smoke inhalation had to be every wildland firefighter's nightmare. The story of the Mann Gulch Fire of 1949, where firefighters had been caught in a blowup that swept over them suddenly, killing thirteen—twelve of them smoke jumpers— was as indelible a part of Montana history as the Lewis and Clark expedition or the Battle of the Little Bighorn.

Thornhill shook his head. "There hasn't been any significant movement in that area. Even if there had been, someone on the ground would have called it in."

"Could there be a problem with their comms?"

"The team carried two of these." Thornhill unclipped a handheld radio from his belt and passed it to Redd. It was a BK KNG2 unit, a slightly better version of the radios Blackwood's department used. "Hard to believe that both of them failed, but I suppose anything is possible."

"All right, let me get out there and start looking."

Redd offered the radio back, but Thornhill shook his head. "Keep it. You'll need it to coordinate with me here. You're also going to need some PPE." He gave Redd an appraising look as if noticing for the first time how tall and broad he was. "I just hope we have something in your size."

THREE

The crew chief of the Bell 206 gave the signal, and Redd began moving toward the helicopter. He hunched over, bent nearly in half as he moved under the sweep of the still-turning rotor blades, mindful of the fact that all it would take was a sudden gust of wind to tilt the rotor disk down and lop off his head. He'd gotten in and out of a lot of different kinds of aircraft during his years in the Corps but had never become complacent about the dangers of leaving the ground. He was particularly distrustful of helicopters.

Now attired in a spare long-sleeved Forest Service green firefighter's shirt and brown trousers and wearing a borrowed hard hat, Redd stepped up into the rear compartment of the helicopter and took one of the four empty seats. The shirt was a little too small across the chest, and the pants somehow managed to be both baggy and too short, but the Nomex fabric would protect him if he got too close to the flames.

If things really got bad, he had an emergency shelter in his backpack. Before heading out to the helo, Thornhill had shown him a video on how to deploy the shelter in the event of a sudden burnover. The shelter, which looked a little like a bivy sack made out of aluminum foil, did not inspire confidence, but supposedly it could reflect up to ninety-five percent of radiant heat and withstand convection temperatures up to five hundred degrees.

"How hot can the fire get?" Redd had asked.

Thornhill had grimaced. "A lot hotter than that," he admitted. "But the shelters do work. Most of the fatalities that have occurred when a shelter was deployed happened because the firefighter didn't use it correctly or tried to get out too soon."

When he saw that this assurance had not produced the desired effect, he added, "The shelter is required personal protective equipment for anyone going out there, but you're not a hotshot, so there's no reason for you to be anywhere near the actual fire. If it starts coming your way, run. That's your best bet."

Run. That seemed like a better option than wrapping himself up like a potato about to be put on the grill.

The helicopter crew chief, attired in a green flight suit and wearing a bulbous flight helmet, remained outside to observe that Redd followed the buckling-in procedures. When that task was completed to his satisfaction, he stepped up and took one of the other seats, and within seconds, Redd felt the aircraft shift and tilt as it left the ground.

From the air, Redd got a much different perspective on the fire. He could see the clearly delineated front, where the burn bisected the forest. Ahead of it were summer-dry but still-green trees, mostly lodgepole pines, which had grown up out of the ashes of another fire that had consumed 47,000 acres in 1988. Like many pine species, the lodgepole was fire-dependent, its cones needing the heat of a wildfire to open and release seedlings. Behind that front was only a sea of smoke, and under it, burning trees. In another thirty years, perhaps a new forest of lodgepole pines would rise, but just now, it looked a lot like hell on earth.

Just where I wanna be, Redd thought sarcastically.

The flight was mercifully brief. Less than ten minutes later, the helicopter descended to just a few hundred feet above the treetops, giving Redd an unrestricted view of the clearing the smoke jumpers had used as their drop zone.

The crew chief waved to get his attention and then pointed to the headset resting on the back of Redd's seat. Redd held one of the earcups up under the brim of his hard hat, momentarily muffling the engine noise in that ear.

"We can't get low enough to drop you here," explained the other man. "But there's a little hilltop about half a klick further south. I think we can put down there. Or at least get close enough for you to step off."

"Sounds good," replied Redd. A five hundred-meter trek was a small price to pay for exiting the aircraft in the safest manner possible.

The Bell swerved away and moved to a new position, a bald hilltop that had somehow escaped colonization by anything bigger than sagebrush and cheatgrass. The helicopter shifted back and forth a little as the pilot fought the wind and lowered to within about four feet of the ground. At a signal from the crew chief, Redd unbuckled and crawled backward to the open entry port, lowering himself first onto the skid and then making the big step down onto solid ground. As soon as he was down, he dropped into a crouch and covered his head, just as he'd been instructed to do, while the helicopter's rotor blades kicked up a dust storm.

A not altogether unpleasant silence fell over the landscape. With trees rising up on all sides of the hilltop, Redd couldn't see the smoke from the fires. But for the ambient haze overhead and the eerie red transformation of sunlight, it might have been just another day in the woods.

He took out the handheld radio and called in to the ICP, reporting that he was on the ground and about to start moving, then switched to his Garmin GPSMAP67 navigation unit.

The estimate of half a klick hadn't been far off the mark. According to the GPS, the waypoint he'd used to mark the smoke jumpers' drop zone was 516 meters away.

Moving through the forest understory required some trailblazing. The trees weren't crowded, but the vegetation was waist-high in some places. Redd bashed through it, making as much noise as he could so that any rattlers lurking nearby would slither away at his approach. Finally, after about twenty minutes on the move, he arrived at the waypoint and, a moment later, spotted a stack of cardboard boxes and large nylon packs, all stacked up like a wilderness resupply stop.

Hopeful that the simplest solution to the mystery—a mere communications breakdown—would prove to be the case, Redd cupped a hand to his mouth and shouted, "Hello!"

He waited a full thirty seconds, listening intently for anything that might be an answering call, but heard only birds and bugs and, occasionally, the crackle of trees igniting in the distance.

He tried again. "Hello! Any smoke jumpers here?"

No reply.

He hadn't really been expecting one, but at the same time, it was hard to believe that eight men could just evaporate into thin air. Sure, one or two might have met with some kind of accident, but all of them? And if something had happened, wouldn't they know to return here, to where they'd left their supplies of food and water?

Shaking his head, Redd pocketed the Garmin and began examining the area for clues. He quickly picked out trails of recently disturbed vegetation leading away from the resupply point. Some of these showed distinctive drag marks, probably the result of the smoke jumpers hauling the heavy boxes from where they'd landed. Four of the less distinctive trails, however, led in the direction of the fire. Redd picked out the one farthest to the left and began following it.

In order to preserve the integrity of the trail, Redd moved parallel to it, staying two or three feet away, close enough to be able to spot boot prints and other signs that definitively placed the smoke jumpers on this path.

As he followed the track, which occasionally veered around small trees and clumps of sage, Redd soon began to witness the effects of the fire. A haze of smoke, smelling strongly of burning wood and vegetation, swirled about him, stinging his eyes. The much larger column of smoke rising into the atmosphere partially blotted out the sun, leaving the forest shrouded in gloom. The air was charged with a faint but distinctive sound like the distant roar of a blast furnace or a jet engine—which, in fact, wasn't far from the truth—punctuated by gunshot-like pops as superheated pockets of pitch and moisture exploded out of burning trees.

The trail then turned and began running across a rising slope parallel to the fire, which seemed to be burning higher up the same hill. It was another twenty minutes before Redd encountered the first sign of firefighting activity when the trail brought him to a section of forest with several fallen trees, most of which had been cut into smaller sections with a chain saw. A cursory glance indicated that the work had begun farther down the trail, possibly as much as a hundred yards away. The smoke jumpers had evidently been working their way back from a starting point.

"Hello!" Redd called again. "Anyone here?"

He stepped over one of the fallen trees, searching for more clues, and caught a glimpse of color—a shade of orange that didn't look natural.

It was the plastic housing of a STIHL chain saw, lying on its side in a small pile of white sawdust alongside a partially sawed-through tree bough. Redd stared at the tool, trying to determine why its operator had apparently abandoned it.

Then he saw more color, staining the sawdust.

Not orange.

Not plastic.

Red.

Blood.

Redd felt his heart begin to hammer faster, a primal reaction. Blood meant violence, and violence meant there was a threat somewhere.

There were predators in the forest. Animals that had been known to attack humans. Mountain lions. Bears.

He did a quick turn, searching for any sign that the source of the perceived threat might still be nearby. That was when he spotted the body.

It was a firefighter. There was no mistaking the uniform. He lay face down only a few steps away from the discarded saw. Redd wondered why he hadn't noticed the unmoving form sooner. It was almost as if, with his essential life force gone, the man's very reality had begun to dissipate.

Careful to maintain his situational awareness, Redd moved closer to the body. He expected to see slash marks from claws and teeth, but there was only a single dark, wet spot in the center of the man's back and, in the center of that, a tiny hole.

A bullet hole.

"Who shot you?" Redd whispered. "And what the hell is going on out here in the middle of a wildfire?"

FOUR

Emily Redd positioned the heels of both hands on her lower back and pressed, grimacing a little but also savoring the momentary relief from the dull, persistent ache in her tense muscles. At times like this she had to consciously remind herself that her present tribulation was temporary and that in days, months, and years to come, it would seem like a small investment with a grand return.

An only child, Emily had always dreamed that one day she would live in a house full of children. When Matthew had disappeared from her life during their senior year in high school and she had thrown herself first into her studies and then into her career, that dream had somehow lost its immediacy. But the little bundle of joy and lower back pain who was presently shifting and squirming in her womb was a near-constant reminder that her dream was finally well on its way to becoming a reality.

"Just a couple more weeks, baby girl," she murmured, gazing down at the great round bulge protruding from her abdomen.

Her due date was actually ten days out, but she was at the point in the pregnancy where labor could begin at any time. As a physician, Emily knew that with few exceptions, mostly relating to the health of both mother and child, babies came out when they were ready. Due dates were just ballpark guesses.

"Got one coming in!"

Emily looked up from her swollen belly to the nurses' station, where the charge nurse, Joanna Delmer, had a telephone handset pressed to one ear. "ETA, two minutes," Joanna went on, repeating the information being relayed to her over the line. "Twenty-nine-year-old female found down. CPR was initiated on the scene before the EMTs arrived." She paused a beat, then added, "Suspected opioid overdose. Naloxone was administered on the scene. No apparent effect."

Emily's heart sank.

Opioid overdose.

It wasn't the first time she'd heard those words here in the emergency department of the Stillwater County Health Center, nor would it be the last, but the frequency with which she'd heard them over the last six months was both troubling and depressing.

Drugs were a problem everywhere in America—had been forever, it seemed—and rural communities were by no means immune. In fact, the problem was often worse in the hinterland, where economic and social prospects were limited, which led to both dependence on narcotic substances as a way of self-medication and the illegal production and trafficking of those substances—a far more lucrative enterprise than working the family farm. But in the last few years, drug abuse and dependency had graduated from being merely a social problem and was now considered a disease epidemic, with more than a hundred thousand deaths annually.

Many factors contributed to the broader problem, but the one thing that had turned it so deadly was the synthetic opioid fentanyl. Opioids worked by interfering with the nervous system, preventing the brain from receiving pain signals and other sensations, but they also slowed both heart rate and respiration. When a person took a dose higher than what they were accustomed to or had some underlying health condition, they might stop breathing and die within a matter of minutes. Eighty times stronger than morphine, fentanyl was a potent medicine used clinically for pain management. Unfortunately, it was also readily available as an illegal street drug. Because it was so potent and because there was no regulation of dosages, the number of overdoses and overdose deaths had been steadily rising.

Emily had nothing but sympathy for those caught in the web of addiction. Many of them were just ordinary people who had gotten hooked on prescription pain meds like oxycodone, and then when their doctor stopped writing the scripts, they turned to illegal sources. She had been able to help several of them get into treatment programs, but she'd signed a lot more death certificates.

The information about the incoming patient was not encouraging. *Found down* meant that the initial overdose had not been witnessed. Someone, probably a husband or a boyfriend—*please, God, don't let it be one of her kids*—had found the woman unresponsive, not breathing, and after calling 911, had initiated CPR.

When the EMTs arrived, they had administered naloxone, a powerful opioid blocker that could almost instantly reverse the effects of an overdose, but had not observed any change because, in all likelihood, the patient was long gone.

However, because CPR had already been initiated, the EMTs were required by law to continue the lifesaving measure until the patient could be transferred to the hospital . . .

Where it would fall to Emily to give the order to stop compressions and then break the bad news to the woman's loved ones.

The families were the real victims because their pain did not end with the signing of the death certificate. Time softened grief, but it never completely went away. She saw it often in Matty's eyes, that ever-so-subtle flinch of pain when he saw a young boy interacting with his mother in a store or restaurant or in a movie. He didn't talk about his mother very often, how her drug dependency had hurt them both, how he had found her dead with a needle in her arm. When he did, he was stoic, controlled, but she could tell he was still hurting nearly twenty years later.

When she saw the flashing lights of the ambulance through the glass door of the emergency entrance, she pressed her lower back again and thrust her shoulders back, trying to stretch out the ache.

Twenty-nine, she thought, shaking her head. *Same age as me. What a shame.*

"Okay, let's do this," she said to no one in particular and began moving to one of the empty treatment bays where the code team was already assembling.

The glass doors opened a moment later, and in an instant, the energy level in the emergency room went from zero to sixty. A gurney materialized in the doorway, guided by an EMT who was also working the Ambu bag affixed to the tracheal tube that had been inserted into the patient's airway. Two patient care assistants from the ER staff were positioned on either side, pushing the gurney along. The patient lay supine, and another EMT who Emily recognized and knew from other encounters in the emergency room sat astride the patient, sweating profusely as he performed rapid and rhythmic chest compressions. His name was Jayden, but for reasons she wasn't aware of, everyone called him by his nickname, Midnight. As the gurney was rolled into the treatment bay, the other EMT began giving Joanna a verbal account of the interventions they had provided and the medications that had been given. Emily meanwhile settled the earpieces of her stethoscope into place and signaled for Midnight to pause compressions. As soon as he did, Emily placed the bell of the stethoscope on the woman's bared chest.

Nothing.

She stepped back to allow Midnight to continue compressions while one of the PCAs began placing the AED leads, and Joanna disconnected the Ambu bag and connected the tube to the wall ventilator. Everyone moved efficiently, professionally, but Emily felt their underlying sense of futility.

She shared it.

Compelled by a sudden and unexpected need to humanize the patient—*no, the person,* she corrected—she let her gaze drift to the woman's face.

With eyes closed, muscles slack in unconsciousness, mouth obscured by the trach tube taped in place, she was barely recognizable as a human being, but Emily nevertheless felt an immediate sense of familiarity.

I know her.

That wasn't really unusual. Emily knew most of the people in Wellington and its surrounding communities because, eventually, they all had reason to visit her.

She looked over at the other EMT. "What was the name again?"

"Raina Cole."

The name, like the face, rang a bell.

A former patient, maybe?

Then she remembered her earlier observation, *same age as me,* and it clicked.

Raina Cole, of course!

They had gone to school together all the way from kindergarten to senior year. Not friends exactly, especially not once they got to high school, but they were not enemies either. Raina had been one of those girls who liked a lot of attention from boys, while Emily preferred the attention of just one.

Emily had not made much of an effort to keep track of her schoolmates. A lot of them were still around, caught in Stillwater County's gravity well. Those who had escaped usually didn't look back, and Raina had always seemed like she'd be one of those.

Looks like you didn't get away after all, she thought. *Poor thing.*

"Pads are on," said the PCA. "Ready to start the AED."

Emily tore her gaze away from the woman's face. "Stop compressions."

An exhausted Midnight took advantage of the pause to swing down from his perch, and one of the ER staff moved to the patient's side, ready to take over compressions as soon as the AED collected enough information to determine the course of treatment. The interruption, of necessity, had to be brief, but a few seconds was all it took.

The AED monitor screen did not display a perfectly flat line—that only happened in movies—but it might as well have. Instead, the device, designed to shock the heart back into rhythm, simply read *No Shock.* Technically speaking, that could mean one of three things: That the patient believed to have no pulse did indeed have a normal, albeit faint, heart rhythm. That there was no "shockable" pulse detected. Or that the patient recently regained a pulse. But while the information was limited, Emily didn't need to see anything else to know the truth.

Raina's heart had stopped beating.

Asystole.

"How long was she down?"

"Short answer," replied the EMT, "too long." And then, as if he realized how callous the answer sounded, he added, "Dad found her. He said he called her, and when she didn't answer, he went over to her place. Started compressions right away. If he hadn't . . ." He trailed off, leaving the rest unsaid.

If the father hadn't started compressions, the first responders would have passed it along to the county coroner's office because Raina Cole, by any medical definition, was already deceased.

Emily closed her eyes, feeling something in the pit of her stomach that wasn't, for once, the baby doing acrobatics.

The decision to end the code was her responsibility now. As a physician, Emily had been taught the importance of pursuing every kind of treatment. Asystole *was* reversible. A shot of epinephrine, in combination with another dose of naloxone, might be enough to jolt the woman's heart into a shockable rhythm. It was possible, however unlikely, to bring Raina's body back to life.

It was also possible, and very likely, that the woman's brain, deprived of oxygen for who knew how long, was already irreversibly damaged, and all those interventions would do nothing more than prolong the pain and suffering of her survivors. Not to mention racking up an astronomical medical bill that would probably bankrupt them, compounding the tragedy.

Emily never allowed questions of cost to influence her medical decisions, but she was not oblivious to their impact.

But she's my age. She has so much more life to live. I have to try.

"Resume compressions," she said, her voice cracking a little. "Push two mils of naloxone and one of epi. *Now!*"

Hang in there, Raina. I'm going to do everything I can for you.

FIVE

In the instant that he identified the nature of the wound that had ended the smoke jumper's life, Matthew Redd switched into combat mode. Someone had murdered the smoke jumper, and that someone might still be in the area.

He did another three-sixty spin, searching the surrounding area for any signs that the threat was extant before kneeling down to check the unmoving figure for signs of life.

The man had no pulse and wasn't breathing. The blood staining his shirt around the bullet hole was already dry, indicating that the shooting had happened some time ago.

Probably right after the last reported contact with their team.

Redd leaned back on his haunches, considering what to do next. This wasn't a rescue mission anymore. It was a crime scene.

Who would shoot a smoke jumper in the middle of a raging wildfire? And why?

Those were the obvious questions, Redd knew, but maybe not as important as *how* someone had managed to pull off such a crime.

He was no investigator, but he knew enough to realize that this crime, like any, was the sum of motive, means, and opportunity. In this instance, the biggest mystery was opportunity.

The fire line was miles from the nearest road. *"It might not be the middle of nowhere,"* as J. B. might have said, *"but you can't see it from here."* There were no trails, and the terrain wasn't suited for off-road vehicles or horses, which meant the killer would have had to hike cross-country on foot, a journey that would have taken several hours.

Unless he was here all along.

That brought him back around to the question of motive.

Why kill a smoke jumper? Redd turned, doing another three-sixty scan of the perimeter. *Especially one who's actively fighting a fire?*

Then it hit him.

Unless you wanted to make sure the fire wasn't put out.

While he couldn't dismiss the possibility that this was a crime of passion . . . maybe the smoke jumper had hooked up with the killer's girlfriend or something like that . . . Redd's gut told him this was something else. Something related to the place.

Not everything is a conspiracy, he reminded himself.

And he was right. Though, since he'd been back in Montana, all Redd had done was inadvertently uncover conspiracies.

Maybe the smoke jumper had surprised a poacher lurking at the edge of the fire, hoping for an easy kill. Hunting out of season was illegal, but was it something worth killing over?

Not your job to figure it out, Redd told himself.

He took out his phone, checked to see if there was a signal—there wasn't—then put it away and instead unclipped the radio Thornhill had supplied from his belt. He took note of the frequency it was currently set to and switched to the channel used by the sheriff's department. "County One, this is Redd. Do you read, over?"

After a brief delay, a voice that he did not recognize came back over the line, advising him to stand by. About half a minute after that, Blackwood's voice issued from the radio.

"Matthew. I hope you have good news for me."

"Just the opposite, I'm afraid. I found one of the missing smoke jumpers. Dead. Shot in the back."

There was a long pause, during which Redd could easily visualize Blackwood's stunned expression. To his credit, the sheriff didn't ask Redd to repeat the message. "Was it accidental?"

"Are you asking me if he was *accidentally* shot in the back while fighting a fire in the middle of nowhere?" Redd couldn't imagine any circumstances where someone might accidentally shoot another person in the back. Maybe during hunting season, but definitely not during fire season. "Not a chance."

There was another brief pause. "What about the rest of them?"

"No sign of them yet. I called in as soon as I found this one. How do you want to deal with this?"

"Can you secure the scene?"

Redd looked through the smoky haze, trying to judge how close the fire was. "Honestly, I can't make any guarantees. If the wind changes, the fire could come through here pretty quick."

"All right," said Blackwood. "I want you to do what you can to preserve the scene. If you've got your phone, take as many pictures as you can. Then get out of there."

Redd glanced down at the motionless form on the ground, trying to decide how best to carry out the sheriff's directive. "I'll put him inside his fire shelter and tag the location," he said. "Then I'll continue the search."

"Absolutely not." Blackwood's response was as quick as it was forceful. "Forget the search. The shooter could still be out there."

"All the more reason for me to find the other smoke jumpers. They might have targets on their backs as well." He didn't voice his speculation that the reason for the loss of contact with the smoke jumpers might be that they were all dead. "Don't worry," he added. "I'll be careful."

"You'd better be. I don't want to have to face Emily with the news that something happened to you."

Redd laughed. "You and me both."

"Let me know as soon as you find anyone else. County One, out."

Redd returned the radio to his belt, then took out his phone again and used it to photograph the body from several different angles. Only then did he roll the dead smoke jumper onto his back, getting his first look at the man's face.

He was young, early twenties, Redd guessed, snapping another picture.

The man's chest had been torn open by the bullet—probably a hollow-point round—exiting the body. The mere fact of an exit wound indicated that the shot had been fired at close range. A handgun, not a hunting rifle. A forensic examination of the entry wound would probably confirm that, provided the remains weren't consumed by the fire. Redd photographed the exit wound as well, then put the phone away.

It took less than a minute to deploy the smoke jumper's survival shelter but considerably longer to shift his body into it. As he did, Redd couldn't help but think about the times he had performed a similar duty, packaging the remains of fellow Marines who had died in combat overseas. The last thing he did was mark the location in his GPS. Then, with that task complete and still keeping his head on a swivel, he moved on from the spot, looking for the other missing smoke jumpers.

He found the next one only about fifty feet from the first.

A single bullet hole in his back.

SIX

It was the worst part of the job.

Losing a patient—formally making the necessary decision to stop treatment and document the time of death—was hard, but having to go out into the waiting room and tell the family members, with their faces silently pleading for news of a miraculous recovery . . .

That was just brutal.

"Mr. Cole?"

The man, late fifties, with dark hair and a salt-and-pepper beard, wearing what Emily thought of as the Wellington Uniform—flannel shirt, faded Wranglers—looked up at her, then stood. There was a flicker of hope in his red-rimmed eyes, but it was extinguished before she could say a word. "It's Jessup, actually. Bob Jessup. Raina took her mother's last name . . ." He trailed off. "She's gone, isn't she?"

"I'm so sorry, Mr. Jessup."

He sank back into his chair and hung his head. "I guess I knew when I found her."

"Would you like to be with her?" Emily asked. Even though delivering the bad news was the worst part of her job, there was some comfort in helping the survivors begin the healing journey.

He looked up again as if surprised by the question but then nodded. "Yes, I'd like that very much."

She led him back into the examination bay where Raina lay on the padded table. The trachea tube had been removed, but an IV remained in her arm. A hospital sheet now covered her torso and lower extremities, but her face had been left uncovered.

Jessup took her hand in his. "She looks like she's just sleeping," he said, his voice breaking a little. "Like I could just say, 'Wake up, honey,' and she would."

Emily didn't respond but, after a respectful pause, moved on to the second worst part of losing a patient. "Mr. Jessup, this might be a hard question, but do you know if Raina was a registered organ donor?"

She braced herself for his reply. Most families supported the legally binding decision of their loved ones when it came to organ donation, but Emily had more than once been accused of being a ghoul, or worse, for broaching the subject.

But Jessup seemed to brighten at the question. "Yes, I'm pretty sure she was. I'd have to go back and find her driver's license to be sure. But, ah, can you actually . . . you know, use her . . . her organs? I mean, because of the drugs."

"Thanks to the CPR you started, there's a good chance most of her organs and tissue are still viable. Do you happen to know if she used intravenous drugs?"

He shook his head. "No. Just pills. She was in so much pain all the time."

The comment felt like a stab to Emily's heart.

If someone could have gotten to her sooner, helped her . . .

"I can let you have a few more minutes with her," said Emily, turning away as much to hide her own grief as to begin making the necessary calls to initiate the organ harvesting process, but then her curiosity got the better of her. "How did it start?"

"It happened when she was overseas," said Jessup, not looking away from his daughter's face. "Afghanistan. A suicide bomber rammed her truck."

"She was in the military?"

Jessup nodded. "Army. Eighty-eight Mike. Truck driver."

"I didn't know she served."

Jessup now gave her a questioning look. "You knew Raina?"

"Not well. We went to school together."

He accepted this with a nod. "After she graduated, she . . . she struggled. To find herself, I mean. Married too soon. Married the wrong guy. But then, after she left him, she got it in her head to join the Army. She was going to use the GI Bill, go back to school, and do something with her life."

"I had no idea."

Jessup shook his head sadly. "Then she got hurt. Messed up her back something bad. She spent months at the VA hospital learning to walk again. But the pain . . . It just never went away. When the VA docs took her off her pain meds . . ." He shrugged then gazed at his daughter's face again. The tears he'd been fighting back started to fall. He composed himself just long enough to say, "I guess she found another way to get them."

I couldn't save her, thought Emily. *But maybe I can find out where she got the drugs.*

But would that even help?

She looked over to Raina's dad. He held a hand over his mouth while staring at his daughter. Eyes red. Filled with grief.

"We're going to find out who gave those drugs to your daughter," said Emily, her own words surprising her. "And they're going to answer for this."

SEVEN

The smoke jumpers had worked in pairs, or at least that was how Redd found them.

After discovering the second pair, about two hundred yards east of the first, he didn't bother radioing Blackwood with any more updates. He just took the pictures, put the bodies into the emergency shelters, then tagged the location and moved on.

He had two reasons for doing this.

First, it didn't seem necessary to provide a blow-by-blow account of what had become a hunt for the victims of a mass murderer. When he found the fifth and sixth bodies at a similar interval from the third and fourth, both shot point-blank in the back, he lost what little hope he'd still nurtured that he might find some of them alive.

The executions had been methodical. The killer had just walked up behind each of them and pulled the trigger. While the unknown shooter's motive remained opaque—Redd didn't think it was a panicked poacher anymore—his intention was crystal clear. Not a single smoke jumper would be left alive.

The firefighters probably hadn't even realized they were in danger. The roar of their chain saws had likely covered the sound of the report, and at a distance, the noise of a pistol might not be distinguishable from the pop of pitch exploding in a burning tree trunk.

Redd's other reason for eschewing further calls to Blackwood was more urgent in nature. The wind had shifted. The fire was advancing.

At first, he hadn't been sure. It wasn't like he suddenly saw a wall of actual flames coming his way. But when the smoke seemed to grow thicker, making it hard to both see and breathe, he decided it was time to check in with Thornhill.

"Redd! Where on earth have you been? Why haven't you checked in?"

"Nothing to report," Redd lied. He would leave it to Blackwood to deliver the bad news.

"Well, I've got something to report. The wind has shifted. The fire is doing exactly what we were afraid it would do. If you can't find those guys soon, I'm going to have to drop in another team."

"Don't do that."

Redd knew he'd answered a little too quickly and feared that Thornhill would demand an explanation, but the incident commander was already talking.

"You really should think about getting out of there. I can send the helo back for you. They can't land, but they can drop a line and hoist you up."

"Give me thirty minutes." Thirty would give him enough time to locate the last pair of jumpers, provided that the interval remained about the same, and then make his way back to his original insertion point.

"I can give you thirty," replied Thornhill. "I can't promise the fire will."

So, despite the unresolved threat of the unknown killer, Redd sprinted down the last set of tracks leading away from the smoke jumpers' resupply point. Because he already knew what he would find two hundred or so yards up that trail, he wasn't at all surprised to spot the body sprawled across his path.

But he was surprised when the body let out an anguished moan.

When he overcame his initial shock, Redd rushed over and knelt to begin assessing the man's condition. He immediately saw that there were other differences. This smoke jumper, a young, dark-complected man—Redd guessed he was Native American—had not been shot in the back. His attacker had struck with a Pulaski, one of the axe-adze hybrid tools used by the firefighters. The horizontal adze blade was buried to the hilt in his chest. But for the fact that he was stirring, Redd wouldn't have believed the wound was survivable. The killer had probably thought the same thing, which was why he had moved on after striking the blow.

A closer examination of the wound provided a partial explanation to the question of survivability. The blade had missed the smoke jumper's heart by several inches. That was the good news. The not-so-good news was that it had sunk deep into his chest cavity. Had the killer removed the blade, the young man would almost certainly have bled out within minutes, but the blade itself had sealed the wound or at least slowed the bleeding. Even so, judging by the difficulty of his breathing, his chest cavity was almost certainly filling up with blood.

If he didn't get medical attention—not merely what little first aid Redd could administer, but Level I trauma care, and soon—he would be joining the rest of his team. Making sure he stayed alive long enough to get that treatment was now Redd's primary focus.

He broke open his medical bag and began laying out the materials he would need to hopefully stabilize the smoke jumper. He'd have to work around the Pulaski blade. In an impalement situation, removing the object in the field was the worst possible thing to do, even with medical gear. Instead, after donning a pair of nitrile gloves, he began swabbing the firefighter's forearm in preparation to insert an intravenous catheter.

The touch of the cool alcohol on his skin roused the smoke jumper. His eyelids fluttered open, and he made a moaning sound that might have been a question.

"Hey, you're awake," Redd said, trying to sound upbeat. "We're gonna get you patched up, so just hang on and try not to move around too much. I'm going to start an IV and get some fluids in you, then we'll see if I can't do something to help you breathe easier."

"Uhnnn."

Interpreting that as permission, Redd tied a rubber-band tourniquet just above the kid's elbow and tapped the antecubital hollow until a vein popped out. With a deft move, he slid the needle into the vein and advanced the catheter until he saw a flash of blood in the tubing. The hard part done, he connected the tubing to a bag of saline solution, which he placed on his patient's abdomen, and then untied the tourniquet, letting normal blood flow resume.

Starting an IV line was something Redd had learned to do in the Marines, and while he had not had much opportunity to exercise that particular skill in a real-world setting, he had done it plenty of times in a training environment. The same could not be said for what he was about to do next.

Redd had judged that the young man's difficulty breathing was the result of fluid and possibly air accumulating in the thoracic cavity. The treatment for this, a procedure known as a tube thoracostomy, involved cutting a small hole in the chest, between the ribs, and then inserting a piece of surgical tube through the chest wall and into the pleural space to drain off the fluid. It was a procedure normally reserved for emergency room doctors, but Redd's recently earned Wilderness EMT certification allowed some latitude when it came to the scope of practice. In the wilderness, where rapid transport to a trauma center wasn't always available, the first responder had to be able to do whatever it took to stabilize the patient.

But while that meant he was legally covered in the event that things went wrong, it did not mean that he felt especially confident in his ability to perform the procedure. He had only ever practiced it on mannequins.

Using trauma shears, he cut open the side of the firefighter's Nomex shirt, careful not to disturb the Pulaski, and then began swabbing the area where he intended to make the incision.

The sealed thoracostomy tray included a diagram showing the location of the fourth intercostal space between the ribs—roughly nipple level on a male patient—but Redd had to push and probe to locate the ribs. Doubting himself and remembering the age-old advice—*measure twice, cut once*—he moved his fingers back up to the nipple line, found the ribs, and, holding his finger in place, moved it down the man's side.

"That's the spot," he said aloud, wishing he felt as confident as he tried to sound. The truth of the matter was that he was a lot better at taking lives than he was at saving them. "Okay, this next part might sting a little."

The smoke jumper's only response was a wheezing, gurgling sound.

Better get it done, Redd thought.

With one finger on the spot, he took a scalpel from the tray and placed the edge right below it. "Please, God, don't let me screw up," he murmured, and then he pushed the blade into flesh.

The scalpel sliced through the skin and deep into the muscle with hardly any resistance at all. A trickle of blood began to stream from the incision. Redd laid the scalpel aside and inserted his finger into the cut, probing to make sure that he'd gone deep enough.

"I think that's it," he said.

The kit included two pairs of needle forceps. Redd used one of them to clamp the outflow end of the French 16 tube and then used the second to insert the working end into the incision. The rest was textbook. He put in a couple of sutures to hold the tube in place, applied a glob of petroleum jelly and gauze to prevent air from getting sucked through the incision, and then connected the clamped end of the tube to the drainage collection device. When he was sure that everything had a good seal, he unclamped the tube, which immediately filled with a bloody froth.

Although the entire procedure had taken less than ten minutes, Redd felt as if he'd aged ten years. He felt mentally exhausted, but as the young firefighter's breathing began to improve, a wave of relief buoyed his spirits.

This must be how Em feels every day, he thought.

His task was far from complete, however. He'd bought the kid some time, but it would be in vain if he couldn't get him to a hospital.

He gripped the smoke jumper's hand and was reassured when the kid reflexively squeezed back. "Now, let's get you out of here, okay?"

The smoke jumper winced a little, but then his eyes met Redd's, and for the first time since Redd's arrival, he seemed to show some awareness. His lips moved, trying to form words, but Redd couldn't make out what he was saying. Redd wondered if the kid was trying to tell him something about the man who had attacked him, and it occurred to him that, in saving the smoke jumper's life, he had saved the only eyewitness to the killing spree.

Maybe not the only one, he thought, remembering that there was still one smoke jumper unaccounted for.

As he put out a radio call to Thornhill, he moved away from the injured firefighter and began searching the area. There was no sign of the missing man anywhere in the vicinity, but that was not the only difference. Unlike the other sites, where the smoke jumpers had made a start of creating a firebreak, there was no evidence of any work done here. He did, however, locate what looked like another recently blazed trail moving off toward the east, parallel to the line of the advancing fire.

Thornhill's voice barked from the radio. "Redd, you there? What's going on?"

Redd keyed the transmit button. "I have a badly injured firefighter here who will need air transport ASAP."

"Injured? You found them?"

"Only one of them," lied Redd. "But he's in pretty bad shape. I'm not sure it's safe to move him."

There was a pause. "Where are you?"

"About four hundred meters east of the original drop zone." Redd checked his GPS and then supplied the UTM grid location as well.

When Thornhill came back, there was an edge of desperation in his voice. "Listen, Redd, the fire is almost on top of you. There's no way I can get a helicopter to you in time. Even if I could, they wouldn't be able to pick you up. You're going to have to pull back at least a couple klicks and either find or make an LZ."

Redd glanced back at the injured smoke jumper. "That's a no-go. There's no way he'll survive that trip."

"If you stay there, you'll both die." Thornhill's desperation now verged on full panic, but after a moment, he went on. "I don't know what to tell you, Redd. Put him in his shelter and then get as far away from there as you can before it's too late."

Redd shook his head, but it was a gesture of frustration, not dissent. Saving the smoke jumper's life only to turn around and leave him to face his fate wrapped up in aluminum foil like last night's leftovers felt like the worst kind of betrayal. Yet, as cold as the calculation was, Thornhill was right. The shelter was probably the kid's best chance at surviving the fire, and leaving him behind was Redd's.

Maneuvering the injured man into his shelter without aggravating his wounds took longer than Redd would have liked, and when he was finished, he was confronted with another problem. A person was supposed to be face down inside the shelter since there was usually a thin layer of breathable air near the ground, but the smoke jumper's injuries didn't allow for that kind of positioning. Redd solved the problem by outfitting him with a ventilator mask attached to a small bottle of oxygen before sealing him up inside.

Before leaving, Redd quickly cleared away as much vegetation and wood debris from the surrounding area as he could, reducing the amount of ground fuel. Then, satisfied that he had done what he could for the young man, he took off down the trail to the southeast, searching for the last smoke jumper.

With the wind pushing the fire toward him, the air was so thick that visibility was now measured in mere feet. The smoke stung his eyes and burned his lungs. He tried the old firefighters' trick of wetting a bandana and tying it over his mouth and nose to reduce the effects of smoke inhalation, but this barely seemed to help.

Five minutes, he told himself. *You can hold out for five more minutes.*

If he couldn't find the missing smoke jumper in five minutes, he would have to abandon the search and start putting some distance between himself and the fire.

It soon became apparent, however, that this estimate was overly optimistic. The fire was no longer an abstract, unseen danger but a living monster—a roaring dragon that devoured both wood and oxygen. The smoky air was full of glowing cinders that alighted upon him like burning snowflakes. He realized that his Nomex firefighting attire, by insulating his extremities against the heat, had given him a false sense of invulnerability, making him think he could pass through fire unscathed like some Old Testament prophet. After just a couple more minutes, in which he covered only about three hundred meters, he knew it was time to prioritize his own survival.

"I'm sorry," he gasped, apologizing to the last smoke jumper as he turned his back to the fire and stepped off the trail. "I have to go."

That was when he heard the gunshot.

EIGHT

The report was loud. So loud that Redd ducked his head reflexively. Loud meant close, and close meant that the fire was no longer his most immediate concern.

It also meant that the killer had just struck again, and that changed everything.

The subsequent rush of adrenaline did not immunize Redd against the very immediate threat of the fire, but it did tip the balance. He pivoted back onto the trail and took off at a full sprint, running toward the source of the sound.

Toward the gunshot.

The thought of running away did not even enter into his head. There was a killer out there, responsible for at least six and now possibly seven deaths, and while he couldn't bring back the victims, he *could* make sure that their murderer was brought to justice. Though he wasn't armed, save for the old Case folding knife he'd inherited from J. B., Redd had one thing going for him.

The killer didn't know that he was now the one being hunted.

A few moments later, the trail Redd was following began sloping downward. The fire was still close, still advancing, igniting the understory and setting pine boughs aflame, but because of the tendency of heat to rise, the air became noticeably cooler and clearer with each foot of vertical descent. With the increase in visibility, Redd now saw that the trail continued downhill, disappearing into a dense stand of lodgepole pines.

Without the smoke to provide concealment, Redd came to a full stop and took a moment to listen for any sound of movement ahead. For several long seconds, the only sound he heard was the crackle and pop of the fire behind him. Then, just as he was about to keep going down the trail, the sound of another gunshot split the air.

This time, Redd threw himself flat. The shot had definitely come from the valley below and sounded like it might only be twenty or thirty meters away. His first thought was that the killer must have spotted him. But when there was no follow-up and no sign of the killer moving up the hill to check on the results of the shot, he raised up for a quick peek. Just long enough to draw fire.

Nothing.

So, if he wasn't shooting at me, who was he shooting at?

Redd knew he wouldn't get an answer by staying put, so he popped up and made a quick dash for the closest tree. He stopped there, but only long enough to see if he'd been noticed, then moved again, zigzagging his way from tree to tree down the hill.

As he neared the valley floor, Redd glimpsed a man-made structure through the screen of trees—a small log cabin.

Redd recalled that there were a few such lodges scattered throughout the Elkhorn Recreation Area and along the course of the Trask River—rustic, off-the-grid structures, built by locals early in the last century on public land and then eventually bought back by the Forest Service and rented out to visiting fly fishermen and hunters. But he had not realized there were cabins in the path of the fire.

The presence of the cabin and the fact that the trail had led almost directly to it raised a host of new possibilities. Had the eighth smoke jumper known about the cabin and tried to shelter there when the killer came after him? Or was it the killer who had been using the cabin, maybe for some secret criminal enterprise, a secret worth killing to protect?

Redd continued forward as stealthily as possible, making a final dash to the back of the cabin, a solid wall of stacked logs without windows or doors. As he approached, he used a military tactic known as *slicing the pie* to edge slowly around the corner and detect any threats that might be waiting beyond. It was a technique ideally performed with a rifle in hand. Redd would have to settle for the old folding knife, which, although razor-sharp, was only lethal at very close range.

He didn't find an enemy waiting beyond the corner, but there was something, or rather someone, there. Another body lay stretched out on the ground at the front corner of the cabin. The body's upper half was just out of view, so that only the legs and lower torso were visible from where Redd now stood, but even a partial view was enough to reveal that the victim was not a smoke jumper. Instead of Nomex trousers and heavy leather boots, this figure wore blue jeans and Nikes. And though he couldn't say with absolute certainty, something about the style of the clothes and the shape of the body suggested femininity.

A woman, he thought. *Maybe a tourist staying at the cabin. But was she targeted or just an innocent bystander caught up in the violence?*

He couldn't begin to guess. This discovery was another unexpected variable, a twist in the unfolding mystery narrative that only served to further obscure the emerging picture.

And there had been two shots.

"Come on out, kid. I'm not going to hurt you!"

It was not the shout so much as the mere sound of another human voice that nearly caused Redd to jump out of his boots. Heart pounding from the spike of adrenaline, he almost fell down in his haste to scramble back to the rear of the cabin.

It was a man's voice, slightly hoarse but otherwise unremarkable, and yet Redd knew with certainty that it belonged to the killer.

"Come on out, kid . . ."

The killer was stalking another victim.

Holding his breath and trying to slow the runaway train that was his heartbeat, Redd closed his eyes and tried to focus on what he could hear.

Footsteps. Barely audible. The soft crunch of pine needles and dry soil underfoot. The interval was almost a full second. A slow walk. And getting . . . louder? Softer?

Definitely softer.

The killer was moving away.

Redd let out a breath, then pied the corner again and continued along the side of the cabin. He eased around the front corner even more slowly, trying to ignore the corpse at his feet—it was a woman lying face down, her long blonde hair mostly covering her face—and focused on what lay beyond.

The cabin sat in a clearing, perched on the edge of a shallow creek—a minor tributary of the Trask River, Redd guessed. He did not see anyone moving in the near-to-middle distance but thought he glimpsed something moving in the trees at the far end of the clearing. He also saw that the front door of the cabin stood wide open.

"So, we're gonna play hide and seek, is that it? Come out, come out, wherever you are."

Redd froze. The voice, which seemed to be coming from the woods, wasn't as loud as before. This wasn't due to distance but rather a softening of the man's tone—a parody of playfulness.

"*Come on out, kid.*"

Redd felt a seed of apprehension begin to germinate in his gut. The pieces were coming together, forming a terrible picture.

The dead woman outside the cabin. The killer's beseeching tone. The false promise, "*I'm not going to hurt you.*"

He's hunting a child.

The heat from the fires burning around them paled in comparison to the white-hot anger Redd suddenly felt surge through his body.

Without even realizing it, his fingers clenched into fists.

It was time for him to act.

NINE

For a fleeting moment, Redd considered charging into the woods, relying on surprise and violence of action to level the playing field, but common sense won out over bravado. Getting himself killed wouldn't do the kid any good.

He looked down at the three-and-a-half-inch blade of the folder clenched in his right fist.

I need a better weapon than this.

He cast a quick glance around the clearing, looking for anything that might serve, and then his gaze fell on the open entrance to the cabin.

Mindful of the fact that the killer in the woods might not be working alone, Redd eased up to the doorway and sliced the pie before entering. The interior of the one-room cabin was unlit, but there was enough ambient illumination streaming in through the doorway to confirm that there was nobody inside the cabin.

Or rather, nobody alive.

There was no question that the man seated upright in a chair near the back wall, arms and legs held fast with duct tape, head tilted back as if gazing up at the rafters, was dead. Redd could see the hole just above the bridge of the man's nose and the spray of blood and tissue on the wall behind him.

Like the woman outside, the man was attired in blue jeans and sneakers and wore a short-sleeved button-up shirt.

Not the missing smoke jumper, thought Redd. *So, where is he? And what happened here?*

A quick visual scan of the cabin revealed nothing that might be useful as a weapon, not even a kitchen knife. But it did offer a glimpse into the lives of the people—the family?—who had been residing there.

There were three cots, with a sleeping bag laid out on each. One was noticeably smaller than the others, adorned with images from one of the Toy Story movies. A twelve-inch-tall Buzz Lightyear action figure lay on the floor next to it.

Aside from the table and chairs, which looked to be part of the original decor, the only items of note were the stack of Mountain House meal buckets against one wall and half a dozen three-gallon water jugs.

They were planning to be here a while, thought Redd. *Hiding out?*

He tried to imagine the sequence of events.

The killer had taken out the smoke jumpers first, sneaking up on them, shooting them in the back . . . except for the guy with the Pulaski in his chest.

Why was that one different? And why kill the smoke jumpers in the first place?

Then he had gone to the cabin. *Following the last smoke jumper? Or was this his destination all along?*

He hadn't shot the man in the cabin right away, though. Instead, he had bound him to the chair. Perhaps to interrogate him?

Was he the real target?

If so, then everyone else . . . the smoke jumpers, the woman . . . the child . . . were all collateral damage. Wrong place, wrong time. Eyewitnesses to the crime who had to be silenced forever.

The woman—the dead man's wife?—had probably been the last to die. Maybe she had been out walking in the woods . . . walking with the child . . . When she heard the first shot, she told the child to run and hide. Then the killer came out and shot her dead too.

It was probably as close as Redd would ever get to figuring out what had really happened. All that was missing was the motive, and that was something only the killer could provide. But in order for him to do that, Redd would have to take him alive, and that wasn't high on his list of priorities.

He took just a moment to capture the dead man's likeness with his phone camera, then turned back to the doorway, edging around the corner and scanning the clearing for any sign of activity. Seeing nothing, he crept along the front of the cabin and then headed into the surrounding woods.

Despite his size, Redd moved with preternatural stealth. Years of stalking elk in the mountains with J. B. and later conducting covert reconnaissance on potentially hostile objectives, first with the Marine Raiders and then with his FBI fly team, had elevated his sneak game. Nevertheless, without knowing exactly where his target was, luck would play an outsize role in determining the outcome of this encounter. If the killer happened to be looking back at the wrong moment, all bets were off.

"Come on, kid. I'm just trying to help!"

Redd froze in place, turning his head slowly, trying to pinpoint the source of the voice. The man was close, maybe only twenty or twenty-five yards away.

"You hear that?" the man went on. "That fire's gonna be here in a few minutes. I just want to help!"

"Liar! You hurt Janelle and Raymond!"

Redd winced when he heard the screamed retort.

Don't say anything. He'll follow the sound of your voice.

That voice, both defiant and full of fear, was high-pitched, but Redd thought it sounded like a young boy.

"No, kid. That was an accident. Raymond had something that belonged to a friend of mine, and he wouldn't give it back. But that doesn't have anything to do with you. You and me, we can be friends!"

Redd used the killer's extended monologue to good effect, moving more quickly than he otherwise might have, closing in on the man's location. He was just starting to edge around a tree when he glimpsed movement on the opposite side of the trunk and froze again. The killer was right there, just a couple of steps away.

Got to time this just right, thought Redd, coiling himself like a rattler preparing to strike.

"I'll never be your friend!"

The boy's angry shout came just as Redd was starting to move. At almost the same instant, the figure on the opposite side of the tree turned and sprang into motion, leaping toward the sound of the voice and away from Redd.

"Gotcha, you little brat!"

Redd corrected course on the move, darting after the killer's receding back, catching up to the man just as the latter thrust his left hand into the hollowed-out trunk of a long-dead tree. With a savage pull, he yanked the hiding child into the open.

Then Redd was on him.

He didn't bother with threats or demands, but he was mindful of the fact that the killer almost certainly had a handgun pointed at the kid, so instead of clobbering him or trying to choke him out, Redd instead clamped a hand down on the man's right shoulder and spun him around.

As he found himself face-to-face with the startled killer, Redd immediately noticed three things.

The man did indeed have a gun—a semiauto, though that was about all Redd could determine at a glance. No surprise there. He'd known the man was carrying.

The second thing Redd observed was the small figure whose right arm was still caught in the killer's grip. A boy, as Redd had earlier surmised, maybe six or seven years old—Redd didn't have much experience judging such things. He was short with a thin build and had black curly hair. His cheeks were smudged with dirt and streaked with tears, and his bright blue eyes were wide with fear.

Poor kid.

It was the third thing Redd noticed, however, that caught him off guard.

The man was attired in clothes almost identical to what Redd himself wore. Forest Service green Nomex shirt and brown trousers. Firefighter gear.

He'd found the missing smoke jumper.

TEN

The man had blond hair, shaved close on the sides, long on top and pulled back in a tight ponytail, and a wispy reddish beard, all of which would have made him look like a Viking warrior from a TV show if not for his slight build and overall unimpressive physique. Redd didn't know if the man was actually the eighth smoke jumper or if he'd just appropriated the fire-resistant attire of the missing man, but one fact was beyond question: This *was* the man who had murdered the smoke jumpers as well as the man and woman at the cabin.

He was the killer Redd had been tracking.

And now I've found him.

The man's eyes went wide in surprise but then seemed to harden, like a missile targeting system locking on, even as the pistol in his right hand swung around toward Redd.

But Redd was much faster. He caught the man's wrist in his own right hand and thrust the weapon up, pointing skyward. The man howled as Redd's grip tightened, crushing the limb, but then he let go of the boy and, twisting around, threw a roundhouse that connected squarely with Redd's jaw.

To say that he had been hit harder once or twice in his life would have been a monumental understatement. Redd was used to fighting men *his* own size. Big men. The killer might as well have punched a brick wall for all the effect it had. Redd absorbed the impact by allowing his head to rock to the side, then he slowly turned back to face the man.

"Big mistake."

Judging by the other man's wide-eyed expression of terror, he had already arrived at the same conclusion.

Still holding on to the killer's right arm, Redd raised his own arm higher, lifting the man up until his feet were no longer in contact with the ground. With his arm hyperextended, the killer could do little more than flail his free hand and kick his legs ineffectually, but somehow, through it all, he kept his grip on the pistol.

Redd drew back his left fist, preparing to end the man's struggle with a single well-placed punch, but before he could deliver the blow, a sudden movement caught his eye. It was the boy, darting past him and sprinting away from the scene of the confrontation as if a pack of wolves was in pursuit.

"Wait!" Redd cried.

The boy didn't look back, but the distraction allowed Redd's captive foe to land another mostly ineffectual punch to his jaw. Redd shook it off and then drove his cocked fist forward into the man's face. The violent blow knocked him out cold.

Redd let the unconscious killer fall in a heap at his feet and then, after relieving him of his pistol, took off after the boy.

You deserve a lot worse than that, Redd thought. *Trying to hurt a kid.*

Then Redd shifted his attention back to the child.

"Wait!" he shouted. "Kid, I'm here to help!"

It occurred to Redd that the killer had said more or less the same thing. The kid had every right to be terrified of strangers dressed as firefighters.

Still, he had to try.

The boy had a good fifty-yard head start on Redd and didn't appear to be anywhere close to running out of steam. He'd passed the cabin—and the dead woman—and was now running parallel to the creek. Redd shoved the pistol into his waistband at the small of his back and charged after the boy.

"Kid, hold on!"

His long strides ate up the distance between them, at least until the kid, hearing the sound of Redd's feet pounding the earth behind him, glanced back and then kicked in the afterburners. Fueled by a burst of adrenaline, the boy began pulling away.

"I'm one of the good guys!" shouted Redd, but the boy paid no heed.

Suppressing a curse, Redd lowered his head and summoned up a matching burst of speed. He wasn't sure what he would do when he caught up to the kid. Physically restraining him seemed like a really bad idea, but if the kid wouldn't even stop to listen to what he had to say, he might not be left with any choice. He was surprised at how winded he felt. He made a point of staying in shape, and there was no way a little jog like this should have made his lungs feel like they were on fire . . .

The realization hit him like a slap in the face. His lungs *were* burning, but it had nothing to do with the exertion. The boy was running *toward* the fire.

The air around them had grown thick with smoke, casting the woods ahead into darkness from which embers glowed like the eyes of a demonic army. Between the rush of blood in his ears and the pounding of his boots on the ground, he hadn't heard the low roar of the advancing blaze, but now that he was aware, Redd couldn't believe how close the fire actually was.

The boy evidently realized it too. He skidded to a stop and then whirled around, his eyes darting back and forth, looking for a new escape route.

Redd also halted, giving the kid plenty of room. He raised his hands in what he hoped was a nonthreatening display. "Hey, it's okay," he said, trying for a soothing tone, something easier said than done. With smoke burning his lungs, he could barely get the words out without choking. "I know I look . . . big and scary, but . . ." Redd gasped, every breath burning, inflaming the lining of his lungs. "I just want to help you."

The boy refused to meet his gaze, but he didn't run. Redd took that as a good sign.

"My name's Matt." Redd's eyes were stinging like he'd been splashed with acid. He coughed again, then drew in a shallow breath. "What's yours?"

For a moment, Redd didn't think the boy would answer, but then, in a small voice, he said, "My name is Jack." His voice was soft, and Redd noted he had a slight lisp.

"Jack," Redd echoed, nodding. "Like Captain Jack . . ." Another coughing fit overtook him. "Jack Sparrow in those pirate movies."

Redd had hoped the reference would help him build rapport with the boy, but he didn't see even a hint of recognition, so he tried a different tack. After another shallow breath, he said, "Maybe you haven't seen those yet. But I'll bet you've seen *Toy Story*, right?"

Jack's head came up, his wide eyes meeting Redd's own gaze. "*Toy Story 2* is my favorite movie."

Redd took some small comfort in the fact that Jack didn't seem to be suffering the effects of the smoke as badly as he was.

Must be because he's shorter. Closer to the ground where the air isn't as bad. I wonder how long that will last.

"Is that right? Mine too." It was more of an exaggeration than a lie. He remembered liking the movies but had been younger than Jack the last time he'd watched any of the films in the series. "My favorite character is Woody because I'm a cowboy, just like he is."

"But Woody's a sheriff," Jack corrected, making it sound like an accusation and regarding Redd with fresh suspicion.

Redd winced inwardly at his mistake. He blinked away stinging tears and hastened to do some damage control. "Believe it or not, so am I. I mean, I'm not *the* actual sheriff, but he's a good friend of mine, and I work for him. I'm sort of like a deputy."

Wrap this up, Redd told himself, his lungs screaming with sharp pain. He had to fight to keep his eyes open to look at the boy.

"Then why are you dressed like a fireman?"

"Well, when there's a big emergency like this fire, everybody has to help out."

Jack continued to take Redd's measure for a few more seconds. Then he shrugged. "I like Buzz the best."

"Buzz Lightyear." Redd nodded and then, in his best approximation of the character's voice, said, "To infinity . . ."

That was as far as he got before a coughing fit overcame him. But the boy actually laughed, and Redd did his best to join in for a moment. Then he became deadly serious. "Jack, listen. We've got to get out of here. I can keep you safe, but we have to stay together. Look out for each other like Woody and Buzz. Think you can do that?"

Jack stared back at him and then looked past him. "But where's the bad man?"

Redd threw a quick glance over his shoulder. The smoke was now so dense he couldn't see the cabin, much less the spot where he'd dropped the killer. "I don't know. But I don't think he'll try anything now that we're a team."

"He hurt Janelle . . . and Raymond too."

Janelle and Raymond. Not Mom and Dad. Redd filed that information away under the heading of *Things to Ask Later.*

"I'm not going to let him hurt you. I'm a lot bigger than him. He tries to hurt you again and I'll hit him so hard he really will go to infinity and beyond, buddy. That's a promise. But right now, what we need to worry about is this fire. Okay?"

Jack returned a hesitant nod, his eyes seeming to say, *You better not let me down.*

Redd thought about offering his hand but decided against it. Instead, he turned, facing back the way they'd come . . . At least, he hoped so. It was hard to tell for certain. "Let's get a move on."

As he began striding forward, he glanced back and was relieved to see Jack jogging to catch up to him.

The feeling was short-lived.

Through the fog of yellow smoke, he saw a flash of orange directly in their path. The air around them was suddenly alive with a noise that was something like the staccato pop of a machine gun and the roar of a jet engine, growing louder.

The fire had caught up to them.

Redd knew he had seconds to act, or they'd face certain death.

ELEVEN

Emily's eyes darted back and forth as she scanned the information on the screen, mentally translating the shorthand of chart notations into a coherent narrative describing the health history of Raina Marie Cole.

She knew she should just let it go. Her job was to help the living. There was nothing she could do for Raina now. But a single thought—*same age as me*—had lodged in her mind like a barbed fishhook.

Same age as me.

How did it all go so wrong for her?

Raina's father had painted the story in broad strokes, and Emily knew she could probably fill in the gaps without too much effort. It was an all-too-common trajectory, a sequence of causal relationships.

A person sustains a serious injury and is given pain medication by a physician.

The patient becomes dependent on those pain meds and then turns to street drugs when their doctor won't renew the prescription.

And because taking street drugs is like playing Russian roulette every day, the fatal overdose is more a matter of when than if.

That story, or something like it, had played out thousands of times, maybe hundreds of thousands of times. It was no different in this instance.

Oh, someone should have realized what was happening and intervened, and maybe they'd even tried, but in the end, it wasn't enough. Someone, probably Raina's doctor, had allowed her to continue taking opioids for pain management and had failed to catch the early warning signs of dependency.

Maybe that was why she couldn't let it go. Raina was gone, but if Emily could understand where it had gone wrong for her, understand the pathology of Raina's addiction, then maybe she would be better equipped to help the next patient.

So, after making the final entries into Raina's medical records, she scrolled through the woman's history, trying to find where that critical failure had occurred.

It was all there. The initial assessment conducted at the medical facility at Kandahar Air Base, and then a few days later a far more comprehensive assessment of her injuries at Landstuhl Regional Medical Center in Germany. Crushed vertebrae, herniated disks, broken pelvis and left femur. She had been transferred a few weeks later to Walter Reed where she spent more than a year in physical therapy.

The chart contained a record of every treatment and every medication prescribed, from antibiotics to pain management. Opioids had been a part of that almost from the beginning.

Nothing wrong with that, Emily thought. Raina had probably been in a great deal of pain, and contrary to what some people believed, toughing it out wasn't necessarily the healthiest thing to do.

Pain management had continued even after her return home to Montana, where she'd continued with outpatient therapy at the Fort Harrison VA Medical Center, outside Helena.

Something caught Emily's eye. She scrolled up, checked an earlier notation, then scrolled down again.

"They changed the dosage," she murmured. "They were trying to wean her off it."

The entries that followed told the tale of how Raina's caregivers had begun addressing Raina's dependence on opioids, both by reducing the dosage of her prescription and by prescribing nonsteroidal anti-inflammatory drugs. At first, it seemed to go well, but then Emily saw notations from the doctors indicating a diagnosis of OUD—opioid use disorder—and that the patient was "resisting further reduction." A slower taper was recommended, along with mental health treatment.

Then something changed. A new set of entries appeared, interspersed with the records from the primary caregiver. At first, Emily thought perhaps a specialist had been brought in to consult, but it almost immediately became apparent that this new doctor's course of treatment was completely at odds with the efforts of the primary care team. While the latter was trying to help Raina gradually end her body's dependency on opioid painkillers, this new doctor was prescribing increasingly higher dosages. Not long thereafter, the entries from the VA doctors stopped altogether.

Unable to shake her dependency, Raina had gone looking for someone willing to do what her caregivers at the VA would not.

"I guess she found another way . . ."

Emily felt cold rage building in her chest. She couldn't believe a doctor, someone who had sworn to "first do no harm," would do something so irresponsible.

"Who is this jerk?" she muttered.

A quick Google search informed her that Dr. Mark Dickerson was a family practitioner in Helena. His part in Raina's story, however, had ended in 2016 when, without any explanation, the entries in Raina's medical record ceased altogether. The timing coincided with the Centers for Disease Control and Prevention's issuance of new guidelines that strongly advised against prescribing opioid painkillers, characterizing the unfolding crisis as an epidemic. Subsequently, many pharmacies had refused to stock them for fear of civil and even criminal liability. The CDC guidelines had, in Emily's opinion at least, only inflamed the problem as patients like Raina, addicted to prescription painkillers, had turned to street drugs. Ironically, the CDC had finally corrected course and refined the guidance, but that was little comfort for the families of the tens of thousands who died of overdoses on drugs like fentanyl during those years.

Emily knew that Raina bore the ultimate responsibility for her fate. She had refused the help that had been offered her, refused the difficult path that would have saved her, and instead had gone looking for instant gratification. If Dr. Dickerson had refused to write her script, she would have kept looking until she found someone who would.

But that didn't excuse him.

Emily stared at the screen of her phone, which displayed the Google page with the information about Dickerson's practice, and then, without really stopping to think about what she was doing, tapped the link to call.

The recorded voice of an automated answering system informed her that if she was calling about a medical emergency, she should hang up and call 911, and then began reciting a menu of options. Emily hit zero, and after several rings, an actual live person answered.

Emily decided presenting herself as a professional was the best way to proceed, so after identifying herself, she asked to speak with Dr. Dickerson about a former patient of his.

"I'm sorry," came the reply. "Dr. Dickerson retired a few years ago."

Of course he did, thought Emily sourly. *He gets to play golf and go fly-fishing while Raina's father has to plan a funeral.*

"Is it something Dr. Glaser can help with?" the woman on the line was saying.

"No, I really need to speak with Dr. Dickerson. Do you have his contact information?"

The woman rattled off a telephone number with a 406 area code and a 444 prefix, which Emily scribbled on a Post-it note. "He's still in Helena?"

"Sure is. He's got a real nice place out in Lakeside. I don't think he'll ever leave."

Emily stared at the phone number for a moment, then made a decision. "I don't suppose you would happen to have that address."

TWELVE

Redd knew he had no time to waste and no room for error if he was going to save himself and Jack. All around them, patches of grass spontaneously ignited practically underfoot, but the real danger now was not from the flames but rather from the heat.

"Don't breathe!" Redd shouted. The air temperature around them had become blast-furnace hot, and inhaling it would blister their lungs, suffocating them long before the flames could take them. "Hold your breath for a second and cover your mouth. Like this." He buried his mouth and nose in the crook of his elbow.

Although wide-eyed with terror, Jack followed his lead. Doing so wouldn't afford much protection from the scorching heat, but it would mentally help the boy hold his breath until Redd could deploy the emergency shelter.

Between a practice session at the command post and packaging the remains of the murdered smoke jumpers, Redd had refined his technique for breaking out the aluminum and silica composite bag, but this was his first time doing it *in extremis.*

His fingers slipped uncertainly on the buckles of his rescue pack. The shoulder straps seemed to bind up, refusing to slide off, forcing him to shake and wriggle out from under them. Once the pack was off, he fumbled to find the pouch where the rolled-up shelter was stored, wresting it open and pulling out the shelter. His lungs continued to burn, less from the heat and more with the fatal impulse to simply breathe.

He was taking too long, and he knew it.

C'mon! his brain shouted.

But then the shelter was in his hands. He gave it a shake, then another and another until it was mostly unfurled, revealing the long opening on one side. He stuck one foot in, anchoring it to the ground, then ducked his head and shoulders inside, using himself like a tentpole. Then he reached out with both hands to Jack.

Jack didn't need to be told what to do. Dropping his own arm from around his face, the boy sprang into Redd's open arms, hugging him around the waist. Redd pulled Jack into the shelter and then, after getting his other leg inside, dropped onto the ground, kneeling on all fours with Jack beneath him, holding the shelter's open side to the ground.

All I can do. Now, it's out of my hands.

The foil cocoon shut out all light, and for a few seconds, it seemed to bring relief from the heat as well. Redd took a tentative breath. The air inside the shelter was as hot as a sauna, but it was a lot cooler than what was outside. Nevertheless, Redd felt the heat on his back radiating through the skin of the shelter and his Nomex shirt. Then another thought occurred to him.

The pistol!

Frantic, Redd reached back and found the handgun he'd taken from the killer where he'd stashed it in his belt. There was some debate about the exact temperature at which handgun ammunition "cooked off"—igniting the primer and either firing the bullet in the chamber or causing the cartridge to explode—but it wasn't something Redd wanted to put to the test. The gunmetal felt red-hot in his hands as he removed it, placing it on the ground where, hopefully, it wouldn't reach that critical threshold.

He supposed if it got that hot, an exploding pistol would be the least of his worries.

Redd thought back on his conversation with Thornhill about how hot the fire could get. He imagined the aluminum melting or even catching fire, or the glue holding the silica composite together breaking down . . . imagined the shell simply disintegrating around them.

What would happen to him and Jack then?

Would they even live long enough to know what was happening?

Redd pushed the thoughts from his mind, knowing that his biggest job at the moment was to protect Jack, and that meant reassuring him they'd be okay.

Even if Redd wasn't sure that was true.

"You good, pal?"

Redd sensed Jack nodding more than he saw it.

"It's going to get pretty hot, but don't worry. It'll be over soon."

Please let that be true, Redd prayed. *At least spare the kid.*

The noise of the inferno rose to a deafening crescendo. Embers rained down on him, striking the exterior of the shelter like hailstones. Then something much bigger and heavier slammed down onto his back, probably a tree limb that had been burned off the main trunk, nearly crushing him against Jack. Grunting, Redd summoned all of his strength and pushed against the debris, arching his back as if doing a push-up, and felt the object, whatever it was, start to fall away.

The exertion left him completely drained. Bright spots flashed in the darkness around him, not flames but phosphenes—seeing stars. Despite his best efforts to hold his position, keeping his weight off Jack's body beneath him, the muscles in his arms quivered and then failed, dropping him down atop the boy once more. He could feel Jack shaking under him, sobbing as death came for them both.

But then, just as quickly as it had escalated, the fury of the firestorm began to abate. The furious roar of the dragon quieted as the beast, having devoured everything here, moved on in search of new fodder. However, Redd knew that the danger was far from over. He recalled something else Thornhill had said.

"Most of the fatalities that occurred when a shelter was deployed happened because the firefighter didn't use it correctly or tried to get out too soon."

But how soon was too soon?

Careful to keep the corners of the shelter pressed to the ground so as to keep the hot air outside from rushing in, he shifted to the side, trying to ease some of the burden off of Jack. He felt the boy stir and take a breath—a good sign, he decided.

"Just a few more minutes," he promised. "Okay?"

"Okay," came the reply in a small voice.

He's talking. Another good sign.

"We're gonna be okay," Redd went on. "How are you doing? Are you hurt at all? Did you breathe any smoke?"

"I don't know. I think I'm all right," came Jack's innocent little voice.

"That's good." Redd knew he needed to keep the boy talking and keep his spirits up, but he had no idea what to say.

Then Jack filled the silence. "Are Raymond and Janelle dead?"

Redd winced at the straightforward question. He had no idea how to talk to a kid about the subject.

Except, you do, don't you?

He hadn't been much older than Jack when he'd found his mother, Linda Redd, dead on the bathroom floor of their dingy little trailer. It was a memory he didn't choose to revisit, but sometimes it came back to him unbidden.

It had been Redd's first real experience with mortality. And something he'd never forget.

Up until that moment, death was something that he had experienced only through books and movies. He understood it in the abstract, just as he had a vague notion of what might happen to a person afterward, but knew nothing of the emotions that came with loss.

He remembered a police officer—a woman—who had taken him aside, hugged him, and when he had asked her almost the same question that Jack had asked him, she had told him, *"Your mama is resting peacefully now."*

She had meant well, but Redd had known, even then, that it was the wrong thing to say.

"Yeah, Jack," he said finally. "I'm sorry, buddy, but they are."

Jack began to cry.

"Can I ask you something, Jack? Raymond and Janelle . . . They're not . . . They weren't your parents?"

"No. My mommy went away . . ." He caught himself. "She died too."

The words felt like a knife to Redd's heart. "I lost my mom too. I was a little bit older than you. How old are you, anyway?"

"I'm six and three-quarters."

Redd couldn't help but smile. "Counting the days until your next birthday?"

Jack nodded.

"Were Raymond and Janelle relatives of yours?"

"Yeah. They're my aunt and uncle. I went to live with them after Mommy died."

Redd nodded in the darkness. "After I lost my mom, I went to live with a man named Jim Bob. Right here in Montana. He became my new dad."

Even as he said it, Redd realized he'd made a mistake in sharing that. Jack was now twice bereft. He'd lost his mother *and* his aunt and uncle.

Redd hurt for the poor child. And he hoped there was someone in Jack's life who could step up and be the Jim Bob he needed.

He decided to change the subject. "Jack, do you know why the bad man wanted to . . . to hurt Raymond and Janelle?"

More movement. Jack shook his head. "No."

Redd visualized the scene in the cabin—Raymond duct-taped to a chair before being executed. Interrogated first? It sure looked that way. "Do you know what Raymond did? What his job was?"

"He worked in a big office."

Big office. Not much help there.

"Why did all of you come out here?"

"Raymond said we were going to go camping for a while. But I think . . ."

Redd prompted him, "Go on. What do you think?"

"Well, Raymond and Janelle were . . . They were fighting a lot. And Janelle was . . . scared, I think."

"Scared of Raymond?"

"No. Someone else. I don't know who. Maybe it was the bad man."

Redd knew that Jack wasn't going to be able to shed any more light on the subject, but so far, everything he had heard and seen suggested that Raymond had been mixed up in some kind of criminal enterprise and something had gone horribly wrong. Maybe he owed money to the mob or something like that. He'd been running for his life when he'd brought his family to a remote corner of the wilderness, but it hadn't been enough.

Death had found him in the end.

Now Redd needed to make sure Jack didn't suffer a similar fate and silently vowed to do everything in his power to protect the kid.

"Well, we can talk about all that later," he said, trying to sound upbeat. "I think it's probably okay to get out of this thing. How does that sound to you?"

Jack tensed. "Is the bad man still out there?"

Redd had been wondering that as well. The man had been unconscious when Redd left him to chase after Jack, so if the burnover had reached that far, he was done for. But wildfires didn't always move predictably.

Still, Redd had taken his weapon. Even if he was alive, he probably wouldn't attempt anything.

"I don't think we have to worry about him. Like I said, I won't let anyone hurt you," he answered. "Okay, I'm going to raise one corner just a little, and we'll see if it's safe. Ready?"

"Ready!"

Redd lifted the corner of the shelter he'd been holding with his right hand just a few inches. Hot, smoky air blew in, replacing the cooler air inside, and for a fleeting moment, Redd feared that he'd doomed them, but then the temperature seemed to equalize. He waited another couple of seconds, then lifted the corner higher to reveal the aftermath of the burnover.

The world outside the shelter had been transformed into something resembling an alien landscape.

A layer of ash covered the ground like fresh snow. A few feet away, the tree branch that had struck Redd's back was mostly charred, but flames continued to dance on its surface, as they did on the trunks of several nearby lodgepole pines. The smaller limbs and foliage had all been burned away, leaving the main boughs blackened but still upright—smoking black spires that disappeared into the yellow-orange haze that seemed to blanket everything.

Redd spotted another smoldering object a few feet away, an unrecognizable lump that nevertheless looked vaguely familiar.

"What's that?" Jack asked, pointing at the blackened mass.

Redd groaned. "I think it was my backpack."

The pack contained all his survival gear, extra food and water, and the somewhat depleted medical bag. Fortunately, his radio had been clipped to his belt, and the GPS receiver had been in his pocket—both were still intact and functioning.

Redd unclipped the radio and called Thornhill.

The Forest Service official was ecstatic. "Redd! Thank God you're still with us. What's your situation?"

"Well, I've been better," admitted Redd. "Listen, there's a lot going on out here, and I can't get into it right now, but I need you to send that helicopter in here for a pickup ASAP. I've found a . . ." He glanced over at Jack. "A civilian. A minor child."

"You've got a *kid* with you?"

"He was staying at an old fishing cabin. His guardians didn't make it."

There was a long silence on the line. When Thornhill came back, he sounded a little defensive. "Those cabins were supposed to be vacant."

"That's a problem for later. Right now, I need you to send the helo and get us out of here. We got caught in a flash fire and had to ride it out in the shelter."

Thornhill gave a response that made Redd wish he'd covered Jack's ears.

"All right," he went on. "Where are you right now?"

Redd gave him the UTM coordinates from his GPS unit, and after a few minutes, Thornhill replied with a different set of numbers, which Redd plotted into the device. The map showed a location about a mile away on the other side of the creek.

"That's your LZ," said Thornhill. "Can you make it there?"

"As long as the fire doesn't get in the way."

"You should have a clear path to it. I'll have the helo there in thirty minutes. Radio in if you can't make it in that time."

"I'll be there," replied Redd, silently adding, *Even if I have to carry the kid on my back.*

As soon as he signed off with Thornhill, Redd switched frequencies and called Blackwood.

The sheriff's voice boomed from the handset. "Matthew! You had me a little worried."

"You and me both," admitted Redd. "Listen, there's been a new development." He quickly recounted the events at the cabin, finishing with his overpowering and disarming the killer but stopping short of describing the burnover. It wasn't really relevant, and he didn't feel like reliving those few hellish minutes.

"Do you still have the suspect in custody?" asked Blackwood.

"No. I had to leave him and run after Jack."

"Ah. Tough choice. But you did the right thing going after the boy."

"I took his gun. And I can give you a description. He's miles from the nearest road. If he can even make it out of here alive."

"I'll get that description out to the deputies and the highway patrol. We'll find him."

"There's a helicopter coming to evacuate us back to the command post. I'd like you to have a couple of deputies waiting there. Until we know for sure what this is all about, I think Jack should be in protective custody."

Feeling the boy's eyes on him, Redd gave what he hoped was a reassuring smile. "I'll see to it personally," said Blackwood. "You have my word."

Redd signed off and then turned to Jack. "All right, buddy. We've just got to walk a little ways, and then you're going to get to take a ride on a helicopter. How does that sound?"

Jack's eyes went wide with wonder as he contemplated the prospect, but then his expression changed. "Wait!" His little arms shot up in protest. "I forgot my Buzz toy!"

Redd knew exactly what Jack was talking about. "Your Buzz Lightyear toy?" He shook his head. "I'm sorry, but I don't think we can go back for it. The fire—"

"But I *need* Buzz." The demand came out like a wail of grief. Fresh tears fell from his big round eyes, causing streaks of wet ash to cake to his face.

Redd knelt so that he was at eye level with the boy. "Jack, listen. There's a really good chance that the cabin isn't there anymore. Your old Buzz might be gone. But I promise, as soon as we get back to town, I'll get you a brand-new—"

"Please." Jack's lip quivered, and his chin fell to his chest. "I want *my* Buzz."

The boy's posture broke Redd's heart. Suddenly, he wished Emily was there. Or even Mikey or Liz Derhammer. All of them were better with kids and would know just what to say.

Redd scanned the surrounding area once more.

There's no way that cabin is still standing.

But he didn't have the heart to say that out loud. And he knew this was about more than just the toy, especially for a boy who had lost as much as Jack had.

"Was Buzz a present from your mom?" he asked.

Jack's head bobbed an affirmative.

"I see." Redd took a breath. "I'll tell you what. I wasn't kidding about the fire. It's not safe to go back to the cabin right now. But I'm going to have to come back out here in a little while, and I'll do my best to bring Buzz back for you. Deal?"

Jack continued to stare at him as if looking for some hint of duplicity. Then he seemed to reach a decision. He wiped his face with his arm, then said, "Promise?"

Redd smiled and offered his hand. "I promise, Jack." Then sensing the boy needed a reassuring hug, Redd pulled him into his arms. "Let me get you to safety first, and then I'll come back for Buzz."

THIRTEEN

It wasn't until Emily was behind the wheel of her white Chevy Tahoe on the highway and heading north, just beyond the turnoff that led out to the ranch, that she finally began to grasp the sheer size and proximity of the Trask River Fire.

Matthew had talked about it that morning, just before she left for work, and she had nodded sympathetically when he worried aloud about *"losing another house to fire"* or something like that. Truthfully, she had thought he was overreacting.

Wildfires in late summer were a fact of life in Montana. In a state that was mostly wilderness and open range, with a climate and topography that favored lightning storms on hot afternoons when the prairie grass was stick dry, fire was just another type of weather. In fact, it was part of the natural cycle, necessary both for reducing the fuel loads and for maintaining the natural equilibrium of the ecosystem, a scientific fact that rangeland managers understood but could not always convey to the average person who thought only in terms of acreage burned. In the very rare instances when a fire did pose a threat to populated areas, it was quickly brought under control, and she'd felt certain that this one would be no different.

But now, as she beheld the wall of smoke looming heavily overhead, looking like nothing less than the surface of a rogue planet poised to collide with the earth and smash everything into oblivion . . . Now she was . . . less certain.

The fire was close. So close, if she let her imagination run wild, she could almost feel its heat radiating through the Tahoe's window.

But that is just your imagination running wild, she chided herself. The fire couldn't be *that* close.

Could it?

I hope they don't close the highway.

If they did shut down traffic along the highway, she would have to call Matthew and ask him to pick up Junior, and then she would have to explain why she wouldn't be home on time.

When she had made the decision to drive up to Helena and confront Dr. Dickerson, it had felt so . . . so right.

Dickerson would never have to face any consequences at all for his role in Raina Cole's death. Any attempt to prosecute would run aground upon the simple reality that Raina's death, while tragic, was the result of her own choices. The same would probably go for a wrongful death lawsuit. Dickerson had, in fact, stopped writing the prescriptions, a detail which would likely absolve him of blame.

A case could be made that he had committed an ethical breach by treating her in the first place, but because he was retired, any kind of formal censure, up to and including losing his medical license, would be purely symbolic.

No, Dickerson would never be held to account. Which was why Emily had felt so compelled to tell him to his face that *she* knew what he had done. *She* cared, even if no one else did.

Now, however, confronted with the ominous spectacle of a world on fire and the very real possibility that she might get stranded in Helena, she couldn't help but wonder if perhaps she had been just a little . . . hasty.

But she didn't turn back.

Gradually, the wall of smoke receded into the rear view, and not long thereafter, open range gave way to semi-urban sprawl as she entered the outskirts of the state capital. Ten minutes later, the onboard GPS advised her to take the next exit, and then she was heading east on East Custer Avenue. Another turn left onto York Road seemed to transport her out of the city and into what was, for Emily, undiscovered country. Although she had lived most of her life in Montana and made frequent trips to the state capital, mostly for shopping or other business, she rarely had cause to go exploring.

Helena was a city in the same way that a chihuahua was a dog. It met the technical definition, but that was where the similarity to places like London or Chicago stopped. With a population of just over 35,000—bumped up to more than 80,000 if the far-flung metropolitan area was included—it was more of a big town than a small city. The area of greatest population density was north of Mount Helena, west of the highway, but one didn't have to stray too far from the highway and its corridor of big box stores to lose any sense of being in an urban center.

Although a few suburban communities had sprouted up like weeds out in the hinterland, there wasn't much to see along the ten-mile drive to Lakeside, the residential neighborhood where Dr. Mark Dickerson had elected to retire in style.

Dickerson's home looked like something out of an Eddie Bauer catalog. A big two-story lodge built of cut stone and rough-hewn logs, it was the Hollywood ideal of what a house in Montana should look like—faux rugged. With so many Hollywood elites falling in love with and moving to Big Sky Country, it had become an increasingly common and costly aesthetic. As Emily turned into the driveway, the mere sight of the opulent lodge swept away any lingering sense of doubt about her course of action, replaced by boiling rage.

She grabbed the folder containing a printout of Raina Cole's medical record and got out of the Tahoe—an undertaking that had become increasingly difficult since she could no longer see her feet—then made her way up the stone steps to the front porch.

The door opened before she could ring the bell. Evidently, her arrival had been noticed. She was surprised to see not a man in his sixties but rather a stunningly beautiful woman.

Emily's first thought was that she was gazing upon the Snow Queen from the Hans Christian Andersen fairy tale. Pale and blonde, with icy blue eyes the same color as her lilac-blue appliqué jacquard dress—an Oscar de la Renta, if Emily was not mistaken.

Slender, almost willowy, but with a bustline that Matthew's best friend Mikey Derhammer would have jokingly described as "aftermarket," the Snow Queen towered over Emily. She was as tall as Matthew, maybe even a little taller, though a glance down revealed that five inches of her height could be attributed to her silver Louboutin So Kate heels—Emily didn't think they were knockoffs.

Who wears heels to answer the door? Emily wondered.

The woman's appearance was so striking, not to mention unexpected, that Emily was momentarily at a loss for words.

The Snow Queen gazed down at her with an expression that fell somewhere between bemusement and contempt, with more of the latter as her eyes dropped to Emily's bulging midsection. Then she broke the spell of silence. "Can I help you?"

The words were uttered with a distinctly Slavic accent.

Definitely not a local girl, thought Emily. She cleared her throat and launched into a variation of the introduction she had rehearsed. "I'm Emily Redd, head of emergency medicine at the Stillwater County Health Center. I'd like to speak with Dr. Dickerson, please."

The Snow Queen arched one eyebrow. "My husband is retired."

Husband? Emily managed, with an effort, to hide her reaction. *Forget Snow Queen,* she thought. *More like Trophy Wife.*

"I realize that. This concerns one of his former patients. Is he available?"

The woman gave Emily—and especially her belly—another appraising glance. It occurred to Emily that Mrs. Dickerson was probably spinning jealous fantasies in her head to explain the presence of a very pregnant woman on her doorstep. With a melodramatic sigh, the woman said, "I will see if he wants to talk to you."

Emily wasn't at all surprised when the door was closed firmly, shutting her out, but she wondered if the woman would actually tell her husband that he had a visitor or if she intended to let Emily stand on the porch until she gave up and went home.

She was about to ring the doorbell when the door opened again, this time revealing the older man she had expected.

Dr. Dickerson, I presume.

Based on how she'd been received by the man's wife, Emily had expected a level of wariness or even suspicion from the doctor, but the gray-haired man standing at the threshold greeted her with a genial smile. "How do you do? I'm Mark Dickerson. Anya said that you're an emergency room doctor, but . . . ah, she didn't catch your name."

"Emily Redd. I'm the director of emergency medicine at Stillwater County Health Center down in Wellington."

"That must have been a bit of a drive. What can I do for you, Dr. Redd?"

"Earlier today, I treated one of your former patients. Raina Cole." Emily watched to see if the name would produce a reaction. It did not.

Dickerson shook his head. "Doesn't ring a bell. Sorry, but I haven't seen any patients in years. If she was one of mine, you should probably talk to Ken Glaser. He took over my practice." He paused a beat, then added, "I hope she's all right."

"Unfortunately, she's not. She died. And you stopped treating her before you retired."

For the first time since he'd opened the door, Dickerson's smile slipped. "That's too bad." Another pause. "But if what you say is true, then she hasn't been my patient for several years. I'm sorry you came all this way, but I'm afraid I can't help you."

He took a step back, one hand on the door handle, but before he could pull the door shut, Emily thrust the folder at him. "According to her medical records, you treated her for chronic pain. She was a disabled veteran injured in an IED explosion in Afghanistan. She was receiving treatment at the VA, but when they tried to taper her use of opioid painkillers, she stopped going to them and came to you instead. You prescribed sixty milligrams of oxycodone, extended-release, and you kept writing her scripts for several months thereafter. After you stopped, she turned to street drugs.

"It's all here." She shook the folder. "What I can't figure out is why any medical professional would continue prescribing opioids to someone who had been diagnosed with opioid use disorder."

As she'd spoken, Dickerson's face had grown redder, his nostrils flaring as his breathing quickened. "We're done here," he said. "You need to leave."

"It's a simple question, Doctor," Emily pressed. "You knew she was an addict. Why did you keep writing her scripts? The VA was trying to get her off the drugs. You made sure that she stayed hooked."

"You don't know what you're talking about." Dickerson's voice had risen an octave, his protest sounding like a child throwing a temper tantrum.

"Then explain it to me. Tell me how it was medically necessary to keep giving drugs to a drug addict. I'm sure it didn't have anything to do with kickbacks from the pharmaceutical company."

"It's time for you to leave." Dickerson shoved the folder away with one hand and grabbed the inside door handle with the other.

"I'm sure Raina's father would like to hear your answer."

The door slammed shut so hard that the sound of it seemed to echo across the lake like a gunshot.

Feeling hot all over and just a little lightheaded, Emily leaned against the porch rail and tried to slow her breathing. As she did, she pondered what to do next. She doubted Dickerson would open the door to her again, so ringing the doorbell probably wasn't going to accomplish anything. Besides, he might call the police to accuse her of harassment or trespassing.

Let him, she thought. *And I'll make sure everyone in Helena knows what he did.*

Except she knew that once law enforcement and the courts got involved, things had a way of going sideways.

If it came down to it, Dickerson would probably hide behind some high-priced lawyer who would make sure that *she* was the one who got punished.

She and Matthew didn't have the money to fight a battle like that, and losing might cost them everything. Her job. The ranch.

I shouldn't have come here, she thought, and this time, there was no righteous indignation left in her.

And as if she wasn't feeling bad enough, her body chose that moment to remind her that she was not only pregnant but closing in on her due date with a vicious cramp. The spasm, which hit hard and fast, sent her grabbing at the porch rail for support.

It wasn't the first time she'd experienced a cramp like this. Braxton-Hicks contractions, sometimes called "false labor," were common and often increased in frequency and intensity in the final weeks of a pregnancy. She'd experienced plenty of them with Junior, so she wasn't overly concerned about it being the start of labor. Nevertheless, the momentary discomfort only added to what had proved to be a pretty terrible day already.

When the contraction eased after about ten or fifteen seconds, she straightened and gathered her wits. She glanced down at the folder in her hand, considered leaving it on the porch, then thought better of it.

Dickerson had been right about one thing. It was time for her to leave.

✕ ✕ ✕

Inside the house, Dr. Mark Dickerson was shaking as he leaned back against the door, bracing it with his body as if he feared that the pregnant doctor might try to force her way inside.

What was her name again?

He couldn't remember. Couldn't even think straight.

This had always been his greatest fear. A reckoning so long delayed that he had dared to believe the danger was past.

But it wasn't. It had just laid there like an unexploded land mine, waiting to be triggered, waiting to blow up in his face.

He would lose everything. The house. The Range Rover. Anya.

He was not so foolish as to believe that she loved him any more than he loved her. She loved his money, and he loved the envious looks he got when he paraded her around at the country club and society events.

Without his money, she would leave him in a heartbeat.

He might even go to jail.

Anya appeared at the end of the hallway. "What did that woman want?"

He looked up at her, reading the suspicion and jealousy in her eyes. He knew what she was thinking, but the truth was so, so much worse.

"Nothing," he said too quickly. "It was a misunderstanding."

"Misunderstanding?" Anya's voice dripped with sarcasm.

Just then, he heard the low rumble of an engine starting. Dickerson pushed away from the door and moved to the nearest window, tugging the blinds aside just enough to peek out at the driveway where a white Chevy Tahoe was rolling back toward the main road.

"She's leaving," he said.

Anya folded her arms over her considerable bosom. "And will we see her again?"

The question brought unexpected clarity. He let the blinds fall back into place, and when he turned to face his wife, he was smiling. "No. No, I don't think we will ever see her again."

Her suspicious demeanor softened, but only a little.

"Anya, my love, it just occurred to me that all this smoke in the air isn't good for our lungs. Let's get away for a while." He knew that the suggestion would make her think he was running away from the problem, but she wouldn't care because she loved going places and spending his money. "Somewhere tropical. How about Miami Beach?"

She would find the thought of Miami Beach—or, more accurately, Sunny Isles Beach, known informally as Little Moscow—irresistible.

"You'll need something to wear." He straightened. "I need to have a meeting with my business partner before we go. Why don't you head to Denver and do some shopping. I'll come down later tonight and meet you there."

Her eyes narrowed again at the mention of the business partner, but she knew better than to ask. After just a moment's consideration, she gave him a seductive smile. "You are too good to me, *miliy*."

He matched her smile. "Only because you're worth it, *milaya*."

As she floated up the stairs, eager to begin packing for their impromptu getaway, Dickerson let his smile harden. He took out his phone, brought up his contact list, and tapped a name. The phone rang twice before a gravelly voice said, "Yeah?"

"There's a problem. I need you to fix it."

FOURTEEN

Jack tired quickly once they crossed the river, leaving behind the scorched woods where the fire had nearly claimed them, so Redd offered to give him a piggyback ride. He wasn't sure how the boy would respond to that—was six and three-quarters too old for piggyback rides?—but Jack accepted the offer, and Redd let him climb aboard.

Jack weighed only a little more than the pack Redd had lost to the fire, so carrying him this way wasn't especially burdensome. The only real difficulty was when Jack's arms tightened around his neck. Because he had to use his own arms to hold Jack's knees above his hips, Redd couldn't just reach up and gently loosen the boy's death grip.

"Jack, buddy. Relax. You're choking me out."

He felt the pressure ease as Jack moved his hands down a little. "Sorry."

"It's okay. Don't worry. I'm not going to let you fall."

But just a few minutes later, Jack's arms had found their way back across his throat. "Jack. You're doing it again."

No answer.

"Jack!"

He could feel the boy's steady breathing, but there was still no response. Redd realized then that Jack had fallen asleep while hanging on for dear life. Redd sighed and decided he could tolerate the discomfort. The kid had been through a lot and probably needed the sleep.

It took most of the allotted thirty minutes to reach the designated LZ, and Jack slept soundly through it all. When Redd finally reached the coordinates, he decided to let the boy go on sleeping until the helicopter showed up. Five minutes later, when he heard the distant sound of engine noise and rotor blades beating the sky, Redd began tapping Jack's leg.

"Wake up, buddy. Our ride's here."

Jack stirred then started, jolting awake with a low wail as if caught in a nightmare. He let go of Redd's neck and tried to push away. Redd felt the boy's weight shift back and quickly dropped to one knee, shortening the distance between himself and the ground so that, when he released Jack's legs, he did not have far to go. In the same motion, however, he twisted around and swept Jack into a one-armed hug to prevent him from bolting.

"Hey, Jack," he soothed. "It's all right. You're all right."

Jack's eyes were wide with panic, but after a moment, recognition dawned, and the fear ebbed. He began looking around, taking in the unfamiliar setting.

"There you go," Redd went on. "Everything's okay. You had a little nap. That's all."

Jack swallowed and then nodded. "I'm awake," he muttered, rubbing the back of his hand across his eyes.

Redd relaxed his hold, allowing the boy to stand on his own. "You hear that? The helicopter? We're going to ride on that. Pretty cool, huh?"

Another nod.

"It's going to be kind of loud, but just stick with me, and you'll be fine."

Right on cue, the noise level escalated, and a few seconds later, the helicopter appeared above them, descending at a low angle until it was right over the clearing, hovering about fifty feet off the ground. Redd saw the crew chief leaning out from the back of the aircraft. Once visual contact was made, Redd and Jack retreated to the edge of the landing zone while the pilot made a cautious descent into the clearing. When the crew chief gave them the signal to approach, Redd bent low and, holding on to Jack in a side hug, moved out under the spinning rotor blades. Redd could feel the tension in Jack's extremities, but to his credit, the boy did not falter or hesitate. When they reached the aircraft, Redd boosted him up into the cabin and then hoisted himself in after.

As soon as they were buckled in, the helicopter rose above the treetops and moved away, staying low to maximize ground effect. Redd was pleased to see Jack looking through the side window, watching their journey with great interest. Redd also looked, studying the transformed landscape and trying to determine how far the fire had spread during the relatively short time he'd spent on the ground. He was especially concerned about the fate of the injured smoke jumper he'd been unable to evacuate. It was impossible to tell if the place where he'd left the man had burned over, let alone how intense the burn had been.

Hang on, he pleaded silently. *I'm coming back for you.*

FIFTEEN

The helicopter touched down at the command post, remaining there just long enough for Redd and Jack to step off before taking flight again, heading for Helena to refill the fuel tanks.

"How did you like that?" Redd asked when the noise had subsided a little.

"It was awesome!"

Redd allowed himself a moment to smile, then gestured across the open area to a pair of black SUVs with emergency flashers on the roof and the word *SHERIFF* emblazoned on the door in letters big enough to read from a hundred yards away. "Remember how I told you I was friends with the sheriff? Would you like to meet him?"

As Jack considered the question, his eyes narrowed. "Am I in trouble?"

"No," Redd replied quickly and forcefully. "Never. We're going to take care of you, Jack. Keep you safe, just in case the bad man is still out there. But the sheriff will want to talk to you about what happened. Think you can do that?"

Jack continued to stare up at him. "Are you gonna be there too?"

Redd frowned. "I've got something I have to take care of first, but I'll come back and check on you as soon as I can."

Jack couldn't hide his disappointment, but after a moment, he nodded. "Okay."

As they made their way toward the patrol vehicles, Redd saw two uniformed figures step out and begin heading out to meet them. He was pleased to see that one of them was Sheriff Blackwood himself and even happier when he realized that the other was Stacy Reller, the department's only female deputy. A mother of two preadolescent boys, she would be the perfect temporary caretaker for Jack.

Blackwood quickly took the lead, reaching Redd several steps ahead of the deputy. After a cursory glance down at Jack, he focused his attention fully on Redd. Tall and lanky, with just a hint of a paunch, Blackwood stared out at Redd from beneath the brim of his khaki Stetson.

"How are you doing?"

"Dealing with it. Could have been a lot worse." Redd cast his eyes down.

Blackwood nodded in understanding, then focused his attention on Jack. "And who is this young feller?"

When Jack did not answer, Redd took the reins. "Jack, this is my friend Sheriff Blackwood. Sheriff, this is Jack."

Jack looked up at Redd. "He doesn't look like Woody."

Redd grinned, shooting a glance at Blackwood's uncomprehending face. "No, he doesn't, but he's still one of the good guys." He then pointed to Stacy. "And this is Deputy Reller."

Stacy leaned down, putting herself at Jack's eye level. "It's a pleasure to meet you, Jack. Say, have you ever ridden in a police car?"

Jack shook his head. "No, but I just rode in a helicopter."

Stacy affected a look of surprise. "Is that right? You know, I'd love to hear all about that. What do you say we ride back to the sheriff's office and get you cleaned up a little? Maybe on the way into town, we can scare up a cheeseburger and a milkshake. How does that sound?"

"Can I get chicken fingers?"

"I think we can do that." Stacy smiled and extended a hand.

Jack looked at the hand, then looked up at Redd questioningly. Redd nodded. "It's okay. She'll take good care of you. And when I'm done here, I'll come see you."

When Jack and the deputy were out of earshot, Blackwood turned back to Redd. "All right, Matt. Tell me everything. Take it from the top."

Although he had made several reports to the sheriff by radio, Redd launched into a much more detailed account of everything that had happened, beginning with his discovery of the first murdered smoke jumper and ending with a brief description of the desperate moments spent in the fire shelter. Blackwood only interrupted a few times, asking for clarification.

"Did you get a last name?" he asked when Redd put names to the victims at the cabin.

Redd shook his head. "Jack didn't say, and I didn't ask. The kid just watched them get executed. He's pretty traumatized."

"Maybe Stacy can get him to open up a little. We need his last name at the very least."

"What will happen to him now?" asked Redd.

"Once we have a name, we'll try to find next of kin."

"I think Raymond and Janelle *were* his next of kin."

"If there isn't anyone else, I'll have to contact Child and Family Services Division."

"So you're going to put him into the system." Redd couldn't keep the bitterness out of his tone. He had spent a few days *in the system* following his mother's death before Gavin Kline had appeared in his life and taken him to live with J. B. "Foster care."

Blackwood gave a helpless shrug. "The law is clear on this. And whether you believe it or not, it's what's best for him. CFSD has the resources to take care of him."

"It's just . . . he's been through so much."

"Which is why he needs the kind of help that only they can provide."

Redd couldn't bring himself to accept that. "He's an eyewitness to a serious crime. He should be in protective custody."

Blackwood gave him a sidelong glance. "You believe he's still in danger?"

Redd wasn't certain, but it was a thread to grasp for. "I think it's a real possibility."

Blackwood considered this for a moment, then blew out his breath and sighed. "Well, it's something to consider. But even if that's the case, the county doesn't have the resources to see to his needs. Physical *and* emotional."

"Can you at least hold off on doing anything until I'm done out here? I'd like to see him again." Redd had no idea why he added the last part, but as he said it, he realized that it was the absolute truth. He felt something for Jack that went beyond mere affinity. It was as if, in finding the boy and saving him from the killer, he had become Jack's sworn protector—a sacred trust not easily renounced.

Blackwood nodded slowly. "I think I can swing that." He paused a moment. "Let's talk about what you found out there. We've got nine dead bodies—"

"Eight," corrected Redd. "At least, I hope it's only eight. One of the smoke jumpers was still alive when I left. Hopefully he still is, but I'm going to need some help to get him out of there."

Blackwood nodded. "The SAR team from Bozeman is on their way here now. I'll leave it to you to coordinate the rescue effort. But we also need to get in there and recover the bodies. Not to mention collect whatever evidence we can. If there's anything left."

"You'll have to talk to Thornhill, the guy in charge of fighting the fire, about that. He doesn't know about the murders yet."

"Right now, the fewer that know, the better. You got any theories about why this happened?"

"A few," Redd admitted. "I think Jack's uncle—Raymond—was the primary target. Everyone else was collateral damage. And I think this was a hit."

"Like a mob hit?"

Redd nodded. "I think Raymond brought his family out here because he knew someone was gunning for him. Jack said that he worked in a big office, but I think maybe what he meant was that Raymond worked in a big office building. Like a skyscraper."

"Not many of those around here."

"Nope. My guess is that they were from out of state. Maybe the hit man was too."

Blackwood immediately picked up on Redd's intention. "You want to bring the Bureau in on this."

It wasn't a question, so Redd didn't respond.

"Well," Blackwood went on, "I suppose the case could be made that the murder of Forest Service employees on public land already makes this a federal case."

"I was wondering about that," admitted Redd.

Under his drooping mustache, one corner of Blackwood's mouth twitched up in the start of a smile. "I'll just bet you were. Well, I appreciate you not giving me the hard sell." He nodded. "Go on. Give your dad a call."

SIXTEEN

As his armored Chevrolet Suburban rolled along Constitution Avenue, Gavin Kline recalled an old Chinese curse: *May you get what you wish for.*

He was probably misremembering the exact verbiage, and in any event, the attribution was dubious, but the sentiment, a variation on another old proverb— *Be careful what you wish for*—was absolutely, universally true.

He had always been ambitious and driven, but when he'd earned his gold shield all those many years ago, the idea that he might one day occupy the top slot at the Bureau had been just that—an idea. Not a goal or a target. Not the focus of a five- or ten- or even a twenty-year plan. Oh, he was going to rise through the ranks, of that he had no doubt. But director? Even if it was only the interim position of acting director, that was the sort of thing reserved for idle fantasies, like making plans for spending lottery winnings.

Nevertheless, here he was, and here, it seemed, he would remain. With the president's nominee for the directorship mired in Senate gridlock, Kline had been told to expect to remain in the position for at least another year or so, during which time he would have to do more than simply keep things on an even keel.

To begin with, there was the not-insignificant job of purging all vestiges of a shadowy conspiracy that had very nearly compromised the entire federal government, like a tree rotting from the inside out. Kline's predecessor had been a key figure in that conspiracy, and despite his very timely demise, his influence was widespread. His cronies occupied a number of senior positions in federal law enforcement agencies, and it was Kline's job to root them all out, with the added challenge of not undermining public support for the institutions of government—no mean feat.

That Herculean task—or was it Sisyphean?—was enough to take the shine off his so-called promotion, but ironically, it was the part of the job he actually cared about.

Not so the rest of it. The politics . . . the administrative details . . . the endless appearances before Congress, begging for more funding to keep the nation safe.

Like this latest quixotic battle, a figurative can that had been kicked down the road time and time again: The J. Edgar Hoover FBI Building—always an architectural eyesore—had been literally falling apart at the seams for more than twenty years. Yet, despite signaling approval for a new headquarters building, the process had dragged on for almost as long, mired in petty political considerations. The latest argument was over where to locate the new headquarters. Several generations of FBI leadership wanted to relocate to Virginia, in close proximity to Quantico, where the FBI academy was located, but politicians throughout the DC metro area wanted the facility built in their districts. Kline had no real preference and knew that if this particular issue was resolved, there would be some other point of contention, but he was nonetheless obliged to spend the rest of the workday defending the Quantico plan in front of a Congressional subcommittee.

May you get what you wish for, he thought as the motorcade approached the security checkpoint on Delaware Avenue. *Definitely a curse.*

The buzz of his cell phone distracted him from his dark musings and immediately put him on his guard. Only a handful of people had this number, and almost all of them knew better than to call when he was on his way to the Capitol unless the situation was a dire emergency. Then he saw the caller's name on the screen and breathed a little easier.

There was no temptation to let it go to voicemail. He did not hesitate to accept the call. "Matt! How are things?"

His son's deep voice boomed from the phone's little speaker. "I'd be lying if I said it's all good."

Worry flooded Kline's system. "Is it Emily? Is everything okay with the . . ." He stopped short of saying it aloud, fearing the worst.

"Em's fine. Everyone's fine. This is something else. There's a situation here, and I think we're going to need to bring in the Bureau."

"I'm listening," said Kline.

As Redd began recounting a story of murdered smoke jumpers and the rescue of a six-year-old boy, the Suburban came to a full stop in front of the steps leading up to the House Chamber. A moment later, the FBI special agent in charge of Kline's protective detail opened the door to let him out. Kline forestalled him with a raised hand. His ambitious career pursuits had wrecked his relationship with his son, and he was only now starting to rebuild. He wasn't going to rush this.

Congress could wait.

When Redd had finished talking, Kline weighed in. "Matt, this probably isn't what you want to hear, but it sounds like this falls squarely in the jurisdiction of the Forest Service Law Enforcement and Investigations."

"The Forest Service has their own investigative agency?" asked a disbelieving Redd.

"Most government departments do."

"Well, I can see how they might want to go after whoever killed those smoke jumpers, but I think the real target was the family staying at the cabin, and I think whoever ordered the hit is somebody the Forest Service cops aren't equipped to deal with."

"You're probably right," said Kline. "Okay, I'll kick this out to the Bozeman field office. Someone will be in touch."

"Gavin, I don't just want 'someone.' I need to know who the victims are. I've got first names—Raymond and Janelle—and I've got a picture. I'm sending it to you now. My gut tells me that whatever they were mixed up in, it's probably the sort of thing that would put them on your radar."

The phone buzzed in Kline's hand as the photo arrived in a text message. Kline winced when he found himself looking at the face of a dead man.

"I also want Jack put in protective custody," Redd was saying. "Blackwood's going to have to turn him over to Child Services, and I'm not sure they'll be able to protect him."

"Sir," intoned the agent at the door. "You're going to be late."

Kline waved him off. "All right, Matt. I'll do what I can from here and get back to you ASAP."

"Appreciate it."

"It's good to hear—"

A double-beep tone signaled the end of the call.

Kline sighed. *At least he called me,* he thought. *That's something.*

He stepped out of the Suburban, and as he made his way up the Capitol steps, he called his secretary, instructing her to have two agents immediately dispatched from the Bozeman field office to Wellington, with orders to report to the county sheriff. Matthew would be able to fill them in when they arrived.

He then forwarded the photo to another number, along with a short message:

Only have first names. Raymond & Janelle. Might be tied to an open investigation. See what you can turn up.

He was almost to the secure entrance when the phone buzzed with a reply.

On it, boss.

SEVENTEEN

From the air, Redd could see that the fire had advanced several hundred yards during his absence. The spot where he had left the injured smoke jumper was now a smoking wasteland.

"Well, that doesn't look good," remarked Dave Rossi, one of the two SAR technicians from Bozeman who had come up to assist Redd with what they hoped would be the rescue of a living firefighter and not the recovery of a dead body. The observation was all the more noteworthy since it was just about the most either man had said since introducing themselves just before boarding the helicopter.

The men had been aloof toward Redd. Not exactly rude, but he got a definite vibe from them, a vibe not unlike that of seasoned military operators interacting with selection candidates. In their eyes, he was an unknown quantity. Unproven, untested. While they weren't exactly dismissive, their quiet disregard spoke volumes. He would have to prove himself if he was going to earn their respect.

But that wasn't a game he had any interest in playing. He didn't need their respect. He just needed their help to save a man's life.

If it isn't already too late.

"No, it doesn't," admitted Redd. He'd tried to remain optimistic about the smoke jumper's chances of survival, but looking down at the scorched earth, it was hard to believe that anything still lived down there.

Still, he had to know for sure.

As it was unsafe to attempt a landing, the rescuers would have to be lowered from a hover. Since it now seemed unlikely that the subject was still alive, Redd, who was still nominally in charge of the effort, decided to go down first to assess the situation.

When the helicopter was hovering about a hundred feet above the ground, Redd clipped his chest harness to the loop at the end of the cable and, at a signal from the crew chief, stepped out into nothingness.

The winch unspooled the cable quickly—the winch's max speed was two hundred feet per minute—slowing only when Redd was about twenty feet above the ash-covered ground for a landing as gentle as taking that last step from a staircase. Even before touching down, Redd could feel the heat radiating up from the ground and from the blackened boughs of trees that were still smoldering. Now that his feet were back on the ground, he could feel that heat rising through the soles of his boots.

"Get in, get out quick," the crew chief had advised when briefing Redd and the SAR technicians back at the base. "Stay down there too long and you'll burn your little tootsies off."

It hadn't been funny then, and it definitely wasn't funny now.

He unclipped and stepped away from the dangling cable end, then began searching the area for the emergency shelter, which, according to the GPS, should have been no more than ten meters from where he was now standing. After walking in slow circles around the spot for almost two full minutes, he spotted a lump that looked to be about the right size for a body in a shelter. He brushed away a layer of ash to reveal a dull, metallic surface.

Barely aware that he was holding his breath, he carefully punctured the scorched foil-like covering with his knife and then tore it away to reveal the human form underneath. As he did, he heard a faint groan rising from the protective cocoon.

A gasp escaped Redd's lips. Impossibly, miraculously even, the smoke jumper was still alive.

Almost frantic, he kept tearing at the shelter, which crumbled like weathered paper under his fingers, until the figure inside was revealed.

The smoke jumper was alive, but judging by his pallor, he wouldn't be for much longer if Redd didn't do something, and quick. The bag that had contained saline solution for the IV line lay flat and empty on his chest, right beside the blade of the Pulaski that was still jutting from his body. The receptacle for the chest tube was almost completely full of blood, and the man's breathing had become shallow and labored. Somehow, he had managed to pull the ventilator mask away from his face, the oxygen bottle long since depleted.

But he *was* alive.

"Thank God," Redd whispered and meant it.

❌ ❌ ❌

As soon as they were on the ground, Rossi and the other SAR technician—Justin Bern—worked far more efficiently than Redd ever could have to get the injured subject stabilized again. With more IV fluids and O2 flowing into him and the chest drain emptied, the man's breathing and color improved considerably.

After inspecting the chest tube, Rossi glanced up at Redd. "You did this?"

Redd nodded.

Rossi didn't say anything more, but his expression—raised eyebrows, a slight nod—conveyed what he did not say aloud. *Not bad.*

Redd took it as a compliment. In truth, he did feel a measure of personal satisfaction, not because he had earned the other man's respect but rather because his efforts had not been in vain. Despite all the death he had encountered, he had succeeded in saving two lives, and that wasn't something to be discounted.

Nevertheless, he felt that there was still unfinished business. Maybe it was too late to save the other victims, but it wasn't too late to see that justice was served.

Careful to avoid dislodging the Pulaski, the SAR techs got the subject into a wire basket litter, securing him in place with crisscrossing strands of one-inch tubular nylon webbing. Two lengths of eleven-millimeter static cord were candy-striped around the rails of the litter and tied with bowline knots. The knots were then secured with a heavy-duty carabiner, which they attached to the hoist cable lowered down from the still-hovering aircraft.

Bern rode up with the basket, making on-the-fly adjustments to keep the litter stable and get the patient loaded aboard the aircraft. When the cable came back down again, Redd indicated that Rossi should take the next ride up.

"Don't wait around for me," Redd told the other man. "Get him to the hospital. Send the helo back for me once he's off-loaded."

Rossi regarded him with a raised eyebrow. "You sure?"

Redd nodded. "Every minute counts, right? Besides, there's something else I need to do out here."

The man accepted this with a shrug, then clipped into the hoist cable.

When the helicopter was gone, Redd took out his GPS again and selected the waypoint marking the location of the cabin. It was closer than he'd realized, at least measured as the crow flies, and with most of the ground vegetation burned away, there was nothing to prevent him from making a beeline toward his destination.

He didn't know exactly what he hoped to find there, but it felt like the place to begin the search for answers. He felt certain that Raymond and Janelle, or possibly just Raymond, had been the killer's true target, so anything that might help Redd understand who the man was and what had prompted him to flee to a remote corner of the Montana wilderness would go a long way toward figuring out who might have wanted him dead.

Redd was not too surprised to see that the cabin was still standing. Ground fires tended to burn fast, consuming grass and other dry vegetation quickly but at relatively low temperatures. Much the same way that a big unsplit piece of wood thrown onto a poorly kindled fire might not ignite, the cabin's logs had been scorched but had not burned.

Something similar had happened to Janelle's remains. The flames had consumed her clothing, burned away her hair, and charred her skin black, yet her body remained intact—enough so that a forensic examination would certainly be able to establish the cause of her death. He regretted not having photographed her earlier.

Before entering the structure, Redd walked the area where he'd left the unconscious killer, hoping—though it was a grim hope—that he would find the man's body in a similar condition, but there was no sign of him. Either Redd was mistaken about where that confrontation had occurred or, more likely, the killer had removed himself from the area.

Redd's gut told him that he had not seen the last of the man.

He returned to the cabin and went inside. With the smoke haze in the air reducing the amount of ambient light, he had to use his phone's flashlight to negotiate the gloomy interior. Aside from the layer of ash that seemed to coat everything, the cabin looked almost exactly as he had left it. Raymond's body still occupied the chair at the back of the space, the spattering of blood on the wall now looking almost black. Redd approached and performed a quick pat down, hoping to find a wallet, phone, or other personal effects, but the man's pockets had already been turned out, presumably by the killer.

A thorough search of the cabin proved similarly futile. He discovered an empty Mountain House food bucket that had been repurposed as a trash can, but it contained nothing aside from empty wrappers, paper plates, plastic cups, and disposable cutlery. There were no notes, letters, or papers hinting at Raymond's career or other activities that might have prompted his flight to the wilderness.

The return to the scene of the crime wasn't a complete waste of time, however. With a smile, Redd scooped up Jack's Buzz Lightyear action figure and headed out the door.

EIGHTEEN

Roughly six miles away, the man who had called himself Josh Harris—his real name was Dean Werner—unconsciously rubbed his bruised jaw as he took out his phone and checked for signal strength.

"Two bars," he murmured. Not ideal, but probably good enough to get a call through. "Guess I better do this."

It had been over an hour since he watched the helicopter vanish into the distance, carrying with it the boy and the firefighter whose unexpected arrival had thrown a great big monkey wrench into his plans, and he'd spent most of that time dreading the call he knew he had to make.

Loose ends, he thought.

His father had been explicit in his instructions.

Kill them all. No loose ends.

And he'd almost pulled it off.

It had been such a perfect plan. His brother, Holt, in typically brutish fashion, had wanted to just go in and ice the targets—*pop, pop,* just like that—but their father had nixed that idea. Dead bodies had a way of bringing unwanted attention. So Dean had come up with a plan that, while admittedly a lot more complex, would nicely divert suspicion away from them. The authorities might not even realize that the couple had been murdered.

He'd started by setting the fire in the Elkhorns not far from the cabin where the couple was staying. Dean had served on a convict firefighting crew a few seasons back, so he knew a thing or two about wildfires and, more importantly, how the Forest Service fought them. Just starting the fire might not produce the desired results. When a new fire popped up, the Service would drop in smoke jumpers to put it out quickly, and that would spell disaster. To make the fire work for him, Dean would have to make sure that the smoke jumpers *didn't* get the blaze under control. And that was the beauty of his plan. All he had to do was infiltrate the smoke jumpers heading out to the fire, kill them quickly, and then head to the cabin to finish off the primary targets.

Getting into the smoke jumper base hadn't been a problem. He knew a smoke jumper—the fool was into Dean's dad for close to ten grand and wasn't likely to ever pay—so acquiring the necessary equipment had been easy. Later, if he got a chance, he'd dump the guy's body out in the burned area so he looked like just one more victim of the fire.

There had been a couple of wrinkles. The Forest Service hadn't sent the smoke jumpers in right away like he'd planned, so he'd spent a very tense few days trying to avoid being noticed, all the while praying that the fire kept going. Eventually, the alert had sounded and he'd simply loaded up with the others. In the hustle and bustle, nobody had even noticed until they were in the air, and even then, that Indian kid had bought his story about being from McCall Base.

Easy peasy.

Jumping out of a perfectly good airplane had been a piece of cake too. He'd learned how to do that in Airborne School—right before he'd gotten himself tossed out of the Army—and while the chute was a little different than what he'd trained with, he'd figured it out on the way down.

Taking out the smoke jumpers had been like shooting fish in a barrel. Except for the Indian, none of them had even known what was about to happen. Taking care of the man and the woman—Raymond and Janelle—had been a little messier, but that was to be expected since Dean was also supposed to recover some kind of key, and he was supposed to try to get Raymond to tell him where it was. He hadn't, and that was another problem. But in the end, he'd scratched everyone off the list.

Except that kid . . .

Dean hadn't known about the kid being out there, and he really didn't feel good about wasting a child, but his dad had said *no loose ends,* so the kid had to die.

And that was where things had gone off the rails.

Of course, it wasn't the kid who had spoiled things but that firefighter, coming out of nowhere and knocking Dean out cold.

He had regained his senses mere seconds before the fire swept through the clearing near the cabin and had only survived by splashing into the creek and hunkering down in the shallow water while the flames sucked all the oxygen out of the world.

It had been a close thing.

He had hoped that the burnover would take care of the firefighter and the kid, but after things died down, he heard voices and realized that they were still alive. Without his gun, there wasn't much he could do against the firefighter—the guy was freaking huge—but he had followed them anyway, hoping that maybe he could sneak up on them and club the guy with a tree limb or something.

No such luck.

Both the kid and the smoke jumper were gone, probably telling their story to the cops already, complete with a description of Dean. Now all the effort he had put into making the deaths look like the result of the fire turned out to be a waste of his time. The cops would know that it was a targeted killing and would start looking into Raymond's business. If they looked hard enough, they might just find a thread leading back to Dean's father's operation.

Make the call, he told himself.

Otis Werner answered on the first ring. "Boy, where have you been?"

Great, thought Dean. *He's already in a rotten mood, and I haven't even told him the bad news.*

"No bars out here," said Dean.

"Bars? What are you doing at a bar?"

"I meant there's no cell reception. Out in the woods. I just finally got a signal."

"Oh," grunted Otis. "Well, is it done?"

"It's done."

"And the key? Did you find the key?"

"It wasn't there." Dean knew better than to answer with a simple *no.* "I tried to get him to tell me where it was, but no luck."

Dean figured this would earn him a verbal beatdown, but Otis surprised him. "But he's dead, right? That's the main thing."

"Yeah, he's deader'n . . ." Dean couldn't come up with an appropriate simile, so he let the thought dangle unfinished. He needed to tell his father the bad news.

Just rip the Band-Aid off.

"Only thing is . . . there was a kid there."

"A kid?"

"Yeah. I didn't know Raymond had kids, but there was a boy. 'Bout the same age as Angie's kid." Angie was Dean's youngest sister. "Six or seven years old, I'd guess."

"And?"

Dean did not fail to grasp the subtext. *And you iced him, right?*

"I went after him," Dean went on, "but then this firefighter showed up out of nowhere. Big guy. Knocked me out."

There was a long silence on the line. Dean braced himself for the expected eruption, but when Otis finally spoke, his cold, flat tone was far worse than any outburst. "Do you remember what I told you?"

"Yes, sir. No loose ends."

"No loose ends," Otis echoed. "By my count, you've got yourself two loose ends. You're gonna need to tie those off, boy."

"I know that, sir. It's just . . . I've been walking for a couple of hours now. I could really use a ride. And that firefighter . . . He's a big dude. I might need a little backup. Holt—"

"Holt is taking care of some business in Helena," snapped Otis. "This is your mess. Fix it."

"Yes, sir," replied Dean. But Otis had already ended the call.

NINETEEN

Even had he not been in a highly agitated state, the harsh knock at his front door would have startled Mark Dickerson. Because he was agitated, he literally jumped in alarm. The motion detector at the driveway entrance usually alerted him to the arrival of visitors long before they ascended the steps to knock or, preferably, push the button of the Ring doorbell.

When he overcame his initial reaction, Dickerson took out his phone and checked the doorbell video, which was also equipped with a motion sensor that should have registered the presence of a visitor. The display showed his front porch, but there was nobody standing in the camera view. Then the knock sounded again—fast, loud, and hard, like the report of a machine gun.

Bam! Bam! Bam!

Although he was expecting a visitor, the fact that he couldn't see the person standing on the porch, banging on the door, left him paralyzed with indecision.

Another rapid-fire knock rattled the door in its frame, this time accompanied by a low growl. "C'mon. Open up, Doc."

Despite the underlying tone of menace, Dickerson was relieved to hear the voice. This was the visitor he was expecting, after all. He hurried to the front door and opened it.

Dickerson didn't personally know the man standing across the threshold, but he was exactly the sort of person the doctor was expecting—a rough man who could take care of dirty business. He was a couple of inches shorter than Dickerson, but this did not make him any less physically imposing. Broad chested and solid, with thickly muscled limbs and a shaved head that seemed to sprout directly from his torso, the man looked like nothing less than a concrete wall on two legs. Even his tattoos, which not only adorned his arms but also crawled up the sides and back of his head, resembled the angry scrawl of graffiti artists.

He stood close to the house—close enough to be out of the cone-shaped field of the Ring doorbell's motion detector. Dickerson could only assume that he had somehow approached the porch from an oblique angle to avoid notice.

"You alone?" asked the man, looking past Dickerson into the house.

Dickerson nodded. "I sent my wife out of town."

"Good." The man did not wait for an invitation but stepped inside and closed the door. "I hear you've got a problem."

"We've all got a problem," countered Dickerson. "If I go down, we all go down."

The living wall grunted dismissively. "Just tell me what's going on."

"One of my referrals down in Wellington OD'd today, and the NP at the emergency room decided—"

"NP?"

Dickerson frowned at the interruption. "Nurse practitioner," he snapped. "Do you need me to explain what that is?"

"Nah."

"Well, this NP got her panties in a twist and decided to look into the dead woman's medical history. Next thing you know, she's standing on my doorstep accusing me of facilitating the woman's addiction."

"So?"

"So?" Dickerson gaped at the man. "So, she's right. That's exactly what I did. And if this woman makes a stink about it . . . and something tells me she just might . . . how long do you think it's going to be before someone starts putting it all together?"

The man's shoulders twitched in a rough approximation of a shrug. "Okay. I'll take care of it."

Finally, thought Dickerson. "Her name is Emily Redd. She lives at Thompson Ranch, just north of Wellington. Here's the address." He held out a folded Post-it note.

The man stared at the note for a moment before taking it. "How did you get this?"

"Very carefully, I assure you. As long as you make sure it looks like an accident, nobody's going to connect it back to me." He hesitated before adding, "You are going to make it look like an accident, right? I don't need the law knocking on my door. None of us want that."

"I don't think you'll have to worry about it."

Then, with a deftness that seemed impossible for someone so bulky, the man reached out with both hands and gave Dr. Mark Dickerson's head a quick twist, breaking his neck.

TWENTY

The hearing was mercifully short. There were only a handful of representatives present, and owing to the fact that it was already late afternoon or perhaps because of the sense that the hearing was a performative measure that would accomplish nothing, very few questions were asked of him. A few political points, likewise performative, were made, and then Kline was dismissed. The whole process had taken less than an hour.

As he made his way out to the waiting Suburban, he turned his phone back on—he had put it on airplane mode to avoid any disturbances during the hearing—and immediately received a text, a simple one-word message.

Done.

Kline couldn't help but smile. There was a reason Special Agent Stephanie Treadway remained his secret weapon. A former intelligence officer whom he had personally recruited into the Bureau, Treadway was the rarest of creatures in government work—efficient and loyal but with hardly any personal ambition. Unlike most agents, even Kline himself, she did not aspire to someday run her own field office or head up a division. When he had been promoted to acting director, he'd expected that she would take over the Directorate of Intelligence— his old job—but she had demurred.

"Are you kidding?" she had said. *"Can you see me sitting at a desk? No thank you."*

Her response had not been much of a surprise, but it did pose a bit of a problem. If she did not accept the promotion, he would have to appoint some-one else to the position, and that person would become her immediate superior, which meant Kline would lose direct access to Treadway and her unique skill set. He had found a work-around solution by creating a temporary position on his own staff, but that arrangement couldn't endure long. Treadway was too good an investigator, too valuable to the Bureau. She needed a permanent assignment.

He tapped out a reply, similarly brief. **Hungry?**

Always.

You order, I'll pay. Heading back to the office now.

Food was a cornerstone of their special relationship. For years, whenever they needed to talk over the details of an investigation in private, they would meet for lunch or dinner at one of the capital's many upscale casual eateries. Now that he was in a senior leadership position, unable to go anywhere without his protective detail, even the simple pleasure of discreetly dining out was impossible, but at least there was always takeout.

Treadway showed up about fifteen minutes later carrying two flat black-and-white boxes emblazoned with a star logo and the words *We, the Pizza.*

"Pizza?" remarked Kline. "That's different."

She set the boxes on a corner of his desk and shrugged. "Takeout is always cold by the time you get around to eating it. Pizza tastes great at any temperature."

"Can't argue with that." Kline walked over to his kitchenette and brought out plates, napkins, and a couple cans of soda—Coca-Cola for Treadway and Diet Dr Pepper for himself. When he returned, he saw that Treadway had both boxes open, revealing two large pies, one traditional—red sauce, pepperoni, sausage, ham, and so forth—and one with a white sauce and some kind of greens. Spinach, Kline guessed.

"I got the spinach and artichoke for you," said Treadway as she helped herself to a slice of the meat pie. "I was going to order you a salad, but honestly, they all just sounded too . . . weird. I figured spinach and artichoke is kind of like a salad, only on a pizza."

A lifelong fitness enthusiast, Kline had always envied Treadway's ability to gorge herself on stuffed burgers and oversize sandwiches with no apparent consequences to her health or physique.

"It's the carbs in the crust that are the real culprit," Kline pointed out, more for his own benefit than hers. She didn't have an extra ounce of fat on her body.

"It's okay to have a cheat day," Treadway retorted around her first bite. "Just run an extra couple miles."

Kline looked down at the spinach pie and thought about her suggestion. Since becoming acting director, his running regimen had suffered. He still managed to log a few cardio workouts on the elliptical trainer, but that was a poor substitute at best, and the thought of spending more time in the exercise room made the idea of a cheat day less appealing. Instead, he cracked open the Diet Dr Pepper and took a sip.

"So, what can you tell me about dead Raymond?"

This time, Treadway finished chewing and swallowing her mouthful before answering. "His name is Raymond Williams. He's the CFO . . . I guess I should say he *was* the CFO of ParaDyme Pharmaceuticals." She spelled the company name.

"Never heard of them," said Kline.

Treadway scooped another slice onto her plate. "They're family owned, not publicly traded. They don't advertise on TV like the big pharma giants, but they're doing pretty well. Corporate headquarters are in Chicago, and they've got manufacturing and distribution facilities all over the world. CEO is Martin Waldron." She paused a beat before adding, "He's kind of a skeevy dude. Just reading about him made me want to take a shower."

"How so?"

Treadway shrugged. "He's one of those guys that gives capitalism a bad name . . . Well, a worse name. Price gouging on lifesaving meds and then being all smarmy about how it's 'just business.'" She made air quotes with her fingers. "Plus, he just looks . . . I don't know. Creepy."

"I take it ParaDyme is under investigation?" It was the only explanation for how Treadway had been able to identify the dead man in the photograph with just his given name.

"Well, yes and no. A few years ago, when the opioid crisis was just hitting the news, the DOJ took a hard look at everyone in the industry for illegal practices. Raymond Williams was interviewed, and in the associated file, it mentioned his spouse, Janelle Lewis Williams. The names were flagged when I did the keyword search, and after that, it was easy to confirm with the picture. The investigation didn't lead to anything."

Kline steepled his fingers under his chin. "And now Raymond Williams and his wife are dead in what looks like an execution."

Treadway stared at him for a long moment. "Boss, I gotta know. Where's this coming from? You send me a picture of a dead guy, and you know his first name but nothing else? That's kinda sus."

Kline gave her a rueful smile. "Matthew found the bodies. They were in a cabin on Forest Service land. I guess you could say he took a personal interest."

"Ah. And so you did too."

"Yeah." Kline was silent for a moment. "Matthew thinks Raymond Williams and his wife were in hiding. On the run. Judging by the fact that someone tracked them down in Montana and killed them . . . along with half a dozen smoke jumpers who were working in the area . . . I'd say he's right."

"Dead smoke jumpers too?"

"That said," Kline went on, "this doesn't seem to immediately fall under our jurisdiction, so officially, we can't investigate."

"But you want me to look into it anyway," said Treadway, as if finishing his thought.

Kline smiled. "You know me so well."

Treadway shot a look at her watch. "I'll leave for Chicago now." Her eyes drifted down to the pizza boxes—one pie was half gone. The other remained untouched. She pointed to them. "Mind if I take those?"

TWENTY-ONE

WELLINGTON, MONTANA

Although he had only been away for a few hours, as he drove back toward Wellington, Redd felt like Odysseus returning from the underworld. Aside from a tinge of smoke in the southern sky, the terrain beneath it looked exactly as it should, but the world seemed somehow different, surreal. It was as if he was seeing it all for the first time. He wondered if his time spent in the fire had somehow altered him at the molecular level.

He wanted to chalk it up to fatigue. He was bone-tired, and even though the ordeal had not been the most physically demanding thing he'd ever done, the emotional toll of what he had witnessed and endured was considerable.

Kline had called to update him with a positive identification for the two victims at the cabin—Raymond and Janelle Williams—but the knowledge that Raymond was a senior executive from a pharmaceutical company did not immediately shine any light on the motive for so much senseless killing.

When he closed his eyes, Redd could easily visualize the face of the killer. He looked like a scrawny street thug, maybe gang muscle, but that in and of itself didn't mean anything either. The killer might have been hired to carry out the executions, with no personal connection to Williams.

But he went after Jack too.

That probably wasn't personal. The killer had been trying to eliminate witnesses. Now that Redd could also ID the man, there wasn't any reason for him to go after Jack, but Redd was still concerned for the boy's safety. Kline had promised to send agents from the Bozeman field office to look after him, but that was only a short-term solution. Jack would need more than just long-term protection. He would need a family.

Redd glanced over at the toy sitting in the Raptor's otherwise unoccupied passenger seat. "I guess he'll always have you, Buzz."

Buzz Lightyear had nothing to say on the subject, but Redd found the action figure's cocky smile strangely reassuring.

Redd made the turnoff toward downtown Wellington and continued along Broadway—Wellington's grandiosely named main street—until he reached the county courthouse. He parked the truck on the street and then headed inside through the sheriff's entrance.

Earlier that year, the seat of local government had been left in ruins following an attack by a group of rogue Homeland Security agents bent on terminating Redd and anyone who stood with him. Thankfully, none of Redd's family or friends had been killed in the ensuing firefight, but the century-old building had nearly been destroyed. Most of the major damage, including a gaping hole that had been blown completely through one wall, had been repaired, and the interior rooms had been given a complete—and somewhat overdue—facelift, but the exterior of the two-story brick structure was pockmarked with little divots gouged out by errant gunfire. The county commissioner had decided against trying to plaster over those, claiming that "battle scars give the building some character." Indeed, for a few weeks after what the news media dubbed "the shootout at the Stillwater County Courthouse" or alternately, "the Battle of Wellington," the little town had been the focus of national attention and had seen a measurable uptick in tourism. Redd had even seen a flyer from the local historical society touting the courthouse as the location of "the last Western gunfight."

Let's hope so, thought Redd.

Mere moments after he stepped through the glass door, Maggie Albright, the department's receptionist, waved a hand in front of her nose. "My goodness, Matthew. You smell like a garbage fire."

Redd self-consciously sniffed the fabric of his borrowed Nomex shirt, then shrugged. "Sounds about right."

"I heard you were out there on the fire line," Maggie went on, a little more soberly. "I'm glad you made it out of there with all your hair."

"Me too. Is the sheriff back?"

Maggie shook her head. "He's out with the patrol. But Stacy's in his office with our young guest. Watching cartoons on TV." She pointed to the doll Redd carried. "I know he'll be thrilled to see that."

Redd nodded and headed past her desk to the open door of Sheriff Blackwood's office. Stacy Reller, sitting in one of the guest chairs, noticed him first and, upon seeing the Buzz Lightyear toy, flashed a smile at Redd. Jack, who was sitting in the big desk chair, eyes glued to the wall-mounted television set, didn't look up.

"There's someone here who'd like to see you," announced Redd.

With what looked like great reluctance, Jack tore his gaze away from the screen and glanced over at Redd. Then he did a double take.

"Buzz!" Jack leaped from the chair and bolted across the room to seize the toy from Redd, just as Maggie had predicted. He threw both arms around Redd's legs and hugged him like a long-lost friend.

"Thank you, thank you, thank you!" Jack said, squeezing tight.

Surprised and more than a little moved, Redd reached down and tried to reciprocate, but because the top of Jack's head barely came up to his waist, he had to settle for ruffling the boy's hair.

Jack finally released his clutch and focused his full attention on the toy, displaying it proudly for the deputy's inspection. "Stacy, it's Buzz. Lookit!"

"I see. That's so awesome."

"I thought he was gone forever." He glanced back at Redd as if wondering what other miracles Redd might be able to accomplish.

"I guess it takes more than a little fire to put Buzz Lightyear out of commission."

Jack then grabbed Redd's hand. "Come on. Watch with me?"

Bemused, Redd shot a glance at the deputy, who gave a nod of approval, then allowed himself to be pulled along. "I guess I can stay for a few minutes."

He grabbed the other guest chair and pulled it over so that he could sit beside Jack. There was a cartoon program playing on the television—something with robots and anthropomorphic animals—but Jack seemed more interested in his toy, posing the action figure and "flying" him around, making little *whoosh* noises. Redd was relieved to see him playing after everything he'd been through that day, but he also knew that Jack was probably using the activity to hide what he was really feeling. To hide his fears.

Redd remembered what that felt like.

Not long thereafter, Maggie stepped into the office. She glanced first at Redd, then at Stacy, and then back again. "There's some folks here I think you might want to talk to."

Redd followed Maggie back to the front desk where two fairly well-dressed twentysomethings—one male, one female—stood waiting. Even before they produced their credentials, Redd knew they were FBI agents.

"Mr. Redd?" said the man, flipping open his badge case. "I'm Special Agent Kennedy. This is Special Agent Nunez. We understand you have a young witness that needs protecting."

Redd sized up the two federal agents before replying. He sensed none of the condescension that urbane federal officers often exhibited toward members of rural law enforcement agencies.

But they both look so young.

Redd guessed the Special Agent in Charge of the Bozeman field office had sent his most junior agents for what he probably considered a pointless assignment. Nevertheless, Redd decided to play the cordial host and extended a hand in greeting. "Glad you're here," he said as Kennedy accepted the handclasp. "I guess you two drew the short straws?"

"Not at all, sir."

"We volunteered," Nunez chimed in. "It's not every day that the director himself calls to arrange a protective detail."

"And we're both pretty good with kids," Kennedy added.

"That a fact?" Redd shook Nunez's hand as well. "So, what have you been told?"

Kennedy was ready with the details. "Six-year-old male child, possible witness to multiple homicides, possible target for the unsub. We're to keep him safe until more permanent arrangements can be made."

Redd raised a hand. "First of all, he's six and three-quarters." He wasn't sure why he added that and felt like it sounded odd when he heard it himself. "And the kid's not just some witness. He watched his aunt and uncle get executed. And he was about three seconds from being the next victim when I showed up. Now he's alone and afraid. He needs more than just a babysitter with a gun."

Nunez spoke up. "Mr. Redd, we'll take good care of him. You have my word. Now, how about you introduce us to . . ."

"Jack."

Nunez nodded. "Jack."

Redd regarded her a moment longer, trying to gauge both her sincerity and her ability to deliver on her promise. He gestured to the hallway. "This way."

When they reached the sheriff's office, Redd caught Jack's eye. "Jack, there are some people I'd like you to meet."

Nunez immediately took the lead, approaching Jack from an oblique angle so as not to block his line of sight with Redd. "Jack? Hi, I'm Alma. I work for the FBI. Do you know what that is?"

After a moment's hesitation, Jack met her gaze. "Like on TV?"

Nunez smiled. "Well, kind of."

"Do you have a badge?"

"I sure do. Want to see it?" She took out her credentials and displayed the gold shield. "Would you like to hold on to it for a minute?"

Jack nodded with wide-eyed enthusiasm.

Encouraged by her success at establishing rapport with the boy, Redd grudgingly admitted to himself that maybe he was being overly protective. "Jack, I've asked . . ." He glanced at Nunez. "Alma, was it?"

She nodded.

"Alma," Redd went on, "and her friend . . ."

Kennedy stepped forward. "Hi, Jack. I'm Preston."

"Alma and Preston are going to stay with you for a little while," Redd finished.

Jack turned to the FBI agents. "Are you going to keep the bad man away?"

Preston threw a questioning glance in Redd's direction, then nodded. "You bet."

Redd knelt in front of Jack. "That sound okay to you?"

The boy's forehead creased in consternation, and for a moment, Redd thought Jack might refuse and instead beg to go with Redd himself.

And if he did, would I be able to tell him no?

But then the boy nodded. "Okay," he said and went back to playing with his action figure.

Redd stood and turned to Kennedy, who seemed to be the senior of the pair. "What's your plan?"

"For tonight at least, we'll put him up in a motel room. We've got reservations at a place called the Diamond T. It's just north of town."

"I know where it is," replied Redd. "Don't you think that location is a little exposed?"

Kennedy looked chagrined. "We haven't actually been there yet. The head office made the arrangements. Though from what I've heard, there weren't a lot of alternatives."

"Why not take him back to Bozeman?"

The agent spread his hands in a gesture of helplessness. "Something about not removing him from the jurisdiction." Noting Redd's frown, he quickly added, "Mr. Redd, we'll keep him safe. You have my word."

The assurance did not lessen Redd's apprehension, but he knew that he needed to let the agents do their job. "All right. I guess I'll let you take over." He turned to Jack. "Okay, buddy. I need to take off now."

Jack looked crestfallen. "You're leaving already?"

"I have to, pal. I've got to get home and do my chores."

"Am I going to see you again?"

The simple question felt like an arrow to Redd's heart. He knew, all too well, what it felt like to lose all sense of continuity, never knowing where he would sleep that night or who would be taking care of him. Live that way long enough, and a kid loses all faith in the promises and good intentions of grown-ups.

"Count on it," Redd promised. "How 'bout I come and see you tomorrow? Maybe I'll even take you out to my ranch. Let you ride my horse, Remington. Would you like that?"

Jack's eyes lit up. "A *real* horse?"

"Remi's the best horse." He cast a meaningful glance at the FBI agents, a silent but easily understood reminder of their promise to keep Jack safe, then looked back at the boy. "See you tomorrow, Jack."

As he started to leave, Jack called out, "Bye, Matt," in an unintentional sing-song that brought a grin to Redd's face.

See you soon.

It was a promise he hoped he would be able to keep.

TWENTY-TWO

Although it hadn't been her worst day at work—not by a long shot—Emily was glad to put the Stillwater County Health Center in her rearview mirror. Losing a patient was always tough, and confronting Dr. Mark Dickerson, which in hindsight she realized might have been ill-advised, had been a unique source of stress, but what had taken the greatest toll was the simple fact that she was nine months pregnant and ready to pop.

Why did I ever think it was a good idea to work right up to my due date? she wondered.

She knew the answer, of course, and it wasn't just that they needed the money, though that certainly was a factor. Mostly, she felt a sense of obligation to both the health center and the community. She was desperately needed at the little rural hospital. When she had taken her family leave to have Little Matty, the emergency department had all but closed down, and unless someone could be found to take over on a temporary basis, it would probably happen again. Anyone with a real medical emergency would have to be transported to Helena or Bozeman, and the time it would take for them to make that trip might be the difference between life and death.

But the closer she got to her due date, the less persuasive that sense of obligation was. And as much as she couldn't wait to hold her newborn daughter, what she was most looking forward to was simply not being pregnant anymore.

Within seconds of Emily's arrival at the home of Mikey and Liz Derhammer—Matthew's and her best friends, respectively—Liz emerged from the house with a pair of trundling boys in tow. Emily was still amazed at how quickly little Matty was mastering the skill of running. It seemed like only a few days had passed since he'd begun tentatively cruising around the house, using furniture and toys for support between bursts of strides. She chalked the rapid progress up to the fact that he had an example to follow. Mikey and Liz's son Lucas was two years older than Matthew Jr., and for most of the last year—ever since Emily had discovered that her son wasn't safe at the hospital's day care center—the two boys had spent almost every day together, playing and napping under Liz's supervision. Liz, who had begun working from home, had eagerly volunteered to take over Junior's day care, claiming that it was easier to watch two kids than just one since they could usually be counted on to keep each other occupied.

When the day care arrangement with Liz had first begun, Emily always went inside to visit with her friend before taking Little Matty home, but as getting in and out of the vehicle became increasingly difficult, that habit had fallen by the wayside. Liz had started bringing the little guy out to her, buckling him into his safety seat in the back to make things easier for her friend. Ordinarily, she would then spend a few minutes chatting with Emily, telling her how the day went, but today, perhaps reading Emily's mood, she cut the visit short, leaving Emily to make the drive home.

As she drove north out of town, Emily's thoughts turned to mundane practicalities. On days when Emily worked, Matthew usually took care of dinner, either throwing something on the outside grill or warming up something on the stove, but as far as she knew, he was still out on his search and rescue call, so it would fall to her. She didn't really mind—she actually enjoyed domestic activities—but it would have to be something quick and easy. Probably leftover chili or stew.

I should have grabbed a pizza before leaving town, she thought.

She resolved to send Matthew a text when she got home, asking if he had any idea when he'd be done. Maybe he would have a dinner suggestion. While she didn't mind the actual cooking, Emily hated having to decide what they'd eat.

When she crossed the last cattle guard, she saw a dark shape on the road ahead, bounding toward the Tahoe on what looked like a collision course. It was Rubble. Matthew's dog.

When the Rottweiler pup was behaving himself, which admittedly was most of the time, he was "their dog" and sometimes even "my good boy." When he was being mischievous, or just a little too playful, as he was now, he was "Matthew's dog." She still loved the big beast, but it always made her nervous when he came out to greet them or chased a moving vehicle.

"I hate it when you do that, boy," she murmured, shifting her foot to the brake pedal. The big rottie veered out of the way at the last second and then commenced doing a little dance of joy, wagging his hindquarters back and forth and leaping into the air as he woofed happily.

With Rubble dancing alongside, she rode the brake the rest of the way up to the house. As soon as she set the brake and turned the motor off, the dog, evidently believing that he had completed his mission to escort her in, spun around twice and charged away, running around to the rear of the house on some new, very important puppy task. Emily couldn't help but laugh.

Moments after she went inside the house, with Little Matty stationed in the gated, kid-proofed living room, she turned to see that Rubble was at the door, begging to be let in. They had decided against putting in a doggie door since any opening big enough to let Rubble through would also be big enough for little Matty to use as an escape route, so at least until there were no more toddlers in residence, she and Matthew would have to play doggie doorman, twenty-four seven.

She was just opening the door for the pup when she felt her phone vibrate in her pocket. She took it out and saw an incoming call from Matthew. As Rubble pushed inside and promptly flopped down on the entry rug, Emily took a breath, forced a smile so that her weariness and general frustration with the day wouldn't come across in her voice, and hit the green button to accept the call.

"Hey, you," she said.

"Hey yourself."

She thought he sounded almost as tired as she felt. "Rough day?"

"Yeah, kinda. I'll tell you all about it when I get there. I'm just leaving town now. Want me to pick up something for dinner?"

Her smile, no longer forced, broadened. "You read my mind. I just got home myself."

"Any requests?"

Before she could reply, she saw Rubble jump to his feet as if coming to attention. He remained statue still, facing the closed door.

"What's up, boy?" she asked.

"What's wrong?" Matthew's voice in her ear was every bit as alert and rigid as Rubble's stance.

"Not sure. Rubble's acting kind of funny."

As if responding to a cue, the dog let out a low, inquisitive woof. She had seen him do something similar in response to a car coming up the drive, but usually, when he did, she could hear the sound of tires crunching on the gravel. She didn't hear anything like that now.

"You said you're still in town?" she asked.

"Em, what's going on?"

"Not sure," she said again. "Rubble's acting like there's someone outside, but I didn't hear a car."

"Could be he heard something in the woods. But don't take any chances. Lock the doors and stay away from the windows."

Emily was already reaching for the door. As she turned the dead bolt, Rubble gave a low growl.

"What is it, boy? What do you hear?"

Suddenly, the door rattled with a hard knock that startled Emily and Rubble both. The dog immediately began barking.

"Rubble! Quiet!"

The command silenced the dog, but his hackles remained up as he continued looking at the door.

There was another knock, softer this time, almost tentative, followed by a gruff male voice. "Hello?"

Emily stared at the door for a moment, unsure of how to respond. They almost never got unexpected visitors at the house. But whoever was out there had obviously heard her speak to Rubble. She couldn't pretend she wasn't home.

Before she could make up her mind, she heard Matthew's voice, small and tinny but no less frantic, erupting from her phone's speaker. "Em. What's going on there?"

"Hello?" came the voice from outside. "Hey, I broke down on the road. I just want to use your phone."

Broke down? Emily thought. *Well, that would explain why I didn't hear a car.* But her early warning system was flashing multiple alerts.

Who doesn't have a cell phone these days? And if he broke down on the highway or even on the service road, he would have had to walk past several houses to reach the drive to the ranch, so why did he come here?

Some part of her wanted this to be exactly as it appeared on its face—a traveler in need, a chance to do a good deed for a stranger—but after everything that had happened to them in the last few years, she had learned to trust that inner warning system.

Something's not right about this.

"Hello?" Another knock, gentler than the first but insistent. "Ma'am, I just want to use your phone."

Emily swallowed, cleared her throat, and then spoke out in a loud but firm voice. "I'm not going to open the door, but I will call a tow truck for you. Go back and wait at your car."

A long silence followed, and for a fleeting moment, Emily thought maybe the visitor had complied.

Bam!

The impact—no mere knock, but a full-on assault against the door—was as loud as a gunshot and, like the report of a gun, reverberated through her body. Emily jumped, a panicked yelp escaping her lips.

The stranger was trying to break the door down.

Rubble, teeth out and mouth open, growled and then, despite Emily's earlier command, let out a menacing bark. This time, she did not silence him. Instead, she turned on her heel and ran for the living room. Behind her, the door shuddered with another blow. She didn't look back but instead focused on trying to open the baby gate that barred the way to the living room.

Rubble, standing his ground, barked again and then let out a low, throaty growl.

A few feet away, Little Matty sat frozen in place, one hand still holding the plastic block that he had been in the process of stacking atop another, eyes wide, lower lip just beginning to quiver in anticipation of an outburst.

You and me both, sweetie, thought Emily as she worked the safety latch.

The third blow blasted the door inward, along with a sizable portion of the doorframe, which had, until that moment, held fast to the dead bolt. Despite herself, Emily glanced back just in time to see the stranger enter her home.

The man was short but powerfully built, a human wrecking ball. Everything about him was thick, as if his entire body had been compressed under extreme gravity. His shaved head, colored with black and indigo, looked like a bowling ball sinking down between his shoulders. His legs were like tree trunks, and his tattooed forearms were as big around as Emily's thighs. Even his fingers looked short and stubby like hammerheads.

He stood there, framed in the doorway, his whole body turning as his dark, malignant eyes scanned the kitchen.

Looking for me.

Then suddenly, a dark mass eclipsed his moon-like visage. It was Rubble, leaping at him, jaws open and ready to close like a bear trap on the intruder's throat. Instead, moving more quickly than Emily would have thought possible for someone so bulky, the man brought his forearm up and blocked the attack.

Rubble did what any dog would do under the circumstances; he clamped down on the forearm, sinking his teeth deep into the man's flesh, and began to twist and thrash. For just a moment, the man was unbalanced and almost went down.

Almost.

With a bestial howl, equal measures of pain and rage, the man widened his stance, lowering his center of gravity, and stayed on his feet. He then raised his arm high and Rubble with it—all 130 pounds of him—and began whipping the limb back and forth, trying to shake the rottie loose.

For a moment, it was almost impossible to tell who was shaking whom. With a bite force well north of three hundred pounds per square inch, Rubble wasn't easily dislodged. Blood spattered the floor and walls as the dog's teeth ripped and tore with the violent thrashing. But despite the damage, the intruder's counterattack seemed only to grow more ferocious until even Rubble's powerful jaws could not overcome the mounting g-force. His teeth tore loose in a spray of blood, and then Rubble flew across the room and slammed into a wall with an agonized squeal. Breathing heavily, the man stood there for a moment, gazing down at his savaged forearm, but then his eyes began to rove about, looking once more for his intended victim.

The fight between man and beast had lasted only a few seconds, but they were seconds that Emily had not squandered. Once she was through the safety gate, swinging it closed more out of habit than purpose, she rushed over to Little

Matty, scooped him up under one arm, and crossed to the far corner of the living room where sat a beautiful maple armoire. She threw its doors open, revealing an inner door of solid metal with a numerical keypad.

Take it slow, she told herself, taking a deep breath to get her nerves under control. *Get it right the first time because you might not get a second try.*

She extended a shaking finger and then, letting muscle memory do the hard part, tapped in the correct sequence. The lock disengaged with a click, and the door swung open.

Across the living room, the human wrecking ball simply walked through the safety gate, his legs smashing it as if it had been assembled from toothpicks, and stalked across the room toward her.

Emily saw his approach from the corner of her eye and knew that he would be on her in mere seconds.

Get it right the first time, she told herself again as she set Little Matty down beside her and then reached into the armoire. It took her half a second to find the item and another to put hands on it. When she had it, she whirled around to find herself almost face-to-face with the intruder.

Despite the fury blazing in his eyes, he glanced down, saw the shotgun in her hands, and hesitated just for a moment. But Emily didn't.

Her target already sighted, she squeezed the trigger.

TWENTY-THREE

It usually took Redd about twenty-five minutes to make the trip from Wellington to the ranch. This time, he made it in under fifteen, and yet it felt like an eternity. Even after Emily got back on the phone to let him know that she had successfully driven off the intruder, Redd kept the pedal to the floor, willing the truck to go faster. He felt utterly impotent. His loved ones had been put in jeopardy, and he had not been there to protect them.

Urgency was his only recourse.

If he correctly understood Emily's account of what had occurred—and given that she was still riding an adrenaline high, that was questionable—she had managed to get the shotgun from the gun safe and blasted her attacker with a load of double-aught buckshot. That should have ended the home invasion permanently, but evidently she had missed, or just winged the intruder . . . that was the part Redd was unclear on . . . and the man had fled the house under his own power.

Her description of the intruder did not match that of the man who had killed the smoke jumpers, but drawing a line to connect them wasn't hard. Hired muscle. Street thugs working for whoever had put the hit out on Raymond Williams. Now, just as Redd had feared, they were coming after the witnesses.

He wondered how they had identified him so quickly. Even if the killer in the woods had made it through the fire alive and made it out to where he could get a signal on his phone, he wouldn't have known Redd's name, only that he appeared to be another firefighter. So how had they figured out who he was and where he lived? Did they have someone monitoring the sheriff's office?

Did they know where Jack was?

He considered calling Kline again, warning him that his worst fears had been realized, that the killers were still intent on silencing the witnesses, that the danger to Jack was very real, but ultimately decided it could wait until he wasn't driving down the highway at ninety-five miles an hour.

When he skidded to a stop in front of the house, he didn't even bother shutting the engine off. Instead, he leaped from the Raptor and bounded up the front steps, even as Emily, with Matthew Jr. in her arms and Rubble beside her, came out to greet him.

Redd threw his arms around his wife. "I'm so sorry," he whispered in her ear as he hugged her fiercely. "I should have been here."

"We're okay," she whispered in his. It wasn't a reply, just an assurance. "We're okay."

With Rubble running in circles around their legs as if trying to figure out how to get in on the tender moment, Redd finally let go of Emily and held her at arm's length. "Okay, let's get you in your rig."

"What? Why?"

"We can't stay here. It's not safe."

Emily was taken aback by the suggestion. "And where exactly do you think we should go?" She shook her head. "No, Matty. This is our home. We're not going to run away every time there's a little trouble."

"Em, you don't know what's happening here. What these people are capable of."

She cocked her head to the side. "What are you talking about?"

"This is all my fault. Something happened today, out in the woods. I . . . I guess you could say I stumbled into the middle of an execution, and now whoever was behind it is sending their thugs after me. Tying up loose ends."

Emily took a backward step, regarding him as if his sanity was in question. "Matty, this doesn't have anything to do with you."

Now it was Redd's turn to be dumbfounded. "Excuse me?"

Emily took on a chagrined expression. "I'm afraid I kind of poked a hornet's nest today."

"I don't understand."

"Come inside. I'll tell you all about it." She took another backward step and gestured for him to enter the house ahead of her. Redd, still a little confused, went in.

He immediately registered the damage to the doorframe. Security had been a foremost concern when building the house, and Redd hadn't skimped on door hardware. Nevertheless, the Schlage 2 ¾-inch backset dead bolt he had installed on the front door did not appear to have slowed the intruder down much. Half of the solid wood frame, along with the steel strike plate, had torn loose in a long, jagged splinter. The floor and walls beyond the threshold were liberally spattered with still-damp blood.

"Rubble went after him," explained Emily. "I thought he was going to take the guy's arm off."

Redd glanced down at the Rottweiler, noticing for the first time the streaks of dark red on his muzzle. "I'm surprised he didn't." He dropped to a squat and petted Rubble with both hands behind his ears. "Who's a good boy?"

"This guy was big, Matty. Not as tall as you, but solid. What's that old saying? Like a brick outhouse. And he was all tatted up. You know, like prison tats."

"You're an expert on prison tattoos now?"

"Believe it or not, I've seen a few. But this guy was like the Terminator. He just kept coming. He tossed Rubble across the room like an old dishrag and then came after me. If I hadn't made it to the gun cabinet . . ." She shuddered as if the thought was too terrible to put into words.

At the mention of the gun cabinet, Redd glanced into the living room and saw the armoire and the gun safe standing wide open. He also saw that the opposite wall was spattered with more blood and pockmarked with half a dozen holes, each about the diameter of a pencil. The pattern told a story. Either Emily's shot had been poorly aimed or the intruder had almost managed to duck out of the way as she pulled the trigger. Two or three of the buckshot pellets had scored a hit, while the rest had simply peppered the back wall.

Still, even a couple of pellets hitting at close range could do serious damage. Between that and what Rubble had accomplished, the intruder had to be hurting.

Redd turned to Emily. "You said you didn't hear a car?"

She shook her head. "He must have left it down at the road and walked up."

Redd did some quick mental math. It had taken him fifteen minutes to drive home. From the house, it was a little more than half a mile to the road, a ten-minute walk at an easy pace. But how long would it take someone who was injured and losing blood?

Redd realized that the intruder might still be on the property, maybe even lying in a field somewhere, bleeding out, if not already dead.

"Keep the shotgun handy," he said as he strode over to the gun safe and took out his pistol belt, which held his Ruger Vaquero .44 Magnum. It had been J. B.'s gun and the first firearm Matthew Redd had ever fired.

"What are you doing, Matty?" asked Emily, her voice full of apprehension.

"I didn't pass any cars when I came up from the highway. That means he might still be here somewhere. I'm going to track him. He's wounded, bleeding. Probably not moving very fast."

"He's got to be long gone by now."

"Maybe. Or he might just be out there waiting for us to lower our guard." He buckled the belt around his waist, drew the Ruger, and spun the hammer to check that it was loaded. He always left it loaded when he put it away, but he always checked before heading out.

"Matty, just call Blackwood. Let him come out and take care of this."

"No time. Besides, he's got his hands full." He faced her and held her gaze with his stare. "Em, you know I have to do this."

She frowned but then nodded. "Be careful. Even hurt, that guy's a monster."

Redd had a history of fighting big men. Two in particular, and both times, he'd come out on top. Then again, he'd taken a beating each time.

He returned her nod and spoke one last word to her—a reminder. "Shotgun."

Then he turned and headed out the door.

TWENTY-FOUR

Redd had been so focused on Emily and Matthew Jr. when he had arrived that he hadn't noticed the blood trail leading away from the porch. Now that he was looking for it, it was impossible to miss. A series of dark red drops, each about the size of a poker chip and some in clusters of two or three, ran across the porch, down the steps, and onto the gravel driveway.

As Redd descended the steps, Rubble raced out to join him.

"Stay!"

Rubble came to a full stop but regarded him with a pleading look.

"Sorry, boy. I need you to stay here and look after the family."

Redd would have liked to have the dog at his side while tracking the intruder. Even though rotties weren't bloodhounds, like all dogs they could follow a scent trail and especially a blood trail. But Rubble was even more valuable to Redd as a fiercely loyal protector, just in case the intruder circled around and made another attempt on Emily and Junior. Rubble uttered a plaintive wail but obeyed the command and stayed put.

Who's a good boy?

The trail was harder to track over gravel, but it quickly became apparent that the man had been moving in an almost straight line, following the driveway, allowing Redd to move at a fast jog.

He expected the distance between the drops of blood to decrease as he went along. A wounded game animal often bolted after being shot, which resulted in a longer interval between the blood drops, but once the initial adrenaline surge passed and pain and blood loss took their toll, the animal usually slowed, increasing the frequency and shortening the interval. Evidently, that didn't hold true for human prey. The blood trail left by the intruder remained more or less constant and consistent with someone running at a brisk pace. The trail brought Redd to the end of the drive, then turned in the direction of the highway and continued along the side of the road another fifty yards before abruptly vanishing.

Redd's shoulders slumped in defeat. Not only had the intruder *not* succumbed to his injuries, but he had also run all the way to a waiting vehicle. A large cluster of blood drops marked the spot, a sign that the man had stood still for a few seconds before getting in and driving away, likely several minutes before Redd made the turnoff from the highway.

He recalled what Emily had said about the man: *"Like the Terminator. He just kept coming."*

Redd had known a few men in his life who could shrug off damage like that, ignore pain and injury, or sometimes, like a wild animal, transform that adversity into rage fuel, but nobody was truly invincible. The man would have to seek medical attention somewhere, and between the nature of his injuries and his physical description, there was a good chance that law enforcement would be able to quickly run him to ground.

"Speaking of which," Redd murmured as he took out his phone.

Kline answered on the first ring. "Matt. I just heard from the Bozeman office. They've sent two agents to protect your witness."

"I've met them," Redd cut in. "Gavin, just listen. Things have escalated here. Someone just attacked Emily here at the ranch."

"Attacked? Is she all right?"

"She's fine. Just a little rattled. Ran the guy off with a hide full of buckshot. But look, if they found me, then you can bet they'll be coming after Jack. You need to let your agents know what they're up against."

"Slow down. Tell me what happened to Emily."

Redd started back up the road, talking as he moved. "Some guy came up to the house and tried to get her to let him in. When she refused, he kicked down the door and came in after her. Rubble tore his arm up, and then Emily blasted him with the shotgun. I think she just winged him, but he took off."

"Was it the same man who killed Raymond Williams?"

"Based on Em's description, that's a negative. She said this guy was short but strong. The guy in the woods was so skinny he'd blow over in a light breeze. Oh, Em said her guy had prison tattoos. Her words, not mine. I'm thinking they're gang muscle, which means there's no telling how many guys they can throw at us."

"All right," Kline said. "I hear you. I've got Treadway looking into ParaDyme Pharma. If we can figure out why somebody wanted Raymond Wiliams dead, we'll be a lot closer to ending this threat."

"Right now, I just want to keep my family safe. And Jack. That kid has been through enough."

"I understand. You and Em should get out of town. Find somewhere safe to ride this out."

"That's exactly what I plan to do," replied Redd. It occurred to him then that Emily was in no condition for an impromptu road trip.

I'll figure something out, he thought and then ended the call.

✖ ✖ ✖

Rubble came out to greet him when he returned to the house, followed by Emily, who Redd couldn't help noticing was *not* holding a shotgun.

When Redd pointed this out to her, adding, "What if I had been a bad guy?" she was ready with an answer.

"If you had been a bad guy, Rubble would have ripped your face off."

He couldn't argue with that. "All right. Let's get Junior loaded up. We're getting out of here."

"And just where are we going exactly? In case it slipped your mind, I probably shouldn't be too far from a hospital."

"We'll go to Helena. Get a hotel. It's perfect, actually, since we'll already be close to the hospital." Although Emily had delivered more than her share of babies at the county health center, it was not a fully equipped birthing center. Emily's ob-gyn was in Helena. Junior had been born at the hospital there, and their plan was for baby number two to be born there as well.

Emily crossed her arms over her bulging belly. "No. I'm not leaving. Not until it's time."

"Em, you have no idea what's going on here."

She looked at him sideways. "Why don't you tell me exactly what *you* think is going on."

Redd sighed. "You know I went out on a search and rescue call, right? Eight missing smoke jumpers right on the edge of the fire? Well, somebody killed them. Shot them in the back. And they weren't even the real target. The real target was some pharma exec who was hiding out with his family in an old hunting cabin. This guy killed him and his wife and was going after the kid when I showed up and scared him off. Now me and that kid are the only witnesses who can identify him. I don't know how he found out where I live, but—"

Emily raised her hands. "Matty, hold on just a second. I told you, that's not what's going on here."

Redd looked at her, recalling what she had said when he'd first showed up.

"This doesn't have anything to do with you . . . I kind of poked a hornet's nest today."

"Okay, I'm listening," he said. "What do you think is really going on?"

"I lost a patient this morning. An OD. She was someone we went to school with, Matty. Raina Cole."

The name meant nothing to Redd, but he nodded for her to continue.

"She was a vet. Got messed up pretty bad in an IED blast and ended up hooked on pain meds. Opiates. When the VA tried to wean her off them, she found some quack doctor up in Helena who would prescribe to her, and then when he stopped doing that, she started using street drugs. Fentanyl. It killed her."

"I don't see—"

"So I drove up to Helena and called him out."

"Him?"

"Her doctor. He's retired now. Living it up with his lake house and his Russian trophy wife, while the people he kept hooked on opioids are dying left and right." She paused a beat, her voice dropping. "I think he must be connected to some bad people. Street dealers. And I think when I called him out, he got scared and sicced his human wrecking ball on me."

Redd had to take a moment to process what he was hearing. "Let me get this straight. You went and yelled at a doctor for overprescribing pain meds, and he sent someone to kill you? Have I got that right?"

"Seems pretty obvious to me."

It wasn't at all obvious to Redd. And yet, was it any harder to believe than his theory that the killer who had targeted Raymond Williams had somehow tracked him down in a matter of hours and then, instead of lying in wait and ambushing him as he came up the driveway, decided instead to go after Emily?

Then something dawned on him.

Fentanyl. Pain meds.

Raymond Williams worked for a pharmaceutical company, and it wasn't a stretch to imagine that his company's product might have had something to do with his murder.

Emily's patient had died from street drugs, but it had been the reckless doctor's prescription to regulated opiates that had gotten her fatally addicted.

Connection or coincidence? Redd wasn't sure. *Only one way to find out.*

"Okay . . . going with your theory that this doctor sent someone after you. I think maybe I should have a talk with this doc and see what's what."

Emily's stance softened, and she wrapped a hand around the back of Redd's neck and looked up into his eyes. "While part of me would love for this doctor to know that I've got my own big strong man to unleash if necessary, this isn't our fight, Matty. Let's just let the police handle it for once."

"I love you, and I don't mean this the way it might sound, but if you tell the police what you just told me, you'll be lucky if all they do is laugh in your face. You've got nothing to connect this doctor to what happened here." He let that sink in a moment before continuing. "I'm already in contact with Gavin about the murders out in the woods, so I've got legal status with the Bureau to investigate this on my own. Don't worry. I'm not going to do anything crazy. I'm just going to ask this doctor a few questions. I'll know by his answers whether he's involved in this or not."

Emily frowned but, after a moment's consideration, assented with a nod. She let go of him, moving back just a step. "Okay. But I'm coming with you."

"Em, I don't think that's a good—"

"I'm coming, Matthew," Emily said, cutting him off. "We're a team, and don't you forget that. We stick together no matter what."

Judging by her tone, the use of his full first name, and the defiant hand placed on her hip, Redd knew better than to argue.

"Fine," he said. "Let's go get some answers."

TWENTY-FIVE

CHICAGO

If Special Agent Treadway had learned anything from her research into Martin Waldron—aside from his reptilian nature—it was that he loved attention, particularly media attention. Whether it was on financial news programs or high-profile podcasts, Waldron never passed up a chance to make a public appearance. Treadway used this knowledge by posing as a producer from the CNBC network's financial news program *Closing Bell* who wanted to schedule him for a remote interview, allowing her to confirm that he was in his Chicago office and would remain there after hours, awaiting the arrival of the news crew.

Upon landing at Midway International Airport, she went directly to the rental car kiosk and picked up the vehicle she had reserved—a Volkswagen Jetta. Whenever she was on one of Kline's special assignments, she always rented rather than using cars from the Bureau motor pool. Not only did doing so afford a degree of anonymity—there was just something about the US government fleet vehicles that shouted "fed"—but it also allowed her to come and go without interacting with the local field office hierarchy, who often took a dim view of anyone operating in their jurisdiction without their approval. Of course, she didn't *need* their approval. She was working on behalf of the FBI director himself. Nevertheless, in her experience—she had come over from a certain intelligence agency whose initials were CIA—it was always best to leave the smallest possible operational footprint.

The corporate headquarters of ParaDyme Pharmaceuticals was located on the seventy-eighth floor of the iconic Willis Tower—the tallest building in the world at the time of its completion in 1974 and still the third tallest in America. Known until 2009 as the Sears Tower, it was still called that by most Chicagoans. It took Treadway about half an hour to make the eleven-mile drive from the airport to downtown Chicago, where she parked in a nearby garage. She then spent another half hour sitting in front of a portable lighted mirror, using the contents of her professional makeup artist's train case to transform herself into someone Martin Waldron would find irresistible.

Treadway was, by almost any definition, attractive, but with the aid of professional-quality cosmetics, high-quality wigs, and the right wardrobe choices, she could transform herself into a woman of breathtaking beauty. In truth, her theatrical accoutrements were only a very small part of the equation. Most of it was attitude, and Stephanie Treadway had plenty of attitude to spare. It was why she had been one of the Agency's most successful case officers until a close encounter with a Taliban suicide bomber had caused her to rethink her career priorities. Now she used her talents to get closer to the subjects of FBI investigations.

She decided to go corn silk blonde for the meeting with Waldron. Not only did his dating history, proudly and publicly archived on social media, indicate an affinity for slender white women with blonde hair, but Treadway had observed that most men tended to underestimate the intelligence of blondes.

Her transformation complete, Treadway walked the rest of the way to her destination, changing from flats to three-inch pumps just before boarding the elevator. The heels were a literal pain to walk in, but for what the lift did to the shape of her calves, she could tolerate a little discomfort. Upon reaching the seventy-eighth floor, she entered ParaDyme's lavishly appointed lobby and strode confidently to the reception desk. "I'm here to see Mr. Waldron. I believe he's expecting me."

The receptionist, who bore an unsurprising resemblance to Treadway's present persona, regarded her with a Medusa stare but then managed an insincere smile. "Of course. I'll have someone escort you."

A few moments later, a uniformed security guard emerged from the double glass doors leading into the complex of offices and, after regarding her with a good deal more appreciation than the receptionist did, beckoned her to follow. "This way, ma'am."

The guard led her through the double doors and down a maze of hallways to another set of glass doors that opened into a smaller reception area where another blonde—younger and slightly more attractive than the first—rose to greet her, tacitly excusing the security guard. The woman, presumably the CEO's executive secretary, led Treadway the rest of the way into Martin Waldron's private domain.

Before stepping through, Treadway took out her phone, to all appearances reading a new text message, then tapped the screen a couple of times before putting the phone away and stepping through the open door.

Waldron occupied a corner office, giving him a panoramic view of the city below. The office was furnished in Scandinavian style, with an emphasis on form over function. To Treadway, it looked more like a showcase than a workplace. Waldron himself was sprawled out on an overstuffed sectional, watching the large wall-mounted plasma screen television like a bored teenager killing time after school. Treadway noted, with a wry smile, that the TV was tuned to *Closing Bell.*

Waldron had dark lank hair that glistened with an oily sheen. He was clean-shaven with a sallow complexion and a mouth that appeared to be twisted into a permanent smirk. There was an immediate flash of desire in his eyes when he beheld her, but he attempted to hide his interest behind a mask of casual indifference, regarding her with a languid nod. A moment later, however, his forehead creased in bemusement.

"Where's the rest of your crew?" he asked.

Treadway affected an innocent expression. "My crew?"

Waldron sat up, swinging his body around to face her. "For the live segment."

Treadway cocked her head to the side. "I'm sorry. I think maybe you've got me confused with someone else."

Comprehension slowly dawned in his eyes, and then his lips curled up into a salesman's plastic smile. "It would seem I've been had."

He stood up and crossed the room to stand in front of her, hands resting on his hips as he made a show of looking her up and down. "You really didn't need to go to all the trouble. If you wanted to get with me, you could have just emailed me your picture. That would have gotten you a date."

"Cute," she said, matching his smile. Then she took out her badge case and flipped it open. "Special Agent Treadway. FBI."

Waldron's gaze flicked down to her credentials just for a moment, then returned to match her stare. His expression remained unconcerned. "FBI? Well, that definitely would *not* have gotten you a date." He narrowed his eyes at her. "That was a naughty trick, Special Agent Treadway . . . misrepresenting yourself to get inside my office. I'm sure that must break some kind of rule."

Treadway shrugged. "I'm sure I don't know what you're talking about."

Waldron made a sound that was somewhere between a grunt and a chuckle. "Maybe I should have my team of overpriced attorneys present before I say anything to you."

"You're welcome to have representation present," replied Treadway smoothly. Then she arched an eyebrow. "If, that is, you're concerned that you might say something incriminating."

Waldron continued to stare at her, and for a moment, Treadway thought he might make good on his threat to lawyer up. Then his head tilted to the side. "Well, I'll probably get an earful from my legal team for talking to you, but what the heck? I've got nothing to hide. What can I help you with, Special Agent Treadway?"

Treadway mentally pumped her fist. Waldron had just tripped over his own ego. "I just have a few questions about a person who, I believe, works for you." She watched his face carefully for any tells as she spoke the name. "Raymond Williams."

"Raymond? Yes, he's my CFO. And a good friend."

"Is he here? In the building?"

Waldron smirked. "Why do I think you already know the answer to that question? No. He's taken some personal time."

"It must be tough to run a big operation like this without your chief financial officer."

Waldron shrugged. "Raymond's assistant is picking up the slack."

"Do you know Raymond's present whereabouts?"

"I don't. I didn't ask. Personal time is personal business."

"What if I told you that he was in Montana?"

Waldron quirked an eyebrow. "Montana? That doesn't sound like Raymond. He's not exactly what you would call 'outdoorsy.'"

Treadway decided it was time to set the hook. "Can you think of any reason why someone might want to kill him?"

Waldron's eyebrows went up in an approximation of alarm. "Kill Raymond? I can't imagine anyone wanting to . . ." He paused a beat. "You're not saying . . . He's . . . Raymond is . . . *dead*?"

It was a performance worthy of a soap opera. Waldron said the right words and had a look of sincere surprise at hearing the news, and yet, somehow, his reaction lacked authenticity. No two people ever reacted to news of a death the same way, but there was something about genuine shock that only an experienced investigator would notice. Waldron's reaction had a rehearsed quality. It wasn't the sort of thing that would hold up in court, but it was more than enough to put him on the radar as a potential suspect.

"I never said he was dead," she replied quickly. "I only asked if you knew why someone might want to cause him harm. Possible enemies or criminal involvement, that sort of thing."

Waldron's eyes widened ever so slightly at the realization that he had jumped the gun, but he recovered quickly. "Then he's still alive. Thank goodness." He shook his head. "If he was . . . If he *is* involved in anything like that, he kept it a secret from me. Raymond is a straight arrow. As straight as they get."

That, thought Treadway, *might be the first true thing you've said.*

She held his gaze a moment longer, then squared her shoulders. "Well, thank you for taking the time to talk to me, Mr. Waldron."

Waldron was taken aback. "That's it?"

"That's it." She proffered a business card. "If you think of anything else, please don't hesitate to call."

Waldron stared at the card for a moment as if contemplating whether the snake he was about to pick up was venomous. Then he took it and, with a forced smile, said, "Look at that. I didn't even have to ask you for your number."

Treadway ignored the comment. "I'll see myself out."

But as she reached the door, Waldron called after her. "Special Agent?"

She turned, half expecting another pathetic come-on. "Yes?"

"Is Raymond . . . you know . . . ?"

"Alive?"

"Well . . . yeah."

"I'm sorry, but I can't comment on an ongoing investigation. Good day, Mr. Waldron."

As soon as the door closed behind her, she took out her phone. From the home screen, she navigated to the app that was running in the background. The screen displayed the words *signal capture* above a progress bar that presently read 78%. She lingered there, all too aware of the secretary's scrutiny.

Come on, she urged, watching as the number ticked up in sudden leaps.

83%

87%

The maximum range of the Bluetooth-based app was only about fifty feet, but the farther she got from the target phone, the slower the signal capture process would be. Still, she couldn't stand in front of the door forever.

She raised her eyes to the secretary and smiled. "Sorry. I'm trying to call an Uber, but my phone keeps trying to connect to your Wi-Fi."

The secretary seemed to accept this explanation. Treadway just hoped that Waldron didn't come out to make sure she was gone.

95%

Close enough.

Still staring at the phone, pretending to look for a cellular signal, she started moving toward the exit door.

100%

Connection complete.

Yes!

Treadway quickened her step, pushing through the glass door and back into the warren of hallways. She wasn't even halfway back to the main reception lobby when her phone screen flashed a new message. *Call sending.*

She quickly put in an earbud and was just in time to hear a slightly irritated female voice say, "What do you want, Martin?"

"An FBI agent just questioned me about Raymond." Waldron's voice was tinged with panic.

Score, thought Treadway.

In the long silence that followed, Treadway reached the main reception area and exited the ParaDyme offices. She continued to the elevator lobby but didn't press the call button. She didn't want to risk losing her data signal in the elevator and missing out on the conversation.

Finally, the woman spoke again. "I'm going to assume that you had counsel present."

"I didn't get a chance."

"What?" The woman's voice erupted into a shout. "You're kidding. Even you can't be that stupid."

"She ambushed me."

"*She?* They sent a woman? Of course, they would. Let me guess. She was so pretty you couldn't say no to her." The woman didn't wait for an answer. "Well, what did you tell her?"

"What do you think I told her? I said I didn't know anything."

"Did she believe you?"

"I think so."

Another pause, then, "Okay. We knew there was a chance this might blow back on us. I just didn't expect it to happen this soon."

"She made it sound like Raymond might still be . . ." Waldron left the sentence hanging. "Are you sure he's really . . . you know . . . taken care of?"

"He'd better be," said the woman. "I'll look into it."

"What do you want me to do?"

"Nothing. You don't know anything, remember? But if the feds come to you again, let legal do the talking."

"I will." Waldron sounded a little less panicked now. "Mar, do you think they found the key?"

What was that? Treadway wondered if she had heard correctly. It sounded like Waldron had said *Mar*, but it might have been *Ma*. *Is he talking to his mother?*

"They better not have," the woman answered. "Because if the feds have it, we're finished." She paused a beat, then added, "I'll take care of it."

A double beep signaled the end of the call. Treadway glanced at her phone screen, which now displayed the number Waldron had called and the duration of the conversation. A tap on the former should have yielded caller ID, but instead of a name, all that showed were the words *No Information.*

Feeling a twinge of apprehension, she checked the registration of Waldron's phone and found that it also showed *No Information.* Waldron and Mar, whoever that was, were both using throwaway prepaid cellular phones, or more likely, a burner app that served the same purpose without the need to actually change phones.

So, they aren't completely stupid after all, thought Treadway.

She would be able to continue to monitor Waldron's phone activity, but her instincts told her that the woman was the real brains of the operation, and unfortunately, all she had was a word—*Mar.*

But even without an identification, her foray into the heart of ParaDyme's empire had yielded a treasure trove of information. Martin Waldron was definitely involved in the murder of Raymond Williams. He was also looking for a key of some kind, which he believed Williams possessed, and that key, whatever it was, had the potential to bring down Waldron and his coconspirators.

Now if I can just figure out who Mar is.

TWENTY-SIX

Treadway was wrong about the relationship between Martin Waldron and the woman on the other end of his phone call. Mar—short for Marina—was not Martin's mother but rather his twin sister, older by six minutes. Treadway was, however, dead-on regarding the power dynamic at work. Martin didn't make a single decision without first consulting his sister. Martin might have been the CEO of the family company, but Marina was the CEO of the family.

Though the physical resemblance between them was uncanny, their personalities and temperaments could not have been more different. Where Martin took an almost lackadaisical approach to everything but flaunting his wealth and living extravagantly, Marina was serious and driven. Unmarried, with little interest in romantic relationships, she was, to all appearances, wholly devoted to philanthropic endeavors. Her official title was president of the Waldron Foundation, a charitable organization dedicated to various humanitarian and environmental causes, operating out of a private office in her 25,000-square-foot mansion in Lincoln Park, only a few miles from Willis Tower. In reality, she ruled over all of the family's business interests, legitimate or otherwise. ParaDyme was the public face of the Waldron empire, but its profits were only a fraction of the money brought in through the family's other pharmaceutical enterprise and subsequently laundered through her charitable organizations.

Now all of it was in jeopardy.

The fact that the FBI was already aware of Raymond Williams's death and asking questions of her brother was certainly cause for concern. But how much did they really know? Were they just fishing?

Marina stared at the phone in her hand and considered what to do next. She opened a drawer, sorted through several hanging file folders until she found the one she was looking for, and took from it a single piece of lined paper with a handwritten list of more than a dozen telephone numbers. Each number was only ever used for a single call, after which the recipient would change to the next number on the list. The first six were crossed out. Using the burner app, Marina changed her own phone number and then called the seventh number on the paper.

The line rang a couple of times before a brusque voice answered. "Yeah, I know," said Otis Werner, eschewing the customary salutations. "I'm taking care of it."

"Well, I'm pleased that you're on top of things," she replied acidly. "But a little heads-up would have been appreciated. The FBI is already sniffing around our doorstep."

"FBI?" This was clearly news to Otis.

"Yes," snapped Marina. "*FBI*. Do you need me to spell that out for you?"

"How did they get involved?"

"I don't know, but they are. Just tell me this: Did you actually take care of Raymond? He's not in protective custody or something, is he?"

"He's stone dead," said Otis. "The wife too. I can promise you that."

"Then what happened? I told you to keep it low profile. Who dropped the ball?"

"Dean was going to use the wildfires out here to burn the bodies and cover things up. I guess some firefighter showed up out of nowhere just as he was going after their kid."

"And?"

Otis made a noise that sounded like he was spitting. "And Dean got thrown around like a girl. He managed to get away, but the kid and the firefighter both got a look at him."

So that explains how the authorities knew that Raymond was dead, thought Marina.

"But like I said," Otis went on, "I'm taking care of it. I've got my boys looking for the kid now."

"Are you sure that's a good idea?" asked Marina. "We're already exposed here. Maybe it would be better to just have Dean head up to Canada for a while."

"The kid and the firefighter are the only ones who can positively ID Dean. If they aren't around to testify, it doesn't matter what the feds think they know."

"I just don't want you making a bad situation worse."

Otis grunted an indifferent reply.

"What about the key?" asked Marina. "Did Dean recover it?"

"No. Williams didn't have it with him."

Marina sucked in an apprehensive breath.

"He must have stashed it somewhere," Otis went on. "Wherever he put it, he took that secret to the grave."

"Are you really that much of an idiot? He could have given it to someone as an insurance policy. For all we know, the FBI already has it."

"They don't," Otis insisted. "If they did, we'd all be in lockup already. Don't sweat it."

"Don't tell me not to sweat it," said Marina in a tight voice. "I didn't get where I am by not sweating it. I don't care what you have to do. Find that key." A sudden thought struck her. "Maybe the kid knows where Raymond put it. When you find him, make him tell you."

Otis was silent for a long moment. "What if he won't talk? I ain't real good with kids. Just ask my own."

Marina considered this. "You know what, you're probably right. Maybe a woman's touch is called for. Take him to the mill. I'll meet you there."

"You're coming here?" Otis asked, surprised.

"Is that a problem?"

"Well, no. It's just . . . I didn't think you wanted to get involved in the operational side of things."

"Maybe if I was more involved, we wouldn't be in this situation," she shot back. "Make no mistake, Otis. This is a crisis. As long as the key is in the wind, we're in danger."

He started to say something, but she cut him off. "I'll be there in a few hours. Just find that kid. And get rid of that firefighter, whoever he is."

TWENTY-SEVEN

Before heading up to Helena, Redd drove the family back into town to drop Matthew Jr. off at the Derhammers' house. Emily had initially objected to leaving their son with Mikey and Liz. She didn't see any reason why they couldn't take Little Matty with them.

"It's not like we're going into battle," she had said, staring pointedly at the revolver still holstered at his hip. "Right?"

Rather than point out that, inasmuch as they were about to confront a man that Emily believed had sent a killer after her, it might very well turn into a battle, Redd tried a more practical argument. "You know how Junior gets on long rides. He'll be a lot happier playing with Lucas."

"I just don't like always having to rely on Liz to watch him. I feel bad, you know?"

This was something on which Redd would ordinarily have agreed. He had a natural aversion to asking for help, even when he needed it most. And for all those times she was quick to urge him to accept help when it was offered, Emily had a similarly independent streak. "I mean, it's one thing to use her for day care," she went on, "but evenings should be family time. For them *and* for us."

"All right then," countered Redd. "Are you going to stay in the truck with Junior while I have a friendly chat with the good doctor?"

"Of course not," Emily said quickly. Then she frowned. "Okay, I see your point."

"And we're not going to leave him in the truck by himself," pressed Redd.

"No, we're not going to leave him in the truck."

"So, it's either take him to Mikey's or to your mom and dad's place."

"Little Matty would run circles around Mom and Dad." Emily's parents were elderly, and as much as they enjoyed spending time with their grandchild, now that Junior was walking he was just too much for them to handle. "Okay," she conceded. "I'll give Liz a call."

Mikey and Liz were, of course, more than happy to help out, which didn't necessarily make either Redd or Emily feel better about asking for the favor, but Redd was secretly relieved that he wouldn't be taking his son into a situation that had even a slight potential for danger. He would have preferred to have Emily stay behind as well but knew that was an argument he would not win.

At least she could hold her own if it turned into a gunfight.

With Junior now safe, happily playing with Luke, and Emily literally riding shotgun, not to mention Rubble sprawled out in the rear of the cab, Redd was finally able to focus on the task at hand. He returned the Raptor to the highway and headed north once more.

Earlier, when he had been racing to get back home in response to the attack on Emily, he hadn't paid much attention to the sky, but now it was impossible to ignore. The column of smoke, looking much bigger or closer than Redd remembered, loomed over the world like something from an apocalyptic disaster movie. The sun, normally bright and blinding, was reduced to a dull red-orange spot that hardly seemed to give any light at all. Then, about fifteen miles past the turnoff to the ranch, Redd saw that northbound traffic had come to a complete standstill.

"What the heck?" he muttered.

"A traffic jam?" wondered Emily as she leaned forward, trying to see how far the blockage extended. "I'll bet that's never happened here before."

"I wonder if they closed the road."

As if to confirm this suggestion, a pickup just a few vehicles ahead of them abruptly swung out of the lineup, did a U-turn, and then headed back in the direction of Wellington, which allowed Redd to advance. More vehicles followed suit, and soon Redd saw that, indeed, the road ahead was partially blocked by a sheriff's patrol vehicle with its emergency lights flashing. Some vehicles were allowed to pass after talking to a deputy—Redd saw that it was Undersheriff Shane Hall, who had fought alongside him during the battle at the courthouse earlier that year—but a few immediately turned back.

When he finally reached the roadblock, Redd rolled the window down. "Hey, Shane," he said. "What's going on? Is the highway closed?"

The deputy shook his head. "Not yet, but it could happen." He looked past Redd, saw Emily, and touched the brim of his hat. "Dr. Emily."

She returned a smile and a wave.

Shane brought his attention back to Redd. "There's a chance they might close the highway if the winds shift, so I'm letting everyone know that if they continue on to Helena, they might not be able to make it back." He leaned in close. "Just between you and me, though, what I'm really doing here is looking out for that suspect you described. Garrison is up on the hill behind me with a scope, watching the folks that pull out of line and head back."

Garrison, Redd knew, was Deputy Garrison Scott. He'd also been shoulder to shoulder with Redd and everyone else during the battle at the courthouse. Redd liked the man, and Hall too.

Of course, thought Redd. *And what better way to get a look inside each and every vehicle than a safety stop?* "No luck, I take it?"

"Not yet, but we're going to keep looking all the same."

Emily leaned over. "Do you think they really might close the highway?"

Shane shrugged. "All depends on the weather. You heading up to Helena?"

"That's the plan."

"Well, if it was me, I'd hold off on whatever business you've got until tomorrow." His gaze drifted down to the bulge of her belly. "Oh," he added quickly, eyes widening in comprehension. "Unless this is something that can't wait."

"Relax, Shane," said Emily. "I've still got a few more days."

Looking relieved, the deputy nodded. "Well, if you do head up there, be aware that you might have to take the long way to get back home."

The long way, Redd knew, involved a lengthy, circuitous journey to the west of the Elkhorn Mountains, down to Butte, then over to Three Forks to catch the highway south of Townsend—a detour that would add several hours to the trip. Redd also knew of several rural back roads that could get them home, but utilizing them would similarly add many hours to the trip, not to mention involve four-wheeling through some potentially hairy conditions. He wouldn't subject Emily to that in her current condition.

Redd glanced over at his wife. "What do you think?"

"I don't like the idea of driving all night, but I would like to have another talk with Dr. Dickerson."

Redd turned back to the deputy. "I guess we'll take our chances."

✖ ✖ ✖

Ten miles farther down the road, Redd was already reconsidering that decision. The fires seemed much closer to the highway than he would have believed. He could even see flames flickering on the upper boughs of distant trees. He knew there were a couple miles of open rangeland between the highway and the forested flanks of the Elkhorn Mountains, but he also knew how quickly the flames could move, especially over dry grass and scrub.

And if the fire made it as far as the highway, there was no reason to think it wouldn't jump across and keep going all the way to the Missouri River, destroying everything in its path, including Thompson Ranch.

Redd kept this dire possibility to himself.

By the time they reached Helena, the sun was beginning to dip beneath the now-distant layer of smoke, painting the sky shades of orange and pink. Under any other circumstances, it would have been a sight to behold, but Redd was too focused on accomplishing his objective and getting back home to appreciate the problematic beauty of a wildfire sunset.

Emily played the role of navigator, directing him along the same route she had followed only a few hours earlier. Her relative familiarity with the area meant that she realized there was a problem before Redd did.

"Uh-oh," she said. "That's not good."

Redd didn't need to ask what she was referring to. Even from a quarter mile away, he could see emergency lights attached to several sheriff's patrol vehicles as well as a couple of unmarked cars, all arrayed in front of a large lakeside house.

TWENTY-EIGHT

"That's the doctor's place, isn't it?" asked Redd.

Emily nodded. "What do you think it means?"

"That many cops in one place means somebody died."

Suddenly, Emily's assertion that the attack at the ranch related to her confrontation with the doctor didn't seem quite as unbelievable. Redd pulled the Raptor onto the shoulder, shifted to park, and then took out his phone.

Thirty seconds later, he had Sheriff Blackwood on the line. Without going into too much detail, he explained that he and Emily had come up to Helena to consult with a retired doctor only to discover a police presence at his residence. Blackwood agreed to put in a call to the Lewis and Clark County Sheriff's Department to find out what was happening.

Blackwood called back in minutes. "Bad news, I'm afraid," he said without much in the way of preamble. "It looks like Dr. Dickerson took his own life."

"Suicide?"

Emily shot Redd a questioning look. He nodded and then, after touching a finger to his lips, put the call on speaker. "Are they sure?"

"Mind you, none of this is official," said Blackwood. "But it sounds like the wife was out of town. When she couldn't get through to the doctor, she called a neighbor who came over and found him hanging off the second-story landing. Neck broke. Body cold. There was even a note. Something about not being able to live with the guilt. I didn't push too hard for the details. Professional courtesy only extends so far."

In the passenger seat, Emily was shaking her head and mouthing, *No way.*

"Do you get the impression that they're going to treat it as suspicious," asked Redd, "or will the coroner just rubber-stamp the suicide ruling?"

"Well, I don't rightly know," replied Blackwood in a thoughtful voice. "Is there some reason why they *should* consider it suspicious?"

Redd paused to formulate his answer. "Let's just say I have it on good authority that the doctor may have been involved in some shady business."

"I could draw that conclusion just from the suicide note."

"Just tell the head investigator to insist on a full forensic examination before letting the ME issue the final ruling."

"What aren't you telling me, Matthew?"

Redd glanced over at Emily before replying. "Em paid the doc a visit earlier today. She found evidence that he had been overprescribing pain meds a few years back. One of his former patients OD'd today. Died in the ER."

"Are you saying that this doctor was selling drugs illegally to his former patients?" Emily shook her head.

"I don't know what he was doing," Redd went on. "But after Em got back home, some thug forced his way into our house and attacked her."

"At the ranch? Is she all right?"

"Just a little rattled."

"When did this happen? Why didn't you call it in immediately?"

Redd grimaced. This was exactly what he had been hoping to avoid. "Honestly, I figured you had your hands full with everything else that's going on. And at the time, I thought it might be related to what happened out in the woods this morning, but Em thought this doctor might have been behind it. Since he's out of your jurisdiction, we decided to come up here and do a little digging on our own. Now I'm starting to think that maybe she was right. Based on her description, not to mention what he did to our front door, the guy that broke into our place could have snapped the doc's neck without breaking a sweat."

"Matthew, if you want to get into criminal investigations so badly, I'd be happy to hire you on as a deputy."

It was not the first time Blackwood had tried to recruit him. So far, Redd had always demurred.

"Okay," the sheriff went on, "let's put aside the fact that you and the missus need to stop playing Hardy Boys and Nancy Drew and leave the crime fighting to the professionals. What exactly do you think is going on?"

Emily began waving her hand.

"I'm going to let Em explain it," said Redd.

Emily jumped in immediately. "Hi, Sheriff. Here's what I think. Dr. Dickerson was prescribing opioids to patients who probably should have been tapering their dependence. When the CDC started cracking down on prescription meds, he retired from his practice, but I think he was supplementing his income by providing illegal drugs to his former patients."

"You're saying the good doctor retired and started dealing," summarized Blackwood. "Do you have any proof?"

"Aside from the fact that he's dead just a few hours after I confronted him?"

"Just for argument's sake," countered the sheriff. "Isn't it possible that when you came calling, he realized the jig was up and took his own life to avoid prison time?"

Redd had already considered and rejected that possibility. "That doesn't explain why somebody came after Em."

"Fair enough," said Blackwood. "So, who killed him?"

"My guess?" replied Emily. "His supplier. I think he freaked out after I called him out. Called his supplier and told him that I had been nosing around. I'll bet he thought I was going to call the cops—"

"Imagine that," Blackwood cut in sourly.

"The supplier probably figured that Dr. Dickerson was a liability and killed him to keep him from talking if he got arrested. Then they sent the human wrecking ball after me. I mean, it makes sense, right?"

Redd didn't like where any of it was leading, but it did make sense. He nodded in agreement.

"All right," said Blackwood. "You've convinced me. I'll pass your concerns along to Sheriff Kostigan. Meanwhile, I'm going to send a deputy out to get your statement and collect any evidence that might have been left at the scene.

Tomorrow morning, I want you to come in and look at some mug shots. Hopefully we'll be able to put a name to your attacker."

"Sounds good," said Redd. "We're heading back now."

After Redd ended the call, Emily glanced over at him. "I can't believe he's dead."

Redd sighed. "These guys don't mess around. Forget the doc, Em. You were supposed to be next. That's our bigger problem."

"So, you believe me now?"

"I didn't *not* believe you. I just didn't have all the facts." He put the truck in gear, made a U-turn, and headed back the way they'd come. "You have to admit, I'm usually the one trouble follows home, not you."

"Okay, you're not wrong."

"The guy that I tussled with out there didn't think twice about killing a lot of innocent people just to eliminate any witnesses, so naturally, I assumed your guy was looking for me."

"What are the odds, huh?"

Redd looked at her sidelong. "What do you mean?"

"You and me both running into ruthless killers on the same day. Makes you wonder how many more of them are out there wandering around."

Redd nodded slowly. "Actually, that's something I've been wondering about too. I think there's a good chance that these incidents are related."

"How so?"

"Let's start with your theory that the doctor was somehow involved in narcotics trafficking. That puts him in bed with some pretty unsavory people."

"Well, yeah, obviously."

"I meant organized crime."

"The mafia . . . in Montana?"

"Who do you think supplied the drugs that killed your patient? And it doesn't have to be the Sicilian mob. There are dozens of organized crime operations running drugs, arms, and human trafficking. It's an international problem. I think the guy I ran into and the guy who came after you could be working for the same outfit," Redd speculated. "The guy they killed in the woods was a pharma exec. A company called ParaDyme. You know anything about them?"

"I've heard of them. They mostly produce off-patent medicines. Generics."

"Opioids?"

"Sure. But lots of other stuff too. From what I've heard, their business model is quantity over quality. They let the big players do the R and D, and then as soon as the patent expires, they cash in." She gave him another sidelong glance. "You think the common thread here is drug trafficking? Well, I can tell you that a lot of doctors, myself included, have always thought Big Pharma is almost as bad as the mobsters. The criminals might be supplying the fentanyl, but it was the pharma companies who created the addicts in the first place. It's a real shame, Matty."

"What if they're also part of the supply chain?"

Emily shook her head. "That seems like a stretch. They're making bank on legitimate prescription sales. Why would they risk everything by getting involved in the production of illegal drugs?"

"Like you said. They created the addicts. Those are their customers. Or they were until the government put the brakes on their legitimate business. They've got the expertise to make the drugs. Why let the career criminals make all the profits?"

Emily remained dubious.

"Look," Redd went on, "this guy was on the run. He knew someone was coming after him. Maybe it doesn't have anything to do with opioids, but whatever he was mixed up in must have been pretty serious."

Emily considered this for a long moment. "What does that mean for us?"

"I think it means this isn't over yet." Redd knew it wasn't the answer she was looking for, so he added, "After we talk to Blackwood tomorrow, we'll head back up to Helena and get a hotel room. Keep ourselves out of circulation until this blows over."

"How are we going to afford that?"

"We'll find a way," Redd replied, with more confidence than he felt. "Safety over money, Em. You know that."

"What about the ranch? And the fires?"

"I'll drive down and check on things every couple of days." Emily seemed to accept this, but Redd could see the worry on her face, so he added, "Hey, it's going to be all right. We'll get through this together."

I sound like Emily right now. When did we swap roles over here?

That brought a smile to her lips. "You aren't going to take off and try to do it all on your own . . . *again*?"

"Nope. No more solo ops."

Just saying it aloud, making the promise, was difficult for Redd. Learning to accept help from his friends and loved ones had been a hard lesson, and even now, it ran counter to his instincts. As far back as he could remember, he had been a lone wolf, facing whatever life threw at him, afraid to ask for help because some part of him feared that doing so was an admission of weakness. It was only now, with the benefit of maturity, that he understood what that kind of thinking had cost him.

As a teenager, when he had decided to drop out of high school in order to take care of the ranch after an accident sidelined J. B., he hadn't told anyone—not Emily, not Mikey, not even J. B. himself. At the time, he had rationalized it as not wanting to burden anyone, but now he understood that what he had really been doing was telling the most important people in his life that he didn't trust them.

He'd almost made the same mistake earlier that year, when he'd been targeted by the rogue Homeland Security agents, but with much higher stakes. In the end, without the help he'd received from all of his friends and family, and even a few strangers, he would have lost a lot more than just a few relationships.

As if to remind himself of that, he reached over the center console and took her hand. "We're stronger together."

I really do sound like Emily. This is getting weird.

Her smile broadened as she squeezed his hand. "Don't you forget it."

Thinking about his trust issues brought Jack's plight to mind. Redd, at least, had finished his childhood journey under the rock-solid guidance of Jim Bob Thompson. Without that, he probably wouldn't have ever met Emily and Mikey, wouldn't have joined the Marines, and wouldn't have found people to love and trust. Jack didn't have a J. B.

Unless . . . But Redd dismissed his own thought. *I'm no Jim Bob, that's for sure.*

The thought struck him like a bolt of lightning from a clear sky. It was, on its face, a ludicrous notion. Jack would soon be in the system, placed with a foster parent if no relatives could be found, but that didn't mean Redd couldn't find a way to help him, did it? Maybe he couldn't be the boy's dad the way J. B. had been his, but he could at least be a friend and mentor and, most importantly, an advocate.

He resolved to pay Jack a visit as soon as they got back to town.

Less than twenty minutes later, however, that plan encountered a snag when he passed a portable electronic notification sign informing them that the highway between Spokane Hills and Wellington was closed.

TWENTY-NINE

WELLINGTON, MONTANA

When he pulled the Billet Silver Dodge Ram 3500 into the parking lot of the Diamond T Motel, Mikey Derhammer immediately noticed the Chrysler 300 parked in front of one of the guest rooms.

"That must be the one," he remarked, even without being able to see the number on the door to the room.

"Why do you think so?" Liz asked.

"That car. It sticks out like a sore thumb." He gestured to the scattering of vehicles in front of the building. There were well-traveled hatchbacks and SUVs, many adorned with a variety of bumper stickers from various tourist destinations, and a couple of pickups with National Rifle Association decals and window stickers displaying a variety of politically charged messages. "Most of the Diamond T's customers are either families on vacation and just passing through or out-of-state fishermen and hunters. That Chrysler doesn't fit. It practically screams 'government issue.'"

"It has Montana plates," observed Liz. "Wouldn't an FBI car have federal motor pool plates?"

"Law enforcement agencies mostly use unmarked vehicles. That way, they don't give themselves away to suspects." Mikey's expertise on this subject derived primarily from his being an inveterate consumer of mystery and thriller novels, but he felt like his reasoning was sound.

"If they really want to blend in, they should drive beat-up old Subarus."

Mikey shrugged. It was a fair point.

When his best friend Matthew Redd called to let him know that he and Emily wouldn't be back from Helena until late and then asked him to check on a certain young witness in protective custody, Mikey had been more than happy to oblige.

In truth, there wasn't much Mikey wouldn't do for Redd. He loved the man like a brother, and when your brother needs help, you lend a hand. It's as simple as that. However, this particular request had felt uncharacteristically personal. Redd so rarely revealed his tender side, even to those closest to him, that Mikey was curious about this boy who had evidently touched his friend's heart.

Redd had revealed that the boy—Jack—had seen his caregivers murdered. Mikey had noted Redd's use of the term *caregivers* as opposed to *parents* but had not asked for clarification. Because Jack had witnessed the crime, there was some danger of further action on the part of the killer, so the boy was being guarded by FBI agents at the only motel in town.

"I was hoping to stop by and visit with him tonight," Redd had explained. "The poor kid's been bounced around like a pinball. There's no consistency in his life. But since we're not going to make it back until late, I was hoping you could just stop by and check in on him."

"What do you want me to tell him?"

"Tell him that you're my best friend and that I couldn't make it tonight, but I will come by first thing in the morning. You're good with kids. You'll figure it out."

Redd had no doubt imagined that his friend would merely swing by and deliver the message, but when Mikey told Liz about the request, she had immediately proposed something different.

"Poor kid," she said. "Going through this all alone."

"Well, he's not really alone."

"You know what I mean. He's surrounded by big tough cops when what he really needs right now is someone who can tell him that it's all right to be sad."

"You mean like a mom."

"Like a mom," Liz agreed.

Mikey had refrained from pointing out that not all cops were big and tough or even male. Liz made a good point. So, after finishing their dinner, they bundled Lucas and Matthew Jr. into Mikey's truck and made the short drive over to the Diamond T Motel to meet the mysterious boy Redd had saved from a killer.

The Diamond T Motel consisted of a single one-story building with a centrally located office. Guest rooms in the front and back, accessible from exterior doors that opened directly onto the parking lot. Mikey had never had occasion to visit the establishment, but he'd stayed in similarly ancient motor lodges on family vacations and knew that they were usually pretty rustic. The sign out front advertised *Color TV in Every Room* like it was some kind of extravagant luxury. There was no mention of a pool or air-conditioning.

With the sun just dipping below the horizon, the motel parking lot—illuminated by a single municipal streetlight and the relatively low-intensity bulbs of the unit porchlights—was as full as it was likely to get, which was to say, not very. The fires appeared to have scared the tourists away, so only a handful of parking slots near the building were occupied. Mikey parked on the side of the lot, away from the building, facing the highway. While Liz began unbuckling the boys, he got out and headed toward the motel unit closest to the Chrysler, confirming that the number on the door was the same number Redd had given him—unit four. As he drew near, however, the door opened, and a young man in dress casual attire greeted him from the doorway.

"Are you Mr. Derhammer?"

Mikey grinned. "Guilty as charged."

"I'm Special Agent Kennedy. Mr. Redd said you might be coming by. Jack's staying in room seven with my partner. She's expecting you. No need to knock. Just walk on in."

Clever, thought Mikey. The FBI agents had rented two nonadjoining rooms and parked the government-issued Chrysler in front of the decoy room.

Not as subtle as just driving an old beat-up Subaru, but nonetheless effective.

He returned to the truck to help Liz finish unloading the boys. With Little Matty holding his hand and Lucas holding Liz's, they went to the door marked with a seven and walked in as if they were the ones renting the room. The first thing Mikey noticed was a boy, six or seven, with dark shaggy hair, sitting on the still-made bed, eyes glued to the television and clutching a Buzz Lightyear doll.

Suddenly, it all made sense to Mikey.

He looks just like Matt as a kid. That and his upbringing . . . No wonder Matt wants to protect him. He sees himself in this kid. In Jack.

Slowly, as if reluctant to look away from the screen, the boy turned his head toward the open door. He briefly made eye contact with Mikey, and then his attention drifted down to the toddler holding Mikey's hand. When he saw Matthew Jr., Jack's eyes lit up, and he jumped off the bed and ran to greet the visitors.

"Please come in," said a female voice with some urgency. "And close the door."

Mikey now saw that a smartly dressed woman with dark hair and an olive complexion stood in the corner of the room adjacent to the door. Mikey hurriedly got out of the way, making room for Liz, and then reached back and closed the door behind them. Jack, meanwhile, was completely focused on little Matty and Lucas.

"Lookit," he chirped. "It's Buzz Lightyear."

Mikey doubted that either of the toddlers had the faintest clue who Buzz Lightyear was, but they both knew a toy when they saw one. Curious hands reached out to grasp the molded plastic action figure.

"You must be Mr. and Mrs. Derhammer," said the woman. "I'm Special Agent Nunez. Sorry to rush you like that, but we don't want to advertise."

"Makes perfect sense," said Mikey. "Thanks for letting us visit with Jack." He turned to face the boy so that he would feel included. "Matt told us all about you. I'm Mikey. Matt's best friend. This is my wife, Liz."

Jack glanced up at the adults and nodded, then returned his attention to the boys. Despite the age difference, he seemed overjoyed to have young playmates. Rather than interrupt the children, all of whom seemed to be enjoying the interaction, Mikey curtailed the introductions and instead moved over with Liz to join the FBI agent.

"He seems to be handling this well," Mikey said in a low voice.

"He's a tough little guy," replied Nunez. "But nobody should have to go through what he has."

"What do you know about him?" asked Liz.

"The head office sent over his records. There's not much, really. His name is John Williams. He's six going on seven. Mother Adeline Williams is deceased. That happened about eighteen months ago. There's no father listed on the birth certificate. After the mom passed, he was placed with her older brother, Raymond Williams, and his wife, Janelle, in Chicago. Visits from state DCFS indicated nothing of concern in the family." She shrugged. "That's about it, really. Except for what happened today. Did Mr. Redd tell you about that?"

"He touched on it."

Nunez thrust her chin in Jack's direction. "Jack says that a few days ago, Raymond packed them all up and drove out to that cabin. He said that both of the adults were acting scared and fighting a lot. Clearly, they were afraid of something. Evidently, they had good reason to be."

Mikey felt Liz nudge him and turned to see Jack ambling toward them with a big smile on his face. Behind the boy, Lucas and Matthew Jr. were engaged in a tug of war for control of Buzz Lightyear.

"Do you want me to get that back for you, hon?" asked Liz.

Jack shook his head. "It's okay. They can play with it."

"Well, I think it's really nice of you to share your toy with them."

Jack beamed at this for a moment, but then his expression fell. Mikey wondered what was going through the little guy's head.

Does he just want other kids to play with, or is it something else?

"He used to talk," said Jack. "Now he doesn't."

It took Mikey a moment to realize that Jack was referring to the toy. "Maybe he just needs new batteries. Want me to take a look?"

Jack brightened again. "Can you?"

"Sure thing." Mikey moved over to the other two boys and gently interposed himself into their struggle. "Okay, boys. I need to borrow this for a second."

The request was met with mild resistance at first, but the two boys seemed to quickly lose interest in the toy when it became evident that Mikey wasn't going to let go. With the action figure at last in his possession, Mikey sat down on the bed and flipped it over to reveal the screw-down battery compartment. Using the short Phillips-head screwdriver that he kept hooked on his key chain, a trick he'd learned early in his career as a mechanic, he set to work loosening the cover. No sooner was the task begun, however, than several loud staccato pops from somewhere outside caused him to look up in alarm.

"Was that a gunshot?" asked Liz, saying aloud what Mikey was thinking.

It was a sound neither of them would ever forget. Earlier that year, they had both fought for their lives alongside Redd and Emily in the courthouse siege.

Even though Mikey was a hunter and accustomed to hearing the sharp crack of a rifle discharge, somehow the sound was different when the shots were being fired in anger and at human targets. Liz was wrong in one respect, though. It wasn't a single gun but at least three or four.

The expression on Special Agent Nunez's face was all the confirmation either of them needed. She unclipped a small radio handset from her belt, but before she could key the push-to-talk, a breathless voice burst from the device. "Alma . . . Taking fire . . . Evac—"

Another round of reports cut off the transmission. Nunez keyed her mic. "Preston. What's going on?"

The only response was another volley of gunfire.

THIRTY

Mikey jumped to his feet, still holding Buzz Lightyear in one hand. With his other hand, he retrieved a small folding blade he always kept in his jeans pocket. Not so long ago, he would have found himself paralyzed by a situation like this, gripped by denial, unwilling or unable to believe that he was in the middle of a worst-case scenario. But he wasn't that person anymore.

Though he lacked formal training, he was battle tested.

He wished Redd was there. Redd was as close to Superman as Mikey had ever seen, and he *did* have the required training for such a scenario. He was a warrior. Lethal from any range.

But Redd wasn't there.

And more importantly, Redd had sent Mikey because he trusted his best friend to handle things. Mikey snapped to action.

This is happening, he told himself. *We're under attack.*

The criminals who had killed Jack's guardians had come to finish what they started, just as Redd had feared they might. Special Agent Kennedy was likely dead, and while the decoy room where he had been installed had evidently served its purpose, drawing the attention of the killers away from Jack's actual location, once those men realized they had been duped, it wouldn't take them long to begin searching the rest of the motel.

Thank goodness most of the rooms are vacant.

Mikey recalled Kennedy's final, truncated transmission.

"Evac."

Evacuate.

"We can't stay here." He said it matter-of-factly, controlling the panic he was feeling.

Agent Nunez, who had drawn her sidearm and moved closer to the door, now glanced back at him. Mikey saw real fear in her eyes. Not just fear for her own life but for the lives of the innocents entrusted to her. "This is the only way in or out," she said gravely.

Mikey looked around and immediately saw the truth of her statement. The old motel had been built at a time when emergency exits were not required by law. The room's only possible egress routes were the front door or the large window right next to it.

"Then I guess that's the way we're going." He turned to Liz, who had gathered the children into her arms and was huddling over them protectively. "Let's go."

She gaped at him in disbelief, but then Nunez gave her support to the plan, her voice grim but determined. "He's right. Get to your car as quickly as you can. I'll draw their fire. Buy you time to get away."

"Draw their fire. Buy you time."

Mikey knew what that meant and vowed not to let her sacrifice be in vain. Kneeling down beside Liz and the three boys, he extended his arms in an all-encompassing hug. "All right, everyone. Time to go."

There was another loud bang from somewhere outside. Not the report of a gun, but something else. The sound repeated twice more and then was followed by a splitting noise and another loud thud. It was the sound of someone kicking down a door. The killers had begun their door-to-door search of the motel.

Mikey brought his attention back to the little group. He handed the Buzz Lightyear toy to Jack. "I think you better hold on to this for now." Then, with the Ram's key fob in hand, he scooped Matthew Jr. into his arms and moved toward the exit.

Nunez grasped the door handle. "When I give you the word, *walk*. Don't run.

Running will just attract attention. Plus, the last thing you want to do is trip and fall. I'll cover you as you move."

Mikey just nodded. Nunez took a breath as if to gather her courage, then, with her pistol at the ready, opened the door. She leaned sideways, edging around the doorframe to check all the angles, then pulled back inside. "Go!"

Mikey didn't hesitate. Holding Jack's hand in his, he stepped out into the open, striding purposefully across the parking lot, laser focused on the truck parked less than a hundred feet away. He resisted the almost overwhelming urge to try to fix the location of the killers, allowing himself only a single backward glance to ensure that Liz was right behind him.

They were halfway to the Ram when someone shouted, "Hey! Stop right there!"

Mikey kept walking. "Don't stop," he said, just loud enough for Liz and Jack to hear. "Don't even look."

"I said, stop!" barked the voice again.

In his mind's eye, Mikey saw the man—a nightmarish, faceless figure brandishing an assault rifle—charging forward to cut him off, but still, he did not turn his head. The truck was just a few steps away.

Then a different voice called out, "Federal agent. Drop your weapons."

Almost before Nunez finished speaking, there was an eruption of noise, and this time, Mikey couldn't help himself. He glanced back, just for a second, and saw the FBI agent, half-concealed in the door of room seven, exchanging fire with a group of individuals hunkered down behind the FBI-issue Chrysler. Mikey couldn't determine how many there were or what they looked like, only that Nunez now had their full attention.

He activated the remote start button on the key fob and then, as the 6.7-liter Cummins Turbo Diesel I6 engine roared to life, hit the unlock button twice and leaped forward to open the rear door on the driver's side—the side that would afford the most concealment from the gunmen. "Liz. Get in back with the boys."

Liz grasped his intent and clambered into the back seat. She set Lucas down in the footwell then reached out for Matthew Jr.. Mikey passed the toddler to her and then boosted Jack inside as well.

"Keep down," he said before closing them in. He slid in behind the wheel, immediately shifting the truck into reverse.

He had parked nose in, just as most people do, with the intention of backing out of the parking spot when leaving. Now, even the few seconds required to perform that simple maneuver felt like a dangerous indulgence.

As he started to move his foot from the brake pedal to the accelerator, he glanced reflexively down at the screen displaying the feed from the backup camera and saw one of the gunmen emerge from behind the besieged Chrysler. The lower part of the man's face was hidden behind a tied black bandana, making him look like an old-fashioned Wild West outlaw, but the semi-auto gripped in both hands and aimed, or so it appeared, right at the camera lens was definitely a twenty-first-century touch.

Mikey thought about jamming down on the accelerator, reversing into the man, and running him over, but he immediately rejected the idea. At that distance, even with the engine redlined, the Ram couldn't go much faster than a running pace in reverse, which would not only give the bad guy plenty of time to jump out of the way but also put the truck and its occupants within his easy reach. Better, he realized, to just put the truck in drive, ride over the curb, and pull directly onto the highway.

In the fraction of a second it took for him to work this out and reach for the gearshift lever, another figure entered the camera frame. It was Special Agent Nunez, breaking cover to engage the gunman moving to intercept the Ram. She fired twice, and at least one of the shots found its target, dropping the gunman. But then, in the instant before the feed from the backup camera was cut off, Mikey saw the FBI agent twisting violently as bullets tore into her.

Mikey squeezed the steering wheel, fighting a tsunami of emotions—horror, fear, despair, blind rage—and stomped on the accelerator. The truck lurched forward and then bucked again as the big Michelin LTX tires struck the curb and rolled up and onto the sidewalk. There was another, smaller jolt as the duallies in the rear rode onto the sidewalk, but by the time the front end dropped down onto asphalt on the opposite side, the truck was going fast enough that it felt merely like hitting a speed bump.

With headlights approaching from both directions, Mikey was faced with a decision—he could either take the path of least resistance and steer to the right or come to a complete stop and wait for an opening to cut over to the southbound lane. Unbidden, a memory of Special Agent Nunez going down in a hail of bullets flashed through his mind, and the decision was made.

No stopping now.

He hauled the wheel to the right, turning into the northbound lane. The driver of a speeding pickup heading in the same direction laid on his horn as he swerved into the center turn lane and blew past, but Mikey barely even noticed. He was completely focused on putting as much distance between himself and the Diamond T as possible.

The big truck was not built for speed, and with adrenaline pumping through his veins, it seemed to Mikey that it took forever to build up a head of steam. Gradually, however, the big Diamond T sign shrank to nothing in the rearview, with no immediate sign of pursuit, and Mikey let out the breath he didn't even know he was holding.

"Everyone okay back there?" he asked.

"We're okay," Liz assured him. "Scared and a little shaken up, but okay. Is it safe to buckle the boys into their seats?"

The request left him deeply chagrined. Here he was, racing down a highway at close to seventy miles per hour, and not one soul in the truck had their seat belt on. If something had gone wrong . . . If that truck had plowed into them or if he had lost control while pulling out onto the highway . . .

Mikey didn't want to think about what might have happened.

Had to do it, he told himself. *The bad guys didn't exactly give us time to buckle up.*

Nevertheless, his foot eased off the pedal just a little. "Can you do it while we're on the move?"

"I can try."

Mikey nodded absently, and even though there was now little danger of a collision, he allowed the truck to coast until the speedometer more closely matched the posted speed limit. As Liz wrangled the toddlers into their safety seats, Mikey spared another glance in the rearview. His heart, which had not really quieted much at all, began racing again.

In the far distance, he saw the headlights of a vehicle closing the distance between them.

There was no reason to think that it was the gunmen from the motel. The highway was the main route in and out of Wellington, used by hundreds of people every day. It might have just been a rancher, one of Matthew's neighbors, heading home after a quick supper at Spady's.

But could he afford to take that chance?

He glanced down at the speedometer and then returned his attention to the spot in the mirror.

Is he getting closer?

"How are we doing back there?"

"Almost done," Liz promised.

Mikey pushed the pedal down a little harder but knew that simply outpacing the killers might not be enough to save them.

"There," said Liz simultaneously with the distinctive click of a seat belt buckle locking into place. "Everyone's safe now."

If only it were that simple, thought Mikey.

THIRTY-ONE

Redd had to fight the urge to slam his fists against the steering wheel. Instead, with his jaw clenched tight, biting back curses that were mostly self-directed, he pulled off onto the shoulder and did his best to focus on the voice coming from his phone instead of the hypercritical voice in his head.

"Two or three guys," Mikey was saying. "They had their faces covered, so I can't tell you what they looked like."

I shouldn't have sent him there. What was I thinking?

"We made it to my truck, but I think the FBI agents . . ." Mikey's voice dropped to a confidential whisper. "They didn't make it, brother."

I knew Jack was still a target. I should have trusted my instincts and insisted that Kline's agents take him somewhere else. Somewhere less obvious. That, or . . . he should have stayed with me.

"But we're all okay," Mikey went on. "Everyone's okay. And Jack is with us."

Redd barely heard him. He was still yelling at himself internally for yet again putting people he loved in danger. Including his own son.

I never should have wasted time going to Helena when the real threat was in my own backyard. And now who knows how many hours away we are, and there's nothing

I can do to protect my family. He glanced over at Emily and could tell by the look in her eyes that she had similar misgivings.

"What should we do?"

Mikey's question caught Redd momentarily flat-footed.

"Matt?" prompted Mikey after a long moment. "A little help here?"

"I'm here, Mikey. Where are you right now?"

"Heading north. But I'm gonna have to turn around soon. I've already passed the signs that say the highway is closed."

"Turn around now," urged Redd. "Go to Bozeman."

"I thought about doing that. I'm not sure it's such a good idea. Those guys are back there looking for us. They saw my truck. They're gonna notice when I pass them going the other way. It's a long way to Bozeman. A lot of open road between here and there."

Despite himself, Redd almost chuckled aloud. Mikey's thinking was clearer than his own. "You're right. That's a bad plan." He racked his brain for a better one. "Did you call 911?"

"Of course. They already knew about what happened at the motel. Someone else called it in."

"Did you tell the dispatcher that you were being chased?"

There was a conspicuous silence on the line for several seconds. "Not exactly in those words." Another pause. "Should I call them back?"

"No. I've got a better idea. Keep heading north until you hit the roadblock. It's manned by a couple of Blackwood's deputies. Tell them what's going on and stay with them. Make sure they know what happened at the motel. They need to know that these guys won't pull their punches. They weren't afraid to open fire on federal agents. If the deputies won't listen or won't take you seriously, call me back, and I'll change their minds."

"Okay," Mikey said, sounding hopeful for the first time since initiating the call. "Okay. That's a good plan. I'll call you back when we get to the roadblock."

"Head on a swivel, Mikey. Be careful."

As soon as he ended the call, Redd checked for traffic. "Hang on," he said and then pulled out into a tight U-turn—the maneuver causing Rubble to slide from one side of the back seat to the other.

Emily clutched at the armrest as the shift in momentum pressed her against the door. "Ugh," she groaned as he steered out of the turn and began heading back toward Helena. "I might be sick."

Redd grimaced. "Sorry."

She sat still for several seconds, eyes closed and breathing deeply until the momentary nausea passed. "Why did we turn around?" she finally asked.

"We don't have time to take the long way home. We're going to take the direct route." It had been only about forty minutes since they'd learned that the road back to Wellington was closed. In that time, Redd had driven back into Helena and followed the detour route west along Highway 12. Even with the added time that backtracking would require, they would still reach their destination more quickly than if they continued on the detour.

"The highway's still closed," Emily pointed out.

"They'll let us through. I'll say it's a federal emergency. Kline will back me up."

"I'm not worried about getting in trouble with the law. I'm worried about the fire."

"They only closed the highway as a precaution. We'll be able to make it through."

I hope, he added silently.

Once he was back up to speed, Redd called Kline.

The FBI director's voice was full of barely restrained anger. "I know why you're calling," he said, preempting Redd's opening statement. "We're already working the problem."

"Working the *problem*?" Redd replied, incredulous. "Do you even have the first clue what the problem is?"

"What do you want me to say? That I screwed up? Fine. I screwed up. But this literally came from out of the blue. This wasn't on anyone's radar."

Redd knew his ire toward Kline was misplaced. "Sorry," he mumbled. "I don't mean to take this out on you. *I* should have seen it coming."

"You aren't psychic, Matt."

"Maybe not, but I knew Jack was still a target. I should have insisted on having him taken to a secure location."

Kline sighed. "There will be plenty of time for Monday-morning quarterbacking after the game. Right now, we've got to focus on our next play. I've received reports that a family was observed fleeing the scene. I'm guessing that was Mikey Derhammer. And is it safe to assume that he has the boy with him?"

"He does," confirmed Redd. "I just talked to him. He's on the highway, heading north. He's planning to connect with sheriff's deputies manning a roadblock."

"Roadblock?"

"The highway is closed due to wildfires. Em and I went up to Helena and got stuck on the wrong side of the closure, but I'm going to bluff my way past and meet up with Mikey. I should be there in about forty-five minutes, tops."

"That's sooner than any of my agents from Bozeman FO, but Matt . . . I don't need to tell you how dangerous these guys are."

"You don't," agreed Redd. "What do we know about them? Are they working for that pharma outfit?"

"Short answer . . . It looks that way. We don't have a read on the trigger men, but we know that someone very high up in the ParaDyme organization is calling the shots. Raymond Williams had something on them . . . We haven't worked out what exactly, but when he absconded, he took some kind of key with him. They want it back, and they think the boy—"

"Jack. His name is Jack."

Kline took the correction in stride. "They think Jack might be able to lead them to it."

"What does this key unlock? A safe deposit box? Something like that?"

"No clue what it's for, but they're worried that if we get our hands on it, it will be enough to bring them down."

"Could it have anything to do with opioid trafficking?" asked Redd.

"That's an oddly specific question."

Redd glanced over at Emily, then briefly recounted the story of her confrontation with Dr. Dickerson and his subsequent death under suspicious circumstances.

"So . . . you're thinking that ParaDyme and this doctor might have been working together to sell unregulated opioids?" Kline said when Redd finished.

"It's a motive," Redd replied, a little defensively. "Maybe Raymond found out about the scheme and didn't like what was going on. Whoever is behind it had to shut him up and destroy the evidence."

Kline quickly backpedaled. "No, I think you're on the right track with this. Let me pass the information along to Treadway. I've got her running the investigation into ParaDyme. She'll tear the place down to the studs if that's what it takes. Bozeman FO will be taking over the investigation in Wellington. I'm heading out there tonight to take charge personally. We're going full-court press with this."

"What do you want me to do?"

"You're already doing it. Keep yourself and your family safe. I'll take care of the rest."

"What about Jack? He's still with Mikey."

Kline considered this for a moment. "Get the boy to the field office in Bozeman. We'll put him in protective custody."

"You tried that already. Didn't work out so well."

"I know," Kline said, chastened. "And I'm sorry about that. It's not an excuse, but we didn't know what we were up against. Now that we at least have an idea of what we're dealing with, we'll be better able to protect him."

Redd remained unconvinced but decided not to press the issue. "I'll make sure Jack gets to Bozeman."

"If you get a chance," said Kline, "see what he knows about that key. It sounds like it could be the . . . well, the *key* to everything."

"Will do," Redd promised and then rang off.

He recalled that Raymond had been bound and presumably tortured before his execution. Had that been the killer trying to coerce him into giving up the key? Evidently, the effort had failed, and now the bad guys were convinced that Jack knew where it was.

It strained credulity to imagine that Raymond would have entrusted the location of his hiding spot to a six-year-old, but Redd supposed it was possible that, if pressed, Jack might be able to retrace the journey from Chicago to western Montana and point out any unusual stops made along the way. But it didn't make sense that Raymond would have stashed the key if his plan all along was to go off the grid. Hiding it would have been a last-minute decision, something done in desperation when he realized the killer had found him.

Redd searched his memory of the cabin, both inside and out, trying to identify possible hiding places. If the key was a literal key, it might be anywhere— under a loose floorboard or jammed into a crack between the logs that formed the walls or . . .

Redd's eyes widened with sudden realization. He knew exactly where the key was.

THIRTY-TWO

Despite several roadside signs alerting drivers to the highway closure, there was still a line of vehicles almost half a mile long backed up at the roadblock. As he took his place in the queue, Mikey wondered what the other drivers hoped to gain by waiting. Did they think they could convince the deputies to make an exception for them? Or that the road would soon reopen, allowing them to continue on their way? Every now and then, a car would pull out of the line, turn around, and head back toward Wellington, which allowed the others to advance forward, but as near as he could tell, nobody was being allowed through.

In the rearview mirror, the headlights of a vehicle that had been behind them more or less the whole time they'd been heading north now began to grow brighter as the intervening distance shrank. Mikey drummed his fingers on the steering wheel, trying to gauge how long it would take for them to reach the roadblock, and made a decision.

"We're not waiting," he muttered and then called out, "Hang on!"

Cranking the wheel hard to the left and stomping on the accelerator, he swung the Ram out of the line and into a U-turn, letting the steering wheel slide through his fingers once the turn was made. As soon as the truck straightened out, he pushed the pedal harder into the floor. The Dodge was still building up a head of steam as it passed the headlights of the vehicle that had been trailing along behind. Mikey caught just a glimpse as it flashed by, enough to determine that it was a late-model beige pickup, but didn't get a good enough look to determine the make or model. There was a second truck, this one white, right behind it.

Mikey kept an eye on the rearview, watching the retreating taillights of the two trucks—two pairs of red spots, glowing like demonic eyes in the descending darkness. He wasn't at all surprised when those lights flared brightly as the drivers applied the brakes. The lights continued to diminish as the Ram surged ahead under constant acceleration, increasing the intervening distance, but there was no missing the flash of headlights in the mirror as both trucks turned around and began heading south.

Mikey muttered a curse under his breath. While it was impossible to say with one hundred percent certainty that the trucks belonged to the men who had attacked the FBI agents at the Diamond T Motel, he couldn't afford to take any chances.

We've got to get away from them, he thought. *But how?*

Mikey was no daredevil behind the wheel. On the open highway, under ideal conditions, he usually drove no more than ten miles above the posted speed limit, not only to avoid a speeding ticket but also out of an abundance of caution. As a mechanic and the manager of an auto body repair business, he had seen more than his fair share of expensive cars transformed into twisted sculptures of fiberglass and steel. He'd also cleaned away a lifetime's worth of bloodstains and knew all too well how easily a few extra miles per hour coupled with a moment's inattention or a sudden obstacle in the road could turn a routine drive into a nightmare.

He was even more careful when he had passengers, especially children.

Testing the limits of his comfort zone, he thought he might be willing to push the century mark, but in his experience, things got weird when you drove that fast. And he didn't doubt that however fast he was willing to drive, the killers chasing them would be willing to go even faster.

It would take more than speed alone to deliver them from their pursuers. He needed a destination. More than that, he needed a plan.

Getting back to town seemed like the obvious choice. Even these cold-blooded killers might think twice before rushing the courthouse with guns blazing. But then again, they hadn't hesitated to shoot it out with the FBI agents; would they be any more likely to balk at the thought of engaging with a few sheriff's deputies?

And that was assuming the bad guys didn't manage to overtake them before they reached the Broadway junction.

He needed to do something different, something the pursuers wouldn't expect.

A check of the rearview mirror showed the headlights of the trailing vehicles, maybe a quarter mile or more to the rear.

Getting closer?

It sure looked that way.

He racked his brain, trying to come up with a better answer. There were car chases aplenty in his favorite books, and the heroes somehow knew exactly what to do and when to do it, drifting through turns under fire, using their own vehicles like weapons to force the enemy into a devastating collision.

Mikey knew better than to believe that reading a fictional account of pursuit would somehow translate into real-world expertise, but wasn't it possible that those stories contained nuggets of practical wisdom? After all, his favorite authors were sticklers for realism, researching their action scenes extensively. A few of them boasted on social media about attending tactical driving academies in the interest of creating verisimilitude in their novels.

It occurred to him that Redd had probably received similar training, either during his time with the Marine Raiders or working with his FBI fly team.

What would Matt do in this situation?

That was easy. Matthew Redd would attack. He would whip the truck around and charge the enemy head-on, daring them to a game of chicken while blasting away at them with his Ruger Magnum.

But Mikey wasn't Matthew Redd.

Can't outrun them, can't attack . . . What's left?

The answer came with unexpected clarity.

Get off the highway.

On the highway, it would be a race that he could not hope to win, but the highway was not the only road available to him. It was merely an artery. A trunk from which numerous back roads branched out, providing access to rural residences, farms, and ranches, extending up into the Elkhorn Mountains. Mikey, born and raised in Stillwater County, knew those roads like the back of his hand, having explored them extensively while scouting for hunting sites.

Okay, where am I?

He flipped on his high beams and began scanning the roadside, looking for anything that might help him orient his mental map. The terrain was mostly rangeland, uniformly flat, and while he could just make out the lights of houses in the distance, the darkness hid any recognizable details. Then, less than a minute after he started looking, he passed a green mile marker with reflective white numbers.

74.

He knew from past experience that the markers counted the distance from the beginning of the highway, west of Helena, all the way to the intersection with an interstate highway, about thirty or so miles south of Wellington. The actual number on the post was not as important as the fact that it allowed him to fix his relative location. He now knew almost exactly where he was. It was as if a map had unfolded before his mind's eye, marked with a big red dot moving along the thick black ribbon of the highway. On that mental map, he also saw the rural roads—some nothing more than private driveways, others put in place by the Forest Service. And if his estimation of his present location was correct, there was a turnoff to West Fork Road about two miles farther down the highway.

West Fork Road began as an asphalt track wandering up into the foothills of the Elkhorn Mountains, where it provided local access for a couple dozen rural homes. A few miles from the highway, the pavement ended, and the road became packed earth, surfaced occasionally with a layer of gravel and graded a couple times a year. The road continued a few miles past the last residence before eventually intersecting with a Forest Service fire road—no name, just a number: 722. The road became increasingly primitive the farther one went, and there were dozens of unmarked branch roads, some of which linked up to roads that ultimately connected back to state and county roads north and east of the Elkhorn Range, while others devolved into overgrown two-tracks that went nowhere. Road 722 wended through the Elkhorns for a distance of more than thirty miles before eventually letting out onto another rural back road on the west side of the range—provided, of course, one didn't get lost in the maze.

That's it, Mikey thought. *That's how I'll shake them.*

The plan quickly took shape in his head, a series of steps that he would have to execute perfectly in sequence if he was to have a hope of losing the pursuers. In about ninety seconds, he would have to slow down in order to make the turn, and if the bad guys saw him do it, which they almost certainly would, they would close the gap considerably, but that would only last a few minutes. Once on the back roads, the unimproved surface would enforce a limit on everyone's top speed, not just leveling the playing field but giving Mikey the home field advantage. Additionally, he had an idea that, if it worked, would effectively wrap his truck in a cloak of invisibility.

It's going to work, he promised himself. *It has to.*

The console screen suddenly lit up, displaying the message *Incoming call from Matthew.*

Mikey grimaced. Matt expected him to be at the roadblock, protected by sheriff's deputies. The change in plans was especially problematic since cellular connectivity was nonexistent on the back roads. If Redd's call had come just a few minutes later, it probably wouldn't have gone through at all, and he would have had no idea where Mikey was or what he was up to.

"Hey, what's up?" He tried to sound upbeat, but to his own ear, he sounded panicked.

"Did you make it to the roadblock?" Redd's voice issued from the truck's sound system, reverberating through the interior.

"Ah . . . no. Not quite." Mikey hesitated, trying to find the right words to explain his decision and expecting a torrent of anxious questions.

Redd, however, evidently misinterpreting his answer, carried on. "When you get there, I need you to do something for me. Does Jack still have his Buzz Lightyear toy?"

Jack's voice piped up from the back. "Hi, Matt! I've still got Buzz."

"That's good," replied Redd, sounding relieved. "I think Raymond might have hidden something inside the toy. A key. When you get a chance, I need you to look for it."

Mikey recalled Jack's earlier complaint. "You know, it might be in the battery box. Jack said that it doesn't talk anymore."

"That's got to be it. Let me know as soon as you find it."

"Umm, yeah. Matt, I need to tell you—" The turnoff to West Fork Road flashed into view off to his right. Frantic, he shifted his foot to the brake pedal, jamming down on it. Even with the antilock braking system, the truck skidded and fishtailed a little as it shed momentum, finally coming to a stop about fifty yards past the turnoff.

"Mikey?" asked Redd. "What's happening there?"

Mikey didn't answer, couldn't answer. His brain was too occupied with the immediate crisis. Biting his lip in frustration, he threw the truck into reverse, jammed down on the accelerator, and began backing up, even as the headlights in the rearview mirror grew ominously brighter.

"Everybody hold on!" cried Liz, her head turned toward their precious cargo. *There's time,* he told himself. *There's time. Don't panic.*

"Mikey!"

An eternity passed before the junction with West Fork Road slid into view. When it finally did, Mikey braked, changed gears, and cranked the wheel hard to the right. Remembering his original plan, he let go of the wheel with one hand and switched off the headlights.

In an instant, the world outside the truck, or at least what little of it had been revealed by the glow of the truck's low beams, was swallowed in the gloom. Nevertheless, the way ahead remained illumined in Mikey's mind's eye. He slipped his foot off the brake, extinguishing the red glow of the brake lights, and bore down on the accelerator pedal.

"Mikey!" Redd pleaded. "Talk to me. What's going on?"

"He's busy, Matt!" Liz cried from the back seat. "Give us a minute!"

Although her tone was a little strident, she sounded surprisingly calm given the circumstances, and her unexpected intervention helped steady Mikey's nerves as he charged forward.

On Mikey's mental map, West Fork Road ran perpendicular to the highway for a distance of about half a mile, at which point it hooked to the right and began meandering on a generally northwest heading, with branching roads and driveways interspersed along the way. At forty miles per hour, a speed that would have been sedate under normal operating conditions but seemed beyond reckless in the near total darkness, Mikey estimated he would reach that turn in just under a minute. On the straightaway, keeping the Ram on the pavement without the benefit of visual cues was really more a matter of faith than skill—as long as he held the steering wheel steady, the truck would hold true—but making the turn would be a gut check.

Fortunately, the darkness was not as absolute as it had seemed. There was just enough ambient light in the night sky for him to differentiate the black asphalt from the graveled shoulder and to make out the irregular shape of vegetation on the roadside. Moreover, his eyes were already beginning to adjust to the low light conditions, and with each passing second, he found his natural night vision improving.

From the corner of his eye, he saw a flash in his side mirror—headlights. The pursuers had made the turn onto West Fork Road.

Resisting the impulse to look back, Mikey focused his attention on the road ahead, searching for the subtle cues that would herald the approach of the turn. He knew it was close. He also knew that he had to make the turn without slowing. They were well beyond the effective range of the pursuers' headlights—high beams were typically aimed so as to illuminate an area only about four hundred feet ahead of a vehicle—but if he so much as tapped the brakes, the Ram's brake lights would give away their exact position.

Now! Do it!

Through some combination of muscle memory, night vision, and spatial awareness, Mikey felt the subtle change in the road surface as it banked into the turn and, with deft assurance, rolled the steering wheel a few degrees to the right.

Redd's voice, taut as a garotte, issued from the darkness. "Minute's up, Mikey. Talk to me."

Mikey let out the breath he hadn't even realized he'd been holding in a low hiss. "Matt. Don't have a lot of time, so just listen . . ."

He broke off as the road undulated through a series of serpentine curves, which, under the best of circumstances, would have demanded his full attention. Clenching the steering wheel so tightly he thought his tendons might snap and fighting the impulse to brake, Mikey wove through the turns, all the while reconciling his mental map to the reality on the ground. Very soon, he knew, they would leave the paved road behind.

When he got a chance to breathe again, he went on. "They're right behind us. I had to turn off the highway. We're on West Fork Road."

"West Fork Ro—" Redd started to say, but Mikey cut him off.

"Just listen. I'm going to head up into the mountains. Take 722 over to the west side. I'm hoping I'll be able to lose them up in there, but even if I can't, there's no way they will be able to overtake us."

He paused to take a breath and quickly checked his mirror. The headlights of the pursuers were no longer visible in the reflection. All he could see was a faint, diffuse glow rising above the irregular silhouette of roadside foliage.

"All the same," Mikey went on, a little surprised that Redd hadn't replied. "I'd appreciate it if you could arrange a little welcoming committee on the other side. You know, just in case they're still hot on our heels."

Redd didn't reply.

"Matt? Are you there?"

Nothing.

A flicker of light inside the cab drew his attention to the console screen where a new message appeared.

No service.

"You've got to be kidding me," Mikey muttered. He knew that his friend had heard at least some of what he'd said, but had the last part gotten through? Did Redd know what he was planning to do?

Shaking his head, he brought his attention back to the more immediate problem of navigating the back roads in darkness. With no cellular service and no way of knowing if help was coming, he had to accept that, for the moment at least, they were on their own.

THIRTY-THREE

When he saw the silver pickup's lights wink out, Dean Werner knew he was dealing with a canny opponent.

He stopped, backed up, and then . . .

He had no idea.

"What do you think he's up to?" he asked.

Holt, seated across from him in the passenger seat, gave a noncommittal grunt.

"Well, that's a lot of help," muttered Dean.

Truthfully, he hadn't expected much from his brother. Holt wasn't a talker under the best of circumstances, and right now, with one arm all torn up from a tussle with a big dog and the other pocked by a too-close encounter with a twelve-gauge, it was a wonder he was even conscious. By all rights, he should have gone straight to Doc—the former Army medic who worked for Dean's dad and took care of all their off-the-books medical needs—to get patched up, but after getting embarrassed by the lady doctor he was supposed to have killed, Holt was more interested in finding an outlet for his frustration than he was in seeking medical attention.

That was just how Holt was.

The more he hurt, the meaner he got.

It was a trait that had come in handy when they'd gone up against the feds guarding the kid, though the fact that the kid had slipped through their fingers had only made Holt angrier.

Dean tapped the brakes, slowing as he neared the approximate spot where the silver truck had stopped, and quickly divined the significance of the other driver's strange behavior when he spotted the junction with West Fork Road.

But did he actually turn off, or is he just trying to make me think he did?

Dean rode the brake to a full stop. "Scotty, you see him?"

Scotty Terrel, sitting in the rear of the cab, peered through the side window for a few seconds before answering in the negative. Dean then picked up his phone, which was running a walkie-talkie app, and tapped the push-to-talk icon on the screen. "Chris, do you see him? Did he make the turn?"

"Don't see nothing," replied Chris Combs, driving the trailing pickup.

Marty Miller, riding shotgun in the same truck, answered similarly a moment later. Both men sounded a little high-strung, which was understandable since their buddy, Kevin Downey, had taken a couple of rounds in the gut during the shootout at the motel. Kevin was presently sprawled out in the back seat of Chris's truck and wasn't looking good at all.

Chris had begged Dean to let him take Kevin to Doc or even to the closest hospital, but that was a definite no-go. Not only did finding the kid and bringing him back to the mill alive take priority over everything else, but the hard truth of the matter was that Kevin was circling the drain, and nothing Doc could do would change that. It sucked, but sometimes that was just the way the cookie crumbled.

Oh well.

Dean weighed the possible courses of action a moment longer and then made a judgment call. "I think he took the turn," he decided out loud, taking his foot off the brake and steering into the turnoff. "Keep an eye out for him. He might have pulled off somewhere, hoping we'll drive right past."

He rolled down the straightaway, looking for any indication that the big silver pickup had gone off the road. With his high beams on, he had a pretty good field of view to either side—good enough, he reckoned, to spot disturbed vegetation or clouds of dust stirred up by tires rolling down graveled driveways. He didn't see anything like that, though, and it occurred to him that maybe the guy in the pickup hadn't just randomly decided to turn off the highway.

"Chris, hold up a second." He braked to a halt and opened the map application on his phone. It took a few seconds for the screen to load, and a quick check of the signal bars indicated that the connection wasn't the greatest. Another mile or so and he would probably lose coverage altogether. Finally, the map finished loading. He pinched his fingers on the screen to zoom out and then began moving it around to get an idea of where the road went. The more he saw, the more certain he became regarding the other driver's reason for leaving the highway.

"I think I know what this guy's up to," Dean said. "Open up your map." He paused a beat to let the other man catch up. "I think this guy probably knows his way around these roads, and I'm betting he'll use one of them to come back out onto a main road somewhere else."

"Where?"

"Well, that's the problem. The fire has burned over a lot of these roads, but he might not know that. And that still leaves a couple places where he might be heading, and we're gonna need to cover them."

"How are we supposed to do that?"

Dean rolled his eyes. Chris wasn't the brightest bulb in the chandelier. "Obviously, we'll need some help. I'll call my dad and have him send some guys out to cover all those exits. You and me are going to push out along Fire Road 722. That's the most obvious way to get through the mountains. I'll head west. You go northeast. I'm sending you the route I want you to follow."

He tapped the desired destination into his phone and then sent it to Chris in a text message.

"Our phones aren't going to work up there," Dean continued. "So you won't be able to check in until you reach the other end. Just follow the map, and if you find them . . . well, you know what to do. We need that kid alive. Everybody else?" He paused a beat and then repeated the same instructions his father had given him. "No loose ends."

THIRTY-FOUR

"They're right behind us."

The words kept running on a loop in Redd's mind.

"Right behind us."

Redd clutched the steering wheel, forcing himself to stay calm. He replayed the rest of what Mikey had told him in his head.

"Had to turn off the highway . . . West Fork Road. I'm going to head up into the mountains. Take 722 over to the west side. I'm hoping—"

That was the point at which the signal had begun cutting out. A few more word fragments had slipped through, but nothing coherent. Then, a moment later, the connection was lost altogether. Redd had tried calling back, but the attempt had gone straight to voicemail, and Redd knew why. Mikey was outside the coverage area, and if he followed through with his plan . . . or with what Redd thought his plan was, it might be a couple of hours before he would be able to get a signal.

"They're right behind us."

Redd took a long, slow breath. *Okay, think,* he told himself. *What can you do to help him?*

Mikey had a plan. That much was clear.

"Going to head up into the mountains."

Mikey knew those mountains, knew all the roads and trails, even the ones that weren't marked. And he was an experienced off-roader. That would give him an edge.

"West Fork Road."

Redd knew exactly where that was. He passed the turnoff every time he drove to and from Helena.

"Take 722 over to the west side."

722?

What is that? A fire road?

He looked over at Emily and saw by her pained expression that she was just as worried as he was and feeling just as helpless. "Em, can you bring up a map of the Elkhorns?"

The suggestion, or maybe having something to do, seemed to energize her. She immediately took out her phone, and in a matter of seconds, her display showed a topographical map.

"Find West Fork Road. It's a little ways north of Wellington."

"I know where it is," she said, not looking up from the screen. "Okay, got it."

"Follow it up into the mountains. It should eventually intersect with Fire Road 722."

"Found it," she said after a few seconds of searching.

She held the phone up, showing him the map. Redd glanced at it but couldn't make out much in the way of detail. "Where does it come out?"

"Uh . . . hold on . . . It looks like it goes in two different directions. One way goes northwest and comes out just past Spokane Hills. The other way goes way up into the mountains and comes out east of Jefferson City."

A ray of hope shone from the darkness. Jefferson City was just a few miles behind them. "That's where Mikey is heading. We can intercept."

He checked ahead and behind to make sure the coast was clear and then jammed on the brakes.

Realizing what he was about to do, Emily cried, "Matty, don't you—"

But Redd was already steering into the median again. As the truck jounced violently down the incline, he cranked the wheel over, braking, then accelerating out of the U-turn and up the slope on the far side of the median. The truck slipped and fishtailed on the loose ground, throwing up clods of dirt and grass, but then the front tires grabbed pavement, and the Raptor shot forward onto the northbound lane.

Suddenly, air began rushing noisily into the cab. Redd glanced over just as Emily leaned head and shoulders out her now-open window. Despite the engine noise and the rush of air moving around, he could hear her retching.

"Sorry," he said when she finally drew back inside, glowering at him for a moment before pressing her back into the seat cushion and closing her eyes.

"Don't do that again," she breathed without looking at him.

Redd felt a pang of regret, not only at having aggravated Emily's motion sickness with the unexpected maneuver but for having brought his pregnant wife along in the first place and, for that matter, for once again having gotten his family and friends caught up in something that never should have touched their lives. He ought to have put his foot down, refused to let Emily tag along with him . . . should have just stayed home with her and let Kline and the FBI do the investigative work.

What was I thinking?

But then he shook his head. How had Kline put it? There would be plenty of time to second-guess his choices later; right now, all that mattered was finding Mikey and his family and Junior and Jack as quickly as possible, protecting them from the killers who had already left a trail of carnage in their wake.

Emily said nothing more as they raced down the interstate but remained motionless, eyes closed and breathing steadily, presumably still battling the lingering effects of motion sickness. Redd left her alone until, about ten minutes later, they drew near the Jefferson City exit.

"Em?"

"What?" She did not look over at him, but her terse delivery told him she was still feeling queasy.

"I could use a little help navigating."

She gave a low growl but opened her eyes and picked up her phone. After a few moments of studying the screen, she closed her eyes again but then proceeded to give him detailed instructions on how to reach the back roads that would eventually link up with Fire Road 722. Even before she finished her recitation, they arrived at the exit. He slowed as he veered onto the ramp and then braked to a full stop at the intersection.

"I'm making the turn," he warned.

She nodded, but Redd saw apprehension twisting her features as he depressed the accelerator and began steering to the left. Once across the overpass, he made another left, as she had prescribed, once more alerting her in advance.

When they were heading north on the local access road that ran parallel to the interstate, she spoke again. "I'm really not feeling so good, Matty."

The admission both surprised and dismayed Redd. Emily's motion sickness was a side effect of her pregnancy, but in the past, her episodes had always been mild. The fact that she was still queasy ten minutes later did not bode well, especially knowing what lay ahead for them. The twisty, rugged back roads they would soon be traveling on would only aggravate her condition.

He soon realized, however, that his wife's carsickness was the least of his problems. As he made the turn onto the first of a series of back roads that would eventually lead to Fire Road 722, he noticed for the first time an orange glow lighting up the sky to the east.

When Mikey had first indicated his intention to use the back roads to traverse the southern end of the Elkhorn Range, Redd had assumed his route would keep him well clear of the wildfire. But the truth of the matter was that neither he nor Mikey knew for sure how large the affected area might be or whether it might now be blocking Mikey's intended course of travel. With no way to contact Mikey or warn him, all Redd could do was continue with his original plan and hope for the best.

The going was slow, and not just because Redd was trying to give Emily a break. The county roads were unpaved, and the farther they got from the end of the asphalt, the poorer the road conditions became. Long sections of washboard ripples were interspersed with low areas where rocks the size of both of Redd's fists put together had accumulated. The Raptor's big lug tires smoothed the ride considerably, but Redd was still obliged to take it slow, creeping along barely faster than a walking pace.

Then an obstacle—one that should not have been entirely unexpected under the circumstances—was illuminated in the Raptor's headlights. The Forest Service road that should have taken them up into the mountains was closed, blocked by a white tubular steel gate secured with a padlock.

Redd stopped short of the barrier and stared at it for a moment, trying to decide what to do. He had bolt cutters in the bed of the truck, and even if he didn't, one look at the gate told him that it stood no chance against the force of his Raptor if he chose to ram it, so the lock didn't pose a real physical limitation. And while cutting the lock and proceeding into the closed area might make him criminally liable for the destruction of federal property and trespassing, he felt certain that a phone call from Kline to the right government official would make that problem go away. What gave him pause was the fact that if the road was closed on his end, it was likely closed at the other end.

Would Mikey have plowed through the gate? Even if it had a Forest Service padlock on it?

Redd suspected his friend would have done exactly that if needed. But he couldn't be sure. There was at least a chance that Mikey might have already been forced to change his plan, and if he had done so, the likelihood of connecting with him was practically nil.

"They're right behind us."

Redd shook his head.

No, Mikey would do whatever was necessary to protect everyone.

The only real question now was how Redd would bypass the obstacle. Just as he was about to stomp the gas pedal and make quick work of the gate, he glanced over at Emily. She was pale and sweaty, and her eyes were still closed.

Changing his mind, he put the Raptor in park.

Emily looked up when Redd opened his door. "Where are you going?"

"Gotta get the gate."

THIRTY-FIVE

Even though the truck was stationary, Emily continued to sit motionless in the passenger seat, performing the technique known as box breathing—inhaling steadily for four seconds, holding for four, exhaling steadily for four, and then waiting four more seconds before drawing breath again.

It was a relaxation technique designed to modulate the body's natural response to stress—elevated blood pressure and heart rate. But while there was promising research to indicate that sustained diaphragmatic breathing could reduce the effects of motion sickness, that wasn't why Emily was doing it now. In truth, the queasiness she had experienced more than twenty minutes earlier had long since ceased to be her greatest concern. Even though part of her didn't want to admit it, the practicing-physician part of her knew with absolute certainty that she was in labor.

The unusually strong contraction that had hit almost simultaneously with Matthew's second hasty U-turn had not been the first of its kind. If she were honest with herself, she had been having contractions for a couple of hours, the first possibly being the one she'd felt on Dr. Dickerson's porch, which she had chalked up to Braxton-Hicks.

She'd experienced a few more contractions during the drive home, all of them far less intense and at irregular intervals and so easily dismissed as false labor. But then, not long after the intruder had forced his way into her home, the contractions had become more regular and frequent.

The mere fact that she might be in the first stage of labor—called early labor—was not overly concerning to her. Early labor often lasted for several hours, which meant there was plenty of time for her and Matthew to meet up with Mikey and Liz and get everyone to safety, especially Junior, before she would need to check into the hospital. And until Matthew started driving like a maniac, the contractions had been mild enough that she could get through them without even clenching her fists.

She was a little worried that the ordeal of driving around on rugged, unimproved back roads might further accelerate the process. It certainly wouldn't do anything to reduce her stress level. The fact that she wasn't able to change positions wouldn't make it any easier, which was why she was doing her level best to find and maintain inner calm by regulating her breathing.

The sound of the driver's door opening drew her attention back to the moment. She opened her eyes and looked over as Matthew slid in behind the wheel. In the glow of the overhead interior light, he seemed to be wearing a guilty expression, like a kid caught with a hand in the cookie jar, but she decided it was probably just his worried face.

"All good?" she asked.

He managed a weak smile and a nod. "All good. How are you doing? Still feeling carsick?"

"It's better," she said. It wasn't exactly a lie. "I know it's not something you can really control, but I'd appreciate anything you can do to keep the ride smooth."

"I'll do what I can," he promised and then fired up the engine. As the truck began rolling forward, rocking a little as it negotiated the irregular road surface, she closed her eyes and resumed her box breathing.

The one thing she didn't dare do was tell Matthew. He was dealing with enough right now, and adding that wrinkle would put him in an impossible position. He would see it as a forced choice between the safety of their son, not to mention their dearest friends, and the health of his wife and their unborn baby. It was a false choice for the simple reason that she wasn't in active labor and wouldn't be for a couple more hours, but he wouldn't see it that way. Better, she reasoned, not to tell him.

I'll just have to hold this kid in here until we can save our other one.

Easier said than done.

Not long after the stop to open the gate, she felt the beginnings of another contraction. She willed herself to keep breathing, but as the cramping sensation intensified, she couldn't help but quicken both her inhalations and exhalations with no break in between.

"You doing okay?" asked Matthew.

She didn't answer, couldn't answer. It was taking all her willpower just to keep from crying out as the pain undulated to ever-increasing peak intensities.

Not good.

But then, almost miraculously, the peaks grew less intense, and the valleys separating them grew longer. After a few more pulses, the sensation faded altogether.

"I'm okay," she managed to say and even looked over at him with a smile. As she did, she surreptitiously checked the dashboard clock, marking the time. Roughly ten minutes had passed since the last contraction, and by her best estimation, this one had lasted about a minute.

Early labor. There was no denying it.

But I've still got plenty of time, she told herself. *And Matthew doesn't need to know . . . yet.*

THIRTY-SIX

After nearly ten minutes of driving in the darkness, with no sign of immediate pursuit, Mikey decided that the risk of going off the road outweighed the danger of revealing their location and switched on the Ram's headlights.

Illuminating the world outside the truck brought an immediate sense of relief. The strain of trying to follow the road ahead in the near total darkness of night had been exhausting, but now that he could actually see where he was going and, more importantly, recognized where he was, Mikey felt reinvigorated. He also decided that he could afford to push the Ram a little harder. Still, while the big truck's suspension smoothed out what would, in an ordinary car, have been a tooth-loosening ordeal, the irregular surface—alternating between hard-packed earth and loose gravel—obliged him to keep his speed under forty miles per hour, even in the straight stretches.

Liz, who had remained in the back seat ostensibly to comfort the children, all of whom were now sound asleep, seemed to intuitively grasp that Mikey needed to focus on the task at hand and did not attempt to engage him in conversation. So, aside from the persistent rumble permeating the cab and the machine-gun-like staccato of loose gravel pelting the truck's undercarriage, the ride proceeded in relative silence even after Mikey turned on the lights. It was Mikey himself who filled the verbal vacuum when, after an interminably long fifteen minutes of driving, they arrived at the junction with Fire Road 722 and found the way ahead blocked by a sturdy tubular steel gate.

"Uh-oh," he said as he brought the truck to a halt. "That's not good."

"What do we do now?" Liz asked tentatively, as if fearing that the question might provoke an angry response.

Mikey *was* angry, but not at Liz. He knew about the gate from his previous sojourns in the area, and while he could not recall ever having seen it closed, he should have taken into account the possibility that the Forest Service might restrict access to the area because of the wildfires. His failure of foresight had brought them to a dead end.

He checked his mirrors, half expecting to see the glow of their pursuer's headlights rising above the treetops.

Nothing there, he thought. *Not yet.*

That wasn't necessarily a good sign, though. It occurred to Mikey that, during the brief period when he'd been driving without lights, he might have missed a posted sign warning of the road closure, a sign that the men hunting them would not have failed to see. Forewarned about the dead end, the killers might have decided to simply lie in wait for their quarry's eventual return.

"We're not going back," he said. And then, realizing it wasn't an answer to her question, he added, "I'll figure something out."

Going around the gate wasn't an option. The ground to either side of the road was wooded, the trees dense enough to prevent passage by anything bigger than a dirt bike or maybe an all-terrain vehicle.

If we can't go around, thought Mikey, *we'll have to go through.*

In a movie or one of his thriller novels, the hero might have simply rammed the barrier, relying on the vehicle's mass and momentum to smash through. Mikey's experience with repairing impact damage made him less than optimistic about the efficacy of such an approach. Even if the truck was powerful enough to break through the steel barrier, doing so would likely produce significant, even catastrophic, damage to the truck or, worse, injure the people inside. And the gate was hinged to swing out, which would make breaking through that much harder.

But then he realized that he didn't need to beat the gate. He just needed to defeat the lock that held it shut.

"Be right back," he said as he unbuckled his seat belt.

"Where are you going?"

"I'm gonna check out the lock. Maybe there's a way to jimmy it open."

As soon as he opened the door, he was all but overwhelmed by the smell of smoke and realized that while it might be possible to get through the gate, it might not be advisable. There was a reason the road was closed, after all. And he had not failed to register the red glow in the sky behind them.

Are we jumping out of the frying pan and into the actual fire?

He shook his head, trying to dismiss the concern. The closure was probably just precautionary, and besides, if they ran into the fire, well, then they could just turn around and head back the way they'd come.

The lock holding the gate shut was out of reach of the Ram's headlights, so Mikey took out his phone and activated the flashlight before leaning over to take a look at the lock. When he did, he couldn't help but laugh.

There was no lock. The gate was held shut with a twist of wire.

Mikey didn't waste any time pondering the deeper significance of this lucky break. It took all of two minutes to open the gate, drive through, and then secure it exactly as he'd found it. But as he returned to the Ram and began driving west on Fire Road 722, he couldn't help but notice the whorls of smoke gathering in the truck's high beams.

THIRTY-SEVEN

Despite the brief stop to coordinate their efforts, Dean and his crew of killers quickly made up for lost time. Picking up the trail of the big silver truck was easy once they left the asphalt. The headlights of Dean's truck illuminated the still-settling dust cloud raised by the truck's duallies, confirming that the fleeing family hadn't pulled off somewhere along the way. After that, it was just a matter of catching up.

"You can go faster, you know," growled Holt.

"I know what I'm doing," replied Dean.

"That a fact?"

"Yes, it's a fact. The further we let them get from the highway, the easier it's gonna be to hide their bodies. Might even be able to make it look like they got caught in the fire."

Holt shook his head. "You always have to make things complicated."

Dean glanced over at the hulking form filling the passenger seat. "*I* make things complicated? If we had done things my way, we wouldn't be in this mess."

Holt just grunted.

After that, they continued in relative silence, following the dust trail for several more miles before coming to a closed gate.

"What the heck?" muttered Dean, bringing the pickup to a full stop. "No way did these guys have the key."

"Maybe they pulled off somewhere," suggested Scotty from the back seat.

Dean shook his head. "Nah, we would have seen them. Scotty, go check the gate."

Scotty did as directed, and after making a cursory inspection, he returned to report his findings. "There's no lock," he said. "It's wired shut."

"Wired?" Curious, Dean got out and went to have a look for himself. As soon as he saw the twist of bailing wire holding the gate shut, understanding dawned. The gate and the fire road beyond were probably being used to shuttle firefighting crews out to the fire line. With people coming and going at all hours, someone had decided that instead of issuing keys to everyone who might need to get through, they would just fake it.

He turned to Scotty. "Get that gate open."

"You want me to close it when you're through?"

Dean shook his head. "Nah. I got a better idea."

When he returned to the truck, he went to the passenger side and opened the door. Holt regarded him with a sour look but said nothing as he leaned in and opened the glove box. There, buried under sundry receipts, warranties, and extra napkins, he located the object of his search, a brand-new Master Lock heavy-duty outdoor padlock, still in its plastic clamshell package. He popped it open, separating the two accompanying keys.

"What are you going to do with that?" asked Holt.

"Gonna lock the gate once we're inside. That way, if they slip past us, they won't be able to get out this way."

Holt grunted again.

Dean returned to the gate and instructed Scotty to put the lock on as soon as both trucks were through, then gave one of the keys to Chris in the second pickup. "Once we're through the gate, you go right. We'll go left. If you catch up to them or if you can't make it through because of the fire, turn around and come back. Lock the gate behind you."

"What if I make it through?"

"Then don't worry about it."

✷ ✷ ✷

Once past the gate, Dean pushed his truck harder, though he was less certain than before that the silver Ram pickup had taken this route. He could no longer differentiate the dust raised by recent vehicle traffic from the smoke and particulate matter swirling in the beams of his headlights. Furthermore, he was no longer confident that his quarry was heading west. While that might have been their original intention, there was a good possibility that the fire had burned across the road, potentially cutting off that avenue of escape, and if the other driver realized that, he might very well have decided to take his chances heading the other direction. But, whether or not that was the case, the only way to be sure was to drive as fast as possible until they either caught up to the fleeing vehicle or reached the interstate to the west.

His diligence paid off. Less than fifteen minutes after turning onto the fire road, Dean spotted a strange white glow rising above the treetops—the headlights of a vehicle, refracting in the ever-present smoke cloud.

"There!" he cried, pointing forward. "That could be them."

"Could be a forest ranger," countered Holt. Coming from his brother, this utterance verged on loquaciousness.

"Could be," agreed Dean. "Only one way to find out."

He pushed the gas pedal a little closer to the floor. The ride got rougher for a moment, but then, counterintuitively, it seemed to smooth out. With the increase in speed, the tires were not spending as much time in contact with the road surface, which meant the truck was effectively hydroplaning, only instead of gliding over water, it was gliding over gravel. Unfortunately, as Dean well knew, the improved ride came at a cost. Just as when hydroplaning, there was a very real risk of losing control, not to mention the potential for real damage to the vehicle. But Dean wasn't worried about that right now. The white glow was getting brighter. The target was almost within reach.

Aware that his own headlights might betray them, Dean borrowed a trick from their quarry and took the precaution of switching to his parking lights. The amber bulbs didn't provide anywhere near as much light, but with all the smoke in the air, they weren't really doing much good anyway. It was only in the sudden absence of white light that Dean saw flames in the near distance.

At first, it was just a single tree, its boughs wreathed in a red-orange halo, a few hundred yards ahead on the right side of the road. Then he saw another on the left side. Suddenly there were burning trees everywhere. In their light, a scorched landscape was revealed. The ground fire had already flashed through, jumping across the road and quickly consuming the tinder-dry vegetation, leaving the trees to burn slowly like logs in a fireplace. With their branches and foliage burned away, the trunks looked like pillars of fire lining the roadside.

Almost without volition, Dean eased the pressure on the accelerator. He could feel the heat radiating through the window glass and could hear the jet-engine roar of the fire as it devoured not only the dry wood fuel but all the oxygen in the forest. A flurry of bright embers blew across the road, brushing against the hood and windshield like red-hot snowflakes.

This was getting a little too real.

"Why are you slowing down?" asked Holt. "We're catching up to them."

Dean gaped at him. "Are you kidding? We'll get roasted if we keep going. I've already been through the fire once today. Once was enough."

"If they can get through, so can we."

"I'm not sure they can get through. They'll probably have to turn around. Either that or *they're* gonna get themselves roasted."

Holt shook his head. "Can't let that happen. Dad wants that kid alive."

Dean scowled at his brother. Since when did Holt start thinking things through? Still, the thought of returning to their father with yet another report of failure was almost more frightening than braving the flames.

Almost.

But Holt had a point. If the guy in the silver Ram could keep going forward, so could they. And while Dean was pretty sure that the other driver *would* turn around, there was no reason not to keep going.

No sooner was the thought formed than Dean saw a burst of embers erupt from near the base of a burning tree trunk just a hundred or so feet ahead on the right. The little explosion—a pocket of burning pitch or maybe the sudden overpressure of water reaching the boiling point and flashing into steam—must have weakened the already-damaged tree because a moment later it was toppling toward the road, right in the path of Dean's truck.

Dean wrenched the steering wheel to the left and punched the accelerator in a desperate bid to outrun the falling tree. On pavement, the maneuver would probably have gone off without a hitch, but on the uneven surface of the fire road, the abrupt acceleration caused some of the tires to spin on loose gravel while others gripped the hard-packed earth, causing the truck to fishtail and then slew to the right. Dean frantically steered the other way, pushing the gas pedal to the floor, and by some miracle, he regained control. The truck shot forward, a fraction of a second ahead of the falling tree.

Even though he'd managed to dodge that particular hazard, Dean did not slow down, fueled by adrenaline and an almost manic belief that he might be able to outrun not just the next falling tree but the fire itself. Scotty, in the back seat, was turning the air blue with terror-induced profanities. Holt barely reacted at all.

And then, from out of the dull red gloom, two bright red points of light shone out from a thick cloud of dust and smoke like demonic eyes staring back at him.

Taillights.

"We got 'em!"

THIRTY-EIGHT

The fire was all around them before Mikey even recognized the threat. Focused on the road and the restricted visibility from the thick smoke, he was slow to notice the trees, burning like torches, lining the roadside.

"Mikey!" Liz cried out. "We're going into the fire!"

"I see it," he said, though in truth, he was still playing catch-up.

It was as if they had turned a corner and found themselves transported into hell itself.

Radiant heat permeated the cab, turning it oven hot. In the back seat, Lucas and Matthew Jr. began to wail, more out of fright than actual pain, but it wouldn't be long before the interior temperature rose above the point of merely being uncomfortable. Mikey heard Liz trying in vain to comfort the children.

"Mikey, it's too much." Liz had to shout to be heard over the din. "We have to turn around."

Mikey's first instinct was to agree. What if the fire got worse? What if the road was completely blocked? Worse still, what if the fire closed off their escape route, trapping them?

But then a line from an old poem played in his head. *The best way out is always through.*

The bad guys were still back there.

Better to take our chances with the fire.

He gripped the steering wheel, determined to stay the course, but no sooner was his choice made than it was taken away from him.

Focused as he was on avoiding flaming debris in the road, Mikey didn't see the pickup until it was right beside him.

The road was barely wide enough for two vehicles to pass each other, and because Mikey had been keeping to the center, the driver of the other vehicle had to thread the needle between the Ram and the conflagration at the roadside, but somehow he managed, and when Mikey, in a pure reflex reaction, cranked the steering wheel to the right and slammed on the brakes, the pickup shot past and swerved into the center.

The sudden braking maneuver sent the Ram into a sideways slide, the big truck veering uncontrollably toward the side of the road. The blazing forest suddenly filled Mikey's forward view. Desperate to regain control, he wrenched the steering wheel in the opposite direction. It was another reflex decision, but it was the right one; the Ram swung back toward the center of the road. But any sense of relief he felt at having avoided a fiery demise was short-lived. The pickup, after passing, had come to a complete stop, cutting the road diagonally to block it.

Mikey had two choices and a fraction of a second to decide between them. He could either try to bulldoze his way past or he could stop, turn around, and head back the other way. Shoving the pickup aside was a gamble. He was pretty sure his truck had the horsepower and mass to do the job, especially if he rammed the pickup's bed—the lightest part of the vehicle. But if he was wrong . . .

The best way out is always through.

Except when it isn't.

At the last possible instant, he balked, depressing the brakes again. Because he'd already given up most of his forward velocity, he didn't skid or slide this time, but the Ram still continued forward a couple lengths before coming to a full stop, just ten yards from the pickup.

The doors of the pickup flew open, and two figures erupted from its interior. The man who had been sitting in the front passenger seat, a squat, troll-ish figure, moved with preternatural quickness, crossing the distance in the time it took Mikey's hand to leave the steering wheel and grasp the gearshift lever. Before Mikey could shift into reverse, the man slammed something against the window right beside Mikey's head.

Mikey didn't need to look to know it was a gun, but he looked anyway.

It was a mistake.

The man jammed the pistol's muzzle against the glass, pointing it right at Mikey's head. He was shouting something, but Mikey couldn't hear him through the glass, not over the screams of terrified children and definitely not over the sound of blood rushing in his ears. Nevertheless, the message came through loud and clear.

Surrender, or I'll shoot you.

They're going to kill us anyway, thought Mikey. *Better to take our chances.*

As if reading his intent, the man drew back his hand and then slammed the pistol into the window again. The tempered glass exploded inward, showering Mikey with a spray of fragments, glittering in the firelight like perfectly cut rubies and topaz. Heat and smoke rushed in as well, but it was the hard metal of the handgun jammed into his ear that brought the most pain.

"Don't even think about it," growled the troll. "I'll splatter your brains all over your family."

Mikey did not believe for a second that surrender and a show of compliance would improve their chances of survival, but he was a believer in the credo "while there is life, there is hope," and so he slowly lifted his hands.

"Shut it off. Then get out. Slowly."

Mikey followed the troll's orders, killing the engine and easing the door open. The initial shock of exposure to the intense heat of the fire was already subsiding, but the hot, dry air seemed to suck the energy out of his body, leaving him unsteady on his feet. His heart was racing, pounding away in a desperate attempt to regulate his body temperature. Any thoughts he might have entertained of trying to physically overpower or outrun the troll evaporated in the heat. He felt like he was on the verge of passing out.

But they're probably feeling it too, he thought. *Don't give up.*

The other man from the pickup had the rear door open and was brandishing his pistol. "Everybody out!" he bawled.

Mikey managed a weak protest. "They're just kids."

The troll, unmoved, shoved him against the front fender, pinning him in place with one extended arm while keeping the pistol aimed directly at his face. "Shut up."

A third armed man—a scrawny blond guy with a ponytail—rounded the front end of the pickup and hurried over to join the second man in menacing Liz. "Get out," he snarled. "Now."

Over the wailing of the frightened toddlers, Mikey heard Liz pleading, "They're just babies."

To Mikey's complete astonishment, the blond man seemed to have a change of heart. "Fine. Leave them. But you and the boy better get out right now."

For a long moment, nothing happened, but then Liz emerged from the rear of the cab. Holding her hand, Jack followed. As soon as he saw the blond man, Jack's eyes went wide in a look of recognition. He shrank back in terror, uttering a low cry. "You're the bad man."

Ignoring the accusation, the blond man stepped forward and seized Jack's arm, dragging him along.

"Don't you dare," Liz cried out, gripping Jack's hand, trying to pull him back, but her show of resistance only earned her a backhand slap from the blond man. The blow knocked her back against the truck and broke her hold on Jack's hand, after which the man dragged Jack away, striding toward the truck without giving her a second look.

Mikey started forward. "Leave her alone, you—"

Suddenly, he was face down on the gravel, spangles flashing before his eyes and a sharp pain spiking through his head. He clenched his fists in impotent rage, but when he tried to get up, the troll growled, "Stay down."

Mikey complied, remaining prone, but turned his head to watch a still-struggling Jack being shoved into the back seat of the pickup.

I'm sorry, Matt, he thought. *I tried.*

Then the troll knelt beside him, blocking his view of Jack. "This isn't personal," he said, sounding almost apologetic. "If that helps."

"It doesn't," Mikey said through clenched teeth.

"Too bad." The man shrugged. "No loose ends."

He extended the hand with the pistol, pressing the muzzle of the weapon to the base of Mikey's skull.

Mikey turned away, searching for Liz. When he caught her eye, he whispered, "I'm sorry."

She returned a weak smile, and then her lips moved, forming the words *I love you.*

At least, that was what Mikey chose to believe she had said.

THIRTY-NINE

Dean shoved the boy down into the rear of the cab and pinned him in place with one hand. He did this partly to maintain control over the squirming kid and partly to shield him from what was about to happen.

He felt bad about everything the kid had gone through. He'd seen his guardians killed right in front of him, and now more people who had decided to take care of him were about to die.

He shouldn't have to see that, Dean thought.

And while he knew that eventually the kid would have to die, just like everybody else—*"No loose ends"*—maybe it would go down a little easier if the kid wasn't completely traumatized. So he kept himself between the kid and the execution in progress.

"Stay still," he said. "I don't want to have to tie you up."

The kid paid no heed and kept trying to wriggle out of Dean's grasp.

"Have it your way." Dean set his pistol on the floorboards, then reached forward to the center console where he kept sundry items that often came in handy doing jobs for his father—useful things like duct tape and zip ties. After grabbing one of the latter, he caught both of the boy's wrists in one hand and deftly looped the plastic tie around them. Threading the end of the tie into the little slot in the low light and without the full use of both hands was a little tricky, but after a couple of false starts, he managed to snug the loop tight, binding the kid's hands together. Only then did he look back, wondering why he hadn't heard any shooting.

What's Holt waiting for?

Suddenly, the cab was filled with white light. Dean swung his head back to look and saw a pair of headlights blazing out of the crimson gloom on the opposite side of the pickup.

Dean muttered a curse under his breath as the newly arrived vehicle ground to a halt a few feet away. What were the odds of someone showing up out here, in the middle of nowhere and in the middle of a wildfire, just when they were trying to take care of business?

Probably some hotshots coming off the fire line, he thought, reaching for his pistol. *Too bad for them.*

But as his hand closed over the butt of the weapon, he saw a dark shape burst from the vehicle. He caught a fleeting glimpse of the thing as it crossed into the vehicle's headlights—not a man, but something else, something bestial, low to the ground, moving on all fours. Moving fast.

A dog, Dean realized. *A big one!*

He lost sight of it as it passed around the front end of his pickup, then glimpsed it again as it shot out into the open, moving with a purpose, like a guided missile homing in on a target.

That target was Holt.

Still kneeling over his hostage, Holt raised his head, and in the instant that he beheld the onrushing rottweiler, Dean saw his brother's eyes go wide in a rare look of horror . . . or was it recognition? Holt pivoted on his heel, trying to bring his gun to bear against the dog, but he was too slow. The animal bowled him over, clamping its jaws around the forearm of Holt's gun hand.

Dean tried to extricate himself from the rear of the cab in order to help his embattled brother, but before he could, another figure—this one very much human—rounded the front end of the pickup and charged into the fray. Dean froze, gaping in disbelief at the newcomer. It was the firefighter—the man who had prevented him from killing the boy the first time.

What's he doing here?

The symmetry of this development troubled Dean. He was unapologetically superstitious, a believer in the inescapable nature of fate. You couldn't cheat death, and if you tried, you only made it harder on yourself. That this man should appear from out of nowhere, intersecting Dean's life not once but twice, and under similar circumstances, was nothing short of ominous.

Is he here for me?

While Dean wrestled with his misgivings, the tableau continued to unfold before him. Holt and the dog were locked in a furious struggle, rolling on the ground in a savage flurry. The big firefighter, clearly seeing no way to intervene in that fight, had turned his attention—along with a rather large revolver—toward Scotty, who had spun the woman hostage around in front of him to use as a human shield and now had his pistol pressed against the soft flesh beneath her left ear.

Dean shook his head, trying to brush off the premonition. There was an easy explanation for this seeming coincidence. The firefighter had obviously appointed himself the kid's savior. No mystery there.

Maybe it's the other way around, he decided. *Maybe I'm the one who's supposed to kill him.*

The thought brought a smile to Dean's face. It was, he realized, perfect. Other than the kid, the firefighter was the only person who could identify him as the man who had killed Raymond Williams and his wife and all those smoke jumpers. This was his chance to tie up all the loose ends at once. And the best part was that the firefighter would never even see it coming.

Moving slowly, deliberately, so as not to betray either his presence or his purpose, he raised his pistol and took aim.

FORTY

As bad as the fire was, and it was *really* bad, the uncertainty was even worse.

As they'd crested the first of several mountain passes and gotten a look at the affected area—a veritable sea of flames lapping at the flanks of the mountains below—Redd had known that they would have to pass through it. There was no uncertainty about that.

Everything else was a crapshoot.

Was Mikey on this road, or had he been turned back by the fire?

Could they make it through, or would they have to turn back?

Would they even be able to turn back on the narrow path, or would this be a one-way trip no matter what?

Redd could not share his concerns with Emily. She was dealing with enough as it was, sitting as still as a Sphinx, eyes closed tight, gripping the armrest with one hand and the center console with the other, breathing with an almost clockwork rhythm to keep her motion sickness under control. Or mostly under control. The road was twisty and the ride rough, so it was no wonder that every few minutes, her breath pattern would quicken and a groan would slip past her lips.

"Sorry," he would mutter. That was the extent of what he could do to reassure her, and as they descended into the burn, even that became more than he could manage.

Because it was relatively free of vegetation and, therefore, fuel, there were no flames on the road, though as the Raptor passed through the leading edge of the fire, Redd would have been hard-pressed to make this distinction. The graveled track was too narrow to serve as an effective firebreak, and the fire had easily leaped across to ignite the dry grass on the far side, creating a wall of flame through which he would have to take them.

As the temperature inside the truck spiked, Redd heard a pathetic whimper from the rear of the cab and glanced back just in time to see Rubble curl up in the footwell, covering his eyes with one paw.

"Sorry, buddy," he muttered. And then the fire was all around them.

The next few seconds felt like a replay of sheltering in the burnover, except this time, he was denied the comfort of darkness. Instead, he saw only the bright oranges and yellows of fire.

The passage was mercifully quick, yet the nightmarish hellscape beyond brought no respite from the uncertainty of the path he had chosen. Everywhere he looked, there was only devastation.

Up ahead, something moved and flashed across the road . . . An animal . . . An elk, perhaps, though wreathed as it was in fire, it was impossible to say. It had an unsteadiness about it, as if it was favoring its right side, and Redd thought the animal must have been hurt. Injured and now running, desperate to escape the flames. Redd knew it would never make it. If it had been within his power, he would have stopped and ended the poor creature's suffering with a bullet, but the animal was long gone before he could even begin to seriously consider such a course of action, so he kept driving, and his doubts continued to multiply.

When he saw the old pickup parked diagonally across the road, blocking his way forward, his uncertainty transformed into dread.

Am I too late?

There might have been any number of explanations for why someone would block the fire road with their truck, but Redd discarded them all. There was not a doubt in his mind that this truck belonged to the men who had killed the FBI agents at the Diamond T and chased Mikey halfway across the county. The only thing he wasn't sure of was what he would find on the other side of that pickup.

Fearing the worst, the next few seconds were a blur. He was vaguely aware of bringing the Raptor to a stop just a few feet from the pickup, grabbing the Ruger and opening the door, and then, just before exiting, telling Emily, "Stay here!" He barely noticed Rubble's explosive exit. The rottie had leaped through the center gap and out Redd's door, blowing past him like a dog on a mission, disappearing like a shadow into the night.

When Redd rounded the front end of the pickup and saw Mikey and Liz, embattled but still alive, all the uncertainty and dread evaporated.

If they were alive, then Junior, Jack, and Lucas were too.

I'm not too late.

Off to his side, Redd heard Rubble let loose with a vicious snarl, followed by a series of growls. He turned just in time to see the rottie locked in mortal combat with the man who had been menacing Mikey. One look at the short ogre and Redd knew this was the same man who had assaulted Emily in their home. Little wonder that Rubble had gone right for him; the canine was simply trying to finish what he'd already started during their last fight. Redd brought the Ruger to bear on the man, but with Rubble attacking and Mikey right behind both of them, he knew he didn't have a clear shot. Judging by the ferocity of Rubble's attack, it would all be over in a few seconds anyway, so Redd switched his focus to the other gunman, who was presently holding Liz in front of him as a human shield.

The man was mostly hidden behind Liz's body, but his head was bobbing in and out of view as he tried to monitor Redd's approach. Redd positioned his body in a Weaver's shooting stance and took aim.

"I'll kill her!" the man warned, shouting to be heard over the noise of the fire and Rubble's snarls.

Redd's aim did not waver. "Let her go and drop the weapon. That's the only way you're leaving here."

The gunman gave no indication that he was even considering the choice, so Redd focused on the narrow portion of his skull that was exposed right beside Liz's ear and tightened his finger on the trigger.

He had already done the math. If he didn't shoot first, Liz would die. It was as simple as that. At this range, the only way he would hit Liz by mistake would be if the gunman jerked her in front of the bullet in the millisecond it would take Redd to pull the trigger, and given the circumstances, it was a chance he would have to take in order to save her life.

He looked away from the target and met Liz's gaze, giving a subtle nod that he hoped would communicate his intention. To his dismay, she answered with an equally understated head shake, followed by an exaggerated eye movement in the direction of Mikey's truck.

What's she trying to say?

She repeated the look, holding it and bobbing her head slightly in what he took to be a silent shout.

Something about the truck . . .

Then he understood.

The kids!

Liz was trying to warn him that the children were in the truck's rear seating area and that if he took the shot and missed, his bullet might hit one of them.

That was a chance he wasn't willing to take, but the gunman didn't know that.

"Last warning," said Redd, taking a sideways step toward the truck, changing his angle of approach. The gunman, following his every move, pivoted, keeping Liz in front of him.

One more step to the right, thought Redd, *and you'll never walk again.*

But before Redd could take another step, there was a sudden flurry of activity off to his left. He risked a quick glance and saw the ogre somehow rising to his feet, with both arms wrapped around Rubble's thrashing form.

Redd couldn't believe what he was seeing. The rottweiler's attack had been brutal. His powerful jaws had flayed the skin from the ogre's arms and torso, tearing away chunks of flesh and opening veins and tissue. Blood was gushing from a dozen or more bite wounds. By all rights, the man should have been dead already, but not only was he still in the fight, he had somehow managed to wrestle Rubble into a bear hug, restricting the dog's movement and his ability to attack. It was like trying to wrestle a tornado, but the man held on. Arms quivering with the strain of holding Rubble and seemingly oblivious to Redd and the threat he posed, the ogre staggered away from the truck.

Redd quickly took a step to the right so that he could keep an eye on both men. He kept the Ruger trained on Liz's captor but remained ready to switch targets at the first sign of a direct threat from the ogre. He knew that if he shifted his aim, the gunman holding Liz would take a shot at him, so he began mentally rehearsing what he would have to do to take both men out.

With his attention divided, it took Redd a moment to realize what the ogre was trying to do.

"Rubble!" he shouted, turning away from the gunman despite the threat, desperate to save his dog.

But it was too late.

Rubble yelped, his loud cry cutting through the thick night air. Redd watched helplessly as the ogre heaved the massive rottie away from him, hurling the thrashing animal toward the roadside and into the waiting fire.

FORTY-ONE

It took Mikey a moment to fully grasp what was happening. He had not been hoping for any sort of last-minute reprieve, and so, having made his peace and said his goodbyes, if only in his heart, he did not expect to hear anything but the sound of a gunshot, and maybe not even that.

He'd seen a television show once where the characters debated whether or not someone shot in the head would even hear the sound of the gun firing.

'Bout to find out, he told himself.

Instead, he felt the pressure of his executioner's pistol ease and then vanish altogether, followed immediately by what sounded like the snarl of a wild beast. He wasn't sure what to make of it all.

But as the noise of the disturbance intensified, with no sign of his tormentor's return, Mikey risked raising his head for a look around. His eyes were drawn immediately to the savage struggle between the troll and a large dog.

Is that Rubble?

Forcing his eyes away from the fight between man and beast, Mikey quickly began to notice other new developments, not the least of which was his best friend standing with his gun drawn and aimed at the man who was holding Liz hostage.

Matt! Oh, thank God.

Mikey felt a surge of relief, but the feeling quickly gave way to other emotions—rage at the man who was threatening his wife, frustration at his own helplessness, fear over the very real possibility that things might still go horribly wrong.

Matt's outnumbered, he thought. *I have to do something.*

He spotted the pistol the troll had been threatening him with, which had been dropped at the beginning of Rubble's attack. Mikey didn't know handguns the way Redd did, but he recognized the pistol as an M1911 or possibly the M1911A1 variant. Despite being based on a century-old design, the .45 caliber semi-auto remained a favorite with many special forces operators—or at least that was the case in some of Mikey's favorite novels.

He closed his fist around the warm metal of the pistol grip, hefting the weapon. It felt like an alien artifact in his hand. Mikey was deadly with a long gun, a trait he'd mastered as an avid hunter providing wild game for his family to eat, but his comfort level with handguns was pretty low. He'd gone with Redd to the shooting range more than a few times. He'd even seen live combat on several occasions, always side-by-side with Redd, and he certainly understood the basics of aiming, firing, and reloading. But he was not exactly an expert shot with a pistol and had only a rudimentary understanding of the M1911's unique characteristics. He knew that the handgun had a thumb safety but couldn't remember whether it was supposed to be up or down in order to fire.

Which is it . . . Up? Down?

Then Mikey looked up and saw Liz with a similar weapon jammed against the side of her head, and his instincts took over. He rolled over into a crouch, bringing the pistol up in a two-handed grip, the fingers of his left hand cupped over the fingers of his right to steady his aim. He didn't have a shot, so he aimed off to the side, careful not to point the gun at Liz. From what he could tell, the gunman hadn't noticed him yet, but he knew that might change at any second.

Suddenly, he remembered that there was another gunman—the blond who had seized Jack.

Where is he?

He swiveled his body around, searching the open doors of the pickup, and spotted the blond gunman perched in the back seat, taking aim at Redd with his own weapon.

Mikey lined the man up in the .45's sights and curled his finger around the trigger, but then he hesitated.

What about Jack?

Jack was in the pickup, hidden from view behind his captor. If Mikey took the shot and missed, he might hit Jack instead. Even if he scored a direct hit, the bullet might go through the blond man and still hit Jack.

Can't risk it, he thought. *But I can't let him shoot Matt.*

He decided the best he could do under the circumstances was a high warning shot—what Matt would probably call "suppressive fire." Close enough to make the gunman think twice about sticking his head out but not close enough to endanger Jack.

Before Mikey could pull the trigger, however, everything changed. Despite being torn to shreds by Rubble, the troll had somehow managed to wrap the dog up in a bear hug and then, to Mikey's complete horror, hurled the dog into the flames.

Bad move, thought Mikey, his eyes already searching for Redd. Mikey knew how much his friend loved the loyal rottie, and he knew seeing his dog go down would spark something in Redd. *He's going to John Wick these guys. For sure.*

A second later, several things happened all at the same time.

Redd let out an agonized howl as he brought his Ruger around and took aim at the troll.

The troll, despite looking like the victim of an industrial accident, turned and, heedless of the large-caliber revolver pointed right at him, charged Matt.

The man holding Liz thrust his hostage aside and took aim at Redd, while the blond gunman in the pickup, now unable to shoot at Redd without hitting the troll, raised his pistol, checking fire.

Mikey saw it all unfolding and, in a fraction of a second, made a judgment call.

Swinging the .45 around and aiming at Liz's former captor, he pulled the trigger.

Bang!

The weapon bucked in his hands as the pistol spat out a round, but Mikey's two-handed grip kept the weapon steady, and he squeezed off a second shot.

Bang!

Both shots, fired point-blank, hit center mass, knocking the man backward off his feet and tearing clean through his upper torso, splattering the side of Mikey's truck with dark gore.

"Liz!" he shouted as the man fell dead at her feet. "Get to cover!"

Although he was relieved to see her dive into the rear cab area, pulling the door shut behind her, Mikey knew the danger was far from over, so he quickly pivoted back, assessing targets as he moved. But in the time it had taken him to dispatch Liz's captor, the troll had closed with Redd, tackling him before he could get off a shot.

The report of a pistol and the simultaneous sound of a bullet punching into the Ram's front fender right above his head provided a sudden and jarring reminder that the troll was not the only enemy still in play. Mikey threw himself flat and then, knowing how exposed he was to the shooter in the pickup, squirmed under his truck, putting its front tire between himself and the gunman.

From that vantage, Mikey could see Matt and the troll on the ground in a tangle of limbs, grappling for dominance. Mikey was both astonished and horrified to see that the fight wasn't going well for Redd. He'd been counting on his friend to come to *his* rescue, but now it looked like Matt was the one in need of rescuing.

FORTY-TWO

Despite his bulk, to say nothing of his injuries, the ogre moved with unnatural quickness, closing with Redd before he could get off a shot and slamming into him like a charging bull. The hit knocked the Ruger from Redd's hands and put him on the ground with the wind knocked out of him and phosphenes swirling in his vision.

It wasn't the hardest hit he'd ever taken, but it was definitely in the top ten. Even so, he knew he had to get back in the fight and launch a counterattack to prevent his foe from seizing the advantage during his momentary disorientation. So even though he couldn't quite see straight or even draw a breath, he flung his arms out, trying to lock up the other man's arms while simultaneously pushing off with his legs in order to flip both of them over with himself on top.

The attempt was a complete failure. With no leverage and a questionable grip on his foe, Redd's efforts to get into a superior position were easily thwarted. The man's squat torso, thick limbs, and the fact that he had no neck to speak of left him with almost no vulnerabilities for Redd to exploit. He broke out of Redd's hold with little more than an indifferent shrug, and before Redd could try again, *he* was the one caught in a bear hug. He tried to wriggle one arm free, but the ogre was prodigiously strong, crushing both of Redd's arms into his chest. Redd tried driving his knee up into the man's crotch, but the significant height disparity kept the blow from landing where it would have a meaningful effect.

Nevertheless, he must have hit something because the man gave a grunt of pain, and his grip loosened just enough for Redd to slide his arms around to encircle the man's abdomen. He then brought his arms up under his foe's embrace, ramming against his opponent's arms, loosening the other's hold, if only for a moment, allowing Redd the opportunity to draw a breath for the first time in what seemed like forever. In the same motion, Redd drove his forehead down into the man's unprotected face. The blow landed just below the man's right eye socket and, if the spike of pain that shot through Redd's skull was any indication, hit with enough force to fracture the man's cheekbone. The ogre, however, just grunted and then redoubled his efforts to squeeze the life out of Redd.

Through the haze of struggle and pain, Redd thought he heard gunshots and feared the worst for Liz and Mikey, but with the sound of blood pounding in his ears, he couldn't trust his senses. One thing was certain, though . . . if he didn't turn things around and win this fight quickly, he wouldn't be the only one to suffer.

He twisted and squirmed, desperate to find a weak point in his foe's simplistic but ruthlessly efficient attack. He drove short but powerful strikes into the other man's kidneys and lower abdomen, but nothing he did seemed to have any effect. It was like trying to tear a two-hundred-year-old tree out of the ground with nothing more than brute strength. The human wrecking ball was utterly unyielding.

A ring of shadows tunneled Redd's vision, and he knew he was close to blacking out. Clenching his teeth, he rotated his arms within the embrace and, using every reserve of willpower he possessed, began driving his elbows into the ogre's biceps.

He gained an inch, then another, but had to fight for both of them. With the man's bulk pressing down on his chest, he was barely able to draw breath, and the circle of darkness continued to close.

Then the miracle he hadn't even thought to pray for happened.

He didn't see it, not at first, but he did hear it—a low, ominous growl—and despite the immediate peril, his heart soared.

Who's a good boy?

The ogre heard it, too, and his reaction was diametrically opposite to Redd's.

His hold on Redd did not weaken noticeably, but Redd sensed a fear in him that had not been there before.

Redd looked up as the bloodthirsty rottie closed in. Rubble had not come through the fire untouched. Large patches of his coat had been burned away, the light-brown skin beneath blackened with ash and, in a few places, glistening from fresh second-degree burns. Nevertheless, he began barking fiercely and snapping at the face of Redd's assailant, though, with the two men in such close contact, the dog seemed hesitant to press the attack.

The other man reacted by heaving his bulk to the side, rolling over with Redd still in his embrace. Caught off guard, Redd missed an opportunity to get on top and was rolled completely over, then rolled a second time. Rubble followed, snarling ferociously but still holding back. At first, Redd thought the other man was just trying to get away from the dog's snapping jaws, but after the second roll, he realized his foe had a different purpose. The man was rolling them both toward the side of the road.

Toward the fire.

They were just a couple yards away from the edge of the road, where fallen tree trunks now formed a bed of glowing embers. Down at ground level, the heat was less intense even this close, but Redd knew how quickly that would change if the ogre succeeded in pitching him into the fire. So when the man attempted another roll, Redd planted his knee against the ground, stopping their momentum with himself on top. The move caught the man by surprise, and Redd quickly took advantage by breaking the hold and maneuvering into a full mount. Straddling the man's chest, he immediately began raining down blows, striking not only at the man's unprotected face but at the raw, bloody flesh already ravaged by Rubble's teeth and the buckshot pellets from Emily's shotgun.

The blows elicited more than just indifferent grunts. The man roared like a crazed bear and began heaving and bucking, trying to dislodge his attacker. Redd thought he was ready for anything the man might throw at him, but the violence of the counterattack overwhelmed him, and in a matter of seconds, he was hurled off the man.

And into the fire.

Even as he flew toward the blazing coals, Redd twisted his body like a cat reorienting in midfall to land on its feet. Redd didn't quite land on *his* feet, but he did manage to come down on hands and knees in the bed of coals. Just as quickly, he pushed back, heaving himself away from the blaze.

Strangely, he had felt no pain and barely even any heat when his hands had come down on the hot coals. His contact with them had been so fleeting that, aside from scorching the fabric of his jeans, he sustained no damage at all. But he was still too close to the fire for comfort, and even as he was regaining his balance, he caught a glimpse of the ogre charging him again.

There wasn't time to get out of the way, nor even to turn and stand his ground. All he could do was lean away from the imminent impact.

It was enough. Instead of knocking Redd off his feet and into the furnace of burning coals, the man struck only a glancing blow—more cue ball than wrecking ball—spinning Redd away at an oblique angle. He still might have gone into the fire if not for the fact that, even as he reeled from the hit, Redd snared the other man's arm, arresting his fall, and whipped himself away from the conflagration.

For a moment, the two men were like warring black holes, caught in a gravitational spiral, dancing toward mutual destruction. But as his maneuver put the ogre between him and the fire, Redd caught the man's other shoulder with his free hand and, as if mounting a horse, heaved himself onto the man's back and rode him down into the blaze.

The impact sent up a flurry of cinders and smoke. Redd buried his face against the other man's back to keep from accidentally inhaling the superheated miasma, but for a moment or two, not much else happened. The ogre lay motionless beneath Redd, as if stunned or even dead.

Then, with the suddenness of a lightning strike, the heat arrived.

Redd felt the skin on his hands and forearms sizzling like bacon in a frying pan, but he gritted his teeth against the pain and held onto his foe, determined not to let the man escape. His determination, however, counted for little. Roused by the pain, or perhaps by the fact of his imminent immolation, the ogre erupted into motion, bucking Redd off and scrambling backward, desperate to escape the inferno. But he was too late. The inferno already had him. Contact with the coals had ignited his clothing, almost instantaneously enveloping him in flames.

As Redd crashed down onto the graveled roadway, he beheld the other man transformed into a creature of living fire. Defiant to the last, the man did not cry out, nor did he fall to the ground in an attempt to smother the flames. It would have been a futile effort, for he had already breathed the fire into his lungs. Nevertheless, he stayed on his feet a few seconds longer, turning slowly, arms outstretched as if searching for Redd, before finally collapsing in a flaming heap. Amidst the ever-present aroma of woodsmoke, an odor to which Redd had long since become nose blind, a new smell intruded—a smell like burning garbage and rancid barbecue.

Redd looked away, his gaze falling upon the crumpled form of the gunman who had been holding Liz captive. The man was unquestionably dead, but there was no sign of Redd's friends.

"Mikey?" he croaked. "Liz?"

As if in answer to his question, the pickup blocking the road suddenly rumbled to life. Redd whirled around toward it, just as the vehicle's unseen driver put it in gear. Redd watched it begin rolling forward and was trying to decide whether it was worth attempting some kind of interdiction when he heard Mikey's shout.

"Matt!"

He turned to see his friend crawling out from under his big truck, pointing frantically at the departing pickup. Then he uttered the three words that explained everything.

"He's got Jack!"

FORTY-THREE

Despite the heat, Dean was shivering so badly that he could barely turn the steering wheel. The image of his brother consumed by fire still burned in his mind's eye. Yet it wasn't the horror of Holt's demise nor even the grief of losing his own flesh and blood that provoked this reaction.

Truthfully, Dean had never really liked his brother all that much. Holt had bullied him mercilessly throughout their childhood, so while he felt an obligatory sense of familial outrage, he wouldn't be shedding any tears for the brute.

No, what he was feeling right now was something else. Something far more terrible.

Dean felt fear. Cold, heart-pounding, hand-trembling *fear*. The kind of fear that was nearly incapacitating. His pulse was racing, and one thought kept running through his mind.

Dad's going to kill me.

It was not hyperbole.

It didn't matter that it wasn't his fault. Holt, believing himself invincible, had bullheadedly charged into a fight just like he always did, only this time, he had gone up against someone better than him and had paid the ultimate price. Nothing Dean might have said or done would have changed the outcome. But that wouldn't matter to Otis Werner. He would hold Dean responsible, and in his grief and rage, there was no telling how he would react.

At least Dean wouldn't be showing up at the mill completely empty-handed.

He shot a glance over his shoulder, checking to make sure the kid was still securely bound on the floor behind him, then cranked the wheel hard, steering around the big Ram truck. He saw the firefighter and also the guy who had been driving the Ram—he was crawling out from under the truck—and knew he should probably stop and try to take them both out.

No loose ends.

But the way his luck was running lately, he didn't like his chances. Holt and Scotty were both dead, which meant the other side had the numerical advantage. He might be able to kill one or the other, but not both.

And if I get killed, who's gonna get the kid to the mill?

That was his rationale, but truth be told, he just wanted to stay alive. There was the difference between him and Holt. Holt didn't think . . . or hadn't thought . . . that anything could really hurt him and so wasn't afraid of death.

How'd that work out for you, big brother?

He threaded the pickup into the narrow gap between the Ram and the edge of the road, barely even noticing as the side of his truck scraped past with a torturous shriek, snapping the side mirrors off both vehicles. Then he felt a slight tremor ripple through the cab, the truck bouncing on its springs for no obvious reason. He glanced back again to check on his captive and glimpsed movement in the bed. A second look revealed the towering figure of the firefighter clambering over the tailgate.

Dean's first impulse was to stomp on the gas pedal, as if he might outrun the big man, but it was too late for that. The guy was already on board, crouching down in the bed, keeping his center of gravity low as he advanced toward the cab.

The chill of dread he had felt upon witnessing Holt's immolation flashed through him once more. "No," he whispered. "No. No. No."

The pickup shot down the gravel road, juddering noisily over the washboard as it gained speed, but the firefighter was still coming, reaching out for the rear cab window.

Where's my gun? Dean looked around frantically but didn't see his pistol. In his haste to get away, he'd left it . . . Where? In the back seat with the kid? He had no idea, but shooting the guy was not an option.

There was a loud thump as something crashed against the rear window. The firefighter was trying to smash through.

If he gets inside, I'm dead, thought Dean.

He whipped the steering wheel from side to side, causing the pickup to careen back and forth across the road. The truck skidded on the loose gravel, fishtailing and almost going into a spin. Dean curtailed his attempt to shake his unwanted passenger off, bringing the vehicle back under control, and then looked back to see if it had worked.

For a moment, he thought it had, but then something slammed into the rear window hard enough to pop the glass out of its frame. The firefighter, lying on his back in the bed, had not only hung on through the wild ride but had just used his bootheels to smash through the window.

Dean whispered a curse through clenched teeth. The man would be inside the truck in seconds.

He considered slamming on the brakes, getting out, and trying to make a run for it on foot. Maybe if the firefighter got the kid back, he'd leave Dean alone.

But then Dad really would kill me.

Then a crazy idea came to him. So crazy that he didn't even stop to consider all the ways it might go horribly wrong. If it didn't work, it wouldn't matter anyway.

He picked out a flaming tree to the left of the road and swung the truck toward it on a collision course. It was not his intention to hit the tree head-on. He wasn't that crazy. Instead, as he neared the road's edge, he slowed and veered away from the tree just enough to avoid a direct collision and his front fender merely kissed the charred trunk. The pickup bounced back onto the road, but the glancing contact was enough to shake the tree, releasing a storm of flaming embers that cascaded down onto the truck. Bright red coals fell like fiery rain on the hood and windshield, then blew away just as quickly as the pickup rolled onward. The shower of coals that had fallen in the bed, however, swirled around in the eddy caused by the slipstream, fanned into bright but transient flames by the rush of air.

Dean kept one eye on the rearview mirror, expecting the firefighter to rise up out of the ashes like some unstoppable, semi-immortal villain in a slasher flick. But as five, then ten, then a full thirty seconds passed with no sign of the man, Dean allowed himself a relieved sigh. His crazy idea had worked.

The firefighter was gone, and he was home free.

FORTY-FOUR

Even as he threw himself over the side from the pickup's bed, a fraction of a second before it struck the burning tree, Redd regretted his decision.

If I had just been a little faster . . .

He had been so close. A few more seconds and he would have been inside the pickup. But when he'd felt the truck swerving toward the roadside and the flames, he had immediately grasped what the driver was attempting and had done the math. If he hadn't bailed out, he would have burned, maybe to death. That left only one option, and so he had jumped.

And in doing so, I abandoned Jack.

Redd hit the ground in a modified paratrooper's landing roll to minimize injury, and between that and the adrenaline, he barely felt any pain. He rolled several more times until his borrowed momentum was spent. He lay motionless in the middle of the road for a few more seconds, waiting for his equilibrium to return, watching the pickup's taillights diminish into the distance.

When the world around him finally stopped moving, he bolted to his feet and took off at a full sprint, running not after the pickup but back to where Emily and the others waited.

Back to his own truck.

I can catch him, he told himself. *There's still time.*

The pickup had borne him about a quarter of a mile down the fire road, a distance that he now covered in under ninety seconds. Rubble met him at the halfway point, yipping ecstatically. He ran in a circle around Redd before falling in beside him. The rottie's singed exterior prompted Redd to consider his own condition. The backs of his hands throbbed, but in the dull red glow from the fire, he didn't see signs of real damage. First-degree burns, he decided. Nothing worse than a bad sunburn.

As he drew near his goal, he saw Emily standing in front of the Raptor. She was bent over awkwardly with both hands cradling her swollen belly. Mikey and Liz stood beside her, Liz holding Emily's shoulders.

She's sick again, Redd thought, not unsympathetically. But he couldn't worry about that right now. The clock was ticking. His chance to catch up to Jack's captor was slipping away.

Mikey and Liz both looked up as he closed the final distance, but Emily kept her head down.

"I can catch him," he shouted, veering toward the driver's side of the truck.

Mikey called out to him, "Matt! Wait."

"No time. You guys drive Em and the kids out of here. I'll catch up to you . . ."

He trailed off as a strange noise reached his ears, fast but rhythmic. It was not unlike the sound of a dog panting, but Rubble was right beside him, breathing normally.

Not Rubble, he realized. *Emily.*

And then it hit him. Emily wasn't sick. She was . . .

He skidded to a stop, then ran back to the front of the truck, staring at her in disbelief. "Are you in labor?"

By way of an answer, a low cry slipped past her lips, momentarily breaking the rhythm of her breathing. Redd just stared at her, dumbstruck.

She's been having contractions this whole time, he realized. *How did I miss that?*

After a few more breaths, she raised her eyes to meet his stare. Perspiration beaded on her forehead and ran down her cheeks like tears. "It's okay," she said a little breathlessly. "I'm okay."

She straightened, the intensity of the contraction evidently fading, and nodded. "Go after him, Matty."

He recoiled at the suggestion. "What? No. I'm not leaving you."

But I can't leave Jack either.

"Matty, it's okay." She took his hand and squeezed it, showing her strength. "Yes, I'm in labor, but there's plenty of time. You go after Jack. Mikey can take me to the hospital."

Redd didn't move. His heart was being pulled in two directions. He couldn't *not* be there for his wife and their children. But at the same time, he couldn't *not* go after Jack. The poor kid had nobody. Nothing.

I'm all he's got. But Emily . . . the baby . . .

Matthew Redd had been to war and seen the horrors of the battlefield. He'd seen men go down and faced terrifying moments—but even so, he always knew which way to run and faithfully charged headfirst toward any problem, willing to try and be the solution, even if it meant putting himself in harm's way.

This was the first time he'd ever been paralyzed by indecisiveness.

He didn't know what to do.

And in that moment, Redd was lost.

Suddenly, he felt Mikey's hand on his shoulder. "We got this, Matt. You go get Jack. You're the only one who can, man."

Redd turned slowly and saw that Mikey was holding something out to him— his Ruger. Redd stared at the weapon, then looked back at Emily, searching her face for any indication that her assurance was just bravado, that she really did need him to stay with her. But even as he did, his sense of compelling urgency returned.

She's right. There's plenty of time. For her. But not for Jack.

"You're sure?"

Emily nodded again and then took a deep breath, straightening her back. "Get the boy, Matty. *Go!*"

Redd took the Ruger from Mikey and then, without any further delay, ran back to the driver's side door. As he opened it, Rubble barked and bounded past him, leaping over the center console and into the front passenger seat, ready to provide backup for whatever situation they were riding into.

Ready for round two.

✖ ✖ ✖

As the Raptor roared away down the road, Mikey—who had already checked to make sure that both Little Matty and Luke were still secure in their car seats— turned to Emily. "Come on," he said. "Let's get you to the hospital."

He felt terrible about not being able to protect Jack or prevent his capture but was at least heartened by the fact that he could do this one thing for his friend.

Emily nodded and allowed herself to be led—Mikey on one side, Liz on the other—to Mikey's pickup. He decided to steer them around to the passenger side in order to avoid having to step over the body of one of their attackers, which was presently sprawled out in front of the rear door on the driver's side, but then grimaced when he saw the passenger side of his truck. It looked as if someone had taken a giant cheese grater to it.

Good thing I know someone who can do the bodywork cheap, he thought.

He opened the rear door for Emily and then offered his arm to assist her with the climb up into the cab. She stepped onto the running board but hesitated when she saw Matthew Jr. still buckled in his car seat, looking fussy but otherwise in good health.

"Hey, baby," she said with a weak smile. "We're gonna get you—"

She broke off with a sudden gasp and then seemed to almost fold over on herself.

Mikey caught her and eased her down off the running board. Liz took Emily's hand and gave it a squeeze. "Another contraction?"

Emily, who was already trying to modulate her breathing, just nodded.

"We got you," said Liz. "Just keep breathing. We'll get through this."

Emily didn't reply but continued breathing and riding out the waves of pain. Mikey knew there wasn't much any of them could do until the contraction passed. With her medical background, not to mention prior experience, Emily knew better than anyone what to do to get through it.

Finally, after what seemed like an eternity, Mikey felt Emily's rigid muscles begin to slacken. The contraction was over.

Liz wiped the sweat from Emily's forehead with a sleeve. "Okay, hon. Let's get you in before the next one hits."

But Emily shook her head. "No," she breathed. "Can't."

"Emily," Mikey said, trying to sound patient. "I promised Matt we'd get you to the hospital."

Emily shook her head again. "No time for the hospital."

No time for the hospital?

"What do you mean there's no time? We need to go!"

Mikey looked at Liz just in time to see her eyes go wide with recognition.

"She's not going to make it, Mikey," Liz said as she pulled off her jacket and sprang into action. "The baby's coming right now."

"Now?" asked Mikey. "Are you sure? Liz—"

Emily cried out in agony.

Liz dropped to her knees while guiding Emily down to the ground before placing her jacket, now rolled into a ball, under their friend's head. Then she looked back at her husband.

"Right now, Mikey. Baby girl is coming right *now*."

FORTY-FIVE

With Emily no longer in his truck, Redd drove the Raptor hard. The truck skidded through turns and shuddered over washboards. Gravel rattled against the undercarriage like machine gun fire. But Redd did not relent.

He figured that the pickup carrying Jack had at least a three-minute lead on him. That didn't sound like much, but given the road conditions, it was a gap that he would be hard-pressed to close. At his present speed, pushing beyond the upper limit of what could be considered safe or sane, he might be able to gain as much as fifteen seconds per mile, meaning it would take about twelve miles for him to catch up—nearly three-quarters of the distance back to the highway. That assumed the other driver wasn't also pushing the envelope.

Catching up to the pickup and rescuing Jack was by no means a foregone conclusion.

Five minutes passed with no indication that he was any closer than when the pursuit had begun. The air above the road remained thick with smoke and dust, making it impossible to determine when the pickup had come through and limiting visibility to the point where he might not have noticed the other vehicle's lights even from a hundred yards away.

The transition out of the fire zone happened so quickly that Redd almost missed it. The fire had already consumed most of the fuel in the area, leaving a few hot spots here and there, but the landscape to either side of the road was mostly just ash. Then, as if the fire had hit some kind of invisible barrier, the zone of devastation ended, giving way to undamaged forest.

Visibility improved quickly as Redd left the fire behind, and while he couldn't see the glow of the pickup's headlights yet, dust motes, stirred up by the pickup's tires, swirled over the road. He was closing in on his quarry. He felt that in his gut.

But he was also running out of road.

When he came to the junction where Fire Road 722 connected with the county roads, he noted the padlocked gate and continued east on the fire road. Since there was no way that the fleeing killer had the key to that lock, it seemed obvious which way he'd gone.

Redd knew that if he stayed on this fire road, in another fifteen miles or so, he would come out somewhere north of the roadblock on the main highway. Fifteen miles was plenty of time to close with the pickup and rescue Jack. Nevertheless, as he left the gate behind, his instincts began nagging at him.

Mikey had come up here by way of West Fork Road, south of the roadblock, and had followed the county roads up to the junction with Fire Road 722—the junction Redd had just passed.

How did he get past that gate?

It was a minor aberration, a single pebble thrown into a river, and yet Redd couldn't shake the feeling that it was important.

Mikey got past that gate. So did the bad guys. But it's locked now. Who locked it?

He tried to tell himself that it didn't matter. The gate was locked. That avenue of escape had been cut off. There was only one way the pickup could have gone.

If they came this way, where's the dust?

The nagging doubt bloomed into a blaring alarm.

Redd swore aloud and jammed on the brakes. When the Raptor stopped skidding forward, he shifted into reverse and floored it, holding the wheel steady as he drove backward to the gated junction.

In the beams of the Raptor's headlights, Redd could see that the padlock securing the gate was not the same type as the one he had cut off at the western gate. The Forest Service bought their locks in bulk, keyed alike. Even from a distance, Redd could tell that this was not one of theirs.

He got out, retrieved the bolt cutters, and had the lock off in less than thirty seconds. Once he was on the move again, it wasn't long at all before the Raptor's headlights illuminated dense shafts of settling dust above the road.

Redd estimated that the mistake had cost him another minute, one he could ill afford, but he did not allow himself to believe that his cause was hopeless. If it had taken him a minute to back up and cut the lock, it would probably have taken just as long for the pickup's driver to get out, close it, and lock it up in the first place.

He pushed the Raptor harder, all but flying over the graveled roadway. Redd found himself leaning forward in his seat, as if by so doing his eyes might be able to penetrate the haze of dust. Several minutes passed, but there was still no sign of the pickup.

A thump shuddered through the truck, and then all of the road noise and vibration vanished, as did most of the dust. The road surface had just transitioned to asphalt. With the increased visibility, Redd hoped to see the pickup's taillights in the distance or even the reflected glow of its headlights, but the only light he saw outside the Raptor was from the stars. Still, he did not relent. With relatively smooth pavement under the tires, he rocketed through the straightaways and straightened the curves, slowing only when the road and the laws of physics left him no choice.

Then the headlights illuminated a diamond-shaped yellow advisory sign with the words *Intersection Ahead*. He had reached the highway.

He waited too long to apply the brakes, skidding out into the main road before finally coming to a stop, but there was no risk of a collision. No traffic moved in either direction, as far as the eye could see.

"If he went north, he'll have to stop at the roadblock," Redd said aloud, glancing over at Rubble. "But does he know about the roadblock?"

Rubble evidently had no opinion on the matter.

"South, then," Redd went on, nodding. He started to turn the truck in that direction but then stomped his foot on the brake.

There were just too many variables. Now that Jack's captor was on the open road, he might go anywhere.

"What am I doing?" he said, glancing down at Rubble again. The poor dog had been whipped back and forth on his seat.

Rubble gave a little woof.

"I can't do this alone, boy."

It was a hard thing for him to admit, even if only to himself and Rubble, but it was the unvarnished truth and a lesson he kept having to learn over and over again, not because he was stubborn, and not because he believed that asking for help was a sign of weakness, but because deep down, he was terrified that if he asked for help and the answer was no . . . *what then?*

But the truth of the matter was that the people who loved him had never told him no, had never let him down. They'd stood with him during the gunfight at the Stillwater Courthouse and against the Infidels Motorcycle Club.

And they were still standing with him.

"Gotta do it," he said. "Jack's counting on me."

Redd took out his phone and called a number from his contact list.

"Matthew!" Sheriff Blackwood's voice boomed in his ear. "Where are you?"

"Out at West Fork Road. It's a long story, and I'll tell you all about it later. Right now, I need your help. The bad guys have Jack. They're somewhere on the highway north of town. Can't be more than ten miles from here, but I don't know which direction they're heading."

Blackwood didn't need him to spell it out. "I'll put my deputies on it right away. Can you describe the vehicle?"

"Late-model pickup. Can't tell you make or model, but it's pretty beat up." He recalled the damage it had sustained scraping past Mikey's truck. "Body damage on the driver's side."

"We'll find it," assured Blackwood.

"There's just one guy," Redd went on. "But he's got Jack with him."

"I won't tell you not to worry. But we'll do everything in our power to keep that boy safe. We're not alone on this. We're up to our ears in FBI agents."

Redd knew he should take a measure of comfort from this news, but his thoughts kept going to all the different ways things could go wrong, from the bad guys somehow slipping through the net to a violent confrontation with the authorities and Jack caught in the crossfire.

"You gotta let go, Matty. You can't do everything yourself."

It was Emily's voice he heard, and for some reason, that made the pill easier to swallow.

"I should be with her," he said aloud and then looked down at Rubble as if for confirmation.

The rottie just gazed up at him expectantly.

✖ ✖ ✖

As he made his way back up to the fire road, Redd kept expecting to encounter Mikey's Ram making its way back out at a more sedate pace. He was a little surprised when, after ten minutes, there was no sign of his friend's big truck. After fifteen minutes, he started to worry that something might be wrong. His foot grew heavy on the accelerator pedal.

Visions of the fire suddenly intensifying around them, cutting off their avenue of escape, flashed through his mind. Had Mikey been forced to turn around and head out by the west gate? Had another truckload of bad guys shown up and intercepted them?

I shouldn't have left them. I never should have left them.

But his thoughts were also with Jack. Five minutes after that, he started praying.

Please let them be okay. Please, God, let them be okay.

By the time he saw Mikey's truck, exactly where it had been when he'd left, he was nearly frantic.

He skidded to a halt a hundred feet back, leaving himself plenty of stand-off distance, and exploded from the Raptor with his Ruger at the ready. Redd whistled, and Rubble bounded out and charged toward the Ram, eager to meet whatever danger waited there.

An agonized cry tore apart the night, and despite the heat, Redd's blood ran cold.

Emily!

He took off in a run, the Ruger leveled in a firing position. He was halfway there when a figure stepped out from behind one of the Ram's open doors.

In his military career, one concept that had been drilled into Redd's head was the importance of PID—positive identification of a target before pulling the trigger. Hours of shoot house training had honed his reflexes to the point where he could not only make PID but aim and pull the trigger in three-tenths of a second.

It was that training that kept him from pulling the trigger.

"Mikey!" Redd hauled the Ruger down, shoving it in his waistband before his friend could even realize that the weapon had been pointed at him.

"Matt!" Mikey called out. "You came back?"

Mikey's face was streaked with sweat, and he wore a concerned expression, but not *that* concerned. Not life-or-death concerned.

"Our boys are in the truck. They're tired but good. Come on," he urged. "You made it just in time."

Just in time?

Redd didn't ask the question aloud but ran forward to join his friend. The first thing he saw was Rubble, who was sitting on his haunches beside the open door. Next, he saw Liz leaning against the truck but with her head and shoulders inside.

Then he saw Emily.

His first thought was that she had been injured, grievously wounded during the earlier firefight. She half lay, half sat in the doorway as if she had collapsed while trying to get out. Incongruously, there was a blanket across her lap. Her skin was pale in the firelight. She looked absolutely exhausted, her face streaked with perspiration, strings of hair plastered to her forehead. And yet, when she saw Redd, she smiled.

"Matty," she said, her voice a hoarse whisper. "You made it."

That was when it finally sank in. "You're having the baby."

She managed another weak smile and a nod.

"No way were we gonna make it to the hospital," Mikey said apologetically. "Thank God the fire shifted and we were able to hole up."

Redd glanced back at him and shook his head. "You did the right thing, Mikey." Then he turned to Liz. "How close are we?"

"Ask Em," said Liz. "She's calling the shots. I'm really not doing much more than offering moral support."

"Not true," Emily retorted, but before she could offer further encouragement to Liz, she doubled over with another contraction.

Liz quickly grabbed Emily's hand and began murmuring words of encouragement. "Breathe. Breathe through it. Don't push yet. It's not time."

Emily let out a sound that was somewhere between a scream and a growl, then shook her head and, in a voice that belonged in a horror movie, said, "It's time!"

"Then push!" Liz said without missing a beat.

Redd had been present at Matthew Jr.'s birth, so there was nothing unfamiliar about the process, but somehow, in this context, he felt completely bewildered. A little voice in his head kept saying, *No, we need to get to the hospital first.*

But when Emily reached out to him, he took her hand as if his body knew exactly what to do. He felt her entire body go rigid, every muscle tensing. Her fingers tightened on his, squeezing with bone-crushing force, and a low growl tore past her clenched teeth, rising with the intensity of her effort.

Liz, kneeling between Emily's legs, cried out, "I can see the baby," and Redd felt adrenaline surge through him.

It's happening. It's really happening.

He wanted to kneel down and see for himself, but at that moment, Emily's hand went slack in his.

"Keep pushing, babe," he exhorted, but she had nothing left.

"You got this!" said Liz. "One more big push!"

Emily managed a nod. "Next one," she gasped.

Liz glanced up at her husband. "Mikey, give her some water."

Mikey quickly grabbed a bottle from the front seat and handed it to Redd, who held it to Emily's lips, letting some of the liquid trickle in.

Emily did not deliver with the next contraction, nor the one after that. With each successive push, she seemed completely depleted, but during lulls in between, she found untapped reserves. Simply watching her endure the ordeal, unable to do anything more than hold her hand and whisper words of encouragement, left Redd feeling emotionally spent. And when, after nearly half an hour of hard labor, his daughter came into the world, he didn't even bother trying to blink away the tears.

✖   ✖   ✖

Wrapped in one of her father's sweatshirts, Lauren Redd—Emily had picked the name the moment she laid eyes on their daughter, and Redd loved it—had just started to settle down after the long process of coming into the world and was already taking her first nap snuggled in her mother's arms. Redd held Emily in his and almost laughed at the random absurdity of the whole situation.

Forget baptism by fire, he thought to himself. *More like birthing by fire.*

It certainly wasn't how he'd imagined bringing his daughter into the world, surrounded by fire and gunfights, but in a weird way, it was kind of perfect. At least for them. They had each other, and that's what mattered most. Even Mikey and Liz—their best friends in the world and the godparents to their children—got to be there for the birth of their little girl.

And, once again, they were there for Redd and Emily too.

"Sorry to interrupt," said Mikey, poking his head over the back of Redd's truck, where he, Emily, and Lauren lay, "but we might wanna head out pretty soon."

Redd nodded his agreement. "Thanks again for everything, Mikey. Really."

"Of course, brother. We love you guys, ya know. That little girl too. She sure is something." Mikey smiled. "You're lucky she got Emily's looks, though."

Liz appeared next to Mikey, joining the conversation. Like the rest of them, she looked exhausted but still wore a big relieved smile on her face. "Before we take off, I think someone's big brother wants to meet his new sister."

"Of course," said Emily. "Bring Luke too!"

A minute later, Mikey and Liz returned with Matthew Jr. and Luke. Little Matty beamed with pride when he saw his sister and gave her a tender kiss on the top of her fuzzy head. Lauren's hair was the same reddish-chestnut shade as Emily's, and all four adults agreed that they'd never seen an infant born with such a full head of hair.

Taking his eyes off his children, Redd noticed for the first time that Luke was carrying something in his arms. Suddenly, his heart sank.

Buzz Lightyear.

The realization jarred him out of the serene moment and sent a pang through his heart.

Jack . . .

Though he knew he'd done all he could to get to Jack and save him, it felt horribly unfair that one child was entering the world surrounded by people who loved her, who would do anything for her, even give their lives to protect her . . . and another one was in the hands of bad men, alone, scared, and facing certain death.

Worse yet, Jack didn't even have Buzz to keep him company.

Then Redd recalled his conversation with Kline.

"Raymond Williams had something on them . . . Some kind of key . . . They think Jack might be able to lead them to it."

"Can I see that, buddy?" Redd asked Luke.

The boy agreed and extended his arm, Buzz in hand, toward Redd.

Redd took the toy, turning it over to inspect it. Hadn't Mikey said something about the battery box?

Realizing what Redd was looking for, Mikey extended his key chain, holding up the small screwdriver attached to it. Redd thanked him, then unscrewed the cover and popped it open, revealing a battery compartment that, while containing no batteries, wasn't quite empty.

Taped inside, where three AAA batteries should have gone, was a microSD card. Redd turned the toy over, dumping the small memory chip into his palm.

"What is that?" asked Emily.

Redd stared in disbelief, a plan already forming in his head. "It's the key."

Mikey, Liz, and Emily all exchanged glances.

"The key . . . to *what*?" Mikey finally said.

Redd's eyes narrowed. He closed his fist over the chip and met his friend's gaze.

"The key to me getting Jack back."

FORTY-SIX

A sheriff's deputy found the pickup, abandoned and in flames, on a back road ten miles north of town less than half an hour after the call went out. With no emergency crews available, the deputy could do little more than watch the vehicle burn itself out, but from what he could tell, there were no human remains inside.

Redd got that news almost forty minutes later when, after a considerably slower-paced drive down from the mountains, his phone finally reconnected with the network. Sheriff Blackwood was optimistic that, despite the damage, there would be identifiable parts in the wreckage that would eventually lead back to the owner, but Redd found little comfort in the assurance. Tracing serial numbers from engine parts would take days—days that Jack didn't have. He only hoped that the microSD card would prove to be a better lead.

At Emily's direction, Redd drove straight to the clinic in Wellington. Although she had earlier judged the facilities less than adequate as a birthing center, with the hard part already done and baby Lauren the very picture of health, she deemed it suitable for postnatal and postpartum care and observation. "I'd say just take us home," she told Redd, "but you know . . . probably better to be close to medical care, just in case."

Redd had nodded.

Just in case.

Although he didn't tell her—she was still exhausted, drifting in and out of sleep during the long drive—he had reasons of his own for wanting to head into Wellington. The FBI agents from Bozeman had set up an ad hoc command center in the sheriff's office, and that was where the search for Jack would be coordinated.

Shortly after settling Emily into a room, with Lauren in a hospital bassinet next to her bed and Matty Jr. curled up beside her, Redd stepped out to hand the SD card off to Special Agent Todd Lyons, who self-identified as "Bozeman FO's resident cyber geek."

"I'll crack this ASAP and get back to you," Lyons had promised, leaving Redd to return to his family.

Half an hour later, Redd's phone buzzed with an incoming call from Gavin Kline. Redd stepped out of the room before accepting the call.

"Too soon for you to be on the ground," Redd said. "I hope this means you have some good news for me."

"Jury's still out," replied Kline. "That data card you brought us is looking like a gold mine of information, but we're still unpacking exactly what it all means."

"I take it that's the 'key' these guys were after?"

Kline hesitated before answering. "Well, it's *a* key," he explained. "A 256-bit encryption key, to be precise. What it unlocks is an offshore bank account, which is almost certainly being used for illegal activities. We're talking billion-dollar transactions funneled through a chain of shell companies."

Redd sensed that Kline was still holding back. "Does it give us anything we can use to find Jack? Names? Addresses?"

After another conspicuous delay, Kline said, "This thing has more layers than an onion. That's what I meant about still unpacking it. Given its provenance and what we already know, I think it's safe to say we'll be able to use it to shut ParaDyme down. It's just not clear yet exactly *how* we'll do that."

"I don't care about ParaDyme, Gavin." Redd's initial hopefulness had already given way to frustration. Now he felt anger flaring like heat in his extremities. "I want something that'll lead me to where they're keeping Jack."

"Matt, I know this isn't ideal—"

"Ideal?" Redd exploded. "The kid has lost everyone he's ever loved. Now he's by himself, probably being . . ." He couldn't bring himself to finish the thought

out loud. "He can't even give them what they want, and when they figure that out . . ." He stopped short again, reining himself in. "Isn't there someone at ParaDyme you can arrest? Lean on them until they give up whoever's working for them out here?"

"Right now, they don't know that we have the key. That gives us time to map this organization out. Figure out who the players are. If we move now, they'll circle the wagons. And you're right. Once they realize we have the key, they won't have any reason to keep Jack around."

Redd, feeling his temper flare once again, took a deep breath to steady his nerves. "Gavin, please. You gotta give me something here. I know it's your job to investigate ParaDyme and all that, but I just want the kid."

When Kline didn't respond, Redd added, "Are you telling me there's *nothing* we can do . . . no hornet's nest to kick or trail that'll lead us to Jack?"

Kline's long sigh was audible over the line. "There might be a way, but . . ." Redd could almost visualize the FBI director shaking his head. "It will mean showing our cards. Once we do that—"

"Do it. If there's a chance, do it."

"Matt, listen to me just a second, okay?" Kline paused a beat. "You literally *just* had a baby. This is going to be dangerous. There are other ways. It'll just take time. But," he said quickly before Redd could interrupt him again, "if you want to move on this now . . . are you really willing to risk your life to bring this boy back home? Because I need to know that honestly before I even think about playing the only card I have."

Redd's anger slowly subsided. There was a part of him that appreciated Gavin's forthrightness. In the past, Kline had made a decision to keep Redd out of harm's way without ever consulting him. Maybe it was the fatherly thing to do, but that hadn't made the situation any easier for Redd to swallow.

At least he's letting me have some say now, even if he disagrees with me.

"I'll do whatever it takes to make sure the kid is brought back safe."

"Okay," signed Kline. "But just know that we're not only betting with that boy's life but yours too."

Redd set his jaw. "Then let's make sure we win."

FORTY-SEVEN

Jack wasn't afraid.

He had been at first. When the bad men showed up at the hotel, and then later, when they'd driven into the fire . . . But each time, he had thought about Matt. How Matt had saved him, both from the bad man and the fire. So when that same bad man had grabbed him, dragged him into the back of his pickup, and then tied him up, he'd been a little afraid, but not like before. And then, when he caught just a glimpse of Matt, already fighting the other bad men, his fear had mostly left him.

The bad guy had driven off before Matt could rescue him, but the simple fact that Matt *had* come for him filled Jack with hope.

Matt will come for me again, he kept telling himself. *He's gonna find me.*

I've got to be strong. Just like Matt.

Everything that happened after that had been like a bad dream he couldn't wake up from. Not a nightmare, though. Not anything that filled him with terror or made him shake with fear. He didn't pee his pants—though he *really* did have to go—or even cry. He'd just had to lay on the floor in the back of the pickup with his wrists tied together so tight he couldn't feel his fingertips anymore while the pickup rattled and bumped down the road.

The bad man had stopped twice. Jack didn't know why he'd stopped the first time, but the second time, he'd dragged Jack out and made him get into another truck with more bad men.

"I have to go to the bathroom," he said, trying to hide the quaver of fear in his voice.

"Go in your pants," growled the bad man, the man who had killed his Uncle Raymond and Aunt Janelle and who had tried to kill *him*. "I don't care."

But then another one of the men spoke up. "C'mon, Dean. If he does that, it'll stink up the truck."

The bad man—Dean—snorted but then pulled Jack to him. "All right, kid. I'm gonna cut you loose for a minute. Don't even think about doing anything stupid."

Jack didn't know how to answer that, so he said nothing. He felt a slight surge of fear when Dean took out a big knife and used it to cut the plastic ties holding Jack's wrists together. For a few seconds after his hands were free, Jack couldn't make his fingers work, but then he felt pins and needles shooting through his skin. The feeling was so intense he almost cried out, but instead, he began rubbing them in an attempt to stop the sensation.

"Come on, kid. We don't have all night."

"Where should I—"

"Git," snarled Dean. He jerked his thumb toward the side of the road. "Go over there somewhere, but I'm warning you—if you do something stupid and I have to chase you down, you're not gonna like what happens."

Jack hadn't even been thinking about trying to run away, but when the suggestion was made, he started to.

Should I run? I'm pretty fast.

But he didn't know where he was or where he should run to. And if he did run and they caught him . . . this time, Matt wouldn't be there to save him.

Not yet, he told himself.

When he came back to the truck, Dean didn't tie him up again. Instead, he just told him to get in and lie on the floor. Then he threw a smelly old blanket over him. After that, there had been more driving, but this time on regular roads. The gentle hum of road noises made him drowsy, and before long, he was fast asleep.

He awoke to the sensation of someone tugging at his foot. "C'mon, kid. Rise and shine."

Jack looked up and saw a world glowing orange, not with firelight but illuminated by what looked like big streetlights. After a few seconds of confusion, he remembered where he was and how he had come to be there.

The truck was no longer moving, and the person trying to rouse him—Dean—was standing outside the vehicle, reaching in through an open door. The pickup was parked next to a big building. Jack's first thought was that it was a factory, but it was different than the factories he was used to seeing in Chicago. It was too quiet. And, instead of being surrounded by other factories, it looked like it was out in the country, surrounded by tall trees. The only really familiar thing he noticed was a couple of boxcars sitting on some train tracks near the factory building.

"Come on out," said Dean, stepping back.

Jack did as instructed, scooting to the door and then hopping onto the gravel of the parking lot. That was when he saw that in addition to Dean and the men who had been riding with him, there were two more people. One of them was a big man with gray hair who kind of looked like Dean, only fatter and with a white mustache that came down on both sides of his mouth all the way to his chin. Jack thought the man looked angry.

The other person was a woman. Most of the women Jack had known were nice to him, even if they did treat him like a little kid sometimes. As a result, he usually trusted them. There was something about this woman, however, that made him wary.

She wasn't scary looking, like a witch from a cartoon or movie. But when she smiled at him, he felt a chill go down his spine. "Hello, there. You must be Jack."

Her voice was sugary sweet, but Jack knew there was poison underneath it. He imagined that, just under her skin, she was a snake, trying to draw him closer so she could sink her fangs in.

He didn't have the breath to speak, so he just nodded.

"Well, Jack, I know you've been through a lot, but all that's over now. You're going to be okay. Understand?"

He knew she was lying but nodded again anyway.

"But there's something I need you to do first." She held out her hand with something pinched between her thumb and finger, but Jack couldn't tell what it was. "Have you ever seen one of these before?"

Jack definitely had not. He shook his head.

"Are you sure?" pressed the woman. "Maybe somebody that you know had one? Maybe your Uncle Raymond?"

He must have reacted somehow because a moment later, the woman nodded. "That's right. I know Raymond. He worked for me. He took something that belonged to me, and I need it back. It's very important, Jack. So, if you know where it is, you need to tell me."

Jack shook his head again. "I don't know where it is."

The denial came out like a squeal, and Jack instantly felt ashamed. He should have been tough and strong like Matt, not crying like a little baby.

The woman stared at him for several seconds. "All right, Jack. Maybe I believe you. But tell me this. When you left Chicago, did Raymond stop anywhere?"

The question confused him. Why did she want to know that? It had taken them a few days to drive out to Montana, and they had stopped a bunch of times. He gave a tentative nod.

"Where did you stop?"

He answered with a shrug. "Lots of places. McDonald's. Gas stations. Parks."

The woman glanced over at the man with the big mustache, then looked at Jack again. "If we took you back there, do you think you could point out all the places where you stopped?"

Jack just stared at her. He didn't think he could do what she was asking but was afraid to admit it.

"This is hopeless," grunted the man with the mustache. "He doesn't know anything. This is a waste of time."

The woman stared at Jack for several more seconds, then turned to the man again. "You could be right."

"So, what do we do now? We've got exposure on this. My boy—" His voice broke, leaving the sentence unfinished.

"I know," snapped the woman. "Let me think."

The man crossed his arms over his chest. "You'd better come up with something. And quick."

The woman's forehead got all wrinkly, and her face screwed up, making her look a little bit like the evil witch that Jack knew she was. Then she straightened. "We have to sanitize the operation. Destroy everything. Just in case."

"Destroy it all?" the man said, clearly not happy about this decision. "What good will that do?"

"The trail might lead back to us, but if there's no evidence, they've got no case."

"What about the money trail? If they've got the key— "

"We can't do anything about that," said the woman, her voice rising with anger. "All we can do is cover our tracks here." She paused a beat, then added, "We knew this might happen someday."

"And what about . . . ?" The man's head bobbed in Jack's direction. "Should I . . . ?"

Jack wasn't fooled by the unfinished questions.

He's talking about me.

"Don't do it here," the woman replied. "Take care of it along with everything else."

Take care of it . . . He's going to kill me.

The woman had lied when she'd told Jack that he would be okay. But then, he had known she was lying the whole time.

The man with the mustache frowned. "You know, if this is a false alarm, we'll be destroying millions of dollars' worth of equipment. Never mind the product. This will set us back years."

"I don't see an alternative."

The man stroked his chin. "What if I could give you one?"

The woman stared at him. "I'm listening."

FORTY-EIGHT

CHICAGO

One of the best perks that came with running a pharmaceutical company, Martin Waldron had discovered early on, was access to a . . . well, a whole pharmacy worth of clinical-grade mood-altering chemicals. Whatever a situation might demand—something to pick him up or help him focus, something to calm him down, something to get the blood flowing to the right places, or something to take his mind away—all it took was an informal visit to the R and D lab, and he could get whatever he needed or, as was often the case, try out some new concoction cooked up by one of the techs.

After his visit from FBI Special Agent Treadway, Waldron had known he needed something. He just wasn't sure what.

Marina probably would have told him to take a sedative—maybe a benzo or even some oxy—and then go home and keep his head down while she took care of the problem. But as tempting as that sounded, he knew that what he really needed most was some distraction. So, after popping a couple tabs of a little designer product from his friends in the lab—"like molly mixed with cocaine"—he'd left the office and had his driver take him straight to The Manse, his new favorite club.

He was flying high by the time the limo pulled up at the unmarked entrance to the club, down an alley on Clark Street. Feeling like a human plasma ball—he could literally see streamers of energy radiating from his fingertips—he bypassed the line of prospective clients waiting to be judged for fitness to enter and, returning a casual salute from the bouncer stationed at the velvet rope, went inside, his heart already beating in time with the house music pumping from the sound system.

His heightened senses sucked in the energy of the place like a sponge. The throbbing beat reverberated through his body, setting his nerve endings on fire. The flashing lights and lasers, the swirl of bodies on the dance floor, the mélange of perfumes and body sprays barely covering body odor . . . It was just the sort of stimuli overload he needed to take him away from his troubles.

As if on autopilot, he floated through the crowd, seeking out the VIP section situated on a balcony overlooking the main floor. He was vaguely aware of the women—beautiful, stacked, scantily clad women who had no difficulty getting past the velvet rope—circling like sharks, looking for someone to take care of them for the rest of the night. But in his present euphoric state, they were merely part of the tableau. Maybe later, when he came down a little, he'd dip his toe in those waters, but right now, he was content to simply float on the ether.

He barely even noticed a waitress placing a tumbler filled with amber liquid atop a cocktail napkin on the table in front of him.

"I didn't order that," he mumbled dreamily.

The waitress was already gone, but another voice said, "You look like someone who drinks scotch."

The woman had to shout to be heard over the music, but something about the voice seemed familiar to him. Dangerously familiar. He looked up and into the smiling face of a stunningly beautiful woman.

This was not an especially remarkable development, not at The Manse and not for someone with Martin Waldron's net worth, but there was something familiar about this one.

Where have I seen you before?

When he figured it out, he immediately wished he'd done what Marina would have wanted him to and gone straight home. Strangely—or maybe not, owing to the chemicals in his bloodstream—he felt no trepidation.

Actually, he felt like Superman.

"Special Agent Treadway." He waggled an accusatory finger at her. "You aren't supposed to be talking to me without my lawyer."

Treadway stepped around the table and took a chair opposite him. "Can't a girl just buy a guy a drink?"

The line probably would have sounded more sincere had she not been required to practically shout it at the top of her lungs, but the result would have been the same. "Nice try." He threw a mocking wave. "Buh-bye."

Treadway didn't take the hint. Instead, she began scooting her chair around to get closer. Waldron knew he should probably do something—either get up and leave or try to have security show her out—but he found himself enjoying the game.

Once she was right beside him, she leaned close and spoke directly into his ear. "We've got the key."

The declaration cast a cold shadow over his euphoria. He was still flying too high to feel anything remotely like fear, but he knew this was catastrophic news.

If they've got the key, they know everything.

"I know you know what that means," the FBI agent continued. "I'm here as a courtesy, with a one-time offer. You can get out ahead of this and save yourself. Or . . ." She shrugged. "Take your chances."

She leaned back and then, pitching her voice to a shout again, said, "I'm going to need an answer right now."

Waldron felt a surge like electricity in his veins as raw adrenaline supercharged his chemically induced state. He felt like his heart was going to explode.

The FBI agent was offering him a deal. But what kind of deal? Complete immunity? Not likely. Then again, what was the alternative? Go to prison for the rest of his life?

This was all Marina's fault. It had been her idea from the start. She had used him like a puppet. Set him up to take the fall if things went sideways.

He didn't owe her anything.

Gotta think this through. What do they really know?

They had the key. They knew everything.

Treadway shrugged again. "It's your funeral." She pushed away from the table, stood up, and started to leave.

Waldron reached out with a restraining hand. "Let's talk."

FORTY-NINE

MONTANA

Like its namesake, the Raptor flew through the night with Redd at the wheel, Mikey riding shotgun, and Rubble curled up on the floor in the back. They were heading west on Interstate 90 toward Missoula, the last leg of a long journey that, Redd hoped, would end with the safe return of Jack from his captors and justice for their many victims.

He glanced down at the Buzz Lightyear action figure resting on the center console.

I'm coming, Jack. Just hang on, buddy.

In the early days of his marriage, Redd had felt conflicted whenever FBI business took him away from home. Even though Emily had never been anything but supportive of his secondary career, he had always thought of it as a separate part of his life, one that too often made demands that carried over into his "real" life—his life with her.

Now, he didn't feel like he was making a choice between being with his family and saving the world from the bad guys. This was different even if Jack wasn't part of his family.

There's something about this kid, thought Redd, pushing his foot harder into the Raptor's accelerator.

When Redd had gently roused Emily to let her know what was going on, she had once again been unequivocal with her support. "Go get him back," she had told him. "We'll be fine here."

That conversation had come shortly after the second phone call from Kline, detailing the information that Stephanie Treadway had been able to elicit from Martin Waldron, the CEO of ParaDyme Pharmaceuticals.

Waldron had sung like the proverbial canary, providing names and details to supplement the picture that was emerging from a forensic examination of the bank account unlocked by the encryption key Raymond Williams had taken from ParaDyme.

Waldron had sung loudest when implicating his sister, Marina, as the real mastermind of an illicit narcotics manufacturing and trafficking network. Using Martin as her proxy, she had made extensive use of ParaDyme's resources to build her organization, tapping the expertise of scientists and technicians to streamline production, utilizing the company's access to foreign suppliers of precursor materials necessary for the manufacture of drugs like fentanyl, and capitalizing on their relationship with physicians like Mark Dickerson who, constrained by federal guidelines, were no longer able to recklessly prescribe opioid painkillers but could refer their former patients to a new source of the drugs. The ill-gotten proceeds had been funneled into Marina's nonprofit charitable foundation—little more than a money-laundering operation hiding behind a veneer of philanthropy.

If Marina Waldron was the brains of the operation, then a Missoula man named Otis Werner was the muscle. And pretty much everything else.

The file on Werner was thin. Aside from a couple of brushes with the law in his early twenties—petty crime, assault, none of which had resulted in felony convictions—he had stayed out of trouble. Or at least had kept any illegal activities well below the radar. For most of his adult life, he had worked for BNSF Railway, but in 2016, he had taken early retirement and purchased a controlling interest in a struggling lumber mill outside Missoula. According to Martin Waldron, the mill produced only a token amount of lumber—just enough to maintain the illusion that it was still a functional operation—camouflaging its real purpose as a fentanyl production and distribution center, supplying product from the Pacific Northwest to the Midwest.

That law enforcement agencies were unaware of the operation was nothing short of astonishing and a testimony to Otis Werner's efficiency and ruthlessness. Martin Waldron, who had no direct interactions with Werner, was unable to illuminate the means by which the man maintained control of the organization but did indicate that it was a "family operation." That information had yielded two more names of interest: Werner's adult sons Dean and Holt, both of whom had been considerably less adept at avoiding legal entanglements. Redd recognized them instantly from their mug shots.

Both men had done hard time at the Montana State Penitentiary. Holt, the older of the two, had reportedly gotten involved with a white power gang during his stint, and it was unclear if that allegiance continued outside the institution. Although Waldron could not confirm it, Kline suspected that Otis Werner was sympathetic to the white supremacist cause and used former inmate gang members as enforcers in his organization.

Kline had wasted no time mobilizing his forces in preparation for a raid on Werner's mill. Armed with a federal warrant, he began coordinating with the Bozeman FO while still in the air, and by the time his plane set down, nearly every agent assigned to the region was geared up and ready to roll out.

The lack of detailed intelligence about Werner's operation posed a real problem. Under any other circumstances, the FBI would have taken their time, gathered intelligence, and built an airtight case against Marina and Werner before moving in and rolling up the operation in one fell swoop. Unfortunately, time was the one thing they didn't have. According to Martin Waldron, Werner was already alerted to the possibility that his operation might be compromised. His sister had, in fact, traveled to Missoula earlier that evening to sound the alarm. Moreover, Werner had Jack, and if there was even a chance of rescuing the boy, the raid couldn't wait.

Redd had asked to participate in the takedown, but Kline had vetoed the suggestion. "We don't need more frontline shooters," he had told Redd.

As much as he wanted to be at the tip of the spear, Redd understood the tactical reasons for Kline's position. The FBI SWAT team that would conduct the raid functioned much like a military team, training and rehearsing together until there was an almost psychic bond between them. To add an outsider, even a highly trained military operator like Redd, at the last minute had the potential to be fatally disruptive.

But Redd had suggested a different role for himself. "I want to be there for Jack. When the dust settles, I want him to see a friendly face."

"I don't have a problem with that," Kline had replied. "But I want you to give me your word that you'll stand by until we give the all clear."

Redd gave his word. But he also brought along his guns.

Before leaving, Redd had called Mikey to ask him to check in on Emily and the kids. Mikey, however, had a different idea. "I'm going with you," he declared flatly. "Don't even try to talk me out of it."

Redd didn't. He understood the helplessness that came with failing to protect the people he cared about.

They'd driven down to the FBI's newest field office, located a few miles south of Bozeman Yellowstone International Airport, where Kline was conducting the final briefing before moving out. To avoid possibly tipping off Werner, the raid would be conducted exclusively by FBI agents with no support or input from local law enforcement agencies—a move that would certainly generate political blowback, but with the life of a hostage on the line, Kline was confident that he could handle it, provided the operation was a success.

They moved out in a convoy of unmarked vehicles with Redd and Mikey trailing behind. Owing to the late hour, there was hardly any traffic on the freeway. Aside from the occasional eighteen-wheeler and a southbound train on the tracks that ran parallel to the highway, Redd might have believed they were the last human beings on earth. They drove in relative silence, though Redd suspected Mikey would have preferred anything—music or an audiobook—to Redd's stoic quiet. Redd, however, wanted no distractions. In his mind, the mission had already begun.

The lumber mill was located about ten miles west of Missoula, on a county road just off the highway. During the briefing, Kline had circulated aerial photographs of the complex, designating the various assembly and rally points, as well as the overall tactical plan.

The photo, downloaded from Google Earth and cross-checked against government satellite imaging, showed a large multistory rectangular structure with a few smaller satellite structures. There was also a long chain belt for moving cut timber into the building and a couple of smaller conveyor belts that evidently shuttled chips and other waste material to hoppers where they could be loaded into trucks. The image, which was a few years old, showed only a few vehicles in the parking lot; otherwise the mill looked abandoned. No supply of logs in the yard, no piles of wood chips around the conveyors. The apparent absence of activity might have been merely a matter of timing, but if Martin Waldron had not been misled, the mill was producing something other than wood products.

Even though he and Mikey wouldn't be part of the raid, Redd had committed the site plan to memory, and as they drove, he ran through various scenarios, not only imagining himself as part of the assault team but also putting himself in the shoes of the bad guys. The iterations played out in his mind's eye like a first-person shooter video game. He was particularly concerned with egress points, specifically the fact that there were too many of them. In addition to the main road, the satellite image showed evidence of several dirt tracks along with an overground and apparently disused railroad siding. Once the shooting started, it would be nearly impossible to lock down all the escape routes.

After war-gaming dozens of possible outcomes, Redd decided the best place for him and Mikey was at the junction with the highway. The one drawback to this position was that he would have to follow the progress of the raid from a distance. But if things went sideways or the bad guys tried to make a run for it with Jack as a hostage, he'd be in a prime position to move in if needed.

Sitting in the darkness, he listened to the traffic on the primary tactical frequency, the same frequency Kline would be using to orchestrate the assault. Redd was used to listening in on radio chatter and had little difficulty following along, but it was a new experience for Mikey, so Redd provided commentary.

"They're using drones to recon the objective," he explained. Then after a few more transmissions, he said, "That's odd."

"What's odd?"

"No vehicles on the grounds. The place looks completely abandoned."

Mikey sat with this for a moment before offering a suggestion. "Maybe they pulled them all inside. Like a garage or something."

The agents operating the drones had suggested something similar. There was a large roll-up door on the west side of the mill building, which probably served as a maintenance bay for the mill's fleet of vehicles and heavy lift trucks.

As the drones moved all around the mill, the SWAT team adjusted their assault plan in real time, making note of open areas where they would be exposed and identifying potential choke points and escape routes. What they did not say aloud, but what Redd sensed based on the reports, was that the operation was already a bust. The drones, equipped with infrared cameras and directional microphones, weren't picking up any signs of life inside the mill buildings. While it was possible to fool such technologies, the likelier explanation was that the bad guys had already fled the scene, if they had ever been there at all.

Redd's initial guarded optimism evaporated quickly as the reports came in. He tried not to let his increasing despair bleed through into his commentary on the raid. Eventually, Kline ordered the SWAT team to begin movement onto the objective, but as reports continued to come in, Redd's heart sank to new depths.

The mill was a dry hole. If Jack had even been there, he was now long gone.

FIFTY

When Kline gave the all clear, signaling that it was safe for the main force of FBI agents to move in and begin collecting evidence, Redd drove up the road to join them. The FBI vehicles were lined up outside the main gate, their occupants proceeding on foot into the complex. Redd parked the Raptor at the end of the line, and after Rubble marked the wheel of a government-issue Suburban, they all headed inside.

The mill looked almost exactly as Redd had imagined it would based on the satellite photos and the reports from the drone operators and SWAT team, with one big difference. It was completely abandoned. The parking lot, illuminated by the pink-orange glow of overhead sodium-vapor lights—the only sign that some-one was still paying the electric bill—was empty of vehicles. The large building that housed the sawmill was dark inside. Its doors stood open, as did the doors of the satellite buildings—modular prefabricated structures that looked like old double-wide mobile homes—but these, too, did not appear to have been used in years. The yard was completely devoid of either cut logs or banded stacks of lumber waiting to be shipped out. Tumbleweeds and growths of wild grass and other weeds suggested that the mill hadn't been operational in some time.

Dozens of FBI agents were deployed throughout the complex, moving in and out of the buildings carrying out their assigned duties. A few of them looked askance at Rubble, probably worried that his presence might inadvertently destroy some critical piece of evidence, but none of them said a word to Redd. He watched them go about their business for a few minutes until he located Kline.

"What happened?" Redd asked, striving to keep the anger he was feeling in check. He knew the FBI director wasn't to blame for the failure.

Kline, looking similarly frustrated, waved his hand in a *look around* gesture. "Our intel was bad. Either Martin Waldron lied to Stephanie or his sister wasn't keeping him in the loop."

Redd took another look around the mill. "You said that the sister came out here to warn them. Could they have cleared out before we got here?"

"Maybe. If they did, they took everything. There's no indication that this was ever a processing facility."

Redd bit back a curse, took a breath, and asked, "What do we do now?"

"We'll hit Werner's residence, but I doubt we'll find him there. I'll have Stephanie take another swing at Martin Waldron. Maybe there's something he forgot to tell us. Any deal he might hope to make is contingent on us bringing in Marina and the Werners."

"And Jack? What about him? Is he part of the deal?"

"Matt, I know it's frustrating, but we're doing everything we can."

"You said they took *everything*?" said Mikey, speaking up for the first time.

Kline shot him a sidelong glance. "If there was ever anything here to begin with . . . yeah. The place looks picked clean. I'm going to bring in dogs to see if we can at least find some trace evidence."

"I'm just wondering," Mikey went on. "What would an operation like that look like? I mean, what sort of equipment would you need? How many people would it take to run it? Would you need a place to store your materials and the finished product? Or is this something that you could operate, say, in an old Winnebago?"

A faint smile touched Kline's lips. "Based on the numbers in that bank account, I'd say the volume of production would somewhat exceed the capacity of a mobile laboratory in the back of an RV."

"So it would take a while to pack up everything, right?" continued Mikey, sounding very much like a detective in a murder mystery—Poirot or Columbo— parsing the details to get at some critical and heretofore overlooked clue. "I mean, you couldn't just load it all in the back of a pickup and drive off."

"No, I don't imagine you could." Kline's answer was thoughtful, as if he was just starting to grasp the significance of what Mikey was driving at.

"Figure they had . . . what, a four-hour head start on us? Would that be enough time to pack up and move out?"

Kline shook his head. "That would be cutting it close. But that just leads me to believe that they were never here to begin with. Or they moved the operation somewhere else a long time ago."

"Then why did Otis Werner hang on to this place? Why not sell it? Or start cutting lumber again?"

"Maybe he held on to it as a decoy."

"A pretty expensive decoy," remarked Redd. "Have you seen lumber prices since the pandemic?"

"All right," said Kline, addressing Mikey. "I take it you have an alternative explanation?"

Mikey's grin was answer enough. "If I was going to set up a super-secret drug lab, I would make it mobile."

Despite himself, Redd couldn't help but laugh aloud.

Mikey shot him a withering glance.

"Sorry," said Redd. "I'm just picturing you slinging drugs. Liz would probably kill you."

Mikey rolled his eyes and then continued. "All right, so not a Winnebago, but maybe put it inside some shipping containers. I've read about people doing that. Burying shipping containers and using them for underground meth labs and mushroom farms. But why bury it when you can operate aboveground?"

Kline listened without comment, but Redd could see the wheels turning in the FBI director's head.

"I figure I'd need one or two containers dedicated to production. Bring in more of them full of whatever chemicals you need to make the drugs. Store them right here." Mikey gestured to the empty yard. "And then load the empties up with product and ship them out. Easy peasy. The best part is, if I ever got wind of the law sniffing around, I could just hook up to a few big rigs and move the whole operation off-site until the heat dies down."

Mikey glanced over to Redd as if looking for a vote of confidence. Redd turned to Kline. "I gotta admit, it makes sense."

Kline remained silent for a long moment, his gaze moving between the two men as he considered Mikey's theory. "If you're right," he said, "if that's what happened, they could be a couple hundred miles from here."

"I'd say no more than a hundred," said Mikey. "Even allowing them a four-hour head start, it would take an hour or two to bring in the big rigs and get everything hooked up. And that's assuming they didn't just pull into a truck stop or Walmart parking lot to wait this out."

Kline nodded slowly. "I'm not one hundred percent sold on this idea, but at the moment, I don't really have anything better." He took out his phone. "I'll need to bring local LEOs in on this. MHP can set up floating inspection points on all the highways within a one-hundred-fifty-mile radius, and Missoula County Sheriff's Department can start checking out long-term parking areas. We won't tell them what we're looking for. Just to report anything suspicious."

As Kline began making calls, Mikey turned to Redd. "I'm sorry."

Redd stared back at him. "Why? Your idea is solid."

"I mean, I'm sorry we didn't get here sooner."

"Yeah. Me too." Redd sighed. He gazed out across the desolate yard of the lumber mill.

Was Jack ever here? How long ago? Did we miss him by hours or just minutes? Is he even still . . .

He shook his head, banishing the thought before it could take root in his head.

He's alive. Hold on, Jack, I'm coming . . .

He turned back to Mikey. "Come on. There's something I want to check out."

Mikey followed him across the yard and around to the rear of the mill building, where Redd stopped and stared out across the tumbleweed-strewn railroad tracks.

"What are you thinking?" asked Mikey.

Redd didn't answer right away but instead kicked at the nearest tumbleweed, sending it rolling away from the tracks. Rubble, apparently believing that this was some new game, began nosing the beach-ball-size orbs back onto the tracks, forcing Redd to give him a sharp "sit" command. Redd gradually uncovered a section of the siding about ten yards long, after which he knelt down and examined the track. The tops of the rails, polished by the friction of rolling train cars, reflected the orange glow of the overhead light like embers.

"There's no rust on these rails. And there isn't anything growing on the track bed." He straightened and moved farther down the siding, kicking away more tumbleweeds and easily clearing another ten yards of track. "Somebody covered the tracks to make it look like they're not in use."

Mikey nodded as comprehension dawned. "They weren't using shipping containers. They were using train cars."

"Before he bought this place, Otis Werner worked for BNSF. He knows the railroad. He probably still has connections."

"We passed a train on the way up here."

Redd nodded. "That was . . . what, forty minutes ago? Maybe twenty miles south of here? The timing would be about right."

Mikey started to nod but then shook his head, his enthusiasm giving way to skepticism. "You really think he could just whistle up a train on a moment's notice? I mean, it can't be as simple as that, can it?"

Redd had been aware of trains his whole life, but especially during the years he'd spent growing up in Montana. The railroads often ran parallel to interstate highways but also connected with rural small towns. There was a line that passed through Wellington. He had seen trains on cross-county hauls that seemed to stretch out for miles, pulled by five or six locomotives working together, but more often than not, what he saw were long chains of boxcars and tankers sitting idle on tracks, like orphans holding hands and waiting for someone to pick them up. Yet, even though trains were ubiquitous in the American landscape, Redd knew next to nothing about how the railroad system was organized.

He shook his head. "I don't know. But I'll bet Gavin can find out."

FIFTY-ONE

Carson Pruitt had just pressed the start button on the lunchroom microwave—beginning the three-minute cooking sequence that would, if past experience was any indication, almost completely desiccate the edges of his Lean Cuisine Fettuccine Alfredo while leaving the center a semifrozen glob—when his phone began buzzing in his pocket.

"Perfect timing, Carla," he muttered, fishing the device out, expecting to see his wife's name on the display.

She didn't usually stay up late enough to call him on his break, but when she did, it was almost always to complain about his schedule. When was he going to get off the graveyard shift so they could have a normal life?

As night shift supervisor for Big Sky Rail Link, a Missoula-based short line railroad servicing western Montana with connections to the BNSF Railway and Union Pacific Railroad, Pruitt had what many Americans did not—a stable, dependable job with a reasonably good income—and when he'd asked Carla Long to marry him, he'd thought she would appreciate that. But almost from the start of their life together, she had complained about him never being home at night and sleeping all day. She didn't need him to explain that there weren't any openings for a supervisor on the day shift or that losing his shift differential would mean cutting back on many of the things that constituted the "normal life" she was so envious of. Nor did she need to be reminded that she had known all of this before they got married.

But at three a.m., alone in bed and feeling lonely, none of that mattered.

He sighed, bracing himself for the expected tearful commiseration session that would devour his too-short break, and looked at the screen.

The call wasn't from Carla.

A wave of trepidation came over Pruitt. An after-midnight call from his department head was never a good thing, but the fact that the call was coming in on his personal phone was especially ominous. It meant that, whatever it was, it couldn't wait.

He hit the button to accept the call. "Mr. Cooper. What can I do for you?"

"Pruitt?" The chief dispatcher sounded irritable and a little confused, as if still not quite awake.

"Yes, sir."

"Uh, Pruitt, I've got someone from the FRA on the line. He needs some information about one of our trains. Can you handle it?"

Pruitt's anxiety eased, but only a little. Whatever this was about, it didn't sound like anything catastrophic, but still, why would the Federal Railroad Administration be calling in the middle of the night?

"Of course, sir." Leaving his Lean Cuisine in the still-humming microwave, Pruitt strode quickly down the hall to his workstation in the dispatch office.

"Just tell them whatever they need to know," Cooper went on. "You can tell me what it's all about tomorrow."

"Sounds good, sir."

"All right, I'm connecting you now." Cooper's voice dropped to a low grumble. "Hang on. I'll probably screw this up."

A double beep on the line indicated some kind of change, so Pruitt ventured a "Hello? This is Carson Pruitt."

A new voice came over the line. "Pruitt? Dave Mercer from FRA. I've got an interagency request for information about a possible pickup you might have made."

Pruitt settled into his workstation and brought up the screen that showed the scheduled activity of all BSRL trains. "Go ahead."

"I need to know if you accepted any consignments originating from an outfit called Bolton Lumber in the last twelve hours."

Pruitt switched to the customer database and typed *Bolt* into the search bar, bringing up the customer information for Bolton Lumber. He clicked through to the Orders screen, noting that Bolton Lumber was an infrequent customer of Big Sky Rail Link, sending and receiving only a few shipments each month. At the top of the list was the information his caller was looking for.

"Mr. Mercer? Yes, I can confirm that we did accept a consignment from Bolton Lumber earlier tonight. Three boxcars of cut lumber to be delivered to the UP yard in Butte."

"Boxcars?" asked Mercer, mildly surprised.

Boxcars, once a mainstay of the American railroad, were slowly disappearing from the landscape, replaced by specialized train cars like tankers or flatbeds that could be used to transport intermodal shipping containers full of freight. Most lumber mills loaded their outgoing shipments onto open gondolas, which were far more accessible than enclosed boxcars.

"That's what it says," replied Pruitt.

"And what time was this?"

"Looks like it was just after midnight." As he said the words, Pruitt was struck by the incongruity. Although BSRL trains ran twenty-four seven, service for small operators like Bolton Lumber usually occurred during business hours and was scheduled at least a couple of days in advance.

There was silence on the line, so Pruitt prompted, "Is there some problem with that shipment?"

Mercer didn't answer the question. "Where is that train right now?"

Pruitt switched back to the dispatch screen, selected the train, and then clicked over to the map display. "Looks like they just passed . . . Clinton."

Clinton?

His hesitancy arose from the fact that Clinton, not even a proper town, was only about twenty miles from Missoula, a distance that the train should have easily covered in about forty minutes. After two hours, it should have been halfway to Butte.

There was another pause, and then Mercer said, "Pruitt, I need you to stay on the line. I'll get back to you."

"Sure," replied Pruitt, but Mercer was already gone.

As he waited, Pruitt returned to the page with the information about the consignment from Bolton Lumber. The unusual timing of the pickup had aroused his curiosity almost as much as the fact that the FRA had singled it out for scrutiny.

What was so special about that shipment that it had to go out in the middle of the night?

The mystery deepened when he realized that the original order had come in only an hour before the pickup was scheduled. Not only that, but the train had been diverted off its original route to make the pickup.

This discovery flabbergasted him. After safety, one of the highest priorities of a train dispatcher was efficiency. Sending a train loaded with cargo meant to go somewhere else on a trip that would take it more than a hundred miles in the wrong direction would end up costing the company thousands of dollars in fuel and operating expenses.

He did a double take when he read the name of the dispatcher who had made the changes. "Hildy?"

The attractive peroxide blonde seated at the workstation to his immediate right was fixated on her own screen and appeared not to have heard him, so he said her name louder. "Hildy!"

She turned slowly toward him as if astonished that he would speak to her and replied with a nonverbal hum.

"Hildy, did you reroute a train to make a pickup at a lumber mill?"

She stared back at him as if confused by the question, but then something seemed to click. "Oh, that. Sales had me push it through. I guess there were special circumstances."

"Special circumstances? What does that mean?"

Hildy shrugged. "You'd have to ask the sales department. Someone probably dropped the ball. Forgot to hit the Submit button on an order, and now we all have to bend over backward to fix their mistake."

Pruitt frowned. It was a plausible enough explanation—it would hardly be the first time someone in sales had screwed up and then expected everyone in operations to clean up the mess. But something like that should have come across his desk first.

And why is the government suddenly interested?

As if on cue, a voice—not Mercer's—issued from his phone. "Mr. Pruitt?"

"This is Carson Pruitt."

"Mr. Pruitt, my name is Gavin Kline. I'm the director of the Federal Bureau of Investigation."

Pruitt sat back in his chair. A call from the Federal Railroad Administration was one thing, but the FBI? All he could think to say was, "Yes, sir?"

"I understand that one of your trains picked up some cars at a lumber mill outside Missoula earlier tonight."

"That's correct." Then, almost guiltily, Pruitt added, "It's all very irregular."

"And the train just passed Clinton?"

"Yes, that's correct. They're running slow for some reason."

"Are you able to communicate with that train?"

"Of course."

"I need you to order them to stop. Can you do that?"

"Stop?" Pruitt instinctively recoiled at the idea of halting a train—any train—without a very good reason but then remembered who he was talking to. "Yes, I can do that."

"Have it stop at . . ." There was a pause as the FBI man consulted with someone, then he came back. "Bonita Station Road. Just west of Ravenna."

"Stop at Bonita Station Road," Pruitt confirmed.

"Don't tell them why," Kline went on. "Say that there's a problem down the line. Something like that."

"I understand." Pruitt selected the train on the dispatch screen and tapped out a short message to the train's conductor, informing him of a delay requiring a safety stop at the Bonita Station Road intersection. After a few seconds, a reply came back acknowledging receipt.

"Okay, it's done," said Pruitt. "Can I ask . . . why?"

He didn't need any reason other than the fact that someone from the FBI was asking him to do it—the company had a policy of willing cooperation with law enforcement agencies—but his imagination was running wild. He visualized boxcars packed with terrorists wielding AK-47s and RPG launchers or crates containing stolen nuclear bombs. Or maybe someone was using the train to transport human trafficking victims.

"I'm afraid I can't give you the details right now, but on behalf of the United States government, let me say your cooperation is greatly appreciated." Kline ended the call on that note, leaving Pruitt to speculate.

Shaking his head, he turned to his coworker. "Hildy, you're never going to believe . . ."

But Hildy was gone.

He stood up, looking around the dispatch center, but there was no sign of the blonde woman. "Where's Hildy?"

"She went out to grab a smoke," answered one of the other dispatchers.

A smoke? Pruitt frowned. Company policy did not explicitly prohibit smoking, but it was discouraged, and employees were only permitted to smoke during scheduled breaks. Hildy wasn't due for one of those until after Pruitt's break ended.

I'm going to have to talk with her about that.

✖   ✖   ✖

Outside in the parking lot, "Hildy" lit her cigarette and took a long drag before taking her phone from her purse and making a call. When it was picked up, she simply said, "They know."

After a brief pause, the man on the other end of the line said, "All right. We knew this might happen. You get out of there. We'll see you in a few days. Just like we talked about."

"You be careful."

"I will. Gotta go."

"Love you, Dean."

But the call had already ended. She put the phone back in her purse, took another drag on the cigarette, dropped it to the ground, and stubbed it out. Then Angie Werner walked over to her car, got in, and drove away, never looking back.

FIFTY-TWO

In the passenger seat of the Raptor, Mikey gripped the armrests, eyes fixed on the road ahead, his right knee unconsciously tapping out a sewing machine rhythm. Redd watched his friend from the corner of his eye, wishing he could share Mikey's sense of excitement and anticipation. All he felt was dread.

The combination of Redd's intuition and Mikey's deduction had uncovered Otis Werner's unconventional escape route, providing a lifeline to Kline and his FBI agents who saw a chance to wrestle success from the jaws of abysmal failure. Werner's fentanyl operation was not only a tangible reality but now within their grasp, and when they caught up to the train and seized those boxcars, it would be a major coup for the Bureau—not just a seizure of product, but the takedown of a manufacturing operation with international reach.

Redd could not bring himself to share everyone's enthusiasm. Though he hid it behind a mask of stoicism, the uncertainty of Jack's fate hung over him like a thunderhead.

When Mikey had floated the idea of the drug lab operating from shipping containers, it hadn't been a stretch to visualize Dean Werner or some other face-less thug driving down the highway in an eighteen-wheeler with Jack bound and gagged in the seat beside him. Trucks needed drivers, after all, and that was a job Otis Werner wasn't likely to outsource. But how many people did it take to drive a train? Would any of Werner's minions even need to ride along? Were they hiding in the boxcars like hoboes of yesteryear riding the rails across America? It didn't seem likely, and if they weren't on the train, neither was Jack.

Kline, judiciously, had covered his bets, sending a small contingent of agents to Werner's Missoula residence. Redd had considered accompanying them, but his gut told him there was even less of a chance that Jack would be at Werner's home than on the train. His gut had not been wrong. The FBI agents had already reported back that not only was the house empty but it appeared as if the occupants had departed in some haste with no intention of ever returning. Otis Werner was in the wind. So was Jack.

Racing down Interstate 90, with the railroad tracks unseen in the darkness not even fifty yards away, Redd kept these forebodings to himself. He didn't want to burden Mikey with his pessimism, and he definitely didn't want to hear any well-intentioned platitudes.

Kline had ordered the train to stop at Bonita Station Road, which crossed under the freeway near a spot on the map called Ravenna, about twenty-five miles southeast of Missoula and about five miles beyond the train's last reported location. Traveling in excess of ninety miles per hour, Redd had estimated it would take them just fifteen minutes to reach that destination, where they expected to find the train and its unsuspecting crew sitting idle. Mikey, tracking their progress on the Raptor's GPS, had been dutifully providing updates on the remaining distance and estimated time of arrival, but as both numbers shrank almost to zero, a note of concern crept into his tone.

"The turnoff is coming up," he said, peering out the side window. "But I don't see the train."

Redd glanced over but, in the darkness, couldn't even see the tracks, much less anything that might have been on them. "Maybe it's still up ahead."

Mikey shrugged. "Yeah, maybe."

Brake lights flared brightly in front of them as the convoy slowed and then veered onto the exit ramp. Redd slowed as well, following the line of vehicles down the gentle grade to the intersection with Bonita Station Road. The FBI vehicles blew past the stop sign and made the right turn, then dispersed left and right, coming to a full stop on either side of the road. As he made the turn, Redd saw the railroad crossing, with its distinctive lights, red-and-white-striped gates, and X-shaped sign. The lights were dark, the gates vertical, the tracks empty.

Redd spotted the SUV Kline had been riding in now idling on the road just short of the crossing and pulled up beside it, rolling down his window as he came to a stop. The window on the SUV's front passenger door lowered as well, revealing Kline with a phone pressed to his ear.

"Where is it?" Redd shouted.

Kline nodded but held up a hand. "Well, is there any way to stop it remotely?" He frowned, the answer evidently not what he was hoping it would be.

"Where's the train?" Redd said as Kline lowered the phone.

"It didn't stop. And the dispatcher can't raise anyone in the locomotive."

Redd didn't need any more information than that. He hit the accelerator, pulled forward, and cranked the wheel hard to the left onto a narrow dirt two-track that ran alongside the railroad. The suddenness of the maneuver caused Mikey to jolt in his seat, flailing for a handhold as if the Raptor was on the verge of rolling over.

"What are you doing?" he gasped.

"Going after that train," Redd replied with calm determination, straightening the wheels and giving the truck more gas. The Raptor shot forward, leaving the FBI convoy in a cloud of dust.

After a moment or two, Mikey managed to unclench his death grip on the armrest. "Wouldn't it be easier to get back on the highway? You could go faster. Get ahead of them."

Redd glanced over at his friend, then brought his attention to the dirt track illumined in the Raptor's headlights. The two-track, evidently some sort of maintenance road, was a little smoother than the fire road he had driven earlier in the night, but the surface certainly wasn't conducive to a high-speed pursuit.

"Something tells me blocking the road isn't going to stop a freight train," he said. "I've got a different plan. Just hang on."

"Us pulling up behind it isn't going to stop it either," countered Mikey. "Tell me that's not your plan."

Redd winced. "Something like that."

"Why do I got the feeling this is about to suck?"

In truth, Redd didn't have it all figured out, but the urgency that had compelled him to begin the pursuit remained undiminished.

To Redd, the fact that the train had not stopped and its crew was not responding to the dispatcher meant only one thing: He'd been wrong to assume that Otis Werner would put the fate of his mobile drug lab into the hands of the railroad. Werner's men were in control of the train. Either they were holding the crew at gunpoint or, more likely, the crew themselves were loyal members of the organization.

And if Werner's men were on that train, Jack might be too.

He was spared having to explain his reasoning to Mikey by the trilling alert tone of an incoming call. The GPS map went black and then the console displayed the name of the caller. Kline.

Redd glanced at the screen, then returned his attention to the road ahead.

"Are you gonna answer that?" asked Mikey.

"Wasn't planning to."

He didn't need to look over to register Mikey's disapproving frown. Then, to his dismay, Mikey reached out and tapped the screen to accept the call.

Kline's voice filled the cab. "Matthew. I don't suppose you'd care to explain what you're doing?"

Kline sounded like a disapproving father, which, Redd supposed, was exactly what he was.

"I thought it was pretty obvious," retorted Redd. "I'm going after the train."

"Are you just mindlessly chasing after it like that dog of yours, or do you have some plan for what you'll do once you catch up to it?"

Redd grimaced at the comparison and glanced over his shoulder as if Rubble might have some insight on the subject. "I'm still figuring that out," he admitted. "But unless you're calling to tell me that you've got a better plan, I think I'll just keep doing what I'm doing."

There was only silence over the line.

"That's what I thought," Redd went on. "I'll call you back when I—"

Directly ahead, the two-track came to an abrupt end, as did the land beneath it. Beyond the precipice, there was only nothingness. The railroad, however, kept going, the tracks transitioning from the crushed-stone ballast of the track bed onto the steel supports of a bridge.

As a long-time Montanan, Redd knew that a section of Interstate 90 between Missoula and Butte ran along the course of the Clark Fork, the largest river by volume in the state and a major part of the Columbia River watershed. Only now did it occur to him that the railroad would also follow the river and occasionally cross it.

There wasn't time to stop and only one way to go, so Redd steered to the right.

The Raptor rode up the slight elevation onto the track bed, and then the front end bounced into the air as the front right tire hit the closest rail. Redd gripped the steering wheel tight, holding it steady as the truck came down, only to lurch again as the rear tire bounced over the rail. A moment later, they were on the bridge, the Raptor straddling the leftmost rail and vibrating fiercely as it rolled across the closely spaced railroad ties. Rubble let out a wail of dismay, and Redd probably would have done the same if not for the fact that he was holding his breath, fighting to keep the truck under his control.

The space between the rails was narrower than he'd realized, only about four and a half feet, considerably less than the Raptor's sixty-seven-inch rear track width—the distance between the centers of the truck's rear tires—which meant that in order to keep the left wheels on the ends of the railroad ties outside the left rail, he was dangerously close to running up against the inside edge of the rail on the right. A deviation of just an inch or two and he would sideswipe the rail. If that happened, the best he could hope for was that the Raptor's tires would simply rebound away, putting him back on course. But it was far more likely that the truck might bounce out of control, careening into or over the low sides of the bridge.

The span bridged a distance of only about a hundred yards, and the crossing was over almost as soon as it had begun, but the punishing ride continued as the Raptor's big tires chattered across the railroad ties. Redd looked left, hoping to find another maintenance road running parallel to the railroad, but beyond the track bed, there was only a steep slope, falling away into darkness and, he could only presume, the river.

Kline's voice cut through the din filling the cab. "Matt! What's going on there?"

Redd couldn't have answered even if he wanted to. Between the incessant rapid-fire thump of the truck's tires skipping over the tops of the railroad ties and the fact that it was taking all of his focus just to keep the truck running in a straight line, conversation was not only impossible but unthinkable.

We've got to get off these tracks.

He knew what he should do—slow down until an opportunity to steer carefully over the rail and off the track bed presented itself. But slowing down

GONE DARK

defeated the purpose that was driving him. It was speed that would save them . . . save Jack . . . not caution, so he maintained pressure on the gas pedal and held the wheel steady.

A few seconds later, he saw solid ground rising from the darkness to the left. *Finally.*

"Matt!" Mikey's voice was barely audible through the din, but the single syllable stretched to a frantic pitch and continued to rise as he repeated the utterance with escalating urgency. "Matt. Matt! *Matt!*"

Redd brought his gaze to the front, expecting to see another bridge looming ahead. Instead, he saw a mountain.

And a tiny round hole into which the railroad disappeared.

If it was possible, the tunnel appeared even narrower than the bridge, but Redd made a snap judgment and held his line, plunging the Raptor into the tunnel.

There was a noise like a gunshot as the driver's side mirror struck the wall and was sheared off. The passage suddenly lit up like daylight as the rough-hewn stone reflected and intensified the Raptor's headlights, like a flashlight beam shining down a rifle barrel. From the corner of his eye, Redd could see the tunnel wall flashing by, so close that it felt like there was nothing—no truck, no glass—between him and it.

Then the thing he was most afraid of at that moment happened.

How it happened, he would never know for certain. Maybe the glancing contact that had torn away the mirror gave the truck an unexpected nudge, or maybe the close proximity of the tunnel wall caused him to momentarily lose his nerve. Whatever the cause, one of the Raptor's wheels sideswiped a rail, and suddenly, the truck was bouncing back and forth atop the track bed.

In the open, the Raptor would almost certainly have flipped and rolled, turning cartwheels across the landscape, but in the close confines of the tunnel, there was nowhere for it to go. Instead, the truck simply caromed from one side of the tunnel to the other, like a golf ball in a downspout.

The cab was filled with the torturous shriek of metal grinding on stone. The fenders tore away in a spray of sparks. The side windows frosted over and then fell into the interior in a rain of diamonds.

Somehow, Redd brought the truck back under his control, only now the Raptor was straddling the right rail. Gripping the wheel so tightly it felt like it might snap, he held on until the far end of the tunnel came into view, and then, blessedly, they were outside again.

Any prayers of gratitude he might have offered were premature, however. No sooner were they out of the tunnel than another bridge appeared in their path. After the chaos in the tunnel, crossing a bridge seemed like a beginner-level task, but Redd took nothing for granted as he guided the Raptor onto the span.

The second bridge was even shorter than the first, and when they were back over solid ground, Redd saw another maintenance two-track veering away from the railroad on the right. Taking that as a good sign, he brought the truck nearly to a full stop and then cautiously rolled up and over the rails until they were off the track bed.

In the relative quiet that followed, he heard Mikey let out a long sigh.

"You okay, buddy?" Redd asked, glancing over.

Mikey didn't answer. He stared straight ahead, eyes wide as if he'd just witnessed the end of the world.

Not sure what else to do, Redd steered onto the two-track and started forward again. That was when he noticed that the console screen had changed back to the GPS map. The call from Kline had dropped, probably while they were in the tunnel. The service road didn't appear on the map, but the blue dot in the center of the display that marked the Raptor's present location floated next to a thin gray crosshatched line, which ran parallel to the yellow ribbon of the Interstate.

Redd looked over at his friend again. "Mikey. I need your help."

Mikey slowly turned his head, wordlessly meeting Redd's gaze.

Redd pointed to the GPS screen. "Check our route. I don't want any more surprises."

Mikey mouthed the word *surprises?*

"Mikey. Focus." Redd snapped his fingers.

The impatient gesture had the desired effect. Mikey jolted a little, then directed his attention to the screen, using his fingers to scroll the display forward. After a moment's scrutiny, he said, "All good."

The words were barely louder than a whisper. He cleared his throat and tried again. "All good. No tunnels. Got some big curves coming up in about a mile. The next bridge is a few miles ahead."

Redd breathed a little easier and put the pedal to the metal, pushing hard on the straightaway to make up for lost time.

As the speedometer needle climbed toward forty, the rush of air swirling in through the destroyed windows swelled to a veritable tempest, but the ride remained smooth, so Redd pushed the truck a little harder.

"Coming up on the turn!" Mikey warned.

Redd waited until he saw the road start to bend to the left before easing off the accelerator, ready to brake if the arc became too sharp. There was no need for the precaution, however. The bend in the two-track followed the bend in the railroad, which had been designed with train traffic in mind. The turn was long and gradual, and as the Raptor rounded the bend and the road ahead began to straighten, Redd renewed pressure on the gas pedal.

"There it is!" Mikey cried, pointing a finger toward the windshield.

Redd, whose focus had been on the road ahead, followed Mikey's line of sight, and then he saw it too.

The train itself was indistinct in the darkness, well beyond the reach of the truck's headlights, but the locomotive's headlamp shone brightly, revealing its location. Following the next bend in the track, the engine appeared to be traveling away at an almost perpendicular angle, but as the Raptor went into the same turn, this perspective changed, and the locomotive's light seemed to swing away and was lost from view.

A moment later, the truck's headlights revealed the rearmost car in the train.

They were close, no more than two hundred yards out, and quickly shrinking the intervening distance. Judging by the rate at which they were closing the gap, Redd guessed the train was only moving at about twenty or twenty-five miles per hour.

Mikey, evidently making the same observation, remarked, "I thought it would be going faster."

"Good thing for us it's not."

Mikey glanced over at him. "Well, now what?"

Redd nodded toward the last car, now less than a hundred yards away. "I'm getting on that train."

Mikey sighed. "I was afraid you were going to say that. Do I even want to know how?"

"Easy. You're going to pull up beside one of the cars and pace it while I climb across."

"I'm going to what now?"

"Once I'm aboard," Redd went on, "I'll make my way forward to the locomotive and order the engineer to put on the brakes."

"Can we go back to the part where you want *me* to drive next to a speeding freight train?"

"You just said it's not going that fast."

"That was before you told me your plan." He shook his head. "I'm not you, Matt. I don't do these things."

"You *can* do it. I'll set the cruise control. All you have to do is hold the wheel steady until I . . ."

He trailed off as the last train car, now less than twenty-five yards away, was fully illuminated by the Raptor's headlights.

It was a tank car.

As its name implied, a tank car was an enormous tank on a rail car chassis. They could be used to transport liquid cargo, ranging from refined oil to hazardous chemicals to raw milk. What was inside the tank was of little concern to Redd. His problem was what he saw on the outside.

When he had conceived his crazy plan to covertly board the train and then make his way up the line to the locomotive, he had imagined running across the roofs of the cars or sidling along on some sort of external catwalk or ledge. But the tank was perfectly cylindrical. There was a ladder mounted on the side of the tank in the middle, rising up to the filler hatch at its top, but nothing that continued down the length of the car and no ledge or platform at the end that might facilitate movement to the next car in line.

"Well, that's not gonna work," he muttered.

"What's not going to work?"

He shook his head and kept driving, passing the last car, only to discover that the next car in line was also a tank car.

So were the next four.

Aside from the obvious problem this presented, there was something about this configuration that nagged at him, but he couldn't put his finger on exactly what it was. Fortunately, the next car in line was not a tank car but something that looked sort of like a low-walled dumpster.

"Perfect." He continued forward until he was even with the front of the car— there was another just like it in the next position—then switched on the truck's cruise control, coasting until the truck matched the train's forward velocity.

"Why not just drive all the way up? Save time and jump onto the locomotive?"

"The idea is to not let them know I'm coming. Okay, take the wheel."

Mike reached across and grasped the steering wheel tentatively.

Redd raised his hands, indicating that he was ceding control. "I'm going out the window. Once I'm out, scoot over and take my seat. I'm going to climb back into the bed. When I give the signal, move in as close as you can. After I jump, just drop back and keep your distance."

He unbuckled his seat belt, then took his Ruger from the center console, absently noting that the Buzz Lightyear toy was gone—probably knocked askew during the wild ride through the tunnel.

Hang on, Jack. I'm coming . . .

He turned to Mikey. "Ready?"

"If I said no, would it matter?"

Redd gave what he hoped was a reassuring smile. "You've got this, buddy."

Mikey swallowed nervously.

Redd twisted in his seat, grasping the top of the doorframe with his free hand, but then an idea struck him. He looked down at the Ruger and then over to his friend again. "It just occurred to me."

"What?"

"Riding down a train with my six-shooter in hand . . . We've gone full Western around here."

A grin split Mikey's face, sweeping away his uncertainty. "Nah. If you were riding it down on horseback, *that* would be full Western."

"I won't tell Remington you said that." He grasped the doorframe again. "See you on the other side."

FIFTY-THREE

Despite Redd's words of encouragement and his subsequent urgent gesticulations, Mikey seemed incapable of bringing the Raptor any closer to the rolling train car than about six feet. Realizing that the mental barrier preventing Mikey from pushing that limit wasn't going to come down any time soon, Redd began calculating his odds of making the leap.

The top of the half wall that enclosed the rail car seemed to tower over him, though, in fact, it was only slightly above head height, and if he stepped off from the sidewall of the Raptor's bed, he would easily be able to see over it. He didn't actually need to leap over the half wall, as there were metal ladder rungs welded to the exterior at the ends of the car. Six feet wasn't an impossible distance by any means. He could, if he stretched a little, almost step across.

Nevertheless, his primitive brain began raising objections.

It's farther away than you think. What if you misjudge and come up short? You're jumping onto a moving object—what if it moves out from under you? What if you slip? What if your grip fails? What if? What if? What if?

Like for Mikey, it wasn't a real physical limitation that fueled his hesitancy but a mental one. His primitive brain was just doing its job, trying to keep him from making fatally stupid choices. But he had veto power.

He knew he would do it, just as years before he had shuffled out the end of a military transport plane with a parachute on his back for the first time. Then, as now, he recalled the Churchill quote: *"Fear is a reaction. Courage is a decision."* *Stop thinking about it and just do it.*

He planted his left foot on the side of the bed and then launched himself over the gap. As he began the jump, he flung the Ruger over the half wall, freeing up both hands to catch himself, which he easily accomplished. He gripped the top rung, and his right foot landed on the lowest, the metal step easily sliding under the sole of his boot until it butted up against the heel, holding him fast. He didn't linger there to savor this accomplishment but quickly brought his back foot up onto the next rung and began climbing. With a single step up, his head rose above the top of the half wall, revealing the car's contents—a load of coarse gravel. The Ruger lay atop it, the blued metal glinting in the starlight.

He rolled over the top of the wall and dropped down onto the gravel, rising into a squat to keep his center of gravity low. Before retrieving the Ruger, he raised his head above the top of the wall and waved down to Mikey, signaling that he had made it aboard. Mikey immediately swerved away, putting several more feet of distance between the Raptor and the train.

Redd felt a pang as he beheld the damage the truck had sustained. His beloved Raptor was unrecognizable. The truck looked like it had run up against a gigantic mandolin.

It's just a truck, he told himself. *Just a truck . . .*

A truck that he had worked and saved for and had already lost once before and that his best friend had poured his heart and sweat into restoring. Redd loved the Raptor but quickly shook off his frustration.

Forget the truck. Jack needs you.

Redd tore his gaze away, retrieved the Ruger, and moved forward, his focus now solely on reaching the locomotive.

Unlike the tank car, the gravel hauler—known in the industry as a *gondola*—seemed to have been designed with ease of movement in mind. There was another welded ladder on the front of the car, from which it would be an easy step onto the exposed coupler hitch connecting the car to the next one in line. The coupler itself didn't exactly look like it was meant to be stepped on. It was irregular and greasy and seemed to be moving back and forth, shimmying a little as the big steel wheels thumped over the track joints, beating out an incessant rhythm.

But Redd knew that even if his foot slipped, he would still be able to maintain positive contact with the rungs to avoid falling. He jammed the Ruger into its holster and swung over the top of the wall onto the ladder.

He made the crossing without difficulty, clambered up into the next gondola—also filled with gravel—and continued forward, repeating the process and then repeating it again and again. There were several more gondolas, some loaded with gravel, others with long sections of large-bore concrete pipe. Then there were half a dozen flat cars, loaded with oversize pallets full of cargo and wrapped in a layer of protective plastic. At the start, he kept a count of the cars but stopped after he reached double digits with the locomotive still maddeningly out of reach. Trains were long, a fact that he was reminded of every time he got stuck at a crossing, but he had never really considered what that meant in terms of real distance. Each car was about sixty feet long, so ten cars were roughly the distance of two football fields, and that didn't include the added vertical distance he had to travel in between each car. Nevertheless, he quickly fell into a rhythm, working through the repetitive effort almost without conscious thought.

He was only aware of being in motion when the train went into a bend, the wheels shrieking as the conflicting g-forces increased friction. Even at the relatively low speed of about twenty miles per hour, Redd could feel the transverse pull, acting not only on his body but on the train itself. Most roads were banked to minimize this effect on cars, but that wasn't the case with a railroad. The only thing keeping the train on the tracks was its not inconsiderable mass and the bevel of the wheels. Redd wondered why the engineer didn't reduce speed for the turns to avoid a potential derailment.

As he continued forward, the low drone of the locomotive grew louder and deeper, not just heard but felt, reverberating through him like a nuclear-powered subwoofer. Then he glimpsed the indirect glow of the big engine's headlamp shining away from him, but still bright enough to be seen from behind, and realized that only one more freight car stood between him and the locomotive.

That was when the thing that had been nagging at his subconscious finally bubbled up into his conscious mind.

There weren't any boxcars.

He mentally reviewed his journey up the length of the train. He had crossed gondolas and flat cars loaded with a variety of cargos, but not one of them had been a boxcar.

Had he misread the signs back at the lumber mill? Had Werner moved the operation out just as Mikey had suggested, in shipping containers on tractor trailer rigs?

He recalled the railroad dispatcher's confirmation that three boxcars had been picked up at the mill. He hadn't been wrong about that. The boxcars should have been at the rear of the train.

But they weren't.

So where did they go?

FIFTY-FOUR

A walkway with a safety rail wrapped around the rear of the engine and continued up its length. Redd made the final crossing slowly, the Ruger in one hand as he gripped the rail and pulled himself over. He saw no sign of a hostile presence.

Holding the weapon at the ready, he began moving down the walkway to the left, passing under the exhaust vents, which poured out an incessant blast of hot air. The noise and vibration reached a crescendo as he moved past the engine compartment. He froze in place when he saw an open doorway directly ahead and, beyond it, a dark compartment, faintly illuminated by the diffuse light from the forward-facing headlight.

Redd remained motionless, watching the enclosure for any sign of activity, but saw no movement in the darkness. He briefly wondered if there was another locomotive ahead of this one—it wasn't unusual to see trains being pulled by anywhere from two to six locomotives—but leaning out a little, he could see only one engine pulling the train. The train's crew and anyone who might be exerting control over them had to be in that compartment.

With no idea what to expect, Redd decided to make a dynamic entrance, sweeping into the compartment as if breaching an enemy stronghold with a fire team at his back. But he had no fire team, and if there were multiple targets in the room, or worse, a blend of hostile and hostage, he would have about a milli-second to establish PID and start shooting. And to further complicate matters, he needed at least one of them alive to tell him what had become of the boxcars.

Still, what choice did he have?

After a mental three-count to focus his intention, he propelled himself forward, up the steps into the compartment. He mentally mapped the space in an instant. The room was cramped and utilitarian, similar in layout to the flight deck of a big jet or the bridge of a boat. There were two chairs bolted to the floor on the right side of the cabin, one in front of the other, and one more chair on the left, positioned in front of a console with illuminated gauges, indicators, and switches. Resting atop the console was a rather beat-up but serviceable M1911A1, and sitting in the chair, idly looking at his phone, was a man in faded jeans and a T-shirt with the sleeves ripped off to reveal a chaotic tattoo intaglio. Eagles, Confederate Army battle flags, and swastikas all vied for pride of place on his exposed skin.

The man seemed to sense Redd's presence but reacted slowly, as if his conscious mind could not accept that someone else was in the locomotive. He turned to look at Redd, then started to reach for the pistol.

"Don't." Redd waggled the Ruger a little to suggest the consequences the man could expect if he continued that course of action.

The tattooed man wisely drew his hand back but did not appear otherwise intimidated. "How did you get on board?" he asked.

Redd ignored the question and stepped in close, seizing the pistol off the console before the man could reconsider his surrender. Shoving the semi-auto into his belt, he took a step back and stabbed the business end of the Ruger in the man's direction. "Where's Jack?"

"Jack?"

"The boy Dean Werner kidnapped."

The tattooed guy shrugged.

"You might be stupid," said Redd, his patience wearing thin, "but trust me, you don't want to play dumb right now."

The man stared back at him for a long moment as if trying to decide how much of a threat Redd posed. Then he nodded slowly. "You're that rancher, ain't ya? Heard all about you on the news and whatnot. Heard you're a preacher's son."

Redd did not correct the misapprehension. "Last chance. Where's Jack?" He holstered his Ruger.

Standing, the man smiled and folded his arms over his chest. The gesture would have seemed more defiant had his crossed arms not been resting atop a substantial beer gut. "I ain't telling you—"

Before he could finish his sentence, Redd unleashed a brutal right hook to the man's body, his big fist landing with enough force to cause a *whoosh* sound to pour from the man's lungs as he doubled over in pain and returned to his seat.

Moments later, when the man could speak again, his bravado had evaporated, replaced by a look that was equal parts concern and indignation. "Hey, you can't . . ." He pressed backward in the chair as if trying to retreat without standing, but the bolted-down chair didn't move.

Redd closed the distance in a single step and struck again. At the last second, he pulled his punch and instead brought his open hand across the man's face. Had he been on the receiving end, Redd would have considered it a light tap, but the man's head snapped to the side as if he'd been hit with a haymaker.

"Where's Jack?" Redd asked calmly.

The tattooed guy rubbed his jaw. "Ow, man. That really hurt!"

"You don't know pain yet. But you're gonna if you don't tell me where Jack is."

Rather than answer, tattoo guy spat at Redd, a giant glob of spit hitting Redd on his cheek. "I ain't tellin' you nothin'!"

Redd wiped the spit off his cheek and let out an almost maniacal laugh. When he looked up, he locked eyes with tattoo guy. His smile gone, Redd said, "You're gonna regret that."

For the first time, the man's eyes widened in real terror. Again making his way to his feet, he pointed his finger at Redd. "You can't—"

Whoosh.

In a flash, Redd struck again. He didn't pull his punch this time, instead opting to put all of his weight behind the blow. He was pretty sure he felt at least one of the man's ribs break.

Tattoo man let out a string of curses. Still bent over, holding his stomach, he looked up at Redd. "You can't do this. You're a preacher's son—"

"Son-in-law, actually," corrected Redd. He reached out, grabbing tattoo guy by the collar of his shirt and lifting him several inches off the ground. "Let's get one thing straight," he growled. "I would go to hell to save my kids, so don't think I won't sin a little to get one back."

Redd had a fleeting thought that the message might not be biblically sound—something to discuss with his father-in-law in a better moment. Still, he'd heard Elijah Lawrence read from Isaiah and Psalms and the book of James, preaching about how all believers were called on to protect orphans and widows.

Right now, there was only one way Redd knew how to do that.

Fear turned to confusion in the man's eyes. "But . . . but . . . he ain't even your kid!"

The statement gave Redd pause.

He's right . . . Jack's not my son.

Then he shook his head, dismissing the thought.

Doesn't matter. He's just a kid. An innocent kid.

"Where," barked Redd, his biceps bulging as he still held tattoo guy in the air, "is Jack?"

There was no response.

"Fine, hard way it is.

After several minutes of enhanced questioning, tattoo guy—having taken more of a beating than Redd initially thought he could withstand—finally started to break. Just as Redd lifted him off his feet again and cocked his free arm back, ready to strike yet another blow, the man threw his hands up and cried, "All right! Stop!"

Redd allowed his fist to hover in the cocked position. "Give me a reason to."

"The kid is still with Dean!"

The answer, as incomplete as it was, brought Redd immeasurable relief. Until that moment, he had not allowed himself to even entertain the possibility that Jack might not be alive, but the likelihood of it had clung to him like a demonic presence.

"Still with Dean."

Jack is still alive.

"And where is Dean?" Redd saw a glimmer of renewed defiance in the man's eyes, so he punctuated his question by slamming the man into the wall of the train car.

"He's helping unload the cars!" bleated the man.

"The boxcars? Where are they?"

"Bonner. There's a siding. We dropped the cars there."

Redd recalled seeing the name Bonner on a sign on the interstate near Missoula and figured that he could find the siding without too much difficulty.

"All right," he said, lowering the man back into the chair but maintaining his hold on the stretched T-shirt. "Now you're going to stop this train."

"Can't."

Redd started to lift the man again, but the latter hastily added, "I'm not saying I won't. I'm saying I *can't*. Mr. Werner did something to the controls. Cut the wires or something. There's no way to stop this train. Can't even slow it down."

Redd glanced down at the console and then turned slowly to take in the rest of the room. He had no idea what any of the controls were meant to do, much less how to fix whatever Werner had done to disable them. Then his gaze fell upon a recessed valve handle partially hidden behind a metal cover and above it a sign that read *Emergency Brake Valve*.

"What about that?" he asked, taking a step toward it.

As he reached for the valve handle, the man's expression became increasingly grave until, just as Redd was about to pull the lever, he cried out, "Don't!"

Redd maintained his handhold and asked, "Why not?"

"Because if you do . . ." Tattoo guy made an explosion with his fingers.

"You're saying the train is rigged to blow?"

The man nodded.

"Where's the bomb?"

"Up front. Close to the front wheels. When it goes off, it will not only take the wheels off the train but destroy the tracks as well. The whole train will derail."

Redd studied the man for any hint of deception. "All right, explain this to me. Werner wrecks the controls and plants a bomb on the train that will go off if anyone pulls the brakes. Have I got that right?"

"It's not wired to the brakes," the man clarified. "But he's watching the train's progress remotely. If he sees a drop in speed, he'll detonate the bomb."

"Never mind that," pressed Redd. "Why are *you* here?"

"To make sure that nobody tries to stop this train."

"And what's going to happen when we reach the end of the line?"

The man shook his head. "He's gonna blow it long before that."

"Why?" Redd gave the man a meaningful shake.

"To hide what he's really doing. When this train goes off the tracks, it'll be hours, maybe even days, before anyone realizes that the boxcars weren't part of the train. By then, he'll have everything moved out."

Redd was almost impressed by the complexity of Werner's scheme. "You're saying this train is going to be destroyed, no matter what? Aren't you the least bit worried about what will happen to you?"

"He's gonna call me first so I can jump off."

Redd raised a skeptical eyebrow. "You're planning to jump off a speeding freight train?"

"We're not moving that fast," countered the man. "I can hit the ground running. Might get a few scrapes, but I'll be okay."

Redd shook his head. "Sorry to ruin your day, but you're not going anywhere."

Then he threw a short, sharp punch that landed squarely on the man's chin and switched his lights out instantly.

"That one was for Jack."

As Redd let the man slump unconscious to the deck, he took out his phone. Not surprisingly, the display showed that he had missed several calls from Kline.

"Just the guy I wanted to talk to," he murmured, tapping the screen..

Kline picked up on the first ring. "Matt! What's going on?"

"Got myself a situation here," replied Redd. "I made it onto the train, but it's been wired to blow. The boxcars with the fentanyl operation were dropped off somewhere up the line. Werner's plan is to cause a derailment to make us think they were destroyed along with everything else."

"Hang on," said Kline. "You're saying he's already dropped off the boxcars? Who's driving the train?"

"Right now? Nobody. Werner ripped out the controls and planted an IED to blow off the front wheels. It could go off anytime."

There was a brief pause. "All right, we need to get you off that train before it blows. Do you think it's safe to jump?"

Redd thought about what the tattooed man had told him. "If I have no other choice, but first, I need to talk to someone from the railroad."

"Okay, give me a second."

Redd heard a beep as Kline put him on hold, but less than thirty seconds later, he was back. "Matt, I've got Mr. Pruitt here from Big Sky Rail Link. What do you need to know?"

"Mr. Pruitt," said Redd, "I noticed some tank cars at the end of the train. Six of them. Do you know what they're carrying?"

"Uh, give me a second . . . Those tank cars are transporting formalin. It's a formaldehyde solution."

Formaldehyde, Redd knew, was the primary chemical component of embalming fluid and was used in a variety of industrial processes, including the production of plywood. It was also a volatile contaminant and a known carcinogen.

"How much do those tanks hold?"

There was another pause as Pruitt consulted his notes. "Thirty thousand gallons."

Kline swore again. "This just keeps getting better."

Redd didn't know what the environmental impact of a formaldehyde spill would be, but the idea of nearly two hundred thousand gallons of the chemical spewing out onto the ground and seeping into groundwater was not a pleasant one.

"Gavin, we have to save this train."

"All right," said Kline after a thoughtful pause. "Do you have eyes on the IED?"

"Not exactly," Redd admitted. He briefly recounted his conversation with Werner's minion. "He said the bomb's on the front of the locomotive. Mr. Pruitt, are you still there?"

"Y-y-yes," stammered the dispatcher. "I'm just . . . just having a hard time with all of this."

"Is there a way to check out the front end of the locomotive?"

"Yes. There's an access door in the center of the front bulkhead."

Redd easily found the door Pruitt had described and opened it, revealing a small, dark compartment. "All right, stand by. I'm going out to have a look."

"Be careful," urged Kline.

Redd ducked inside and, using his phone as a flashlight, located a similar door on the opposite wall. He opened that door to a blast of outside air and noise and was suddenly staring out at the onrushing landscape.

He found himself on a narrow platform, a good six feet above the railroad, which rolled relentlessly under the locomotive. A flight of steps descended on either side, down almost to ground level. Gripping the safety rail with one hand and holding his phone light up with the other, Redd lowered himself down the steps on the right and then leaned out to get a look at the engine's front wheel assembly.

There wasn't much to see. Most of the wheel assembly was concealed behind a heavy steel guard, dark with grime. If there was an explosive device hidden there, Redd didn't see it. He pulled himself back up the stairs and started down the other side.

He stopped short when he saw something on the lowest step.

The object appeared to be a medium-sized cardboard shipping box held in place by several wraps of duct tape. Curiously, the box was open, revealing its contents, which seemed to consist mostly of several smaller cardboard boxes, each bearing the label of the Turneryte company.

The Turneryte company's eponymous product was an inexpensive binary explosive compound—essentially black powder mixed with powdered aluminum. The only way to detonate Turneryte was with a high-velocity impact—as might be caused by a rifle bullet—which was why the product was primarily sold as a reactive target for recreational and competitive shooters. A pound of Turneryte in a cardboard target would produce a small but very visible explosion when hit by a bullet, providing instant feedback on the accuracy of a long-distance shot. More recently, the company had begun marketing the product for gender reveal parties by including bags of powdered chalk—pink or blue—to be added to the target so that, when the bullet struck, the color of the resulting cloud would answer the question for everyone present.

A larger amount of the product—say fifty pounds—could blow up a car, as evidenced by numerous YouTube videos posted by bored and reckless malcontents with too much idle time and too little sense. By some quirk of law, use of the product was unregulated in forty-eight of fifty states, meaning that almost anyone could buy as much as they wanted. This fact, Redd knew from FBI internal memos, concerned domestic terrorism experts since Turneryte could easily be adapted for use in making improvised explosive devices.

The box taped to the step contained seventy-six targets—almost eighty pounds of Turneryte binary explosive.

FIFTY-FIVE

Redd backed away from the homemade bomb, ascending the steps to reenter the locomotive. After closing the doors to reduce the noise, he held the phone to his ear. "Gavin, still with me?"

"Still here. What's the situation?"

"The IED is affixed to the front of the locomotive." He described what he'd found in more detail.

"You have to shoot that stuff to set it off," Kline pointed out.

"Come on, Gavin. We both know how easy it is to rig up a simple detonator. Dean Werner was Army Airborne before they kicked him out. He could do it in his sleep. No telling what the trigger is. Could be a timer, or an antitamper switch. Maybe all of the above."

"I can try to put an EOD team aboard." Kline's tone indicated that even he knew what he was proposing had little chance of success.

"There's no time," countered Redd. He racked his brain to come up with something better. "Mr. Pruitt, is it possible to detach the locomotive?"

"You mean while the train is moving at speed?" Pruitt's tone remained incredulous, but then to Redd's surprise, he continued. "The couplers are designed to prevent that from happening. When the train is in motion, the constant tension of the locomotive pulling forward keeps the locking pin inside the coupler from lifting."

"But if that pin did lift? Would the coupler pop open?"

"It's a little more complicated than that, but yes."

"All right. Talk me through how to do it. Maybe we can't stop the locomotive from going off the rails, but I'm going to do what I can to save the train."

✖   ✖   ✖

The procedure for decoupling a freight car was fairly simple. Simple, that was, if the cars were in a rail yard and the train wasn't in motion. Pruitt's explanation included safety measures, like how to stand—"always keep one foot outside the rails in case you have to get out of the way in a hurry"—that simply weren't applicable. There was no procedure for doing it while on a moving train, but Redd figured he'd be able to modify the steps.

Before heading out to make his attempt, there was one small matter he had to attend to.

He knelt beside the unconscious form of Werner's goon and scooped him up into a fireman's carry, slinging the man over his shoulders like a sack of feed. He then made the short trip to the rear of the locomotive, where he set the man down and rubbed his knuckles against the man's sternum to rouse him.

The man came awake with a start. Then, when he realized where he was and saw Redd hovering over him, he began to squirm with fear.

"Hey!" shouted Redd. "Eyes on me, okay?"

The man nodded.

"This is your stop," Redd went on.

"What?"

"Time to go."

"Go?"

"Jump. Or would you rather stay here and take your chances?"

The man swallowed. "I, uh . . ."

"Let me put this another way," said Redd. "You can jump, or I can throw you off."

The man looked past him. "Maybe I could just—"

"No maybe," countered Redd. "Come on. This was what you were planning to do all along, right?"

"I . . . I . . ."

Redd had had enough. With one fluid move, he seized the man by the scruff of the neck and pitched him out into the night.

A chance at survival was more than the man deserved.

And with that good deed accomplished, he bent himself to the far more urgent task of preventing a disaster.

The first crucial step in decoupling the locomotive was closing the angle cocks on either side of the coupling, separating the air brakes on the rest of the train from the locomotive. The air braking system was designed so that the brakes would engage if the system lost pressure. Under normal operating conditions, the angle cocks were always in the open position. In the event of an accidental separation, the air hoses connecting the cars to the locomotive would separate, and the sudden drop in pressure would activate the brakes, rapidly stopping the train. Both valves had to be closed, and to accomplish this, he had to lay flat on the platform at the rear of the locomotive in order to reach up underneath the chassis and shift the angle cock to the closed position. He then had to cross over to the freight car and repeat the process to close its angle cock.

It was only when he reached down to work the cut-lever to lift the locking pin, which would allow the coupler knuckles to open, that the significance of having a stable position became evident.

The cut-lever was just a long metal rod with an L-shaped bend in it, like the crank handle for a jack, extending from the coupler to the right forward corner of the rail car. Pruitt had explained that raising the cut-lever while there was tension on the coupler would be difficult, like trying to open a sliding latch bolt while pushing against the door. Exactly how difficult, Pruitt couldn't say, but he had advised giving the lever a sharp yank rather than a slow pull. That, he said, was how it was done in the yard.

As he wrapped his fingers around the lever, Redd understood why having his feet under him would have been preferable. From a standing position, he would have been able to use his leg muscles to exert more force on the lever. Lying prone on the platform as he was, he would only be able to use arm strength.

Fortunately, Redd had a lot of arm strength.

Determined to get it done in one, he took a breath and then, letting it out with his own variation on the karate *kiai* shout, he wrenched up on the cut-lever.

The lever didn't move. The violence of his attempt rebounded, searing through his muscles and tendons like a lightning strike. He winced, as much at the failure as the burning sensation that now throbbed all the way to his shoulder, and then tried again.

The second attempt was no more successful than the first. His third try failed as well. So did his fourth.

On the fifth attempt, he took a different approach, rejecting Pruitt's admonition and instead exerting steady pressure. He sustained the effort for five seconds. Ten. Twenty. The breath he had been holding slipped from between his lips in a long groan that escalated into another shout. His biceps swelled, straining the fabric of his shirt sleeve. His tendons felt like they were about to snap. Dark spots began to swim across his vision. But the cut-lever did not budge. Finally, his exhausted muscles failed, and as his fingers slipped from the rod, he rolled onto his back and screamed his frustration into the night sky.

Pruitt was right. It's impossible.

Even as the thought went through his head, he heard another voice—J. B.'s voice.

"Impossible? I don't recall ever teaching you that word."

The ghost of Gunny Miller, the team chief of his Marine Raider squadron, echoed the sentiment, with his favorite quote: *"Impossible is a word to be found only in the dictionary of fools."*

But I've given it everything I've got. I don't have anything left.

"Is that a fact?" argued J. B. *"You're still alive, ain't ya? You must have something left to give."*

"You can quit when you're dead," roared the memory of Gunny Miller.

"Quit when I'm dead," Redd muttered. "Or die trying."

He rolled over, found the cut-lever, and pulled again.

And again.

And again.

He cursed the coupler. Howled at it. And kept pulling. And pulling and pulling and—

The cut-lever suddenly gave, snapping up a few inches. The movement so surprised Redd that he let go of the rod, as if it had shocked him. In the same instant, the joined couplers shifted away from each other, like the end of a long handshake.

But nothing else happened.

"No," Redd howled. "No! Come on. Unhook."

But both locomotive and train continued to lumber forward as if nothing had changed.

Redd rolled over, reversed position, and then lowered himself onto the coupler, driving his heels into the device, shouting curses and prayers in equal measure. One misstep and he could slip down onto the tracks to be sliced apart under the steel wheels, but he didn't care. If he couldn't get the locomotive to separate, he would almost surely die anyway.

But nothing he did seemed to have any effect.

Out of options, he heaved himself back up onto the platform. Sitting with his feet dangling over the edge, right above the coupler, he drew his Ruger and took aim. If a Magnum round couldn't knock the thing loose, nothing could.

He lined up his shot, choosing a spot on the locomotive side, right behind where the two couplers met, and was just about to pull the trigger when he saw a gap appear between the couplers.

They had moved apart.

Redd lifted the unfired Ruger and continued staring at the couplers, half believing that what he was seeing was an optical illusion. But no, the gap was widening. The couplers were separating. The locomotive was pulling away from the train.

Though gradual at first, once begun, the process accelerated. As if only now realizing that it was free of the burden it had hauled for miles, the locomotive seemed to surge ahead. Below Redd's feet, the thick black air hose connecting the car to the locomotive stretched taut and then broke apart with a snap like a gunshot, the separate ends flailing like tentacles for a moment before falling down out of sight.

Redd's howls of frustration transformed into peals of laughter as the locomotive raced ahead under power, leaving the rest of the train behind, still rolling, but losing momentum by the second.

He had done it. He had done the impossible. But his job still wasn't done. Not by a long shot.

I'm coming, Jack. Just hold on a little bit longer.

FIFTY-SIX

Twenty-odd miles away, on a little siding a few miles outside Missoula, Dean Werner sat in the cab of the rented moving truck, alternately monitoring the screen of his mobile phone and checking on his passenger.

The boy hadn't said much since the meeting with Marina Waldron at the mill. It was almost as if he knew what was coming.

Dean wasn't particularly excited about having to deal with that problem. Killing a grown man or woman was one thing, but he took no joy from ending the life of a child. It had been bad enough out there in the woods when he'd iced Raymond and Janelle. Of course, the kid had made things difficult. Then, his coping strategy had just been *Get it over with, quick*. Like ripping off a Band-Aid.

Killing a kid was just plain wrong. Necessary, but wrong. So, if it had to be done, the way to do it was quick. The same advice he'd been given as a boy when he'd been sent out to slaughter one of the rabbits he'd raised seemed to apply in this instance.

Don't look him in the eye. Don't identify with him. Don't even give him a name.

Unfortunately, that ship had sailed. He'd talked to the kid. Learned his name. Even lied to him by telling him everything was going to be all right.

Yeah, this kid's face would definitely haunt his dreams.

Maybe if he'd just killed the kid in the first place, all of this unpleasantness would have been avoided, but it hadn't been his fault. No one could have predicted that big firefighter showing up to save the kid. But keeping the kid alive just to pump him for information he didn't have? That was his father's mistake. And it would be Dean's job to fix it.

Not that Otis was immune from the consequences of Dean's failure. Their lucrative operation was in shambles, and even though they would be able to rebuild and get things going again in six months or so, some of the losses would be permanent.

And not just Holt or the other men who had been killed.

Otis had planned ahead for exactly such a situation, crafting an elaborate escape plan. He'd thought of everything from how to create a minor environmental catastrophe to cover their tracks to establishing new identities for his loyal inner circle. But the mill? Their homes? Their lives in Missoula?

All of that was gone for good.

They couldn't even stay in the United States. The fake personae that Otis had created for them made them native-born citizens of Canada, and while the plan was for them to emigrate back to the States at some point in the future, they wouldn't ever be able to visit the western states.

Dean glanced over at the kid again.

Plus, I'll have his death on my conscience.

He shook his head resignedly, then checked the screen. The display showed a GPS map with a blue dot. The dot wasn't his location, though. It marked the location of another phone, the phone he'd wired up to the detonator in the little IED he'd put together—another handy skill he'd picked up during his ill-fated stint in the Army. When the time came to detonate, all he would have to do was tap a button on the screen.

Eighty pounds of Turneryte wasn't enough to blow up the whole train, but it would be enough to damage the front drive wheels along with a section of track under the locomotive, and that was all he needed to accomplish.

Otis had given a lot of thought to where the detonation ought to occur. Too close to Missoula or Butte and the authorities would be on the scene too quickly to ensure a clean getaway. Blow the train out in the open, and there might not be enough damage to hide what they were actually doing.

The way to maximize the effect—to get the biggest bang for their buck, as

Otis had said—was to take out a bridge crossing, specifically the bridge located about five miles northwest of a little town called Drummond. Blowing the bomb on the bridge wouldn't just send the train off the tracks. It would turn the locomotive into a wrecking ball that would destroy the entire span and dump the train's cargo—including six tank loads of formaldehyde—into the Clark Fork, poisoning the river and everything downstream.

According to the blue dot, the train was almost there, still chugging along at a steady pace of twenty-five miles per hour. Any faster, and it would have already derailed on one of the turns.

He leaned out the window. "Hey, Dad!"

Otis Werner, who had been supervising the unloading of the boxcars into the moving vans that would transport the cargo to a storage unit in northern Idaho, came around to see what his son wanted. "Yeah?" he asked irritably.

"The train is almost to the bridge."

"What are you telling me for? Just blow the thing. I got work to do."

Dean shrugged. "Thought you might want to know."

Otis raised both hands in a shooing gesture and went back to watching the off-load.

Dean zoomed in tight on the moving dot, watching as it closed the distance toward the blue gap of the river. *Almost there,* he thought, moving his finger over the Send button.

The dot touched the blue river, and Dean tapped the button.

FIFTY-SEVEN

When he saw the flash, Redd's elation turned to ashes. There was only one possible explanation for what he had just seen. The IED at the front of the locomotive had just detonated. Whether this was in response to Redd separating it from the train or Werner's plan from the beginning, he could not say. All he knew for sure was that the figurative bullet he thought he had just dodged was now screaming toward him like a radar-guided missile.

It had only been about a minute since he'd successfully uncoupled the train from the locomotive. The engine, still under full power, had pulled away from the long string of heavily laden freight cars, but the latter was still coasting along, carried forward by momentum, and the distance separating them was negligible at best.

By long-ingrained habit, Redd had begun counting immediately after the flash.

One Montana . . . two Mon—

The deep *boom* of the explosion reached his ears, followed immediately by another sound, a combination of heavy impact and the shriek of metal being torn apart as the doomed locomotive demolished itself along with a section of track.

Redd knew that sound traveled at a speed of roughly a mile in five seconds, which meant that the site of the locomotive's destruction was less than a quarter mile away.

He estimated that the train had slowed by five, maybe even ten miles per hour, but it was still rolling onward, and if he didn't do something to slow it down, it would reach the wrecked locomotive in less than a minute. When it did, the train would go off the tracks, and everything he had worked so hard to prevent would happen. Fortunately, there *was* something he could do to slow it down. Rolling back into a prone position, he reached under the platform, found the angle cock, and wrenched it to the open position.

The trailing air hose suddenly came alive and began whipping back and forth as pressurized air rushed out of it. But aside from that, Redd's action had no visible effect on the train's forward motion.

Redd was incredulous. He hadn't expected the train to come to a sudden stop, but he had expected some kind of measurable change. With growing desperation, he began looking around for some other way of stopping the train.

But then something *did* happen. At first, the only difference was a strident hissing sound, which quickly escalated into something like the noise of a circular saw tearing through a piece of plywood. Friction sparks erupted from the wheels as the train's forward momentum exceeded their rotation, causing the wheels to slide along the track. Not just the wheels on the flat car Redd was riding on, but all the wheels, up and down the train. Bright yellow streaks, like glowing worms, rained down on the track ballast to either side of the train.

Redd could *feel* the train slowing, shedding speed rapidly as the friction brakes clamped down tight.

But the train was still moving.

Redd had no way of gauging its speed but felt certain that the long chain of freight cars was still moving faster than he could run. In the moments since the explosion, the train had closed most of the distance to the wreck of the locomotive. It was now less than a hundred yards away, close enough that Redd could see the results of the detonation.

Almost certainly by design, the explosion had coincided with the engine's crossing of a bridge over Clark Fork. The blast had not only knocked the locomotive off the track but had damaged the bridge itself. The runaway engine had done the rest, tearing apart the span and creating a significant gap in the line.

The locomotive had then plunged down into the river where it now lay, half submerged but nonetheless engulfed in flames.

The train continued to slow, but the broken bridge loomed ever closer. Redd watched the landscape roll by alongside the freight car. It was now moving no faster than a fast-walking pace, slow enough that he could have easily stepped off without losing his footing.

"C'mon," he muttered. "Stop!"

Twenty-five yards . . .

Redd knew he should bail out, leap to safety. He'd done everything he possibly could to prevent this disaster. There was nothing left for him to do except save his own life.

So why did that feel like an admission of defeat?

Twenty yards . . .

The wheels had all but stopped turning, but the train's prodigious mass wanted to keep moving forward.

Redd's primal brain was screaming at him. *Jump!* But another part of him remained morbidly fascinated by what was happening. This was a literal train wreck, and he found it almost impossible to look away.

Ten yards . . .

The train was barely crawling, and for the first time since the explosion, he dared to believe that it was going to stop short.

But if it doesn't?

If it didn't . . . If even one car went over the brink, it might conceivably pull the rest of the train along with it.

"Come on, you beast! Stop!"

Five yards . . .

The lead car was on the bridge now. The smell of burning metal and diesel fuel from the wrecked locomotive filled his nostrils.

"Maybe not."

He did jump then, but not so he could escape the train's demise. When his boots hit the track bed, there was hardly any change in momentum, and he easily kept his balance as he darted around in front of the rail car and threw his shoulder into the front, leaning into it like a football lineman hitting a tackling dummy and bracing his boot soles against the last intact railroad tie.

It was a futile endeavor. A display of defiance with no hope of success. He might as well have tried to stop a landslide. The train wasn't moving fast enough to knock him down, but it did push back until he had no choice but to leap out of the way. And then there was nothing between the train and oblivion.

Redd fell back against the side of the bridge, watching as the flat car rolled inexorably toward the breach.

Every railroad freight car rolled on eight wheels, arranged in in-line pairs. When the car reached the break in the tracks, the leading wheels rolled out over nothingness while the rear wheels in the assembly remained on the tracks a few seconds longer until, with a violent thump of impact, the rear wheels also rolled off the broken rail and the front end of the flat car dropped heavily onto the bridge . . .

And stopped.

Finally.

Redd sat there, waiting for the long line of cars to shove the flat car and its cargo forward into the river, an action that would surely pull the rest of the train along into destruction. But the car didn't move.

The train had come to a full stop.

Redd stared at it for a long moment, still not quite able to believe his eyes. Then, as the adrenaline drained away, he began to laugh.

He was still laughing when, seemingly from out of nowhere, Rubble ran up to him and began licking his face.

"I'm okay, boy," he said, still laughing.

Mikey appeared a moment later, stepping out from between the rail cars. "There you are," he said. Then, after panning slowly to take in the train, the bridge, and the burning wreckage in the river below, he added, "Cut it kind of close, didn't you?"

Redd just shook his head, too drained to come up with a clever retort.

"Well," Mikey continued, "don't just sit there. We've still got work to do."

The last vestiges of Redd's laughter died away. Mikey was right. While Otis Werner's scheme to create a major environmental disaster had been thwarted, it had still accomplished its basic purpose, distracting everyone while he made his escape. Redd could only hope that there was still time left to stop him.

As Redd rose to his feet, he repeated his solemn promise.

I'm coming. Almost there.

FIFTY-EIGHT

Lost in thought and anxious about his uncertain future, Dean started at the sound of the truck's roll-up door slamming down on the cargo bay behind him. The closing of the door meant that his truck was loaded and ready to roll out, but to Dean, it felt like a guillotine crashing down on him, severing all connections to his former life.

No going back now, he thought.

But of course, that had been true for a while, and not just since Otis made the hard choice to pull the plug on their operation.

Where did it all go wrong? he wondered.

He had blamed himself for not retrieving the key from Raymond Williams. If that stupid firefighter hadn't shown up and stopped him from killing the kid . . .

But no, that was just one event in a chain that went back much further. Maybe it had been Raymond's attack of conscience that had started the wheels of fate turning. Or maybe it was Dean's own decision all those years ago to join the family business. Maybe this had been his fate from the day he was born.

Otis strode up to the truck, rapping a heavy fist down on the hood. "Get going!" he barked. Dean nodded and started the engine.

Otis, however, wasn't finished. He leaned in through the open driver's side window. "While you're at it, find somewhere to . . ." He thrust his chin meaningfully toward the silent figure in the passenger seat. "Someplace where nobody will ever look."

"Got it," Dean said, making an effort to hide his distaste for the task.

"Good. Don't screw up. I'll see you in Calgary."

Otis took a step back. Dean put the truck in gear and started forward, making the turn onto the maintenance road that ran parallel to the rails. That was when he spied the headlights of a vehicle rolling toward him on the two-track.

Dean felt a sudden rush of apprehension, and as he braked to a stop, he saw Otis and several of his men walking up from behind the truck to investigate. A few walked with one hand behind their backs, hiding the guns they held. Dean took up his pistol as well, holding it across his lap, out of the approaching driver's line of sight.

There was little doubt that the approaching vehicle was law enforcement. The only real question was whether the driver was looking for them specifically or merely investigating a report of unusual activity along the railroad. This section of railroad ran down a strip of land sandwiched in between the interstate and the old Highway 10E, so it wasn't inconceivable that a highway patrolman or sheriff's deputy might have spotted them working and decided to check it out. Ultimately, it didn't matter because there was no way the cop was going to survive the next few minutes.

The vehicle continued its approach, but with its headlights shining directly at Dean, he couldn't make out any details that might reveal which law enforcement agency it was affiliated with. When the vehicle stopped about fifty yards away and the driver shut off the headlights, Dean beheld not an official patrol vehicle but a black Ford pickup that looked like it had been driven in a demolition derby. Even stranger, the driver had one arm extended through the window and was holding something that looked like a rag.

A white rag.

What in the . . . ?

The arm waved back and forth a few times, fluttering the rag to make sure that it was visible, and then disappeared inside the truck. A moment later, a man's head and shoulders emerged, and then the rest of him wriggled through the window opening. Evidently, the body damage to the vehicle had left its doors fused shut.

The man dropped to the ground and then quickly raised both hands, his left still holding the white rag. A moment later, another shape came through the same window—not a man but a monster, large and hideous. It was a dog, a very *big* dog, but because much of its coat was missing, it resembled some kind of unearthly beast.

Dean recognized the dog. He also recognized the man walking beside it.

He wasn't the only one.

In the passenger seat, the kid, his blue eyes wide with hope, sat bolt upright and cried, "Matt!"

FIFTY-NINE

"This has got to be the stupidest idea you've ever had."

Mikey's words echoed inside Redd's head as he began walking forward, still holding up his makeshift truce flag—one of Junior's old washcloths he'd found stashed in the glove box. That had been the last thing Mikey said to him before getting out, but he had merely been repeating what he'd said when Redd explained the plan the first time.

"You're going to walk over there waving a white flag and hope they don't just kill you on the spot? And then you're going to ask them nicely to hand Jack over to you and hope they actually do it and just let you walk away?"

Redd had nodded. "Pretty much."

"This has got to be the stupidest idea you've ever had. You're going to get yourself killed."

Redd shrugged. "You always say that."

"Yeah, well, this time I'm sure of it."

"I don't think so. But if you can come up with a better plan, one that doesn't end with Jack getting killed in the crossfire, I'm all ears."

Mikey had grudgingly admitted that he didn't have a better plan but had nevertheless renewed his objection one last time before getting out.

Stupid was not the word Redd would have chosen. *Dangerous?* Definitely. *Crazy?* Well, that was a loaded word these days.

He was, admittedly, more than a little worried that Otis Werner and his thugs would ignore the flag of truce and gun him down in cold blood. In fact, there was every reason to believe they would do just that. He was banking on the fact that Otis Werner wasn't . . . well . . . stupid. At least stupid enough to kill him without first finding out why he was there.

Truthfully, it wasn't his first choice by a long shot. He wasn't a negotiator. He preferred direct action, bringing sudden and overwhelming force to bear against his enemies. One of his favorite quotes, almost a mantra for him, was from General George Patton: *"When in doubt, ATTACK!"*

During his time with the Raiders, he'd taken to carrying a wood-splitting maul into combat as a breaching tool, and the symbolism wasn't lost on anyone who knew him. *He* was that maul. Hard-hitting, with just enough of an edge to get the job done.

Or at least, he had been.

Maybe it was having Emily back in his life, or maybe it was the maturity that came with experience, but he had come to understand that charging in headlong with guns blazing was not always the best first course of action. There was a time and place for the maul, but sometimes, a more delicate touch was required.

Of all the possible scenarios he'd considered, none had as much chance of getting Jack safely away from Werner's clutches. There wasn't enough cover and concealment to sneak up on the siding, and while a direct assault might succeed in overwhelming Werner's forces, there was too much chance of Jack getting killed, either by a stray bullet or as an intentional final act of retribution.

It wasn't a good plan, but if getting Jack back was the main objective—and for Redd, that was the *only* objective—then this was his best bet at completing his mission.

He had called Kline, of course, advising him of the plan and supplying him with the location provided by Werner's man on the locomotive, but only after he was certain that he and Mikey would reach the Bonner siding ahead of the FBI team. If he was going to get Otis Werner to talk to him face-to-face, he had to do it without a safety net.

So far, the plan seemed to be working. None of the half dozen or so men standing around the moving truck was openly displaying a weapon, though he felt sure all of them had one within easy reach.

Best of all, he'd definitely heard Jack call out to him. Jack *was* alive. Just knowing that for certain filled Redd with both hope and purpose.

One of the men, a big guy with a white horseshoe mustache and a face that bore more than a passing resemblance to that of the late, unlamented Holt Werner, crossed his arms over his prodigious belly and regarded Redd's approach with a look of contemptuous disdain. Although the only photograph he'd seen of the man was more than twenty years old, Redd had no doubt that he was looking at Otis Werner.

When Redd was about ten yards out, Otis growled, "That's close enough!"

Redd stopped and, without looking down, murmured, "Rubble, stay."

Rubble obeyed but remained alert and poised for action.

"You must be stupid or something."

"I've been hearing that a lot lately," Redd replied. "From better men than you."

"You killed my boy. I don't know why I haven't already put a bullet in your skull."

"For your sake, it's a good thing you haven't. I didn't come here alone."

A few of the men began looking around, searching the surrounding area for any indication of an unseen threat.

Otis, however, kept his eyes locked on Redd. "That supposed to scare me?"

"Just thought you should know." Redd shrugged. "Look, you've got to realize that it's over. The FBI is closing in on your operation. They know about this little switcheroo, and they're going to be here soon. When they get here, it'll be up to you to decide whether you walk out of here in handcuffs or get carried out in a body bag, but I guarantee you, those are your only two choices."

"And they sent *you* to deliver terms?"

Redd shook his head. "No. Frankly, I'd rather see you carried out. But you've got someone I care about, and I'd like to make sure he doesn't come to any harm."

"The boy." Otis's eyes narrowed, his visage transforming into a cruel mask. "Maybe I should kill him right now. Then you might know what it's like to lose a son."

Despite his outward bravado, the threat chilled Redd.

Jack wasn't his son. He barely knew the boy. But Otis's words had struck him in the heart.

"You could do that," Redd answered, struggling to hide what he was feeling. "But it's not going to change anything. Might even make your situation worse. On the other hand, if you turn Jack over to me right now, me and"—he nodded his head out at the surrounding darkness—"my friend out there won't lift a finger to stop you. If you hurry, you might even be able to get out of here before the feds show up."

Otis stared back at him, his expression unchanging. After a long moment, he turned his head slowly, glancing toward the idling truck, then brought his attention back to Redd. Something in the man's eyes told Redd that he'd failed to make his case. Otis's next utterance confirmed it.

"You killed my boy."

"Come on, Werner. You haven't gotten this far by making bad decisions. You've got a chance to walk away clean. Are you going to throw that away just out of spite?"

"If you're telling me the truth," said Otis, "there's time for me to walk away clean whether or not I give you the kid. In fact, I think I'm going to hang on to him a little while longer."

He slowly uncrossed his arms. "You, on the other hand . . ." He shook his head. "You're not walking out of here." It was the only warning Redd got.

Suddenly, there was a pistol in Otis Werner's hand, and it was pointing right at Redd's chest.

SIXTY

Redd threw himself flat, rolling to the left, putting the truck between himself and Otis, even as the night came alive with multiple reports. Bullets from numerous weapons creased the air where he had been standing only an instant before.

As he came up on his elbows, momentarily protected by the front end of the truck, he whistled, then called out to Rubble: "Here, boy!"

Rubble responded immediately, leaping over to join his human, even as bullets began chasing after him. Rounds struck the ground, spraying gravel and dirt like shrapnel, but the dog, like his master, was a step ahead of the fusillade.

Redd threw an arm around Rubble's neck, groping until his fingers curled around the grip of the Ruger, which he'd hung from the rottie's collar before venturing out under the flag of truce. No sooner was the weapon in his hand than one of Otis Werner's men stepped around the front end of the truck brandishing a pistol.

Redd brought the Ruger up and fired once, a center-mass shot that toppled the man backward.

So much for the delicate touch, thought Redd. *Now it's time for the maul.*

And yet, he knew he couldn't engage Werner's men with reckless abandon. Jack was still their captive, probably in the cab of the truck. Not only did he have to make sure to have one hundred percent PID before pulling his own trigger, but he also had to draw the enemy fire away from the truck.

He didn't linger there but rolled to the left again, toward the front right corner of the truck. He figured that after witnessing the demise of their buddy and realizing that Redd was fighting back, Werner's men would go around to the other side of the truck in a flanking move. Sure enough, as he rolled past the front corner, he saw two men moving forward along the truck's right side. Both were armed with pistols, but neither of them seemed to know what to do with them. They were carrying the weapons in the up position, elbows bent, barrels pointing skyward, just as they'd probably seen somebody do in a movie. They saw Redd at the same time he saw them, but because they weren't ready and he was, Redd got off the first shot. He fanned the hammer back with his left hand like a gunslinger in an old Western and fired one-handed. The heavy pistol bucked in his hand, but his shot hit the nearest man just below center mass where he'd been aiming. The man staggered backward and fell, clutching his gut. Redd recocked and shifted his aim to the second man, but the latter was already backpedaling, scrambling for cover behind the truck when Redd pulled the trigger. He couldn't tell if the round found its mark or not.

He immediately rolled onto his back to check his unprotected six o'clock and saw another gunman lumbering into view. Before he could acquire the new target, however, Rubble leaped into the fray, clamping his jaws around the man's arm, pulling him to the ground.

But there was another man right behind the first, and with the other gunman out of the way, he had an unrestricted field of fire. The barrel of his pistol dropped toward Redd even as Redd, now in a supine position, brought the Ruger up and simultaneously sighted down the barrel and brought his left hand down on the hammer to cock the weapon. The enemy gunman's semiauto was pointing right at him and would require only a hard trigger pull to loose a point-blank killing shot. Redd both felt and saw the revolver's cylinder rotating ponderously, the moment distorted by a surge of adrenaline that seemed to constrict the passage of time. The Ruger would not be ready to fire until the cylinder advanced the next round into position and the spring-tensioned hammer locked back.

Too slow, he thought, though, in fact, everything was happening in less than the blink of an eye.

The gunman's finger tightened on the trigger, and then . . .

His head snapped to the side, and a fine red mist appeared in the stream of light shining from the truck's headlight. The pistol discharged an instant later, but it was no longer pointing directly at Redd. Almost simultaneous with the handgun's report was the sharper crack of the long rifle that had fired the killing round.

"Thanks, Mikey," Redd murmured. He rolled into the prone and bounded up into a more advantageous shooting stance. Rubble's victim was wailing in pain as the rottie, still gripping the man's arm in his powerful bite, thrashed his head back and forth, shaking the man like a rag doll.

"Rubble," said Redd in a stern command voice, "here!"

Rubble immediately let go of the man's arm, allowing him to slump to the ground, and retreated to Redd's side. Dazed, the man made no effort to reach for the gun he'd dropped. Redd wasn't about to shoot an unarmed man who posed no threat, but as he couldn't risk the possibility that the man might try to rejoin the fight, he swiped the Ruger across the side of the man's head, putting him down for the count.

After checking front and back, then front again, and finding no immediate threat, Redd began moving toward the driver's side of the truck. He thought he heard Otis Werner shouting commands, but with his ears ringing from the noise of gunfire, he couldn't make out what was being said. Whatever was happening seemed to be urgent, so throwing caution to the wind, he came around the front corner, ready to fire.

As he did, he glimpsed movement and a flash of light from inside the cab as the driver's door opened and then almost as quickly slammed shut. A moment later, the vehicle lurched forward. Redd tried to take aim at the driver, but with the interior light now off, he couldn't differentiate a target.

At that very moment, another gunman fired at him from behind the truck. The shot went wide but succeeded in pulling Redd's attention away from the truck's driver long enough for the vehicle to move past him.

The truck lurched, the front end rising as if it had just hit a speed bump, and Redd felt a sudden panic.

Rubble!

But the giant rottie was right behind him, barking ferociously at the vehicle. It wasn't Rubble that the truck had just rolled over but the body of one of the fallen shooters. As the truck continued pulling away, Rubble gave chase, barking and biting at its tires.

Another round snapped through the air right beside Redd, prompting him to drop and roll, but he nevertheless brought the Ruger up and fired from the prone, aiming at the approximate place where he'd seen the muzzle flash. In the dull red glow of the truck's taillights, he saw a human-shaped silhouette stagger and fall.

Redd squinted into the sudden darkness, searching for any more targets, aware with each passing second that the truck and its occupants were getting farther away. Seeing no sign of Otis Werner or any of his men, Redd wheeled around and took off at a full sprint in pursuit of the departing truck.

Had it only been Werner or one of his minions in the truck, Redd might have just let them go. They wouldn't get far, not with the FBI already converging on the location. But stopping a vehicle in motion was a dicey proposition at best. If the driver refused to surrender, the interdiction would, of necessity, escalate. The FBI and highway patrol might employ roadblocks and spike strips or attempt a PIT maneuver, any of which might cause the driver of the truck to lose control with catastrophic results. Because there was a very good chance that Jack was a passenger in that truck, Redd couldn't let that happen. Unfortunately, the truck was steadily outpacing him. Even Rubble, who had valiantly tried to keep up with the vehicle, had been left behind.

Redd dug deep, trying to summon up the energy to push past his limits. He could feel his heart beating out of control. His thighs began to burn as his muscles, being pushed well beyond the anaerobic threshold, swelled with lactic acid. He knew he could not sustain this pace and also knew that even if he did, it wouldn't matter because the truck was moving faster than even the fittest Olympic sprinter. It was now fifty . . . no, seventy-five yards away and increasing that gap with each passing second.

Yet he did not give up. He *would not* give up. Jack's life was in the balance, and he would never, ever admit defeat.

Please, God . . .

As if in answer to that barely formed prayer, the truck's taillights flared brightly, indicating that the brakes had been applied. The truck was stopping.

No, he realized. *Not stopping. Turning.*

The truck had reached the end of the gravel access road and was turning onto the old highway. Redd pushed himself again, knowing that this would be his last chance. Once the truck's tires hit pavement, it would be gone.

The red light softened to its original hue, and then the taillights shifted as the truck began a turn to the left. Simultaneously, the headlights became visible as the truck came into profile, their white light beams illuminating the blacktop on which it now rolled.

Redd skidded to a stop and brought the Ruger up, cocking it and then bracing it in a two-hand grip. He placed the front sight on a spot just below the headlights and began tracking the truck as it accelerated forward.

The vehicle was a good fifty yards away, and fifty yards was the outside limit of the revolver's range for accuracy. Even with flawless technique, the round might drift unpredictably over the distance. When practicing with the weapon on the firing range, with his muscles relaxed and his heart rate normal, Redd's shot group at that distance was about twelve inches in diameter at fifty yards.

He would get only one shot.

He allowed himself a single, deep breath. Held it and then, with another silent prayer, pulled the trigger.

SIXTY-ONE

The gun rose with the recoil, but even with it partially blocking his view, he saw its effect on the truck. The headlights dipped dramatically as the front left tire, perforated by the heavy-duty .44 Magnum round, rapidly deflated. The driver tried to keep going but only succeeded in hastening the tire's disintegration. Chunks of rubber, visible in the red glow of the taillights, were flung out behind the truck, and then a shower of sparks flew out as the rim made contact with asphalt. Unable to continue forward, the driver did the only thing he could—he stopped.

Redd bolted into motion again, running diagonally toward the stalled truck, kicking through roadside vegetation as he charted the quickest intercept course, with the Ruger extended ahead of him, ready to fire the instant the door opened.

He had only gone a few steps when the interior light flashed on again. He briefly saw a figure moving inside the cab, but the door on the left remained closed. The driver was trying to exit from the passenger's side door.

Redd veered to the right, darting behind the truck's cargo bay. He stopped there and pied the corner, easing around the edge by degrees until he spotted a trio of figures, dimly illuminated by the cab's interior light, huddled just outside the open door.

Otis Werner.

Dean Werner.

And Jack.

Jack was between the men, with Dean closest to Redd and Otis just coming out of the truck behind them. Both men had pistols in hand, but neither was actively looking for a target, nor did they seem to be aware that Redd had the drop on them.

Still half-hidden, Redd lined the Ruger up to take out Dean with a head shot, but he didn't pull the trigger. He knew he could kill the man without directly endangering Jack, but unless his bullet magically took out Otis as well, the latter would have time to react, and that *would* put Jack in danger.

He saw only one acceptable course of action. To minimize the risk to Jack, he would have to give the men the opportunity to surrender.

Plus, on some level, Redd knew it was the right thing to do.

"It's over!" he shouted, stepping into the open, the Ruger in a steady, two-hand grip aimed at Otis Werner. "Put down your weapons. Nobody else has to die!"

Almost predictably, Otis reacted by stabbing his semiauto in Redd's direction, but then he did the one thing Redd most feared he would do. He turned the gun on Jack.

"Back off," Otis bawled. "Or the kid—"

Redd didn't let him finish the sentence. With a steady trigger pull, he put a bullet directly between Otis Werner's eyes. The connection between brain and body severed, there was not even a postmortem muscle twitch. Otis simply collapsed, the unfired pistol falling from his nerveless grip.

Well, I tried.

Redd brought the Ruger back down and put its front sight on the blood-spattered bridge of Dean's nose, but even as he did, Dean snapped out of his state of shock and ducked down behind Jack, removing himself from Redd's sight picture. Redd followed him down with the revolver, but Dean was almost completely hidden behind his tiny human shield, with the business end of his .45 semiauto dangerously close to Jack's temple.

Jack stared up at Redd, his eyes wide with equal measures of fear, horror, and hope. Some of Otis Werner's blood had sprayed onto him and now ran down his cheeks like dark tears. The sight tore Redd's heart in two. In less than the span of a day, the poor kid had been threatened, abducted, and witnessed more death than most people experienced in a lifetime, and now, it was happening again. He wanted to tell Jack that it was going to be okay, that it was almost over.

But comforting words wouldn't save the boy.

At least not yet.

Redd focused his attention on Dean Werner. "Drop your weapon."

He expected a display of bravado—like father, like son—but to his astonishment, Dean cried out, "Wait, okay? Just . . . just give me a second."

Redd thumbed the Ruger's hammer back. "Last chance."

"No! Just wait! Okay? Just wait." The pistol barrel lifted away from Jack's head and pointed skyward. "Don't shoot, okay?"

"Drop it," Redd repeated, drawing out the words. From the corner of his eye, he saw flashes of red and blue light, growing brighter by the second. The cavalry was coming, and their timing couldn't be worse. He needed to resolve this standoff *before* a dozen gung ho FBI SWAT officers showed up, eager for a little real-world action. "Drop the gun! *Now!*"

"I don't want to kill him, okay? I never wanted to kill him."

The voluntary admission threw Redd for a moment. What was Dean trying to say? More importantly, what was he trying to accomplish? Was this some kind of stalling technique? A veiled threat or even an attempt to place the onus of Jack's fate on Redd?

The flashing lights were growing steadily brighter, casting a red-and-blue light show across the landscape.

"I don't wanna die!"

"Then put the gun down," Redd said slowly. "I won't say it again."

"How do I know you won't kill me anyway?"

Redd chose his words carefully. He doubted Dean would accept a simple pledge or promise of safety. Had their roles been reversed, Redd certainly wouldn't have. "Believe me, I'd like nothing better. For all the people you've killed, a bullet through the head hardly even seems like justice. Lucky for you, it's not up to me to decide that. Surrender right now, and you'll get your day in court. You have my word. But if you threaten that boy for even one more second, I won't hesitate. And that second starts . . . *now.*"

"Okay!" cried Dean, holding the hand with the pistol up, with his fingers splayed, well away from the trigger. "I'm putting it down, okay? Don't shoot."

The hand came down slowly, all the way to the ground, and then let go of the pistol.

"Step away from him," Redd ordered. "Face down on the ground. Spread eagle."

Dean hesitated a moment, then complied, shuffling sideways away from Jack, away from the truck and his father's dead body. He stretched out in a prone position. "Don't shoot," he said, almost whimpering. "Please don't shoot!"

As soon as he realized that Dean was no longer holding onto him, Jack rushed toward Redd, throwing his arms around Redd's right leg.

"I knew you'd come get me, Matt." The words spilled out in between Jack's sobs.

Redd kept the Ruger trained on Dean but dropped his left hand to clasp Jack's shoulder. "It's okay. It's over, buddy."

As if feeling left out of the moment, Rubble bounded up and began licking Jack's face. Jack let out a little squeal, prompting Redd to utter a stern, "No, Rubble. Sit!" But before the dog could pull away, Jack threw his arms around his neck in a fierce embrace.

They stayed like that for a few minutes, with man, boy, and dog too overcome with emotion to do much else. Redd was dimly aware of the sound of vehicles arriving, of spotlights illuminating the scene like daybreak, of a multitude of footsteps and shouted commands. Then he heard a familiar voice—Kline's.

"All good, Matt?"

He looked over and saw Kline approaching with Mikey at his side, the latter with his Remington long rifle across his shoulder. Redd managed a smile and a nod. "All good."

"Then how about you let us take it from here," said Kline, with a meaningful look at the Ruger.

Redd glanced down at the revolver, still pointing at Dean Werner, then lowered it. As if that was the signal they had been waiting for, two FBI agents in black tactical gear closed in on Dean, searching and restraining him.

"We found a pathetic creature crawling down the interstate about twenty miles back. Looked like he'd just gone fifteen rounds with Tyson. Told us, and I quote, 'That preacher's kid threw me off a train.' Don't suppose you'd know anything about that?"

Redd affected a hurt expression. "Hey, I saved his life."

"Really?" said Kline. "Guy looks like he's got a couple of broken arms and several broken ribs to go with 'em. You wouldn't happen to know anything about *that*, now, would you?"

Redd shrugged. "Like I said, I saved his life."

Kline's eyes flicked to Jack as if to say, *He wouldn't give up the kid's location.*

Redd just nodded once in response.

Nothing else needed to be said.

"On that note," said Kline, as the agents hauled their handcuffed suspect to his feet and began frog-marching him to a waiting vehicle, "I have to admit when you told me you were going after them on your own, I didn't think there would be anyone left to arrest. If you know what I mean."

Mikey chuckled. "Dude, same. Every time Matt goes dark, bad guys stop breathing in bunches."

"Yeah," replied Redd slowly. "Well, there were extenuating circumstances."

He flipped the Ruger up, thumbed the loading port cover aside, and then began rotating the cylinder, allowing spent brass casings to fall into his open palm one at a time. When he was finished, there were six empty shells in his cupped hand.

"You were out of ammo?" gasped Mikey.

"Yeah," admitted Redd, looking down at the Ruger. "But I still got the job done."

Kline shook his head. "I know you're fond of that old cannon Jim Bob gave you, but maybe it's time to consider an upgrade. You know, something that doesn't take half a minute to reload."

Redd chuckled. "Maybe so." Then he squeezed Jack's shoulder again. "What do you say we get out of here, huh?"

Jack looked up. "Where are we going?"

Redd smiled as he picked the boy up into his arms.

"We're going home, Jack."

SIXTY-TWO

He did not go directly to the ranch, but then that wasn't really what he had meant. Home wasn't a fixed place, but something else. Something harder to quantify. It was, Redd had come to understand, wherever the people you loved and who loved you in return were always waiting.

Dawn was just breaking when Redd rolled into the clinic parking lot. The drive back to Wellington had been long, made even longer by the constant rush of air through the Raptor's missing windows and the accompaniment of humming and creaking noises resulting from uncounted deformities to the truck's exterior surfaces and suspension. The frequency of the noises increased in direct proportion to the truck's speed, intensifying into an assault on the nervous system whenever the speedometer crept above fifty miles per hour. Though Mikey didn't remark on the extent of the damage, Redd could see him wince a little whenever the noise got to be too much to handle. Jack, however, curled up on the floor in the rear of the cab and, hugging his Buzz Lightyear toy, slept through it all.

After parking, Redd got out and gently scooped Jack's sleeping form into his arms. Rubble, who had been curled up beside the boy, lifted his head and started to rise, but Redd stopped him with a soft command. "Stay, Rubble." Then he added, "I'll be right back."

The rottie uttered a low, plaintive wail but settled back down.

While Redd was collecting Jack, Mikey made a slow circuit around the Raptor.

"Well," he announced when he finished, "the good news is that it's not nearly as bad as last time. We'll fix her up again," Mikey went on. "Good as new."

Redd nodded absently. He knew he ought to feel at least a little bit dismayed over the truck's present condition, but the weight and warmth of the sleeping form in his arms put everything in perspective.

✖ ✖ ✖

When he stole into Emily's room, Redd was surprised to find her sitting up in bed with their newborn daughter in her arms. She greeted him with a smile and brought a finger to her lips, signaling him to stay quiet. Matthew Jr. was fast asleep on the neighboring bed. Then her gaze fell on the burden Redd carried, and her eyes lit up.

"Is that him?" she whispered.

Until that moment, it had not occurred to Redd that Emily's and Jack's paths had not previously crossed. He turned slightly to reveal Jack's face, which seemed especially serene in repose, then carried the boy over to the bed and set him down alongside Junior. Jack shifted a little but did not stir.

Emily raised the tightly wrapped bundle in her arms. "Want to hold her?"

"Of course I do." He gently took the baby, cradling her close. Little Lauren fussed for a moment but did not cry out. "She's beautiful. Just like her mama."

Emily smiled again and leaned back against the pillow, content to simply watch her husband hold their daughter. After a few minutes, however, she broke her silence. "Was it bad?"

Redd knew better than to lie to her, so he simply said, "I'll tell you all about it later. The important thing is that everybody made it back safe."

"Thank God for that." She regarded him a moment longer. "You must be exhausted."

He laughed. "Which one of us just gave birth to a baby?"

"I got some sleep. You should too."

He handed Lauren back to her. "Later. I've got to head home and get started on the chores."

Her smile slipped into a frown of disapproval, but she didn't object. "All right.

But be careful. I don't want you falling asleep and running off the road. Mikey will kill you if you bang up the truck."

Redd grimaced. "I'll be careful." He leaned over and kissed her. "You okay watching all the kids until I get back?"

"Mom's coming over soon. She can help me ride herd if things get too crazy." She glanced over at the bed where the two boys lay sleeping. "From what I've heard, little Matty and Jack are already fast friends, so I think we'll be fine."

Redd nodded and then kissed her again. "Okay. Back soon."

✳ ✳ ✳

The first thing Redd noticed when he stepped outside again was how blue the sky looked. The air still smelled like the mother of all campfires, but the pall of smoke that had darkened the world the previous day seemed to have dissipated. He hoped that meant the fire was under control and no longer threatening Wellington. He made a mental note to check in with Blackwood.

Later.

As he pulled up in front of the house, the events of the previous twenty-four hours seemed almost like a bad dream. At a glance, everything at the ranch seemed so . . . normal. But the signs of abnormalcy were everywhere. Aside from the damage to the truck, the front door of the house could not be closed due to the fact that the lock plate and a sizable portion of the doorframe had been torn out. There were buckshot holes in the front room wall and multiple spots of dried blood on the hardwood floor.

Most of that could be fixed in an afternoon, but right now, Redd's priorities were of the everyday nature, so he ignored the damage and set to work tending the herd and mucking out Remington's stall. When the work was done, he took a quick shower, dressed in clean clothes, and headed back into town, this time driving Emily's white Chevy Tahoe.

He found Sheriff Blackwood sitting in the clinic's waiting room, along with a middle-aged woman wearing a professional-looking pantsuit and carrying a leather portfolio. Both Blackwood and the woman stood to meet him, and Blackwood seized his hand, shaking it vigorously.

"Glad you made it back," the sheriff said.

"You and me both," replied Redd, eyeing Blackwood's companion with undisguised suspicion. She looked like a lawyer.

"Director Kline told me some of it," Blackwood went on, conspicuously failing to include the woman in the conversation. "You know, I'm just going to say it again. If you want to work in law enforcement so badly, I'd be happy to have you as a deputy."

"Would you believe me if I said I don't go looking for trouble, it just finds me?"

He expected the sheriff to receive this with a laugh, but instead, the comment seemed to elicit a pained grimace. Blackwood shot a glance at the woman before replying. "On that subject, I thought you might like to know that it looks like that smoke jumper you rescued is going to make it through okay. They flew him to Billings. They've got a Level 1 trauma center there. He'll have a long road to recovery, but thanks to you, he's going to get the chance."

Blackwood then turned to the woman. "Matthew leads our volunteer search and rescue program. He went out yesterday and saved an injured smoke jumper who got caught in the fire."

Redd understood that there was some kind of subtext in play but couldn't grasp what it was. Not until the woman took the initiative and introduced herself.

"Mr. Redd, I'm Paula Sturgess from the Child and Family Services Division."

SIXTY-THREE

Redd felt as if someone had just injected ice water into his veins. He shot an accusatory look at Blackwood. The sheriff, grim faced, spread his hands in an *I had no choice* gesture.

"I understand that you've been taking care of a minor child named John Williams, who was the witness to a violent crime. Is that right?"

"He goes by Jack," Redd answered coldly. "And he wasn't just a witness. His whole family was killed. And he was targeted by the same people who murdered them."

"Mr. Redd, I'm not the enemy here." Sturgess's tone was patient, even a bit long-suffering. She was clearly used to being treated with a degree of reflex hostility. "I'm grateful that you were there for John . . . Jack. Especially given the circumstances you just described."

"But you're still going to take him away."

Sturgess sighed. "Mr. Redd, Jack is an orphan with no designated guardian. The law is clear on this. But more than that, he *needs* the stability that only an assigned caregiver can provide."

"Stability? In the foster care system?"

"Contrary to what you've probably heard, the vast majority of foster parents

310

provide a loving, supportive environment for the children placed in their care. The system may not be perfect, but it is the best we can do for Jack right now. And, I might add, it's the law. I don't like having to play that card, Mr. Redd, but the law is on my side. Ask Sheriff Blackwood."

"I'm sorry, Matthew. She's right."

"I *know*"—she stressed the word—"that you're just looking out for Jack. I get it. Believe it or not, so am I. But you need to step aside and let me do my job."

Every fiber of instinct told Redd to stand his ground, but this, at last, was a fight he could not win with physical prowess and bloody-minded determination. "Yeah," he muttered in a small voice. "I get it."

Sturgess did not crow over her victory. Instead, she said, "I can tell you've built a rapport with Jack. Would you like to make the introductions?"

Redd nodded, grateful that he would at least get a chance to explain the situation to Jack. He gestured toward the door leading to the patient care area. "He's with my wife and family in there. I'll bring him . . ." He stopped short, inspiration dawning.

Maybe if she sees Jack with Junior and Em and sees how happy he is, she'll change her mind.

"Actually, why don't we do this in there?" he said.

He was mildly surprised when Sturgess did not object, and he hastened ahead to give Emily a little advance warning.

When he stuck his head in through the door to the room, he found Emily sitting up in bed and Lauren in the bassinet nearby. Jack and Junior were sitting together in a chair beside Emily's bed, watching cartoons on the room's ancient wall-mounted television. The sound was turned down so low that Redd could barely hear the show, but this didn't seem to bother the boys at all.

"Em," he whispered. "There's someone here who wants to meet Jack."

Emily cocked her head to the side for a moment but then seemed to understand. She mouthed the words *social worker* to which Redd simply nodded. Emily took a breath and then returned the nod. "Let's do this."

✖ ✖ ✖

Matthew stepped inside and held the door open to allow a middle-aged woman to enter. As soon as she entered the room and took in the situation, her eyes went wide. Her gaze went from the baby to Emily. "I'm so sorry," she said. "I didn't realize that you . . . why you're here."

Emily regarded the other woman with a kind smile. "It's no problem," she said, trying to act as if the ordeal of giving birth on a backcountry road in the middle of a wildland fire was no more consequential to her than washing the dishes. "As they say around here, it's not my first rodeo."

"Still, I've got two of my own. I know how you must feel right now."

"I'll let you know if it gets to be too much," Emily assured her.

At the door to the room, Sheriff Blackwood said, "Good to see you already looking so chipper, Dr. Redd. Do you need me to stick around?"

Emily wasn't sure if the sheriff was asking because he thought she and Matthew might need additional moral support or because he thought Emily might need some help keeping her husband's sometimes volcanic temper from awakening.

"I think we're good, Sheriff," she said. Then, turning to the woman, she added, "I'm Emily, by the way. When I'm not occupying a bed here, I'm the head of the emergency medical department."

This seemed to impress the woman. "Paula Sturgess. I'm a social worker with CFSD."

As she said it, she glanced over at the two boys sitting in the chair—neither of whom seemed to have noticed her entrance—but said nothing more regarding the reason for her visit.

Matthew, noticing her attention, circled around the bed and knelt down beside the two boys. "Hey, how's it going?"

Jack looked back at him, beaming. "We had waffles for breakfast."

"Waffles? Did you save any for me?"

Emily faced Sturgess and took the proverbial bull by the horns. "I guess you're here for Jack." Her voice stayed low, but her words were direct. "What will happen to him now?"

Sturgess was equally direct. "In the short term, he'll go into temporary foster care. His last home of record was in Illinois, but it's not clear whether we'll have to turn him over to their DCFS. It will probably be up to a family court judge to decide what's in his best interests."

"How long will that take?"

"I won't sugarcoat this. It could take weeks."

"Does he have any family that could take him in?" asked Emily.

"Not that we've been able to determine. The mother is . . ." She trailed off as if realizing that she had already said too much.

"I'm familiar with privacy laws, Ms. Sturgess."

Sturgess considered this for a moment, then opened her portfolio, extracted a file folder, and passed it over. Emily opened it and began scanning. As was often the case with medical files, there was plenty of raw data but little in the way of synthesis. She found Jack's birth certificate, listing his full name and the name of his mother. The line for the father was left blank. There were early childhood medical records for the first year of Jack's life, but after that, hardly anything. Emily recognized this not as an indication that Jack was exceptionally healthy but rather that his mother had neglected regular well-care visits. Then she found the mother's death certificate. The cause of death was cardiac arrest—a nonspecific catchall used by overworked medical examiners who didn't have sufficient time, resources, or incentives to be more thorough. The accompanying police report, however, added a small and all-too-familiar detail.

Suspected opioid overdose.

She glanced over at Jack and her husband, wondering if the boy knew, wondering if Matthew knew.

No wonder he identifies so strongly with Jack. That's something they have in common.

Following that were a few legal documents detailing the transfer of guardianship to Raymond Williams, Jack's uncle. By all reports, Raymond and his wife had taken good care of Jack during their too-brief tenure as his guardians, though they had not formally adopted him. Jack's maternal grandparents were also deceased, and no other relatives on that side of the family were identified.

"So, he really doesn't have anyone," Emily murmured.

"He can stay with us," said Matthew. "And I don't just mean temporarily. Let us adopt him. If there's no one else, why give him to a complete stranger when we're *right here*? You say he needs a family." He spread his arms. "We're a family."

His eyes went to Emily, the unspoken message clear as day.

"I'm sorry. I know we didn't talk about this. Please help me out . . ."

She wanted desperately to help but couldn't find the words.

Sturgess looked at him and then shook her head. "I'm sorry, Mr. Redd. That just isn't how this works. With no blood relations or designated guardians, Jack *has* to be placed in an approved home."

Jack, who had, up until that moment, been more interested in the cartoons than the conversation, turned his big blue eyes toward the adults. He knew that he was the subject of the discussion even if he didn't know the stakes.

"Then we'll get approved. What do we have to do?"

For the first time since entering the room, Sturgess seemed on the verge of exasperation. "Mr. Redd, I can tell your heart is in the right place, but think about it. You've got a toddler *and* a newborn. Do you really think you're in a position to take on yet another family member?"

"We'll make it work."

Sturgess looked to Emily as if asking for a second opinion.

Hiding her own reservations, Emily nodded. "Like he said. We'll make it work."

"Tell us what to do. Sign us up for foster care. We'll do whatever it takes."

"Look, folks, even if you wanted to adopt him . . . you just . . . can't." She lowered her voice as if revealing a scandalous secret. "You didn't hear this from me, but we don't allow permanent placements in homes where the mother is expecting or there's a newborn. That's just a hard limit. Even if I gave you a glowing recommendation, someone—my boss, or a judge, or some adoption rights advocate—would step in and cry foul."

Emily saw some of the fight go out of her husband, and despite her own uncertainty about what he was proposing, she found that she shared his sense of loss.

Then Jack spoke up. "Can I please stay with them? I've never had a mommy *and* a daddy before."

The statement, uttered with the innocence only a child could possess, tore Emily's heart in two.

"I'm sorry, Jack," said Sturgess, clearly striving for a balance between empathy and authority. "I know this is hard, but we're going to find you a family. I promise."

"With what?" Redd rose and swiped the open file off the bed. "You think a bunch of papers are going to—" He stopped, his eyes apparently drawn to something on the first page. "Going to . . ."

He looked again, his eyes moving as he read the name on the file tab again. And again.

Emily saw his lips moving.

Williams, John Bradly.

Wait . . .

Sturgess snatched the file out of his hand and thrust it into the portfolio. "Jack. It's time to go."

"Wait," cried Emily. She turned to Jack. "Your middle name is Bradly? Is that right?" She had overlooked that when she'd read the birth certificate.

Jack looked up at her, his eyes glistening with tears, and nodded.

"Jack Bradly?"

"I don't see what that has to do with anything," declared Sturgess. "Mr. Redd, I don't want to have to bring the sheriff in here, but you're leaving me no choice."

Emily ignored the woman, keeping her focus on Jack. "So, your initials are J. B.?"

"I guess so."

Emily looked to Redd and gave a slow nod.

Trust me.

"I'm sorry, but do his initials really change anything?"

"Actually," said Emily, "it changes *everything*."

"I'm not following you here."

Emily smiled. "Matty, why don't you take the boys to the café for a couple of juice boxes? I'd like to have a moment with Ms. Sturgess."

The social worker started to object. "I can't allow that—"

"Ms. Sturgess, please. All I'm asking is five minutes of your time." She lowered her voice. "You have my solemn promise that Matthew isn't going to make a run for it."

"The thought never occurred to me." Sturgess's nervous laugh, however, suggested otherwise. "It's just that prolonging a scene like this only makes it more painful for everyone involved."

Emily tilted her head in a sagacious nod. "Five minutes."

Without waiting for permission, Matthew took Jack's hand and then scooped Little Matty up in his other arm. "Who wants a juice box?"

When they had left, Sturgess circled around the bed and sank resignedly into the chair. "Dr. Redd, I think we both know that your husband is being unrealistic. I can see it in your eyes. You don't think this is a good idea."

"I had my reservations at first," Emily admitted. "But Matthew's right. Why subject Jack to this process when he's already with a family that loves him?"

"I told you. It's just no—"

"I know we can't adopt him. Not for a few years, at least. But what about long-term foster care? Is that a possibility?"

Sturgess looked hesitant. "It's . . . not impossible. If you had already gone through the process, I might be able to make a case for it."

"Then start the process. And while the process is ongoing, let him stay with us. Call it a temporary emergency placement, and then . . ." She shrugged. "Just keep moving the file to the bottom of the stack until we can clear all the hurdles. You can come check on him every day if you like."

Sturgess sighed. "Dr. Redd, I want to be clear with you about something. There's a very good reason why we don't adopt to families with newborns. The simple fact of the matter is that there's enormous inherent pressure on the parents to give their love and attention to their biological children and to neglect or even resent their adopted children. You can promise me that won't happen, but I've seen it in families that adopted and then had an unplanned pregnancy."

"I understand all that," Emily said. "But there's something else you need to know."

"And what exactly is that?"

"Jack Bradly," answered Emily, as if that explained everything. "J. B."

"I don't get it."

"Then let me tell you the story of Matthew Redd."

SIXTY-FOUR

MINSK, BELARUS
THREE MONTHS LATER

Marina Waldron pulled her fur coat a little tighter around her body as she left behind the still-warm environs of her 2023 Bentley Continental GT. She had a lot of regrets over the way things had turned out in Montana, but as she trekked down the sidewalk toward the building in which the Belarusbank main branch was housed, one of her biggest was the fact that her exile had not brought her somewhere tropical. Granted, winter in Minsk was milder than winter in Chicago, but winter in Barbados would have been more to her taste. Alas, her *persona* was most definitely *non grata* in the island paradises where she had hidden away much of the proceeds of her ill-fated partnership with Otis Werner.

Not that she was complaining. She had certainly come out of it better than Werner, who, she was reliably informed, had perished in a shoot-out with the FBI. She was even better off than Martin, whose cooperation with the authorities was going to cost him three years in a federal prison and the near-complete forfeiture of his assets. She had not only kept her freedom, at least to the extent that being unable to leave her new refuge in Belarus could be considered *freedom*, but also retained access to enough money to live comfortably for at least a few years, and if she invested carefully, maybe even the rest of her life. If that meant trading fruity cocktails poolside for hot toddies fireside at her palatial new residence in Laporovichi on the north bank of the Zaslawskaye Reservoir, well . . . she would just have to grin and bear it.

Unfortunately, the weather wasn't the only source of frustration in her newly adopted homeland.

When she had first opened her account at the national bank, depositing a hefty seven-figure transfer of funds from one of her offshore accounts, she had been treated like royalty. Lately, however, the relationship seemed to have flipped. The initial deference of the bankers had turned into something more like grudging forbearance.

It was, she supposed, mostly a cultural thing. Not only was she an outsider who did not speak their language, she was also a woman. Contrary to what she had been led to believe by decades of American cinema, English was not a common language in Eastern Europe, but early on, at least, there had always been an English-speaking account executive available to assist her with her business. Once it became apparent that she was done making deposits into her account, those executives seemed to have collectively lost their ability to communicate in her language. Requests for routine account service had run up against an impenetrable language barrier.

And now? Now she had been summoned—*summoned*—to a meeting with one of the bank's vice presidents regarding some unspecified problems with her portfolio of investments. No, it couldn't be handled over the phone, and no, he couldn't come out to her home.

It was time to remind these bankers that they worked for her.

She unconsciously loosened the collar of her coat, letting the wintry air cool some of the heat of her rising ire, and made her way toward the building where the main branch in Minsk was located. She was about ten steps shy of her destination when her phone began chiming in her handbag. Already in an irritable mood, she cursed aloud at the interruption and cursed again when she saw the number displayed on the screen.

She hit the button to accept the call. "Yes?"

"Ms. Waldron?" The heavily accented voice mangled her name. "This is Igor Zubarevich from the bank. I spoke to you earlier."

"Whatever you want, Mr. Zubarevich, it can wait. I'm walking into the bank right now."

"I am so sorry, but that's just it. Mr. Kalyuzhny was called away unexpectedly. I am afraid to say we will have to do this another time."

Marina stared at her phone in disbelief. "You're kidding."

"I assure you, I am quite serious."

"I'm literally standing right outside. If Mr. Kalyuzhny isn't available, then have someone else take care of this. I'm done with this runaround."

"I am so sorry," repeated Zubarevich. "There is nobody else. Mr. Kalyuzhny wanted me to ask if you could come in later this afternoon. He suggests you might go shopping to pass the time."

Marina rolled her eyes. "You tell Mr. Kalyuzhny that he can go—"

A double beep, signaling the termination of the call, cut her off.

With a scowl, she shoved the phone into her bag, then turned and headed back to her car. She *would* go shopping, she decided, and then when she came back for her meeting, she would tell Mr. Kalyuzhny to his face what he could do with himself. Then she would withdraw all of her money and take it to his bank's number one competitor.

The thought brought her only a small measure of comfort. Like it or not, this was her life for the foreseeable future.

As she turned back onto the sidewalk, she noticed a tall blond-haired man standing in front of her car, to all appearances gazing at the vehicle in admiration. When he noticed her approaching, he smiled and said something she didn't understand, probably complimenting the Bentley.

The man was good-looking and had a nice smile, but rather than putting her at ease, his apparent interest made her wary. *"Dziakuj,"* she replied—*thank you*—hoping that she'd interpreted his meaning correctly. She added, *"Vybačennie"*—*excuse me*—and gestured toward the driver's door.

The man inclined his head and stepped back, giving her plenty of room to finish her approach, but continued to stand there as if waiting for something else to happen.

Well, he could stand there all day for all she cared. He wasn't going to get anything from her.

She used her remote to unlock and start the Bentley and then locked the door again as soon as she was inside. The blond man continued to stand there and, when he noticed her looking at him, smiled again.

"Whatever," she murmured and reached for the gearshift lever.

✖ ✖ ✖

The sound of someone rapping on the window glass startled Marina out of a somnolence she had not even realized she had been experiencing. She looked up and was immediately confronted by a world she did not recognize. She was still sitting behind the wheel of the Bentley, but everything outside its protective bubble was different. The bank building and the surrounding urban landscape of Minsk had transformed into a rural setting. It was as if she and the car had been teleported into the countryside.

But, of course, that was impossible. Transported, perhaps, but not in the blink of an eye. A glance at the clock in the center of the dashboard confirmed it. She had lost nearly six hours. Her thoughts were still a little muddled, but she wasn't so befogged that she couldn't figure out what had happened.

Someone drugged me!

Her mind immediately began to race as she contemplated all the dire ramifications stemming from that evident reality.

Who did this to me?

A memory of the smiling blond man came unbidden.

Yes, it had to have been him . . . but why?

As the scion of a pharmaceutical company, she had more than a passing familiarity with the drugs that might have caused her to lose time, or more accurately, any memory of what might have happened during that time. A known side effect of the category of drugs known as benzodiazepines was anterograde amnesia—the prevention of the formation of new memories while under the drugs' influence—which meant that a person might remain conscious and seemingly aware but later have no memory of what happened during that time, an effect that had been exploited for sexual assault, earning benzos the nickname "date-rape drugs." Yet while the possibility that the blond man might have dosed her for some carnal purpose was terrifying at a visceral level, there were other, even more terrible explanations.

The hard rap on the window came again, more insistent this time, compelling her to turn her head for a look.

The man standing outside, tapping on the window with the end of a long flashlight, wore a heavy navy-blue parka and a watch cap, both emblazoned with white letters that read *POLICJA*.

Marina's blood went cold. Belarus, like most of the former Soviet Republics, used the Cyrillic alphabet, which she, after only three months, still had trouble decoding. The letters on the police officer's coat were most definitely not Cyrillic, which meant that she was no longer in Belarus.

The policeman kept tapping, more urgently now, and shouting something—no doubt an exhortation to roll the window down or exit the vehicle. With no obvious alternative, she did the former, but as the window began lowering, the policeman's demeanor became more intense. He took a step back, resting one hand on his sidearm, and began gesturing with the other—his meaning now crystal clear.

Get out.

"I don't understand," she said, not caring whether *he* understood or not. Perhaps the mere fact of her using English would serve to explain her slow reaction and thus put the man at ease.

An attractive woman dressed in casual attire stepped out from behind the officer and provided a translation in clear, unaccented English. "He's telling you to exit the vehicle."

"You're American?" breathed Marina, her dread multiplying exponentially.

"That's right." The woman raised her hand to display a badge case. "Special Agent Stephanie Treadway. FBI. And you, Ms. Waldron, are under arrest."

Marina shook her head. "No. You can't do this. It's . . . it's illegal."

Treadway quirked a smile. "That's funny. Coming from you, I mean. But you're wrong. It's all completely legal. You're not in Belarus anymore. You're in Poland, and Poland has an extradition treaty with the US. So . . . congratulations! You're going home."

Marina kept shaking her head. "You kidnapped me. Drugged me and kidnapped me across an international border. You can't do that. It's illegal," she repeated.

"You keep using that word," remarked Treadway. "I do not think it means what you think it means." She paused a beat, then, evidently in response to Marina's uncomprehending stare, added, "*The Princess Bride*? No? Not a fan? You really should watch it. Probably one of the best movies of all time."

"You *can't* do this," insisted Marina.

"*I* didn't do anything," countered Treadway. "The FBI got a tip that you had driven into Poland. I gave the information to the *policja* and let them take care of the rest."

"You sent someone to kidnap me! To drug me! It was a man, a blond!"

Treadway shrugged. "That's a nice story, Ms. Waldron. Good luck trying to prove it in court."

✖   ✖   ✖

Later, after the *policja* drove away with their prisoner, Special Agent Treadway sat back on the fender of the Bentley and did a slow survey of the surrounding area. Seeing no one, she finally shook her head and called out, "Okay, Decker, I give up. Come out, come out, wherever—"

"Hey, Steph."

Treadway almost jumped out of her shoes. Aaron Decker—whom Marina had only been able to describe as "a blond"—had somehow managed to sneak up on her left side while she had been looking to the right.

There was a reason Kline called Decker a ghost.

"Stop doing that!" she said, slugging him in the shoulder. "*How* do you do that, anyway?"

Decker shrugged. "It's a gift."

"Well, I'm just glad you're on our side."

"Always happy to help," replied Decker. "And actually, this has been a nice change of pace."

She didn't have to ask what he meant by that.

Once upon a time, Aaron Decker had been a covert operative specializing in the sanctioned termination of America's enemies abroad—enemies who were beyond the reach of both law enforcement and military interventions. At least, that was the conclusion Treadway—herself a former intelligence officer—had come to believe. In true ghost fashion, there was no paper trail connecting Decker to any official agency. But when Kline had sent her to make contact with Decker, asking him to come out of retirement to help the Bureau take down a global conspiracy of men who had used their wealth and influence to put them beyond the reach of the justice system, and subsequently, those men had met with untimely demises, it wasn't that hard to put two and two together. Decker was Kline's secret weapon of last resort. His assassin.

By "a nice change of pace," Decker simply meant that this time, he had not been required to take a life.

"So where to now?"

"Home," he said. "I don't mind doing these little favors for Gavin, and I definitely don't mind the compensation, but I do not miss living out of a suitcase."

She gestured to the Bentley. "Hop in. I'll give you a ride to the airport."

"You're keeping her car? I'm surprised the *policja* were okay with that."

"You know how persuasive I can be." She grinned. "Come on. When are you going to get a chance to ride in style like this?"

"I just spent the last five hours riding in style," he pointed out.

"Well, yeah, but you weren't riding with me."

He laughed. "Fair enough. Okay, you talked me into it."

WARSAW, POLAND

Sergei Konstantin heaved his bulk onto a barstool and uttered a word that needed no translation: "Vodka."

The unsmiling bartender didn't ask for clarification but deftly decanted a healthy measure of the spirit into an old-fashioned glass and placed it on a cocktail napkin on the bar in front of his customer.

Konstantin downed it in the customary way—in a single gulp—then slammed the glass back down and gestured for a refill. While he waited, Konstantin placed his elbows on the bar and cradled his head in his hands.

It had been a long day, a long trip, and he was beyond exhausted. The war with Ukraine had been good for business, but what was good for business wasn't necessarily good for his health.

At least this job was done. Now, all that remained was the long journey home—a journey made longer now that travel into and out of Mother Russia was no longer as simple as it had once been.

He picked up his glass and rotated on his chair to stare out at the concourse, watching travelers with roller suitcases scurrying about like ants around their nest. In a few minutes, he would have to go join them—just another insect.

Thank goodness for vodka, he thought, tipping the glass back.

And then he froze in place.

"*Nyet,*" he whispered, staring over the top of the glass at a figure moving leisurely along with the crowd. "No. It cannot be. Not possible."

But it *was.*

It was *him.*

He swung back around to the bar, slapped a two-hundred-*zloty* note down beside the empty glass, and made his way out onto the concourse.

He would have to be very careful. This man, if it was who he thought it was, would be able to sense if he was being followed. But Konstantin did not need to know where the man was going. It would be enough to have confirmation that his eyes had not been playing tricks on him. So, instead of hanging back at a distance, he raced ahead, moving almost at a jog as if hurrying to make a connecting flight. He was careful not to look anywhere but straight ahead, and even that was a risk. He did not think the man would recognize him—it had been more than a decade since they'd last been in the same room, and back then, Konstantin had been just a figure in the background—but it was a chance he would have to take.

He kept going until he reached a gate where passengers were just lining up to begin boarding and joined the queue. Only then did he raise his eyes and begin looking around as if curious about the people he would be sharing the plane with.

From the corner of his eye, he saw the man again, moving down the gates, seemingly indifferent to the world around him. Konstantin knew better, though. The man was completely attuned to his environment.

It was definitely him. As impossible as that seemed, it was him.

Konstantin remained in the line until the subject of his interest had passed by. Then he stepped out and moved in the other direction. As he walked, he took out his phone and dialed a number.

The phone rang once. Then a second time. "Come on, chief," he murmured. "Pick up."

On the third ring, the call was picked up, and he heard a low, guttural *"Da?"*

Konstantin, out of breath after his jog through the airport, suddenly found himself at a loss for words. "Chief," he wheezed. "You're not going to believe this."

"Spit it out, Sergei."

Konstantin took a breath. Then another. What he was about to say would change . . . everything.

"I just saw a ghost."

"A ghost?"

Konstantin swallowed hard. "I saw Aaron Decker."

EPILOGUE

CHRISTMAS EVE

As he stood by the window watching thick snowflakes blanket the world around him, it hit Matthew Redd that this was the first time in his life he was truly excited about Christmas.

When he was a kid, Christmastime had been synonymous with disappointment. Once he came to live with J. B., they had found their own understated ways to celebrate. Then a decade ago, Christmas Eve had brought more heartache when Redd's unit, stationed in Northern Iraq, had gone out on a simple mission that turned out to be anything but. As seemingly everything that could go wrong did, Redd and his men spent most of Christmas Eve fighting off waves of ISIS fighters until more help eventually arrived.

Not everyone had made it back, and Redd frequently thought of the men who gave their lives that night. They weren't just the few and the proud . . . They were some of the bravest men he ever rode into battle with. And even now, his heart ached for their families.

The sound of Matthew Jr. squealing in excitement pulled Redd from his thoughts. He turned to see Emily pulling both little Matty and Jack—attired in matching red-and-silver pajamas—onto her lap. She was getting ready to read the boys *'Twas the Night before Christmas*. Rubble, his dark coat now almost completely grown back, was stretched out at her feet. Lauren was fast asleep in their bedroom, bundled up in a pink camo sleeper inside her crib, completely oblivious to the fact that tomorrow would be her first Christmas.

"Jack, do you know this story, honey?" Redd heard Emily ask.

"I don't think so," the boy said softly. "I only know the Grinch."

Each time Jack spoke, Redd found himself in awe of the fact that a child who'd been through so much, who had every reason and excuse to become hardened by the cruel world he lived in, was, in fact, the sweetest kid he'd ever met. The boy didn't have a mean bone in his body. Even with little Matty, who was closing in on his second birthday, Jack displayed nothing but patience and love. He would often play with Junior, teaching him how to zoom Hot Wheels down the hallway or how to hit a plastic ball with their pretend golf set.

Jack had become part of the family, and both Redd and Emily had vowed to cherish their time with him. However long it lasted.

Though their pleas for adoption had gone unheard, Emily had been able to strike a deal with the social worker that allowed them to care for John "Jack" Bradly Williams as his legal foster parents. It wouldn't last forever, but for now, Redd was determined to make the best of it.

A strong wind gust swirled snow across the picture window next to him, the house creaking with the force of the storm. The house was still new, but Redd felt J. B.'s presence, which surprised him because all of the man's belongings— save for a gun or two and everything in the barn—had been lost in the fire that destroyed their original home. Redd took that as proof that it wasn't material *things* that defined someone but rather how they were remembered.

Now that he had a family of his own, Redd was only too happy to revisit the Christmas traditions from his days growing up with Jim Bob. The kids were too young to enjoy the annual viewing of Redd's favorite Christmas movie— *Die Hard*—but they weren't too young to help him pick out a tree. After Thanksgiving, he'd taken them all—Emily, Junior, Jack, and Lauren—out to scour the property for the perfect tree. They'd picked out a nice eight-footer, which Redd had cut and Remington had dragged back to the house, where Emily worked her magic with a display of lights, matching red and green ornaments, and garlands far beyond the basic bulbs he used to hang with Jim Bob.

Redd sighed, letting the scent of fresh pine fill his nostrils. He said a quick prayer for the families of all the men he'd served with who were no longer here to celebrate with their loved ones.

"Matty," asked Emily, "what are you doing over there?"

"Nothing," he said. "Just thinking."

"Well, I *think* you should come over here and help me read to the kids."

Redd smiled. "I think you're right."

"Dada!" yelled Junior. "C'mon!"

"I'm coming, buddy." But then he spotted a pair of headlights peeking through the thick snowflakes. He couldn't see the make and model of the vehicle.

"Matty?"

Redd detected a hint of concern in his wife's voice.

"It's okay, Em. Just someone swinging by."

He said it as reassuringly as he could, but with everything the two of them had been through together, Redd couldn't blame his wife for suspecting something might be wrong. His alarm bells were going off too.

Who would show up this late on Christmas Eve?

Less than ten seconds later, he had an answer as a blue sedan parked under the glow of the floodlights out front, and a familiar figure got out.

"It's Gavin," said Redd.

"*Really?*" asked Emily. "What a surprise!"

Redd squinted at her in mock accusation. "Like you didn't know."

"Who, me?" She pressed a hand to her chest in a show of innocence, then smiled. "Well, let him in."

Redd opened the front door, letting Kline step inside, his arms stacked full of wrapped gifts. He took a moment to stomp the snow off his shoes, then met Redd's gaze. "Hey, Matt. Sorry I didn't call first."

Redd gave a quick nod. "What's up?"

"Well," said Kline, looking for somewhere to deposit his load. Spotting the Christmas tree, he moved toward it, setting all but two items under the boughs with the rest of the gifts. He then turned toward the couch, waving to Emily and the kids. "I, uh . . . decided that I wanted to spend Christmas with my family. I hope that's okay."

"Of course it's okay!" Emily said, her voice full of excitement. "I'd come hug you, but I don't think I could get up if I wanted to."

Kline smiled. "No worries. I'll come to you." He bent down and untied his shoes and slipped them off before doing the same with his coat.

"I'm glad you could make it, Gavin," said Redd, taking the coat from him. And to his surprise, he meant it wholeheartedly.

"Me too. Forgot how cold it is here, though. We've got some snow back in DC, but nothing like this. It's really coming down out there."

Kline stepped into the open living space and walked toward the couch, where Emily was busy juggling both boys in her lap. While adjusting her position, she dropped the book, which thumped onto the floor.

"I'll get it." Kline bent down. "*'Twas the Night before Christmas*," he said, glancing at the title. "Imagine that."

He handed it to Emily, then reached out and tousled Jack's wavy dark hair. "How you doing, buddy?"

"Good, sir," said Jack. "Miss Emily is about to read us a story. You want to hear it with us?"

"I sure do," said Kline. "But first, I need to talk to Matt for a second. That okay?"

Redd grimaced inwardly.

Leave it to Gavin to show up with an agenda.

"Sure," replied Jack, and then went back to looking at the book.

Redd steered Kline into the dining room. "So, what's on your mind, Gavin?"

"Well, for starters, I thought you might like to know that we tracked down Marina Waldron. She was in Belarus."

"I'm guessing we don't have an extradition treaty with them?"

"You guessed correctly."

"And you want me to lead the fly team on a covert mission to nab her." He said it with a decided lack of enthusiasm. Ever since the takedown of ParaDyme Pharma and Otis Werner's fentanyl operation, Kline had been working to create a new role for Redd within the Bureau. To his consternation, Redd had shown little enthusiasm for any job that would take him away from his family.

But Kline shook his head. "Actually, it's already been taken care of."

Redd shrugged, then nodded. "Okay. So . . . what did you want to talk to me about?"

Kline looked down, staring at the floor as if embarrassed. Finally, he raised his eyes and met Redd's gaze. "I just wanted to tell you that I'm . . ." He swallowed. "I'm really proud of you."

Redd shrugged again, unsure what to say back. He realized that, despite all the positive interactions between them over the last few years, Kline had never expressed himself in such a direct, unguarded way. In the past, Redd might have sarcastically dismissed such praise. He hadn't needed or wanted his biological father's approval. Kline had given up that right when he'd let another man raise his own son.

But Redd didn't feel that way anymore.

"I know we don't talk like this very often, Matty . . . Matt." Kline smiled. "I'm sorry that we never connected like father and son. I guess I'm sorry about everything. I really am. All those years ago when I found out your mother . . . that she'd given birth to a child . . . *my* child . . . that she was dead, and I had a son . . . I panicked. I knew I couldn't raise a kid. Not with the life I wanted to lead. So, I called Jim Bob, and . . . well . . . you know the rest."

Redd nodded.

"Truth is, I think I was just scared. I took the easy way out. I'll never forgive myself, but I do hope one day to earn your forgiveness."

Redd thought he had an answer ready, but when he opened his mouth, the words refused to come out.

"You're a great father," Kline went on. "I don't know where you learned it—probably from Jim Bob. But you are. Anyone can see it. A good father and a good husband. And what you've done for that kid? For Jack? That's above and beyond."

"Thanks," Redd managed to say. "For everything, I mean. Being there for me, for all of us."

Had Redd been better at expressing his emotions, he would have told his father that he did forgive him, and that he was ready to move on. He just didn't know how to say it.

Thankfully, though, he didn't have to.

Kline returned a stiff nod. "Well, anyway, I got something for you." He extended one of the parcels he'd held back—a flat, rectangular box, a little bigger than a cigar box, wrapped in red paper with a green bow.

Redd took it, surprised by its weight. "Thanks. If I'd known you were coming, I wouldn't have shipped your presents out."

"Open it," urged Kline.

Redd shrugged, then tore off the paper, revealing an elegant hardwood presentation box. Based on the size and heft of the box, he knew without looking that it contained a handgun, but what he found inside, nestled in red velvet, wasn't just any gun.

"That's a Korth NXS, eight-shot .357 Magnum," said Kline. "Six-inch barrel with a ventilated cooling shroud. Integrated Picatinny rail system. And the cylinder swings out to accommodate moon clips. Heck of a lot faster loading time than that old hand cannon J. B. left you." He chuckled. "For the next time you decide you want to start a war."

"Gavin, I don't know what to say." What he felt like saying was, *I can't accept this.* He'd seen the NXS reviewed in magazines. He'd also seen its price tag.

"You don't need to say anything. As many gunfights as you get into, those extra two bullets should really help," Kline joked. The mood lightened, and even Redd laughed.

Kline held up the other parcel—not a wrapped present, but a simple manila envelope—and then nodded in the direction of the front room. "This is for everyone."

Redd followed Kline into the other room, where Emily looked up at him expectantly. "Gavin has a present for us," explained Redd.

A bright smile spread across Emily's face. "Gavin, you didn't need to. Just having you here is enough. Really."

"Let's see if you feel that way after you see what it is," said Kline. He handed the envelope to Redd.

Redd unsealed the envelope and pulled out a packet of what looked like court documents. It took him a second to realize what he was looking at, but when he did, he was at a loss for words. He even read a few lines over again to make sure it was real.

"Matty?" said Emily.

He didn't respond. His eyes kept coming back to a particular line.

. . . *shall henceforth be known as John Bradly Redd.*

"Matty, what is it?"

Redd looked to his wife, his throat suddenly too dry to form words. Overcome by a wave of emotions, all he could do was hand over the contents of the envelope.

Emily's eyes widened as she read, and then she looked up at him and mouthed, *Adoption?*

He swallowed, then nodded.

"Turns out it's good to have friends in high places," Kline said. He winked at Jack.

"Oh, my gosh," Emily cried and burst into tears.

Junior and Jack, alarmed at the unexpected display, began hugging Emily.

Realizing that neither Redd nor Emily was able to explain, Kline knelt in front of Jack. "Hey, pal . . . What do you say? You want to be part of this crazy family?"

"Gavin," started Emily, tears streaming down her cheeks. "Is this for real?"

"It's for real. Had to call in a few favors and got a little help from some friends to push this through, but it's totally legit." Kline smiled. "So, what do you say, kid? I think Jack Bradly Redd has an awfully nice ring to it."

Redd walked over to Jack and knelt beside Kline.

Jack looked back quizzically. "Wait . . . You're . . . You're going to adopt me?" His big round eyes moved from Emily to Redd. His soft voice cracked. "I'm going to have a mommy and a daddy?"

"And a grandpa," said Kline, standing up.

Redd stood too. "Gavin, I . . ."

Thank you, he wanted to say. But he still couldn't seem to find the words.

Kline put his hand on Redd's shoulder. "I know."

✖   ✖   ✖

An hour later, well after Emily was done reading them the story and following a prolonged teeth-brushing session that Redd thought felt suspiciously like a stall tactic in hopes of seeing Santa arrive, Junior and Jack were tucked into their beds.

Redd had said their nighttime prayers with them and given them each a hug.

"Remember the rule," he said before retreating out of their bedroom. He wanted to get back to the family room and hear more about how Kline had managed to push the adoption through. Plus, he and Emily still had presents to wrap. And with Lauren due to wake any moment for her next feeding, there wasn't much time to get it all done. "We don't open presents until sunup."

That was Emily's doing. She understood most children didn't sleep much on Christmas Eve, the excitement keeping them on edge as the anticipation built all through the night. But from a practical standpoint, she had known that between Redd getting up early enough to knock out the chores around the ranch, and her needing time to feed Lauren, if they didn't set a firm *no presents before sunup* rule, they might not sleep at all.

"Are there any other rules?"

The question came from Jack, and it caught Redd off guard. Letting go of the doorknob and stepping back into the warm, dark room, he asked, "What do you mean, buddy?"

Redd could see Jack's eyes searching, trying to figure out the best way to phrase what he was trying to ask.

"Like, are there any more rules to be part of this family?"

Ah, thought Redd. He walked back over to Jack's twin bed, which was covered in thick flannel sheets and a Christmas-themed comforter. He was tempted to get Emily. She was much better with words and always seemed to know what to say to children. But he sat down.

"Look, Jack. That's just a silly Christmas Morning rule to make sure everyone gets enough sleep so they're not too tired to play with their presents. Okay?"

The boy nodded.

"You are part of this family. Even if you break some rules, that won't change anything. We're gonna love you no matter what, buddy. You can count on that. Always. Okay? There's nothing you could ever do that'll make you *not* be part of our family. So don't worry about that. Ever. All right?"

Jack nodded again.

Redd looked down at him and realized that this must have been what it was like for J. B. all those years ago. Redd remembered feeling insecure for the longest time, worrying that one wrong thing might cause the old rancher to give up on him and kick him out. But Jim Bob assured him, time and time again, that it would never happen. Eventually, Redd believed him and stopped fearing that he'd be cast aside and started loving and appreciating J. B., who was a good and honorable man.

"You just be the best person you can be, Jack. And we'll all love you and support you no matter what. That's what family does."

"I never had a family before."

"Well, you do now. And we're not going anywhere. Good night, pal."

"Good night," came Jack's soft voice.

Redd stood up and walked back into the hallway. But as he was pulling the door shut behind him, he stopped and spun on his heel. Leaning back into the boys' room, he smiled at Jack. "Actually, buddy, there is one rule. Well, not a rule," he said, not wanting to contradict himself. "More like a promise, okay?"

Jack rolled over to face him.

"You have to promise that no matter how old you get, and no matter where you're at in the world, you'll always call home on Christmas Eve. Deal?"

Jack smiled. "Deal."

"Night, J. B.," said Redd—both to Jack Bradly and to Jim Bob, who he liked to think was looking down on him, smiling.

And with that, Redd joined his wife and father, who were already busy wrapping presents without him.

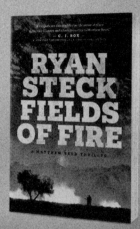
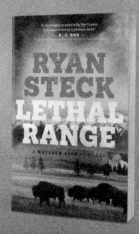
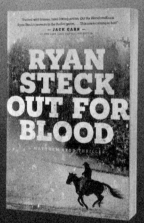

Acknowledgments

As always, I would like to first and foremost thank my Lord and Savior, Jesus Christ, who has blessed me far, far beyond anything I deserve.

It's crazy to think that Matthew Redd has now starred in four books. It seems like just yesterday *Fields of Fire* was hitting bookstores. I'm indebted to **everyone at Tyndale** for their belief in both me and this series, and I am excited to share that, in many ways, we're just getting started. There will be at least two more adventures with Redd and, hopefully, many more beyond that.

Without **Jan Stob**, this series would not be what it is today. After a long career, Jan retired from Tyndale in the spring of 2024. I couldn't possibly share in a few sentences just how much of an impact she's had on me, my books, and my life. Jan was like my "work mom" and not only contributed to the development of my characters but also talked me off many ledges these past few years. When I tested positive for COVID just as my debut novel was coming out, I was in panic mode, knowing I couldn't hit the road as planned. "Ryan, there's nothing you can do," Jan told me when I phoned her late one Saturday night. "Just relax." She made me laugh and calmed me down. A year later, when my wife's health suffered, Jan was a lifeline to me again. Her calming presence and sage advice were invaluable, and she is dearly missed in the publishing world. Jan, I hope you're loving retirement, my friend. Thank you again for all that you've done for both me and Matthew Redd.

To make it in today's publishing game, a new author requires a publisher who has faith in their work and career. Not many get that level of support, unfortunately, but I am one of the few who have. From day one, **Karen Watson** has been a fierce advocate for me and Redd and a believer in this series. Karen, I am so very thankful that you took a chance on me years back and continue to support me today. Being a Tyndale author is important to me because it feels like family. Much of that has to do with you and the way you treat your authors. Thank you for everything.

When it comes to putting a book out, I'm really only in charge of the guts—the words you read and the story that's told. How it's packaged and how you all, the readers, hear about it falls to many others. To that end, I would like to thank **Dean Renninger**, the artist behind all of my covers, along with **Andrea Garcia** and **Natalie Wierenga**. Andrea (Marketing) and Natalie (Publicity) lead the charge when it comes to making sure people know a new book is coming out, and I'm incredibly thankful for all that they've done to spread the word about not only *Gone Dark* but all of my other books as well.

Since Jan's retirement, I've gotten to work with and know **Stephanie Broene** and **Elizabeth Jackson** more this past year. To both of you, thank you for everything. Same for **Andrea Martin**, another invaluable asset to Tyndale authors across the board. Thank you, Andrea. To **Ian Dutcher** and **Cheryl Kerwin**, thank you so much for letting Melissa and me hang out with you guys at PLA 2024. We had a blast, and I can't wait to do it again.

When it comes to delivering a good product for my readers, there is nobody I lean on harder than my amazing, patient, and brilliant editor, **Sarah Rische**. Sarah, teaming up with you for these last four books has been incredible. I mentioned that she's patient because, well, I tend to deviate from my outlines and forget little details far more often than you might imagine. (I've literally listed my own characters' ages incorrectly on multiple occasions, and Sarah *always* catches everything.) I can't imagine that I make your job very easy sometimes, but I know for sure that my books are much, much better because of you. Moreover, what a pleasure it's been to get to know you. Thank you for everything, Sarah, including your friendship, and for being the keeper of all things Matty Redd.

To my agent, **John Talbot**, the best in the business, thank you for . . . well, just everything. I cannot always be your easiest client, and man, there are times I call when I cannot believe you answer the phone, John. Ha! But seriously, I speak to my agent far more than most writers communicate with theirs, and that's because John's advice has been invaluable to me over the years, so I seek his opinion on most everything writing or book related. John, you've also become a dear friend, and you've never steered me wrong. Thank you so much for everything you do for me, man. I appreciate you more than you'll ever know.

It's fair to say that without **Vince Flynn** and **C. J. Box**, I would not be an author today. My two all-time favorite authors, those guys are why I fell in love with thrillers and why I wanted to become a writer. The one and only **Craig Johnson** provided a great quote for *Gone Dark*, which meant a lot to me because I've long been a fan of his Longmire books, but also the television show, which my wife and I have binge-watched numerous times. Craig, thank you. **Robert Crais**, another of my favorite storytellers, also took the time to read an early cut of this book and provided an endorsement. It's crazy to think that heroes of mine are now reading my books. Gentlemen, thank you.

To my author friends **Jack Carr**, **Mark Greaney**, **Brad Taylor** (and **Elaine**, the DCOE), **Brad Thor**, **Nelson DeMille**, **Simon Gervais**, **Jack Stewart**, **Taylor Moore**, **Connor Sullivan**, **Peter James**, **Robert Dugoni**, **Nick Petrie**, **Gregg Hurwitz**, **Andrew Grant**, **James Rollins**, **Brad Meltzer**, **Hank Phillipi Ryan**, **Steve Berry**, **Marc Cameron**, **Claire Isenthal**, **Brian Andrews**, **Jeff Wilson**, and **K. J. Howe**, I have so much love for you all—here's to an even bigger and better year next year from everyone!

Last year, **Brian Freeman** was kind enough to let me crash his event at the famous **Poisoned Pen Bookstore** in Scottsdale, Arizona, and I had so much fun. It is always such an honor to visit with **Barbara Peters**, an icon in our industry, and that stop was certainly one of the highlights of the *Out for Blood* release for me.

To **David Temple** and **Jeff Clark**, the two best podcast hosts I know, thank you both for having me on **The Thriller Zone** and the **Course of Action** podcasts. I had a ball at both stops. You guys are the best.

To **Jen Squires**, who is both my primary care physician and a wonderful friend, thank you for always being there for Melissa, me, and our family. Not many know that I deal with a severe case of anxiety, which is made worse when I'm under stress, and to be frank, I don't know what I'd do without Jen—who goes way above and beyond to take care of me and make sure I'm in good health, especially when I'm on deadline to turn a book in. Love you, Jen. And to **Momma Squires**, Jen's mom, who has taken the time to read my books, thank you for getting to Matthew Redd, but your daughter is the real star.

To my dear friend **John Robinson**, a talented writer, brilliant doctor, and as fine a man as I have ever met, thank you. When I can't reach Jen and have a medical question, John gets the call, and he answers every single time. John, whether it was explaining things going on with my wife or my father or walking me through symptoms during COVID, I am so thankful for your guidance, advice, and prayers. I love and appreciate you, my friend. Thank you.

To **Sherri Foster**, thank you for being so good to me over the years. Truly, I don't deserve a friend like you, Sherri, but I have so much love and appreciation for you. A better person, there is not. You're my hero, my friend. I cannot wait to see your book on store shelves one day soon.

To **Byrdie Bell**, the rock star daughter of the one and only **Ted Bell**, what a joy it's been getting to know you over this past year. I wish you, Mike, and your new bundle of joy all the very best. And, Byrdie, thank you again for letting me carry forward your father's legacy. Writing Alex Hawke adventures has been a thrill, but getting to work *with* you to keep Lord Hawke alive and well has been the real joy.

When I look back at my life, especially my childhood, I realize just how lucky I am to have the family that I do. To my parents, **James** and **Rhonda Steck**, I love you both beyond words and am so very proud to be your son. I apologize for being a . . . challenging . . . child to parent (especially those teen years, sheesh!), but I know that I am where I am today because of you both. So, thank you for never giving up on me.

To my sister, **Joslyn Steck**, I love you dearly. My **Aunt Marlene** has always been there for me and loved me as one of her own. Thank you for that, Aunt Marlene. I love you so much. And to my grandparents—**George** and **Lorraine Steck**, and **Don** and **Darleen Gillespie**, who always cared for me and made summers at Silver Lake and other occasions and holidays so special growing up, thank you. (One of my fondest memories was spending Thanksgiving in Ohio with my grandpa and grandma Gillespie as a child, surrounded by my aunts, uncles, and cousins. What I wouldn't give to go back and get to do that one more time.)

Finally, to my beautiful wife, **Melissa Steck**, thank you for always being my rock, for taking care of me and our kids, for putting us first, and for being my best friend. I am so thankful to be your husband, and I love doing life with you. I am so proud of all that you've accomplished and overcome these last few years. I wish I was as tough as you sometimes, but I am grateful for every single thing you do to support me. Just as Emily Redd understands Matty better than he knows himself, the same is true for Melissa and me. I love you endlessly, forever, and always. Ditto to my children, who've made me the happiest and proudest father on earth. My kids are my heartbeat and the reason why I get up every morning ready to work. **Brynn**, **Chase**, **Ryan Junior**, **Rylee**, and **Mitch**, being your dad will always be my favorite part of life.

Lastly, to **my readers** . . . thank you for taking the time to read *Gone Dark*. I sincerely hope that you loved it because it's my favorite in the series to date. From the moment I set out to write *Fields of Fire*, I knew Redd would eventually adopt a child, which is a topic I wanted to highlight because it is so near and dear to my heart. You might have noticed that I dedicated this book to my daughter, Brynn, who, in many ways, is *my* Jack. That will make more sense in time when you see how Jack fits into the Redd family—so get ready for another adventure next summer.

By the way, the next book brings back a certain fan-favorite character, one to whom Redd owes a favor, and that man, Aaron Decker, is about to cash it in. If you thought *Out for Blood* or *Gone Dark* had a lot of action, just wait . . . the next one will be even bigger. I can't wait for you to see what Redd and Decker are up to in 2026!

About the Author

RYAN STECK is an editor, an author, and the founder and editor in chief of The Real Book Spy. Ryan has been named an "Online Influencer" by Amazon and is a regular columnist at CrimeReads. TheRealBookSpy.com has been endorsed by #1 *New York Times* bestselling authors Mark Greaney, C. J. Box, Kyle Mills, Daniel Silva, Brad Thor, and many others. A resident of Michigan, along with his wife and their six kids, Steck cheers on his beloved Detroit Tigers and Lions during the rare moments when he's not reading or talking about books on social media. He can be reached via email at ryan@therealbookspy.com.

KEEP UP-TO-DATE ON NEWS
FROM RYAN STECK AT

---

therealbookspy.com

TYNDALE HOUSE PUBLISHERS IS CRAZY4FICTION!

Become part of the Crazy4Fiction community and find fiction that entertains and inspires. Get exclusive content, free resources, and more!

JOIN IN ON THE FUN!

 crazy4fiction.com

 Crazy4Fiction

 crazy4fiction

 tyndale_crazy4fiction

 Sign up for our newsletter

FOR GREAT DEALS ON TYNDALE PRODUCTS, GO TO TYNDALE.COM/FICTION

CP0021